Danielle Kidnapped

A Novel of Survival in the Coming Ice Age

John Silveira

This novel is a work of fiction. Names, characters, places, and incidents depicted are the product of the author's imagination or are used fictitiously. Any resemblance to actual persons, either living or dead, and any events or locales, is entirely coincidental.

Published by Riley Creek Books

For information, please contact:

John Silveira
P.O. Box 1646
Gold Beach, OR 97444

PRINTED IN THE UNITED STATES OF AMERICA

Acknowledgements

It's hard to acknowledge all the people who helped me over the years to get this novel to where it is now. I know I'm going to leave some names out and all I can say is, I'm sorry, but I still appreciate your input.

Among those who helped me with their invaluable suggestions and advice are Dave and Ilene Duffy, Dale Myers, Oliver Del Signore, Annie and Erik Tuttle, Laurie Peterson, Christine Mack, Lisa Nourse, Rhoda Denning, Casey Mutch, Holly Davee, Andy Davee, Brandy Mack, Denise Craig, Heather Shinskie, Desirae Yager, Jeremy Livingston, Mark Hamilton, and Clair Wolf.

Though she doesn't realize it, Lacie Wise, by being Lacie, did, in a small way, help me round out who Danielle is.

I also want to thank Christine Mack for the cover idea and Al Boulley, Ilene Duffy, and Sammi Craig for bringing the cover to life with their computer skills. But I especially want to thank Jaime Yager for walking down that lonely road in the middle of nowhere, where the photo was taken, on two lousy days. Despite rain and hail, she insisted on doing it until I got a photo that was right for the cover.

Dedication

This book is dedicated to my daughter, Meaghan Silveira, and her best friend, Lynzi Johnson. If it hadn't been for Meaghan, I'd never have met Lynzi, and if I hadn't met Lynzi, I'd never have known what Danielle was capable of.

Prologue

At the beginning of the first year, despite news stories of record-cold temperatures that resulted in crop failures, the words "ice age" were hardly on anyone's lips. Supermarket shelves still overflowed, though there were spot shortages and prices crept up. But as the year wore on, store shelves started to empty and prices skyrocketed. Though the United States was still the world's largest food exporter, there were calls to reduce exports, and these were followed by resolutions, introduced into Congress, mandating export quotas on most food items and prohibitions on many. Before the year ended, it was illegal to export any food at all.

American agriculture was failing and there was a final bailout. This time it was for farmers, agribusinesses, and sectors of the food processing industry.

Most people were beginning to understand that the once mundane, day-to-day problems of obtaining food, heating oil, and even toilet paper were soon going to become more difficult, until they were all but impossible.

At the beginning of the second year, snow on the ground, usually gone by the end of March, lingered in many of the northern states until mid-May. Motor fuel rationing was instituted as refinery output had to be redirected to heating oil production. On the pretext of national security, American troops invaded the oil fields in the Middle East which led to the United States becoming involved in multiple wars. Industrial production started to decline and jobs evaporated.

Food rationing began in the cities and the first food riot occurred in Detroit where sixty-three people were killed. After that, street violence increased and no large city in the country made it through the second year without at least one major riot over food.

The grid started to fail and electric power was rationed and only available at certain hours of the day. In the spring of that second year, there was a rush to get wheat and other staple crops planted and home gardens sprung up from coast to coast. But, other than in the southern states, little was harvested because the cold weather came too early again.

By the third year, America's cities were eerily quiet. There were massive crop failures and severe food rationing across the United States and around the world. In the Midwest, once breadbasket to the world, wheat, corn, and soybean farmers were completely out of business. Pigs, cattle, chickens, and other agricultural animals were slaughtered until there were almost none left, because there was nothing left to feed them. In Florida and California the citrus industry was obliterated. Further north, Canadian crops were virtually nonexistent and the US-Canadian border, once the longest undefended border in the world, had American troops at every crossing to stem the flow of Canadian immigrants who could not be cared for.

In just a few parts of the lower forty-eight states — the American Southwest and states along the Gulf Coast — there was still a short growing season, and that's where tens of millions of Americans were trying to go, but almost no one in those states wanted them. And in February, citizens of Los Angeles, California, were stunned by a blizzard that left a foot and a half of snow on the city for the first time in its recorded history.

Across the nation, supermarkets were now closed and what little food there was came through "official" government distribution centers where corruption and theft were endemic. Those who had connections — and the Army — still ate well, but almost everyone else lived on starvation rations, if they lived at all.

Each time draconian measures were announced, they were welcomed. "Food hoarders" were cited as having a hand in the mass starvation and an Executive Order was issued authorizing the rounding up of all food stores — including those held privately — for a "redistribution program." Police and military units went door-to-door looking for food that was now considered contraband. Bounties were offered and neighbor spied upon neighbor. Rumors flew as to who had food — to be interpreted as "who was illegally hoarding," now a federal crime. Anyone who didn't look cold and hungry was reported and woe be to those who were even a little overweight, as they soon received visits from the authorities, some of which led to gunfights that left citizens, police, and military personnel dead.

When gun control was called for, at first, only the desperate turned theirs in. When bounties of food were offered for them, once again, neighbor fingered neighbor.

The Mormons were targeted, as they had the tradition of storing against bad times. Temples and churches were ransacked, then burned when the mobs found nothing. Mormon families and anyone else thought to have food were confronted and those who couldn't conceal the goods they had so prudently stored in better times had it taken away, often violently.

In the end, the redistribution program promised from the seized food never materialized. That which was confiscated simply disappeared.

For a while, both police and military units remained loyal to the government and carried out the orders they were given, some out of a misguided sense of duty and patriotism, others because they saw the chaos in the streets and obeyed their orders because it seemed to be the safest course to follow or because it got them and their families fed, but most remained loyal because wearing a uniform was a license to steal. But even that didn't last. When their rations were cut, many police and military units became vigilante groups and sought food from a now largely unarmed population using violence whenever and wherever they had to.

Gangs formed, sometimes with the old police forces and military units at their cores. Other times it was private citizens banding together for survival. In the cities the gangs roamed looking for ever-dwindling caches of food until the caches disappeared, either consumed or successfully hidden. Along those highways that were still open a new phenomenon, collectively called "road pirates," was born. They preyed on those trying to escape south into what was, at least, warmer weather. Often, the armed "authorities" who appeared at your door for "inventory inspections" were actually roving gangs or the road pirates who posed as government officials. It didn't matter, you lost everything in either case.

Though hunger was now rampant across the United States, the rest of the world had it worse. In countries close to the equator, there was still a lengthy growing season, but the only crops that could survive the climate change there were those imported from the temperate zones. However, because they were unfamiliar to the natives, few of those crops were planted, so they, too, starved. According to UN estimates, three to four million people died of malnutrition every day in Asia, Africa, Europe, and North and South America and the rate was increasing. There was nothing anyone could do about it.

In this third year, nearly half of what had once been a burgeoning population of the earth had perished. Governments no longer promulgated the fiction that the change in climate was a freak weather pattern, and politicians ceased promising solutions. No one knew how much worse it was going to get, but it was now clear it would.

But for all the riots, for all the call for gun confiscation "to end the violence," the sad truth was that most people in the United States did not die from violence. Most simply hid in their homes, hoped for help, prayed for miracles, and in the end, almost all of of them drew their shades, climbed into their beds, and quietly froze or starved to death.

It was in the third year of the new ice age that Clayton tried to make a run from Yakima, Washington, to Los Angeles, California, to save himself and his family.

Chapter 1
August 24

The Cascades had been snow-covered from their bases to their peaks all summer long while temperatures in Yakima, typically over a hundred degrees this time of year, had gone over seventy-five just once in three years. It had long been clear to Clayton—and billions of others—the new ice age had begun.

After months of preparation, this morning he was taking his family south to Los Angeles, where they had relatives. Ice age or not, Southern California still had a growing season, and a garden might be all that stood between getting anything at all to eat and starvation.

He considered himself lucky to finally get away. They'd left Yakima just before sunrise. For the first eighty miles the road was no longer maintained so travel along I-82 was slow. But as they reached Hanford the road got better. From here on the Army kept clear a few roads that led west to the coast and south into California.

It was almost 9:30 when he crossed the Columbia River and ten minutes later he turned west onto I-84, at Umatilla, Oregon, a road maintained because it serviced the hydroelectric dams on the Columbia River and the nuclear facilities at Hanford. He glanced in the rearview mirror to see how the kids were doing. Wedged between sleeping bags on the passenger's side, his ten-year-old son, Robert, was trying to go to sleep. Robert had the dark hair and thin lips of his mother and he'd inherited her doleful expression that masked whatever was going on inside either of them.

On the other side of the van was Danielle — beautiful, blonde, thin, and barely five-foot-two. She wore a black T-shirt with red lettering across the front that read:

Fuck Off
or I'll Kill You 'til You're Dead

The shirt was a sore spot with him, but what had him really fuming was the fight she'd put up when he'd forced her into the van.

At sixteen, she shifted back and forth between moments when she was still a child and moments when she was becoming a woman. She had a boyfriend Clayton had never met, and she swore she would never leave Yakima. So she was the last to know, Clayton revealing it to her only as they loaded the van. He had fresh scratches on his arms she'd inflicted when she'd resisted. She had a slight swelling under her left eye from where he'd slapped her. She'd barely spoken since being forced into the vehicle and she now stared glumly out the window.

In her lap, her six-month-old sister, Audrey, slept. Clayton had nicknamed her "Whoops" because she'd been unexpected — testimony that tubal ligations don't always work.

On the front seat, next to him, sat his wife, Emily, her face clouded by that cheerless expression that, after seventeen years of marriage, he'd come to detest. He glanced at her. She'd been quiet since leaving and he had the sense to leave her alone, for now.

It wasn't leaving Yakima that bothered her. She'd have done anything for her husband, and he said they had to go. It was the way they left, without telling anyone, without inviting anyone else to come along, that upset her. Clayton told her she just didn't understand: They had to go alone; they couldn't save the world.

Now, the miles rolled by. Large pieces of debris appeared in unlikely places on the road. Only the Army kept the roads clear anymore, and they didn't do it as a public service; they had their own agenda.

There were stretches where encroaching layers of sand and gravel made driving treacherous. He was careful with his speed, rarely going much over forty, usually doing under thirty. At some point in the future — no one could predict when — the roads would be obliterated, first buried by the ever-accumulating rubble once the Army ceased maintaining them, then torn up by the glaciers when the ice age deepened. Much of civilization was going to be erased once the mountains of ice began to move.

"Are you going to talk to me?" he finally asked.

Emily didn't answer.

"I wish you'd talk to me."

"We could have said goodbye," she said.

"We couldn't. Too many people suspected we were going, already. Word would have gotten around. The police, the damned churches, or the gangs would have come and taken everything away from us: the gas, the guns, the little bit of food we have…"

"I wish you wouldn't swear."

He shook his head in exasperation. "*Damn's* not a swear," he said. They rode in silence for the next few miles.

"We could at least have said goodbye to my family," she said.

"Then your brother, Reverend Jim, would have been there."

"His name is James."

"I don't care what his name is. We'd never have gotten out of there if he'd had his way. The guy's a goddamned communist."

"Please stop swearing," she said softly.

Several more miles passed in silence.

"There were others who wanted to go with us. They'd have given anything to go," she said in a low voice.

He didn't respond.

"My brother-in-law begged."

"You shouldn't have told him what we were doing. The more people who knew, the more chances we had of losing everything when the authorities showed up. We're lucky we got away.

"He should have been making plans himself," he added.

"But he didn't," she said.

"It's like the ant and the grasshopper, Emily. He frittered away his summer."

"That's right. He frittered away his summer. He's an asshole. You've been saying it for years. Not everyone plans like you do. He needed your help. You could have helped him."

Asshole. He'd never heard her use that word before. He pressed on the accelerator a little more and the van went a little faster.

"Why couldn't we have brought Joanie and her brother?" she asked referring to their twelve-year-old niece and nine-year-old nephew.

"We don't have room."

"Why did we have to bring all that stuff back there?"

"We need it. We need the damned gas," he shouted.

"I'm not talking about gas. Clayton, you brought power tools but there's no power. You brought picture albums and left the people behind. You even brought your cell phone, and there's no service anymore. We have room for a dozen or more people back there."

"We couldn't have gotten that many people in here."

"We could have brought three little cars filled with people, filled with the gas we're using for this van and your junk," she yelled.

"Shut up, Emily," he yelled back, "just shut up."

He looked at the thermometer he'd taped to the side view mirror. It read thirty-six degrees Fahrenheit.

They'd seen no one else on the road since they'd left. Not that Clayton expected to. There wasn't enough gas to go around anymore and anyone who had some was more than likely hoarding it until there was a chance to escape south. Gasoline was something you lied to your friends and neighbors about. If you were smart, you lied to your wife about it, too.

He'd started preparing for this trip six months ago, bartering for supplies, monitoring the news, and listening to the rumors. And, when there was nothing else to do, he painstakingly drew and redrew the route they would take. He fine-tuned it with each bit of information he considered significant and finally settled on a route that would take them along I-84 West to Gresham, where they'd turn south on I-205 then get on I-5. From there it was 170 miles until, just beyond Roseburg, they'd cut west on OR-42, at the Winston turnoff, and head for Bandon and the Oregon coast. Where towns appeared on the maps, he'd like to have chosen roads that skirted them. But if they weren't used by the Army, there was no way to tell from the maps which might be navigable, so most of the trip would have to be along the main highways. In the end, the route he chose was exactly that which the Army used.

He knew from the radio that I-5, running north-south through central California, was no longer maintained because of inclement inland weather. But US 101 and US 1, along the Oregon and California coast, were open because the moderating effect of the Pacific Ocean still made for milder weather there.

As he drove through the Columbia River Gorge his CB scanner jumped from one channel to the next. Some signals, because of skip, came from hundreds of miles away. There was no shortage of religion. "Jesus will save you!" "Christ will keep you warm!"

But there weren't enough channels to accommodate everyone and broadcasters spent a good deal of their time feuding and bickering for airtime.

He looked in the rear view mirror again. Robert was still trying to go to sleep. Whoops slept in Danielle's lap. Danielle leaned her head against the window and brooded. He wanted to say something about her shirt, but it would lead to another argument with his strong-willed daughter. It could wait. He still wanted to know where she got it.

He glanced again at Emily. She stared at the road ahead and didn't speak.

Sure, he thought, they'd left Emily's sister and her family. They left her bachelor brother. They left neighbors they had known for years. Some were people who wouldn't leave, who believed the weather would change or the government could save them. Like horses, they wouldn't leave a burning barn. There was macabre irony in that metaphor.

There were others who had already left and even more who wanted to leave. But few down south wanted them because there were barely enough resources, even in California, to support the people already there. The ice age had changed everything.

Until recently, the main roads going south were patrolled by state and federal authorities, and they turned the emigrants back. But once the emigrants got far enough south, they often had no means of getting back. Initially, the authorities put those who made it that far in work camps. But people fleeing the cold and the hunger really didn't care. Work camps meant somebody else had to feed them and keep them warm. However, the camps themselves became strains on the resources available. There were rumors that, when things got bad enough, there were riots and massacres at some of the camps. But who knew the truth? That was one thing there was more of than ever: since the ice age had started, there was no shortage of rumors.

Ultimately, the work camps had to be closed and the travel laws were no longer enforced. So, if you could find the gas, the roads were open. But travel was risky. There were the stories of those whose occupation was to prey on unwary travelers: the road pirates.

§   §   §

Close to noon, and just past The Dalles, Clayton looked in his side view mirror. "Shit," he said. "We're being followed."

A brown station wagon towing a U-Haul appeared in his side view mirror.

"Who is it, Dad?" Robert called from the back of the van.

"I don't know," Clayton snapped. "Sit back and keep down." He took the .44 magnum Blackhawk from beneath his seat and fumbled with it nervously. It felt awkward to his hand. He had never fired it and, though he had paid dearly for it, only fifty rounds of ammunition came with it.

It was loaded and he laid it on the console between himself and Emily. Then he clutched the steering wheel with both hands. He didn't want to appear nervous.

He watched the station wagon quickly gain on them until it was eight car-lengths behind. Then it slowed down and kept pace and followed them west.

In his mirror, he could make out Idaho plates. There were boxes and spare tires tied to the wagon's roof. He wondered what was in the trailer it was towing. He nervously scanned the road ahead concerned that this could be the prelude to an ambush. The CB searched the channels but gave no hint. If the wagon was communicating with anyone, it wasn't by CB.

They passed through Hood River and the wagon followed. The driver matched Clayton's speed on the open stretches and slowed down to keep pace wherever debris slowed their travel.

All the while his CB tirelessly scanned the band, but now there was a lull in the bickering and praying, which left nothing but static, and Emily found the relentless white noise objectionable. Clayton said it had to be on.

Mile after mile the wagon maintained its distance. "They look okay," he finally said and started to relax. "They're heading south, just like us."

"How do you know, Dad? They might be road pirates."

"Shut up, Robert."

They traveled past the Cascade Locks and Bonneville Dam with the wagon following. The few houses they saw from the road seemed empty. The stores were abandoned. They saw no one else.

Just after 2:00, and approaching Troutdale, he glanced in the door mirror again. "They're gone," he said. He wondered how the station wagon could have disappeared so abruptly.

"Oh, God, Clayton, look!" Emily screamed.

The wagon was gradually coming up on her side.

"Oh shit," he shouted. "Everybody down."

Emily pressed herself against the back of her seat. "What are they doing?" she asked nervously.

"How would I know?" he yelled.

He fumbled with the Blackhawk but it fell on the floor between his feet. He reached down to search for it, and the van started to swerve. He found the gun and brought it up and held it below window level. He tried to hold the wheel steady with his other hand.

"Clayton, what are you going to do?" Emily asked.

"Keep back and roll your window down," he commanded.

She didn't move.

"Roll your damn window down!" he yelled.

She rolled it down six inches and cold air surged through the van.

"All the way!" he shouted.

She closed her eyes and opened the window all the way. Her hands came up involuntarily and covered her ears. Clayton thought she was going to scream.

The wagon pulled abreast. He could see the man driving, slowly bring an empty hand up and wave. There were two women and some children in the wagon with him. Clayton felt a swell of relief and placed the revolver back on the console and returned the wave.

"It's just another family," Clayton said and took a deep breath. "They're heading south; just like us."

"A family?" Robert asked popping his head up from behind Emily's seat. "They got kids with 'em?"

Robert pressed his forehead against the window and saw a girl and a boy near his own age in the station wagon. He waved and they waved back. There was a third child, a baby, who sat on the seat between the man and woman in front.

The wagon fell back and followed them again.

"I thought you had to cock it," Emily said derisively.

"What?"

"When Mr. Wheaton sold you the gun, he said you had to pull the hammer thing back for each shot." She turned her head and looked out the window to watch the scenery go by.

She was right. It was a single action handgun and he'd forgotten to cock it. If he'd had to use it, he couldn't have fired it the way he'd been holding it. He left it on the console.

They got on I-205 and he frequently checked the mirrors to keep an eye on the wagon. Sometimes one of the children in the wagon climbed into front seat and sat in the woman's lap. Later, he'd look and the kid would have returned to the back seat.

Given the conditions of the roads, he still felt good about the progress they were making. He had mixed feelings about the wagon and wondered how long it would follow him.

Just after 3:00, Robert said, "I gotta go, Dad."

"What?"

"I gotta go to the bathroom."

They'd been cooped up in the van for almost eight hours already. Clayton winced and glanced in the door mirror. The station wagon still followed. He didn't know if they'd pull over with him.

"Wait a little while," he said.

"I gotta go bad."

Clayton ignored him. He was sure the boy didn't have to go as bad as he made out.

They turned south onto I-5 and Robert said, "Dad, I gotta go to the bathroom real bad." His voice carried more urgency.

"Wait," Clayton yelled.

"I'm gonna wet my pants."

"I have to go, too," Danielle said.

He watched the wagon in his mirror, again. "Shit," he mumbled, but he kept driving.

"*Dad,*" Danielle demanded.

He looked at Emily. She still stared out the window letting him know this was his problem to solve.

He shook his head. She didn't understand the big picture and he needed her on his side.

Up ahead he saw where the shoulder was clear and there were some trees. He let up on the accelerator and, as he gradually slowed down, so did the station wagon.

He coasted to a stop on the gravel shoulder and the wagon pulled in behind him.

"They stopped with us," he said not expecting any comment.

Robert started to pull up the handle on the side door.

"Stop," Clayton shouted. Robert stopped.

Clayton looked in the door mirror again. There was a second man in the back seat of the wagon he hadn't seen before. The driver was getting out.

Clayton leaped out to meet him.

The man smiled until he saw Clayton had the cocked gun in his hand. "Jesus," the man said. "Mister, it's okay." He opened his jacket to show he was unarmed.

"Charles, what's wrong?" a second woman shouted. She got out and stood beside the door on her side of the station wagon looking scared. "Charles, why's he got a gun?"

The man in the back seat was fumbling with a shotgun that was wrapped up in a blanket.

"Stop it, Harry," the driver yelled when he looked back and saw what the man in the backseat was doing. "Put it down. It's okay."

The man finally freed the shotgun but he stayed in the back seat and stared at Clayton through the windshield.

Clayton held his gun, unsure of what to do.

"It's okay," the driver of the wagon repeated.

"What's wrong, dad?" Robert asked. He was standing on the other side of the van looking confused.

"Get back in the van," Clayton said.

Robert didn't move.

"Take it easy, mister," the man said. "We're just like you. We're heading south." The boy and girl were getting out of the wagon. The woman tried to wave them back in but to no avail. Like Robert, they wanted to see what was going on.

Clayton felt as if he was losing control of the situation.

"You are heading south, aren't you?" the man asked.

Clayton didn't answer.

"Dad, I gotta go." It was Danielle. She was walking off into the trees with pages from an old phone book in her hand.

Slowly, Clayton uncocked the gun and put it inside his waistband.

The man in the back of the wagon lowered the shotgun.

"Are you heading south?" the man asked.

Clayton still wouldn't answer. He turned around and got back into his van just as Emily got out.

"Good timing," he whispered sarcastically. But she was already out of earshot.

He watched in his door mirror as she approached the other family. He could see Robert walk up to the other boy. In his hands he held his toy soldiers. The boy ran back to his car and returned with toys of his own. Robert was pulling at his crotch. He still had to go to the bathroom. He and the other boy went off in the woods. The girl stood there uncertainly. Emily must have said something because the girl suddenly went off into the brush in the direction he had seen Danielle disappear.

He turned his head to look into the back seat. Whoops was still sleeping.

Emily's door opened. "We're having lunch," she said.

"We're not stopping for lunch," he said.

"We're having lunch," she repeated and threw him a peanut butter sandwich and slammed the door.

"Make it quick," he ordered.

"Peanut butter," he thought as he started to eat the sandwich. It was one of the foods the government still distributed. "Where in hell did they get all the peanut butter?"

Several minutes later, he watched as Danielle came out of the woods. She was holding the little girl's hand.

"Do you want to monitor each other on the CB?" a voice asked.

Clayton jumped. The driver of the wagon was at his window.

"Sorry, I didn't mean to scare you," he said.

Clayton glared at him.

"I just thought it would be a good idea if we listened for each other on a specific channel."

Clayton didn't reply.

"Seven seems to be pretty empty most of the time," the man said.

"Sounds fine. Just don't make small talk on it."

"Wouldn't think of it," the man replied.

He looked into the van. "You've got a lot of stuff there."

Clayton didn't want to hear about all his "stuff" again. He glared at the man.

"What d'ja do before the ice age started?" the man asked.

"Mechanic," Clayton said.

"Not going to be much of a call for that, anymore," the man said and laughed.

Clayton didn't laugh.

"I was a podiatrist. Guess there'll be a big call for that, now."

Clayton returned to eating his sandwich.

"My friend in the wagon was..." The man paused. Clayton was ignoring him. "Hey, why don't I let you eat in peace." He turned and left.

Several minutes later, Emily opened the passenger's door and got in. "How'd you like them?" she asked. She seemed cheerier than before. The back door slid open and Danielle and Robert got in, too. Whoops woke as Danielle picked her up.

"Well?" Emily asked.

"I'm not interested in them," Clayton replied. "If they want to tag along, fine."

She slumped back into her seat.

He removed the revolver from his waistband and pulled away from the shoulder. The wagon followed.

This part of I-5 wasn't in such disrepair so it was possible to make better time.

The scanner searched the stations relentlessly. At 3:45 a voice on the CB asked, "Carl, you seen anyone coming your way?"

Clayton locked onto the channel.

He didn't hear the reply, but when the speaker returned, he thanked "Carl" and instructed him to keep watching. The channel went dead, sparked only by an occasional transmission from elsewhere and several minutes later Clayton took the manual lock off. He wondered where the transmission originated and carefully scanned the road ahead as he drove.

"What did the driver say his name is?" he asked Emily.

"Charles," she said.

"Are you sure it wasn't Carl?" he asked.

"It was Charles. Are you thinking..." She didn't finish the question and went back to staring out the window.

They passed the turnoff to Albany. Still, they had seen no one else until just north of Eugene a skinny woman with a child beside her watched them from a porch as they breezed by. In the front yard, wooden crosses marked two freshly-dug graves.

Whoops was asleep again, Danielle hummed a song, and Robert played with his toy soldiers. Clayton could see in the side view mirror that Robert and the other boy had swapped some toys.

He glanced at Emily. She still stared silently at the road ahead.

Around 4:30 the station wagon sounded its horn. Clayton looked in his door mirror. Steam gushed out from under the station wagon's front end.

The driver alternately blew his horn and flashed his headlights. Clayton kept driving.

The man rolled down his window and started to wave his hand. Clayton kept driving and the wagon began losing ground. The driver honked more insistently.

"What's happening?" Emily asked.

"There's something wrong with their car," Clayton answered.

He pressed down on the accelerator and the van gradually gained speed. He looked at Emily and their eyes locked for a second. He looked away.

"Help," a man's voice cried from the CB; it was channel seven. Emily locked it in. "We're losing radiator coolant," he said.

In the mirror the wagon faded to a distant speck on the side of the road.

"Washington van, if you're monitoring, please help."

Clayton drove on. The CB transmission stopped.

Emily stared at him.

Whoops started to cry.

"Danielle," he said, "see if Whoops is wet."

She grumbled but she perched the baby on her thighs and loosened the diaper. "Oh, shit," she said. "Where are the towels?"

The odor of the opened diaper flooded the van.

Emily reached to the floor at her feet then passed some rags back.

Danielle, part woman, part child, was learning to swear. Clayton didn't approve. He didn't want her growing up to become a woman who swore. Trashy women swore.

"I want you to watch your mouth, young lady."

She didn't reply but he could imagine her making a face of disgust at the back of his head.

"Why didn't you stop for them?" Emily asked flatly.

He didn't answer.

"Why didn't you help that family?" she demanded.

"There's nothing we could have done for them."

"How do you know that?"

"Emily, we can't save the world. We've got to take care of ourselves."

Tension, suffused with the odor of the baby's loaded diaper, was making the atmosphere in the van unbearable. Clayton rolled down his window and a gush of cold air rushed in.

Channel after channel the CB paused on promises of salvation before moving on. Emily abruptly turned it off. Clayton said nothing. Even he was growing weary of the praying, bickering, and empty noise.

§   §   §

At 6:30 they passed Roseburg and left I-5 for OR-42. Clayton glanced at his gas gauge. He checked the road behind in the door mirror, and surveyed what was coming up ahead. He picked a spot and pulled over onto the shoulder.

"Take another potty stop," he said.

He pulled over, got out, went around to the back of the van, and opened the doors. The others sought privacy in the growth along the north side of the road.

Clayton removed six of the five-gallon gas cans and emptied them into the tank. That gave them another four hundred miles of range. He had nine cans left, another six hundred miles. It would safely get them to Southern California where his mother and his brother's family lived.

As he put the empty cans back, he heard the barking and baying of dogs and looked out into the field to the south where, in the distance, a doe and her fawn were outrunning a pack. He watched the deer clear a distant ridge and go out of sight. The dogs reached the top of the ridge and gave up the chase. They milled around, tired, and sniffed the ground.

His family got back into the van as he watched. He identified with the doe for, like him, she too was trying to escape with her "family." Her recent success might be a good omen for him. He got back in and drove on.

He had to reduce his speed, on this stretch of highway. The Army didn't "clear" the roads so much as they made them navigable.

Soon, they came up on two cars outside of Camas Valley. One was parked on the shoulder; the other was turned sideways and blocked the eastbound lane. Both had their hoods up and their trunks open.

He slowed to a stop a quarter mile away. Emily sat up apprehensively and Clayton turned the CB scanner on again. "You shouldn't have shut this off," he said accusingly.

He listened as a man's voice faded in and out and announced a new church. The scanner moved to the next two channels. Static. From the one that followed those came a hymn. The next explained the ice age was a manifestation of God's wrath.

He cursed the religious nuts for hogging the channels.

Danielle and Robert leaned over the backs of the front seats to look at the cars. Whoops started to cry again.

"Hold Whoops, Danielle, and stop her from crying."

Danielle clicked her tongue in exasperation.

"Is there someone in them cars?" Robert asked.

"How the hell would I know?" Clayton snapped.

The baby stopped crying. In the rear view mirror he could see Danielle rocking her.

The country around them was open. Copses of trees dotted the fields like islands peppering a sea. Clayton knew they could be easy targets for a sniper.

He wondered if that was what had happened to the two cars ahead.

He shifted into park.

"What are we going to do, Dad?" Robert asked.

"We can't turn back," he said and he scanned the trees for danger.

"Why can't we turn back?" Robert asked.

"Shut up," Clayton snapped again.

It would have been good if the station wagon had been able to keep up with him. Three men backing each other up would have had a better chance investigating this than one man alone.

He reached in back and got the M1A rifle. A magazine was in it. The setup had cost him twenty thousand dollars, twelve cases of contraband food, and a set of tires last May. It was easy to part with the tires. There wasn't enough gasoline available to any one person to wear a set out anymore. But he was lucky to get the rifle when he did. Now you couldn't get any rifle for less than fifty thousand, and one as good as an M1A could not be had for money at all. Mr. Wheaton said that before the ice age started a rifle like this had cost two thousand dollars, tops.

He reluctantly opened the door and grabbed a bandoleer of loaded magazines that he slung over his shoulder. He stepped down onto the road.

The air was brittle.

"Get behind the wheel and turn the van around," he said to Emily. "Get it in reverse and back it up as I approach the cars. Stay behind me so I can see both sides of the road. But keep pace with me. If you hear anything suspicious on the CB, toot the horn. If there's any shooting, give me a chance to jump in, then drive like hell back the other way."

"Drive where?" she snapped.

"Just drive, goddamn it," he yelled.

Emily knew he was scared.

He checked the breech while Emily turned the van around. He wouldn't make the same kind of mistake he had made with the revolver. It was loaded. The safety was off.

He stepped to the north side of the road and looked along the ditch. There was no one there. He crossed to the south side and checked the ditch there. Nothing. He started to walk along the shoulder, the rifle ready. But if there was a sniper out there in one of those stands of trees, he was a dead man already. Emily put the van in reverse and kept pace with him.

They got closer to the cars and Clayton yelled, "Stop."

She stopped and the van idled. He covered the last fifty yards alone.

The first person he saw was a woman lying on the ground beside the Ford. Her dress was hiked up over her waist, her underpants tangled around one ankle. She had been shot through the forehead.

In the car, a man lay dead across the front seat. Two young boys were dead in back. All were the victims of head-shot wounds.

In the Accord that rested across the eastbound lane, a man of about twenty lay dead on the front seat, a hole neatly punched through his driver's side window and his brains spattered across the car's interior. A bra was on the seat beside him. There was no woman.

In the back seat a baby lay in a carrier. Clayton leaned closer and could see it was breathing. It was sleeping. He watched for a few moments. Then he checked the cars. Both had been ransacked. The batteries were gone. He knelt behind the Accord and tapped its tank with the muzzle of his rifle. From the hollow ring he knew it had already been drained. From the state of the bodies and the fact that the baby was still alive, he figured the ambush had happened this morning.

He turned and walked back to the van.

"Get back in your seat," he said.

Emily climbed over the engine compartment and Clayton put the rifle and bandoleer back behind his seat. He turned the van around and drove slowly past the two vehicles. Emily sat forward and rolled her window down.

"There's a baby crying," she said.

She looked at Clayton as the van picked up speed.

"There's a baby back there," she repeated. "Stop the van."

He clutched the wheel and stared ahead at the road.

She lunged for the wheel and he pushed her back against the passenger's door.

"*Stop!* You bastard, stop the van!" she screamed.

"No."

"*Stop!* For the love of God, stop!"

He drove on.

She buried her hands, crying in spasms. "You bastard," she said. "You fucking, miserable, hateful, shit-eating bastard."

Without thinking, he backhanded her. It was the first time he had ever heard her use those words. "Shut up, you bitch!" he screamed, then he hit her again.

Danielle lunged across the back of the front seat and started pummeling her father. "You leave Mommy alone!" she shrieked. She began to claw her father's face as he drove.

Emily suddenly had her hands and was pushing Danielle back into her seat.

"Leave your father alone!" she yelled.

"Tell him to keep his hands off of you!" Danielle yelled back.

"If you ever touch Mommy again..."

"What? What are you going to do?" he asked glaring at her in the mirror.

"*I'll kill you!*" she screamed.

They drove on.

Fucking? Shit-eating? Bastard? He was sure he had never heard Emily use any of those words before. His daughter had never threatened him before.

Emily leaned against her door and stifled back her sobs. He turned up the volume on the CB. Let Jesus keep you warm. Let Jesus drown out her crying.

"Will that baby be okay?" Robert asked.

"Shut up!" Clayton yelled, "Just shut up. I want everyone to shut up."

If only the baby hadn't woken he thought. He began to wish he had taken it. It was a mistake to leave it. Every mile drove the truth in deeper. And every mile made turning back more time-consuming, more gas-consuming, more dangerous.

The radio hissed, Whoops slept, and they traveled closer to the coast without speaking until Clayton said, "I told you right from the beginning, it could only be us, no one else. We can't be pissing away our chances with every sorry soul we see."

Emily still stared out her window. She wouldn't acknowledge him.

"I'm not the one that killed its parents," he said of the baby, thinking at first it was a point in his favor. But with each passing mile he wished he hadn't said that, either. Unless someone else stopped, he had just killed the baby.

Danielle sat in the backseat holding onto her sister as if she was never going to let her go.

§   §   §

"Why are we slowing down?" Robert asked.

Clayton had reduced his speed and was scouting both sides of the road. "We've got to find a place to camp pretty soon. I don't want to be looking for a campsite after dark." He didn't want to be driving after dark either; headlights were a giveaway from far away.

He drove even slower.

"Help me look for a good camping place," he said to all of them.

Emily sat stiffly in her seat saying nothing and they drove until Clayton saw a dirt road that left OR-42 going south, where it disappeared in the trees over the top of a hill. There was no snow on the road, so they wouldn't leave tracks. It would be a good camping area, out of sight of anyone going by, and the high ground if they needed it.

He pulled off the highway and drove cautiously along the dirt hoping he wouldn't find someone else already up there. He stopped before the crest of the hill.

"Take the wheel and wait until I signal you," he said.

Emily stared out her window and didn't move.

"Take the wheel," he repeated deliberately.

She slowly turned to him and, when he got out, she crawled over the console, again, and got in the driver's seat.

He walked ahead with the rifle while the van idled behind him.

He reached a point where the road dropped off. Beyond that there was a field. It would be a good place to hide for the night. He walked part way down the hill to make sure they'd be alone. Then he returned to the crest and signaled Emily to follow.

They parked in the trees and set up camp.

Night was already setting in. They ate their supper in silence, then Clayton got their sleeping bags from the van. So there would be room to stretch out, he told Emily that she, Danielle, and Whoops would sleep inside the van and he and Robert would sleep in the tent. What he really wanted was to get away from the scorn of Emily and Danielle—and the cries of the baby if she woke.

§   §   §

At bedtime, he laid the M1A inside the tent alongside his sleeping bag and glanced at the thermometer he'd attached to the tent flap. It was twenty-eight degrees outside.

He lay back on his sleeping bag and stared at the tent ceiling. The sound of Whoops crying in the van was muffled and distant.

Robert sat quietly on his sleeping bag lost in thought. "How long can you live out here with nothing?" he suddenly asked.

"What do you mean, 'nothing'?"

"Like the people we hear about who get robbed."

"You mean, 'How long could someone last this time of year?'"

"Yeah," Robert said.

Clayton thought about it.

"A day. Maybe two. They'd freeze to death during the night unless they kept walking. But you've got to figure they wouldn't find anything to eat. And you know no one is going to help them.

"No one can afford to," he added, hoping Robert would understand why he had left the family in the station wagon, and then the baby in the car. "They'd live two or three days at most," he said.

Robert thought about the answer for a while.

"What if our car busts like the one this morning did?"

"They just blew a hose," he said. "I can fix that."

"How come you told mom there was nothing we can do for them?"

"If I can fix it, so can they," Clayton said sharply.

A long silence followed and Clayton wished he had seen where the questioning had been leading. He could have avoided yelling at his son.

"Does it hurt to freeze to death?" Robert asked.

"Talk about something else," Clayton said.

"Okay."

The boy was quiet for a while, but he was obviously thinking.

"What if someone tries to take our stuff away?" he asked.

Clayton was deliberate this time. "We've got the guns," he said. "We'll be okay."

Robert smiled. He took some toy soldiers from his pocket and started playing with them. Clayton stared at the ceiling of the tent again.

"Will Charlie be all right?" Robert asked.

"Who's Charlie?"

"The boy who was in the station wagon," Robert replied.

"He's all right," Clayton said.

"How do you know?"

Clayton didn't answer him.

Chapter 2
August 25

In the morning, Clayton woke late to the distant sound of barking dogs. He snapped the rifle's safety off and pushed back the flap of the tent with its muzzle. There was a light dusting of snow on the ground and the thermometer read seventeen degrees. It was August twenty-fifth. Across the field he saw a pack of dogs. They were stalking a skinny cow and her calf. The dogs circled as Clayton watched. The calf crowded helplessly against its mother.

A German shepherd antagonized the cow and she lowered her head and charged. The calf tried to keep up with her but a large mongrel rushed in and grabbed its rear leg. The calf broke loose. The dogs were in a frenzy now and the cow panicked. It started to run, lumbering across the field. She and her calf were separated again and the shepherd brought the calf down. The cow turned and drove the dogs off once more. She stood over the calf and waited for it to rise again. Its leg was broken. She waited several minutes watching the calf struggle while the dogs harassed her. Then she turned and bolted off. In a fury the dogs tore into the calf until it stopped struggling. The cow stood at a distance and watched. Then she moved on.

"What is it, Dad?" Robert asked from back in the tent.

Clayton hadn't realized he was awake. "Nothing," he said and let the tent flap drop.

Robert scooted by and looked out. Clayton started to tell him to get back in, but thought better of it.

Robert, he reminded himself, was young and still adaptable. He also had to understand what survival was all about.

After several minutes, Robert let the tent flap drop and he played with his soldiers. Finally, he asked, "Could you have stopped that?"

"The dogs have got to live, too," Clayton replied.

Robert continued to play with his soldiers and they heard the door of the van open. Clayton crawled out of the tent followed by Robert. Emily was standing there holding the baby. He knew she'd seen what happened to the calf and she would be silent now.

"Let's put away the sleeping bags and the tent," he said to Robert.

They rolled up their sleeping bags then took the tent down and returned all the gear to the van. Clayton got the camp stove going and Emily made a pan of some kind of ground wheat mush for breakfast. She mixed some dry milk with baby food and warmed it. She had tried to nurse but stress or something had dried her up. Somehow, Clayton was sure, she could have continued if she'd done it right and they wouldn't have needed to trade for the dry milk to feed the baby. The dry milk had been dear. It had cost him several boxes of the 7.62 ammo that came with his M1A and some of the gasoline he'd had stashed. It was one more of her failings.

While Emily watched the stove, he topped off the van's tank again. When he was finished, breakfast was ready and they sat down to eat in silence.

"What time is it?" Emily finally asked.

He looked at his watch. "Eight-thirty."

She retreated back into her envelope of silence. Unspoken anger. It was her way.

"Let's load up," he said.

They wiped their dishes clean and packed the stove and dishes. By nine o'clock they were driving down the dirt road toward OR-42 and Clayton hit the brakes when he saw a car going by on the highway.

"We'll wait a little while," he said and turned the engine off. "I hope they didn't see us," he added

Whoops cried as they watched the car travel out of sight. The crying was getting on his nerves.

"Check her diaper," he ordered Danielle.

"I just changed her," she said defiantly in her half-woman voice.

"Well, see if she's still hungry."

"She ate."

"Then rock her!" Clayton yelled.

"I am!" Danielle yelled back. But as she rocked her, she leaned toward her sister's face and whispered, "Sissy isn't going to leave you out in the cold to die."

It was just loud enough for Clayton to hear and he exploded and turned in his seat and jabbed his finger in the air as if stabbing at her. "You watch what you say, you little bitch, or I'll smack you again. And you'd *better* get rid of that filthy shirt."

"I'll wear whatever I want!" she screamed and clutching the baby she lunged over Robert and grabbed the handle on the side door. "Let me out of this fucking van."

"She needs to be burped!" Emily screamed. "She just needs to be burped." She turned, kneeled on her seat, and reached back to get Whoops. Danielle held back tears as she handed her mother the baby, and Emily turned and put the baby over her shoulder and patted her back. In seconds Whoops burped and stopped crying. "Close the door," she said to Danielle.

Danielle stared at the door, now cast ajar. Opening it further or closing it was now a major decision. But where would she go? With a slumping of her shoulders, she closed it.

"Don't think I wouldn't have left you," her father barked. It drove her crazy that everything he wanted had to be a demand or threat.

Clayton then looked at Emily. Running through his mind was that she could have said the baby needed to be burped from the beginning. That's all she had to say. What was she trying to prove, that he was wrong again?

He started the engine and in a shower of dirt and gravel they rocketed forward onto the highway and headed west.

Danielle looked out the window and stared at the passing scenery without seeing any of it.

Her father went on about her insolence and "the boyfriend" he'd never met and how she didn't show any respect because he never came around and showed his face..

Once, she looked back at the backs of her parents's heads to see him jabbering and her mother sulking.

Her mother, forever brooding, rarely protested, criticized, or pointed out what displeased her. Worse, she never said what she *really* wanted; Danielle couldn't believe it was limited only to what he father *told* her she wanted.

And why, she asked herself, did he have to control everyone around him? Anyone he couldn't control, he was sure was trying to take advantage of him.

She thought about "the boyfriend," four years older, who had proved to be no less controlling. "If you love me, you'll do this," and, "If you love me, you'll do that." So she did "this" and "that," though she was frequently reluctant, often silently angry as her mother was with her father, and sometimes she was even ashamed. But she did as he insisted to prove she was worthy, afraid he'd find someone better, until she realized it was, and always would be: "To prove you love me, *you must do as I say.*" In a moment of epiphany, she realized the motives behind his demands had not been fueled by love, they had been driven by selfishness and testosterone. That awakening was a week and a half ago and she stopped seeing him but told no one because she wasn't sure the breakup was permanent. Now, of course, *that* decision had been made for her. She didn't like decisions being made for her.

She'd decided men were crazy, selfish, controlling, and manipulative. Yet, she craved their approval. She hated this contradiction in herself. She looked down at the shirt. It had been his. She kept it when they broke up.

She stared back out the window. Though she loved her parents—probably her mother more, she had to get away from them or she'd go crazy. She'd "escape" when they reached Southern California. She'd take care of herself.

They rode to the squawk and static of the CB, again. They passed cars parked on the side of the road, victims of expended fuel. One had a family that tried to flag him down. Clayton roared past.

At nine-thirty they came upon three more cars that were abandoned in the middle of the road. One had been burned. All three had the same dusting of snow the road had. That meant it was yesterday's tragedy. Clayton drove past. He wouldn't make the mistake of stopping again, but Danielle stared, praying there wasn't another baby being left behind.

When they reached Bandon, Clayton turned south onto 101.

Five miles further south they passed a man, a woman, and a boy who were walking south. Walking to keep warm. Clayton wondered why they were without coats. They turned around to face the approaching van. The woman was holding a baby and Emily sunk her head into her hands when she saw them and moaned. Maybe they were from the cars a half hour back. Clayton drove on.

Seven miles later they could see another family on foot ahead. They walked in the middle of the southbound lane. More refugees. The light snowfall continued. The family stopped and faced them as they approached. Clayton drove to give them a wide berth but the man suddenly ran out in front of him waving a rag. Clayton tried to swerve to avoid him and the impact was sickening. The windshield cracked into an irregular mosaic about nine inches across. Emily screamed incoherently and the man somehow held onto the front of the van, getting a foothold on the bumper as it sped along.

"Stop, Daddy, stop!" Danielle screamed.

The man's eyes pleaded as he tried to maintain a hold on the van.

Clayton swerved back and forth across the road trying to shake him loose. But he clung fiercely and his face, bleeding from the impact, was pressed against the fractured glass. The desperation there was a look

Clayton had never seen before. Clayton realized he too was screaming — at the man. Everyone was screaming. Everyone but Robert. Abruptly, the man lost his grip and fell under the van. There was a sickening thump as the undercarriage hit him. Clayton couldn't look in the mirror as he drove on.

"You son of a bitch!" Clayton screamed hysterically at the man. "You fucking son of a bitch!" He was crying.

Emily, Danielle, and Whoops were still screaming. Robert was still silent. Clayton had to grip the steering wheel tightly to keep from shaking.

"You fucking son of a bitch. You fucking son of a bitch," Clayton repeated endlessly.

A voice on the CB came in clearly and promised Christ would save you; Jesus would keep you warm, then another voice, competing with the first, shouted, "Get off my channel, George!" More quarrelling. More savagery.

Clayton turned it off, slowed down to avoid losing control on the sand and gravel that coated the asphalt. He clutched the wheel and drove on. He wouldn't look at his wife.

§   §   §

At noon they pulled off the road behind some trees, just north of Port Orford, and Clayton saw that the temperature had climbed to twenty-two. He set up the camp stove and Emily fixed cereal for Whoops and sandwiches for the rest. Only Whoops and Robert ate.

"What would you have done?" Clayton suddenly asked them. All of them. "We can't stop and help everybody."

"I would have stayed back in Yakima," Emily said.

"We'd die back there," Clayton shouted.

"Maybe that's the way it should be," she said.

"You just don't get it!" he shouted and she said nothing more.

They packed up and drove on. Over the CB they heard a plea for help. Someone offering money, food, and clothing for a lift. They had a baby. Look for a gold Lincoln on Route 18. He didn't know where Route 18 was and, with the skip, it might be hundreds of miles away.

He manually turned to another channel and locked it in.

Miles went by. They passed through Port Orford without seeing a soul, and at 1:00 p.m. they passed through Gold Beach and travelled over the hill called Cape Sebastian. On the other side, as they passed over the Pistol River, a white dog came up from under the bridge and ran along the shoulder on the ocean side of the road.

"Look, Dad, a malamute, just like Buddy," Robert said referring to the dog they had had three years before, but got rid of when the food shortages started.

The dog saw them coming and ran out onto the road.

"Can't we pick it up?" Robert asked.

"There's no room for dogs in this world, anymore," Clayton snapped as he swerved and drove past.

"Could we stop and give it some food? He looks hungry."

Clayton kept driving and Robert pressed his face against the side window and watched the dog disappear from view.

A few miles later two police cruisers materialized like ghosts from behind the trees and blocked the road up ahead. Clayton hit the brakes and skidded to a stop. Two pickups seemed to come from nowhere and moved in to block the road from behind. Men emerged from all four vehicles and quickly surrounded the van. Clayton's instinct was to grab the revolver. But there were at least a dozen men standing there and all were armed. He slid the Blackhawk under the seat.

"What do they want?" Emily asked.

"Just stay calm," Clayton answered.

"Why are there cops out here in the middle of nowhere?" she asked.

"Shut up," he said. "Let me handle this."

A red-headed cop with a moon-face walked slowly up to the van. He stopped and stood back from the window on Clayton's side of the van.

"Get out mister—alone," he said to Clayton.

"I'm staying right here," Clayton said.

"We can shoot that van full of holes then drag your bodies out, if you want it that way."

Clayton took a deep breath then slowly opened the door and cautiously stepped out onto the road.

"What do you want, officer?"

"I want to see your hands at all times," the cop said.

Clayton held his hands up with his palms out and in view.

"Turn and put your hands on the side of the van," the cop instructed.

Clayton did as he was told. The chill of the van's metal was painful to his hands.

The cop stepped up behind him and swung his foot between Clayton's feet, kicking the insides of his ankles.

"Spread 'em good," he said, and Clayton did.

They searched him, emptying his pockets.

"You stay right there," the cop said. "Now, everyone else get out real slow. No coats, I want to see what you got."

They got out and stood on the road: Emily, Danielle, and Robert. Emily held the baby in her arms.

The cop looked them over. He smiled at Danielle. "Get over here with your family," he said to Clayton, and he did.

Several men started to go through the van while two others stood with rifles and watched Clayton and his family. Clayton couldn't bring himself to admit what was happening and instead wondered what they wanted.

"What's your name?" one of the older men asked Danielle. He was the biggest of the cops, with huge hands, large ears, and thick lips. His only uniform was a police jacket with a badge. Otherwise, he was wearing jeans and he looked more like a farmer. She didn't answer him. He kept looking her over and smiling. She looked away. She heard someone call him "Hank."

The men removed the gas cans, the boxes of food, and clothing. They started removing the tools. "What's this shit?" one asked. There were air wrenches, a metal lathe, drills. Two of the men huddled for a moment then they started throwing the tools and the empty gas cans onto the shoulder.

"Look at this," another said and showed his companion a cell phone. They both laughed before the man sent it sailing into the woods like a skeet that gently curved in the air before it dove through the branches and fell to the forest floor.

One of them took the M1A and handed it to another who started walking back to the pickups.

Clayton walked toward the van. "Hey, leave that alone. That's my property."

The big man called Hank stepped forward and punched Clayton in the stomach. Clayton bent over and backed away clutching his gut.

Emily screamed. "Leave him alone, you bastard."

The men turned away and ignored them and Clayton watched as they started loading the van again with the gas cans and tools, the boxes of clothes, and the food. At least they were leaving something, he thought, and hoped they wouldn't find the revolver. Then one of the men climbed in behind the wheel and started the van. A police car backed off the road and the driver drove the van away.

"Where are you going with my van?" Clayton screamed.

No one answered.

"What are you doing to us," Clayton yelled.

"You quiet down, boy," the moon-faced cop said. The others called him Barry. "Things could be worse," he said.

"I want my goddamned van back."

"Hey, mister, you watch your mouth."

"What are you doing to us?"

"Nothing, if you behave yourself."

They started walking back toward their cars and trucks.

"You can't just leave us here with nothing," Clayton yelled.

Three men lingered and conferred. They looked back at Clayton and his family several times. They were talking about something.

"Please, help us," Clayton begged them. "Please, you can't do this."

The three of them walked back toward Clayton. The trucks and the police cars had their engines idling.

"Take us with you," Clayton asked. "We'll carry our weight. Please."

They ignored him but the big man, Hank, suddenly grabbed Danielle's arm and started dragging her away.

"Hey," Clayton shouted and stepped forward but was pushed back.

"Daddy," she screamed.

"Come on," Hank said.

"No," she yelled and kicked him. He threw an arm over her shoulder and got her in a head lock. She was helpless.

Clayton knew what they were doing. "Leave my daughter alone," he yelled and lunged forward.

One of the men hit him with the butt of a rifle and Clayton fell to the ground and the man kicked him. The other two dragged Danielle toward a truck.

Emily cried, baying like a wounded cow. She started walking toward the trucks holding Whoops out. "If you're gonna leave us, take the baby," she sobbed. "Please take the baby."

A man pushed her away.

"Let Danielle take her," she cried.

Danielle screamed to her father and mother and struggled to get out of the cab of the truck. One of the men started beating her with his fist.

Emily dropped to her knees before another man. She wasn't crying now. She held Whoops out before him. Her voice was frighteningly steady and insistent. "Let my daughter take the baby. For Christ's sake, be human."

The man's name was Jerry Brady. He looked at her. His face contorted and he suddenly took the baby and walked to the truck where Danielle sat and handed Whoops to her.

Danielle clutched her sister and screamed, "*Mommy! Help!*"

"Thank you," Emily said to Brady. She pointed to Robert, but the man shook his head.

"*Please!*"

He walked away.

They got into a pickup truck and, just as suddenly as they had appeared, the police cars and the trucks were gone.

§   §   §

Clayton, Emily, and Robert sat on a guardrail alongside the road.

It was a little after four p.m. when a caravan of about forty cars and trucks raced by. Clayton tried to wave them down. He saw faces in the windows as they passed. Faces that would not turn to look at his own. He saw a station wagon with boxes and tires on top that was pulling a U-Haul trailer and he was sure it was the station wagon he had left behind on the road. The caravan disappeared and Clayton and his family were enveloped in silence again.

He sat down on the guardrail again and waited.

The temperature was falling and the snowfall was getting heavy. Robert was crying from the cold and Emily sobbed.

Sometime after 7:00 p.m. Robert stopped crying. Clayton looked at him. He had turned grey and was shivering from the cold. Emily was no longer sobbing. She stared out into the road. It was getting dark. There was nowhere to go, but Clayton knew they would have to walk tonight if they expected to keep warm.

Chapter 3
August 26

The sound of breathing woke Zach. He rolled over in the burrow and reflexively grabbed the Model 60 revolver near his head. He was already squeezing the trigger as he shook off sleep and found himself staring into the eyes of a medium-sized malamute, all white except for a single patch of grey on its right shoulder. The hammer was almost all the way back. A little more and the sear/trigger engagement would break, the hammer would drop, and a bullet would send the canine straight to doggy hell.

Startled by the swiftness of Zach's reaction, the dog backed up but neither attacked nor ran. It stared at him and its tail began to wag. Then, ever so gingerly, it stretched its neck to smell the gun's muzzle.

It almost made Zach laugh. Carefully, he let the trigger return to its original position and the hammer gently came to rest against the frame. He slowly sat up and looked around. There was fresh snow everywhere.

The dog lowered itself onto its haunches and watched him.

Zach couldn't believe his incredible luck. But he didn't want to waste a cartridge, and a shot could draw unwanted attention to him. Loners weren't tolerated by the two gangs that lived along this segment of the 101. Discovery could be fatal.

The dog started to sniff around. This was no feral dog. From the number of tracks in the campsite, it had been exploring for quite a while as Zach slept.

He shoved the revolver into his pocket and grabbed his rifle as he slid out of the sleeping bag and the burrow. Where there was a nonferal dog, there were sure to be people. But there was no evidence of anyone for as far as he could see, and only the dog's footprints appeared in the snow.

The prints went out into the field behind them, then doubled back. Looking down onto the road, he could see where it had come from the north, along the far shoulder. Its tracks were unaccompanied and even now they were disappearing beneath the still-falling snow.

He was sure neither of the gangs kept dogs, they were too expensive to maintain. So he wondered where this one came from.

It was meat and it would be a shame to let it go to waste. He'd already eaten most of the food he'd brought, and with the meat from this animal he could stay out another few days and not have to go back to his cabin. There wasn't much to the dog. It was skinny. But every bite counted.

"Where'd you come from?" Zach whispered.

At the sound of his voice, the dog got off its haunches and came to him.

"Get away," Zach commanded. He didn't want to become friendly with it. The dog backed up a step and sat down, again.

Zach looked around once more to ensure they were alone and the dog got up and sniffed his pack. Zach knew it could smell the goat jerky and rye bread inside. It was hungry.

"Get away from that," Zach threatened.

The dog backed off again, but soon stepped forward to smell Zach's sleeping bag.

"If you lift a leg to piss on that, I'll put a bullet up your ass."

Each time he spoke, the dog regarded him curiously. It was used to people.

The snow picked up. Now, even the dog's most recent tracks would soon disappear.

He would have to be fast. He got out his skinning knife. He'd slit its throat. It would be quick, clean, and quiet. "Quiet" was most important if its master or anyone else was nearby. He would skin it, dress it out, and use its brains to start tanning the hide. He could do all this and have the meat packed in less than an hour.

The dog was now lying on the sleeping bag. It sniffed the pack, again, saw Zach watching him, so he put his head down and pretended to ignore it, though it was mere inches from his muzzle.

Then Zach heard vehicles. He fell down on the snow so as not to be seen from the road. The dog didn't move. He watched it wondering if it would get up. If someone saw it from the road and stopped there could be a firefight. He'd managed to avoid all such confrontations, but for one, in the last three years.

He clicked the safety off on his old M1 Garand rifle and watched from behind some brush as a caravan went by. There were automobiles, trucks, and vans. Three pulled trailers, the rest didn't.

Just as suddenly as they appeared they were gone leaving nothing behind but fresh tracks on the road.

He waited. Nowadays, the caravans usually came in more than one section: twenty or thirty cars and trucks in the lead followed a minute or so later by another twenty or thirty vehicles. Sometimes there were three sections. It was a strategy emigrants had adopted so if part of the caravan got in trouble the others could come to its aid. The road pirates were aware of the strategy and pretty much left the big caravans alone, now. It was the small groups and the loners who almost suicidally tried to make the trip alone that the pirates were likely to prey on.

He pulled the bolt back on his M1 and ejected the round and pocketed it. It was a 165-grain boat-tailed soft-point. He saved these for hunting. He didn't want to waste them in a firefight unless he had to. The remaining eight rounds in the en bloc clip were vintage armor-piercing rounds. He let the bolt slam home.

The dog never moved.

Then they arrived; a second string of vehicles. He lay low until it, too, had passed.

Zach didn't usually set up camp this close to the road. But he'd tracked a deer this far the day before and he'd made camp here before quitting for the night...he told himself it was a mistake he wouldn't repeat.

He waited and listened. There were no other sounds. That was the entire caravan.

He wondered if the dog lived locally. He wasn't aware of any settlement within five miles of where he'd camped that kept a dog like this. But who knew? People had gotten good at hiding in the hills. He had. It could also have been turned loose or lost by one of the carloads of emigrants. Perhaps someone whose car broke down.

He heard a distant motor, again. But it wasn't from the road. It sounded like a chainsaw...or a snowmobile. A snowmobile would be dangerous if he was spotted. That was the last thing he wanted to contend with. The sound stopped. He listened. It didn't start up again. The silence made him more nervous than the sound. He was too close to the road. He had to get going.

He put the skinning knife away and broke camp quickly. He pulled the winter-camo ski mask over his head. There was no time to tend to the dog.

"You're lucky," he whispered.

The dog watched him.

He rolled up his sleeping bag, tied it to his pack, slipped his pack on his back, and donned his skis. He slung the old M1 over his shoulder.

He looked at the dog, again. "Shit," he whispered when he saw the dog staring alertly at the trees to the south. Zach knew it had heard or seen something.

It was time to go. But he wanted the dog. He lay his rifle down, dropped the pack, again, took a length of rope from it, and quickly started to fashion a harness. The dog was becoming more agitated.

That was Zach's final clue. No time for a harness. No time for the dog. It was time to get lost in the forest.

He stuffed the rope back in his pack, slung the pack up on to his back, picked up his rifle and, poles in hand, he skied eastward from the camp and away from the highway. The dog followed him. He wasn't sure why it did. The snow was picking up, but it wasn't picking up fast enough to erase his latest tracks.

He reached the edge of the woods and started down one of the old skid roads. He felt he'd be safe once he was in the trees. The dog ran ahead. But about three hundred yards into the woods it stopped and Zach skied past him. Suddenly, he brought himself up short. He looked back. The dog wasn't going any further. Something up ahead had made it stop. Zach looked further up the road. Maybe skiing in this direction had been a mistake. The dog didn't want to go there. Perhaps he should have skied west, across the highway. But in that direction lay the ocean and that put limits to where he could go. He started to sidestep back up the road while trying to peer into the trees around him. He had a gut feeling the dog knew...

There was the first shot. He couldn't tell where it came from, except snow came down from the branches above his head.

He unslung his rifle from his shoulder and the dog zipped past him.

Follow the dog, he told himself and resumed going east down the road, crouching low over his skis as more gunfire came out of the trees. The dog was getting further ahead. He looked back over his shoulder and saw skiers enter the road in pursuit.

"Shit," he said.

He felt a tug on his pack and a burst of feathers puffed out ahead of him and he realized a bullet had torn through his sleeping bag. If he hadn't been crouching forward over his skis it would have gone through him.

Whoever among them was shooting were not good shots, but it just took one lucky one...or one good marksman in the bunch. His only chance was to keep moving.

He'd been down this road before and he remembered there was a rise up ahead. A decent shooter could take him there when the hill slowed him down.

But he was making good time. Then, there was the rise, looming ahead. He'd never make it to the top before they reached the bottom and they'd have the clear shot they needed. He looked back just as they came into sight. Ahead, the dog had already crested the rise and waited briefly before it suddenly slunk off into the trees.

Zach left the road halfway up the hill and kicked off his skis. He was bringing up his old M1 just as his pursuers were leaving the trail themselves, disappearing into the woods on both sides of the road.

From somewhere someone else started shooting in his direction even though he'd disappeared. Voices yelled for the shooter not to waste ammo. The shooting stopped. You didn't waste ammunition in the ice age.

In the distance he could hear a snowmobile—no, *two*. Things were getting worse, fast.

He peered through the branches and the brush. His pursuers were dressed in winter-camo, as was he. Unless they had cohorts further up the trail, salvation still lay to the east. He picked up his skis and started backing deeper into the trees—and he fell over. He'd tripped over the damned dog. It was back.

"Get outta here," Zach whispered.

Another shot brought more snow down from the branches. He didn't think they could see him. They were trying to panic him out into the open—or to get him to stop moving and try to hide. Stopping would be fatal.

He looked back through the brush.

Someone yelled something he couldn't make out. There was motion through the woods north of him as someone was in and out of sight faster than he could bring his rifle up.

Then he heard more voices from the south, on the other side of the trail. Moving through the trees, they were trying to get ahead of him, attempting to outflank him on both sides. And the snowmobiles were getting closer. They were closing in. Unless he moved he'd be surrounded.

If he could just see one of them—for just a few seconds—he could change things. He didn't know how many there were. But getting east, ahead of them, was still his only escape. He knew he couldn't linger here and he knew he couldn't hide, and if the dog stayed with him, it was going to keep giving his position away. He had to kill the dog—now. He unsheathed his knife and turned. It was gone.

Through the branches he saw something move in the trees to the north. He stared at the spot where he thought he'd seen it. Nothing stood out until it moved once more. Now he could discern a head covered in a winter-camo ski mask like his own. It made the man almost invisible and Zach could just barely make out the contours against the snow-laden branches. He brought his rifle up quickly. He put the bead exactly where he figured the man's face was, then dropped it about ten inches low and ten inches to the left. He didn't want the man dead—yet. He squeezed the trigger gently so that the shot was a surprise to him, as it always was when he placed a good shot. There was a silence that made him think this time he'd missed, but a piercing scream suddenly filled the woods.

A panic-filled voice yelled, "He got Jamison."

"How bad?" another yelled.

More screaming. It had to be Jamison screaming.

"Kill that bastard," another voice yelled.

Now there other voices everywhere.

"Watch out for him," another voice yelled.

That's what Zach wanted to hear.

Though this Jamison would probably die from his wound, right now he was more useful to him alive and screaming. Wounded, at least one of them was likely to hang back to take care of him. And with him screaming they now knew Zach could shoot. This would make them cautious and he hoped it would slow them down. It had to or he was dead.

He started running east through the woods. His skis were getting hung up on branches, making travel difficult, but he couldn't leave them. He still needed to use them to get away.

Men on both sides of the road were getting ever further ahead, trapping him. He could hear orders yelled back and forth. Another voice was clearly one from a walkie-talkie. They were coordinating their attack. He had to keep moving.

If he could just hit another one they wouldn't feel so free to move around and it would give him a chance to make it to the top of the rise so he could get out of the trees and get on his skis, again.

But where'd the dog go?

He saw where its tracks disappeared into the brush and he reflexively followed them into a gully. They went up an embankment and into a small snow-filled glade. He was disoriented, now. He couldn't tell where north-south or east-west lay. The dog's tracks led across the opening. He started across it and heard the click that made him spin around. A boy no more than fourteen was fumbling with an old Russian AKM rifle. Something had jammed it.

Zach dropped his skis and brought his M1 up.

"No, mister, please," the boy pleaded as he lowered his rifle. The look of terror on his face was complete.

Zach walked back to him and wrenched the rifle out of his hands. He removed the magazine and jacked out the cartridge in the breech. Without saying a word he swung the rifle twice against a tree damaging the sheet metal receiver so it would never fire again, then he flung it off into the woods.

"Get the hell out of here," he whispered to the boy. The boy nodded and turned to leave.

Zach went back to where he'd dropped his skis and heard a shot. He spun back and the boy was back out of the trees with a small revolver in his hands and shooting at him.

Bringing his own rifle up quickly, he shot the boy in the head.

"You son of a bitch," he said. He hadn't wanted to shoot the kid. Now the shots would lead the others here. He should have just slit the little bastard's throat the way he should have done the dog.

He grabbed his skis and worked his way further into the forest.

And, suddenly, there was the road covered with the new snow unblemished, except for the dog's tracks, and again he knew which way was east. He put his skis on and followed the dog.

Branches reached out over the road like fingers and slapped at him as he whooshed by. It would only be a few more years and they would obliterate the trail.

As he reached another bend he looked back over his shoulder just as skiers came into view. He made it past the turn before they could get shots off, but ahead was another rise that would slow him down. He kicked off his skis, ran to the top, and put them back on just as his pursuers came back into view behind him. Ahead was a long downhill.

He tried to remember where this road went as another bullet ripped through the trees behind him. They were taking desperate shots. There were chiding shouts to conserve ammunition. Then there was the ominous sound of the snowmobiles.

He skied through another turn then he saw it: the road led into a vast sloping snow-covered pasture that sunk down into a glen, then rose away on the other side. It was either off into the woods or attempt to cross the downside of the field and hope to make it up the other side before they reached this spot from which they'd get clear shots. But safety wasn't in hiding in the trees; it was in getting away. He started down the slope and, suddenly, the dog was back, running through the snow beside him.

He glanced back several times, hit the bottom of the slope, and skied as far up the other side as he could, until he kicked off his skis again, swept them up, and ran as hard as he could up the hill.

Sudden shots told him they'd reached the edge of the field. Snow sprayed up around him where their bullets hit.

"Shit!" he yelled.

He unslung his rifle, and spun. There were two of them, with scoped rifles, trying to acquire him. He drew a quick bead and squeezed off a shot, but he was breathing too heavily to make it accurate. Another shot. He knew he must be hitting close because they turned and disappeared back onto the road. He continued up the hill and saw the dog had stopped with him. Stupid dog he thought to himself as he plodded through the snow. Just as he reached the top more shots rang out. They had to be as winded as he was and were having the same trouble placing their shots accurately, scopes or not.

He threw himself onto the snow, as bullets struck around him, and he rolled over the ridge and out of their view. The dog ran on.

The shooting stopped once he was out of sight. He didn't dare stand. To the east the field sloped gently away. He could ski it quickly, though he'd have quite a bit of open ground to cover. If they made it up to the top of this rise before he made it to the trees on the other side, there'd be nothing between him and their rifles. He had to slow them down.

He crawled back toward the ridge until he could see them. "Shit," he said to himself when he saw three of the men had already skied halfway down the hill. He took careful aim and squeezed off a shot at the lead skier. He missed. He was still shaking and breathing too heavily for good shot placement and each cartridge spent was a round gone forever in a world where no one was making ammunition for civilians anymore. He squeezed off another shot and the lead skier fell. The other two veered off into the woods. The fallen skier lay still for a moment and Zach thought he was dead. Then he started to move.

The dog came back and stood on the ridge in front of him. Zach reached out, grabbed its leg, and pulled it back.

"Get back here, you stupid bastard. Stay."

The dog lay down behind him.

He heard the roar of a motor, again. At the mouth of the road a red snowmobile stopped.

"Shit." He couldn't outrun or out-ski a snowmobile.

He brought the rifle up and placed the front sight on the driver, then dropped it to the snowmobile itself. He squeezed off the shot just as the snowmobile lurched forward and he was sure he'd missed. He tried to acquire his target again, but holding the front sight on it as it raced down the hill was frustrating. Then, halfway down, its engine started to smoke and it seized up. The rider jumped off and started running toward the woods. He tried to draw a bead on the man, but there was no good running shot to make.

Other skiers were now coming down the hill but they were moving fast and staying in the shadows of the trees near the edge of the field. The smoke from the snowmobile was letting up. The skier he'd hit was now crawling towards the woods.

Zach watched him through his sights. He could kill him, but once again, a wounded man was more useful to him than a dead one...though he'd no doubt die, later. He watched the man struggle through the snow until he was almost to the trees. Two men emerged from the woods to drag him to cover. This was what Zach was waiting for. Carefully, he placed the front sight on one of the two. His breathing was measured now, his finger deliberate, and without quite realizing, he pulled the trigger again. The man fell. But, at the same time, he heard the "pling" of the en bloc clip as it flew out of the magazine — one more irreplaceable item from the pre-ice-age world. He reached in his pocket for a loaded clip and jammed it into the magazine well. When he brought his rifle back into play there were two men lying in the snow. The third was already back in the woods. One of the two looked like he may be dead. The other was still desperately crawling his way back toward the trees. He brought the rifle sight to bear on him. His finger gently began to squeeze the trigger, but he again reminded himself the guy was still more useful to him wounded. He took his finger off the trigger and pushed the safety on.

The dog looked confused and began to whine but stayed down on the snow as commanded.

Zach rolled through the snow to retrieve the spent en bloc clip. Suddenly, snow was flying from in front of the spot where he had been lying. They didn't know where he was. They were either trying to panic him so he'd give his position away or it was suppression fire to provide cover to get the wounded man out of the snow. He stuffed the empty clip into his pocket.

To escape, he needed a diversion, and he had one he'd never had to use before. He didn't know if it would work, but now was the time to find out. He scooted back to his pack. From one of its pockets he took a plastic bag that held several M80s, a pack of cigarettes, and a butane lighter. He opened the pack of cigarettes and took two out. One he tore in half and put one of the halves back into the pack. He needed something to put the cigarettes on. They wouldn't burn if he just laid them on the snow. He took a book from his pack and tore off the front cover. He then tore the cover in half and folded each half. He lit the two cigarettes and inserted the fuses of the M80s into the unlit ends of each of them. He nestled one of the cigarette/M80 combos into each of the folded halves of the cover, to protect them from the falling snow, and set them a few feet apart.

Then he scooted further back until, in a crouch and out of sight of his pursuers, he could put his skis back on. He stood a little and peered back at the opposite hill, to the road from where he had come. His pursuers were all below the crest of the hill now and still out of sight.

He started off through the field. He looked back at the dog that was watching him, but hadn't gotten up.

"Come on, stupid," Zach commanded, and it rose to its feet and followed him. "Damned idiot dog," he said as he skied off.

He was sure his pursuers were, even now, making their way through the woods, again trying to outflank him. But he could cover ground faster through the field than they could through the trees. And as he reached the field's far end he heard what he hoped was the first M80 go off. It would make them hesitant to climb the hill. And there was another one set to go off in just a minute or so. He looked back. All that was evident of his passing through the field were his and the dog's tracks. There was nothing he could do about that. What he needed was for the fireworks to buy him more time so he could disappear into the trees.

There was another road at this end of the field. Unlike the skid road from which he'd entered the field, this one was wildly overgrown. That was why he hadn't gone down it his last time here, so he didn't know where it led. But there was no time to ponder that, now.

Travelling down this road was slower, but it would also slow his pursuers—unless they had more snowmobiles.

He kept going. But at one point he stopped, but only because the dog stopped.

Fresh deer tracks. The dog sniffed them.

It may be the deer he'd been tracking the day before, though he hoped it was a different one; the more deer still alive, the better. Zach told himself he might come back here to hunt, later, but only if he could figure out where these guys had come from. He needed that knowledge, if he was going to avoid them in the future.

"Come on, stupid," he commanded, and the dog immediately followed.

§   §   §

The first to reach the top of the hill was a tall man with blonde hair and beard, named Billy Raymond, and he saw Zach and the dog's tracks that led off east across the field. He turned and waved the others up. While he waited he saw the second M80, its fuse stuck in the cigarette, still sitting on the book cover. The cigarette had gone out. He picked it up.

"Son of a bitch," he said. He knew what the man he'd been pursuing had done to stall them.

He picked up the two halves of the book cover. Putting them together he saw it was from an old Army field manual, *FM 21-76, Survival.* On the other side someone had written in ink, *This book belongs to Zachary Amaral.* The name seemed vaguely familiar.

In the snow he saw some of the spent brass the shooter had used. He picked it up and knew right away it was .30-06. He pocketed it.

A blue snowmobile appeared at the mouth of the road and started down into the field. It stopped beside the disabled red snowmobile and the rider dismounted to examine it.

Raymond screamed at the others to hurry up. But the man with the snowmobile, Jim De Angelis, had left its engine running while he inspected the disabled one and he couldn't hear the shouting.

None of the others were hurrying up the hill. They approached the crest warily. They already knew the man they'd been pursuing could shoot. Raymond was livid at their lack of speed.

"Get up here," he yelled.

When they reached him, he pointed to the tracks left by Zach and the dog.

"He's gone. Let's go," he yelled.

"We've got to take Peterson and Jamison back," Ted Foy, a large, older man, countered. "And Anderson is dead."

"No, we've got to get that bastard," Raymond yelled as he started in the direction Zach had taken.

When no one followed, he stopped.

"Come on," he screamed.

"We've got wounded men to get back," Foy said.

"Let the others take them. We've got to get him."

"You go get him," Foy yelled back. "We've got to keep these other guys alive."

The snowmobile finally reached them and the driver, De Angelis, got off. "Jamison bled to death," he said without emotion.

One of the walkie-talkies came to life and a voice said, "We found Kyle...he's dead...head shot."

"Kyle?" Raymond yelled in alarm. "He's just a kid. Give me the goddamned snowmobile," he screamed as he lunged for it.

"No," Foy yelled and blocked him. "We've got to keep Peterson alive. The snowmobile's the quickest way back to the ranch."

"Then you pussies can go," Raymond yelled. "Who's with me?"

"No one," Foy yelled back. "Anderson was leading this expedition and now he's dead. We don't know who the hell we're chasing and I don't know anyone here who wants to be dead, so we're going back."

"LaCroix's gonna be pissed we let this guy get away."

"Then let LaCroix make that decision. This was bound to happen sooner or later; we've run into a meat grinder. How many guys do you want to get killed chasing this one guy? How do we know he isn't meeting up with some friends? We could be going into an ambush."

Foy turned around and yelled at De Angelis, "Go get Peterson and get him back to the compound, *fast!* Then come back for Anderson, Jamison, and Kyle. But get Peterson back as quick as you can."

"What about the other snowmobile?" Raymond asked.

"It's toast, but we can part-it-out." De Angelis said.

"Anyone know this guy…" Raymond asked as he took the halves of book cover out of his pocket and read the name to them, "…Zachary Amaral?"

"Who's that?" Foy asked.

Raymond was agitated. "It's a name on a fuckin' book cover that had a cigarette and firecracker on it," he shouted.

"Cigarette and firecracker?"

"Yeah, that motherfucker tricked us so he could get a lead on us." He looked around. "Anyone know the name?"

After a few seconds, Wayne Dodd, who had been silent to this point, started saying, "Amaral…Amaral…"

"You know who he is?" Raymond asked.

"Hold on…Yeah, he…ah… he married Sandra Gibbons…"

"Sandra Gibbons, the cheerleader from a few years back?"

"Yeah, I think that's him."

"Gibbons is Anderson's damned cousin."

"Second or third cousin, I think," Foy said.

"Who *is* he, though? Who the hell is Zachary Amaral?"

"I hunted with him five or six years ago." Dodd went on. "He was a survivalist-type guy; had a lot of guns and ammo. I can't remember where he came from. But his family owned a cabin out here, somewhere. Kind of athletic. And I remember he won some kind of regional science fair, because that's why Sandra went for him; she liked brainy guys."

"Lotta guys had the hots for her," Foy said.

"Well, I've got the hots for this Amaral, now," Raymond said. "I want him dead. Let's get him."

"We've got wounded to take back," Foy said steadfastly.

"*No!* We're getting this guy, now."

"You're not taking the snowmobile," Foy said.

"I don't need the snowmobile. Who's coming?"

No one volunteered.

"What about you, Wayne? You coming with me?" he asked Dodd, the weakest-willed, a "yes man" who craved acceptance.

Dodd wavered for a second. He didn't want to go. But he didn't want anyone to think he was scared. He was afraid if he said "No" first and others then joined…how would he look?

"What's your decision?" Raymond demanded

Reluctantly he skied toward Raymond.

"Who else?"

No one moved. Some turned their backs to him. They'd lost the stomach to track this guy into the woods.

"Come on, Scott."

Scott Kramer shook his head no.

"Just go part ways with me," Raymond said.

Scott wavered.

"We'll just follow him a little ways. If it looks dangerous, we'll turn back."

Scott didn't know how to say no, either.

"Come on, you guys. We can get him. We can get him for the guys that are down."

"I'm keeping Peterson alive," Foy said and started skiing away. Most of the others followed him.

"Let those pussies go," Raymond said and he started skiing along the tracks Zach and the dog had left.

"Come on," he said to Dodd and Scott.

Reluctantly, they followed Raymond across the field, but they lagged back, afraid bullets would come out of the trees where the tracks led. Once there, they saw where Zach and the dog's tracks disappeared down the old overgrown skid road; they stood out like signposts.

The three entered the road but their progress wasn't as fast as Zach's because Dodd and Scott still lagged, anticipating ambushes every foot of the way. They knew their quarry could and would shoot. Raymond chided them for their caution as they travelled, but even he was cautious and he wasn't willing to get too far ahead of his companions.

Chapter 4
August 26

Zach kept up a good pace getting further and further ahead for the next hour. The dog stayed with him.

He stopped only occasionally to listen for snowmobiles before he'd continue. He'd taken his coat off and tied it around his waist as he heated up from the exertion.

The snow was coming down harder. This was good if it covered his trail, but he wasn't sure how far behind his pursuers were or whether they'd even followed. At various points the dog disappeared only to reappear further along. Zach wasn't sure why it stayed with him.

He was getting hungry and he came to yet another broad pasture the forest would reclaim if the ice age didn't take it, first. He crossed it and finally stopped. He looked back and could see the road where he'd entered the field; where they'd have to enter it if they'd followed him.

He took off his ski mask to expose his ears and he listened again for the snowmobiles.

There was nothing other than the sound of the wind and his own heavy breathing. He unslung his rifle, leaned it against a tree, then let his pack slide off his back until it dropped to the snow. He sat down on a snow-covered log, concealed from view by the bushes that surrounded it. From here he could keep an eye on the entrance to the field. He opened his pack and took out some jerky and a half loaf of rye bread. The dog was at his feet. Zach ate a little. The dog watched attentively.

He broke off a piece of jerky.

"What am I doing?" he asked himself as he held some out to the dog.

The malamute edged close enough to take it. He ate it in one gulp.

Zach ate more himself, then, defying an inner voice that told him he was wasting food, he gave the rest to the dog.

With the jerky gone, Zach folded the plastic bag and put it in his pocket. A plastic bag was one more thing that, once it was gone, was irreplaceable. He broke off some bread, brought it up to his mouth, but hesitated as the dog stared at him. Ignoring the inner voice again, he tore off another piece and held it out.

The dog took it, stepped back, and dropped it on the snow to sniff it, then he devoured it.

Zach continued to watch the clearing. There was nothing moving in the tree line. Gradually, his tracks were obliterated by the new snow. He'd wait here a while to make sure they were completely covered. He wanted to feel that security before he moved on.

He ran his hand over the old M1. He liked it. It was accurate, reliable, and durable. But he wondered if he should have brought his Winchester Model 70. That rifle was scoped. It would have been better for the long-range shots he'd made in the morning. Perhaps he wouldn't have wasted as many rounds. He didn't know. He'd think about that, later.

He thought about the boy he'd killed. It made him sick. It wasn't what he wanted to do. If the little bastard had just left, everything would have been all right, but he had that hidden revolver and he had to start shooting at him. It had been two years since he'd killed anyone. He'd done it to get out of another ambush, just like today. And now there were…he held up his hand and counted off on his fingers, one-two-three-four…as many as four more deaths on his conscience.

He looked down at the sleeping bag still tied to his pack and saw where the bullet had torn through it. Little bits of down were coming out the exit hole. He untied it from the pack and unrolled it. There were several holes, all made by the same bullet as it had travelled through the rolled-up bag. It must have been a full-metal jacketed bullet since it apparently hadn't mushroomed, so the damage to the sleeping bag was minimal. And it must have exited just an inch or two over his head as he was crouched over his skis. Close. Too close.

He could repair the holes when he got home. He was thankful he'd been lucky and all that was damaged was his sleeping bag. He also knew it would take just one errant bullet to change everything.

He looked around. He wasn't quite lost, but nothing was familiar, either.

Across the field, something moving caught his eye through the falling snow. He stared and suddenly realized it was a black bear; the first one he'd seen in a year. Even from here he could tell it was skinny, but it was also big, so there'd be plenty of meat. Given the weather shift, it wasn't going to find enough to fatten up for hibernation, and probably wasn't going to survive the coming winter.

There were almost no big animals anymore. In most areas deer and elk had been hunted to extinction, and in remote areas, where some still survived, they were dying off because there wasn't enough spring or summer to speak of and, without a growing season, most of them couldn't put on summer fat so they simply starved once the snow started falling.

Then there were the roaming farm animals. There weren't many of those, either, but there were still some, though he hadn't seen any in over a month. It seemed forever ago that he'd taken the goat he'd jerked.

Domesticated animals were heading for their own extinctions, too. Over the next few generations, if they could survive in the wild, they'd gradually evolve back to the species from which they came. Horses would revert to something that resembled Przewalski's horses, the tarpan, or the European forest horse; cattle to their Asian and African ancestors; domestic dogs probably wouldn't survive at all, unable to contend with more efficient predators. And cats? They probably had a better chance than most.

There was still some small game and though it was sparse, he still found an occasional squirrel or rabbit.

The bear was too much meat to pass up. He watched it forage in the snow.

The dog began to growl.

"Quiet," he said in a low voice, and it fell silent.

The bear would still have some valuable protein on it. He wouldn't try to make the shot from here but, if he was careful, he could make it back through the field until he was close enough to get a reliable shot. Then he could dress it out and hide part of the carcass and the skin in a tree to return for, later.

He quietly swapped the armor-piercing ammo clip for a clip with the hunting ammunition. He put his outer camo clothing back on so, once again, he blended in with the landscape. He stood and looked down at the dog. It, too, watched the bear. But it was quiet and motionless.

"Stay," he whispered, wondering if it would.

The dog glanced at him, then back at the bear.

He put his skis on and started out into the field. He hadn't gotten far when he heard the dog growl, again. It would scare the bear off.

"Shit," he whispered.

He turned to ski back to the dog. A quick flick of his knife and he'd have two carcasses. It would still be a good day.

He unsheathed his skinning knife. The dog ignored him, but it also ignored the bear and stared off into that part of the field they had come over. It made Zach look back over his shoulder, but there was nothing there.

"Come 'ere," he commanded with a whisper. But the dog wouldn't move. It stood at attention and stared into the field

A shot rang out and Zach went into a crouch.

He looked back at the bear. It was gone.

The dog growled, again.

"Quiet, stupid," he whispered, and it stopped.

He listened, but there were no other sounds. No snowmobiles.

He strained to see through the falling snow and finally he could barely make out one... two...no, three figures clad in winter-camo going to the spot where the bear had been. So, they *had* followed him.

Soon, the three were all huddled down in the field. He knew they were dressing the carcass out. He didn't know how many others there might be behind them. He stayed hidden. If he'd gone out there to take the bear himself, he'd have been in the middle of the field before they'd taken their shot. They'd have seen him and he'd have had nowhere to hide. He felt lucky.

They took the better part of twenty minutes working the bear's carcass. He watched as they took part of it back to the tree line and hoisted it up into a tree.

Finally, taking what they could carry, they all left the field. They'd given up pursuing him. They had no idea they were within a few hundred yards of him.

Zach waited about twenty minutes before he skied back across the field. He found the organs where they'd left them on the snow.

The dog approached the entrails. He was hungry.

"No!" he said to the dog and it stopped,

The entrails were likely to contain pathogens. He gathered them up in a heavy plastic bag.

"Come!" he said and the dog was off in pursuit as he skied to the edge of the field and found the stash they'd put up in a tree. They'd taken the best cuts with them, but there was still enough here to feed him—and even the dog—for several days. He guessed they'd gone to get a snowmobile to retrieve it.

He reached inside his coat and took out the plastic bag. He took what he could carry which was almost all the rest of the usable meat and bone. He'd stash it somewhere else. The rest he spilled onto the snow. Let them think it had fallen. Maybe it would even feed some of the other animals. His tracks would be gone by the time they returned.

All in all it was a good day. He'd survived an ambush, gotten a good part of a bear, and, in the dog, he had meat on the hoof...foot...whatever. Fresh meat for whenever he needed it. So far the dog had earned his keep.

"Let's go," he said and the dog started running.

By nightfall he'd stashed most of what he'd taken in a tree several miles away. In this weather it would keep until he came back. And all of the new tracks he and the dog made were rapidly disappearing.

He could go home, now. But he had mixed feelings about going back to his cabin. He often had terrible dreams when he slept there. His best haven was also his worst nightmare. So, he made another camp about four miles from his cabin and stayed out another night. There were ghosts at his cabin.

He carved a burrow out of the snow and let the dog sleep in it with him.

Chapter 5
August 26

Danielle woke to Whoops's cries and raised herself up onto one elbow to make sure the baby was covered. There was a pink mark on Whoops's face where Hank had slapped her to make her scream. Danielle made her sister as comfortable as she could, then lay back down, pulled the blankets back over her shoulders, and let the baby cry.

The room was cold and stunk of must and mildew. The mattress had the faint odor of old urine. They had taken her clothes. After trying to fight them off, last night, her muscles ached. She didn't know how many had had her. Hank, the big man who had punched her father in the stomach then dragged her away from her family, had been the first. They had undressed her as a gang, then the others stood along the walls of the room and made rude comments while waiting their turns.

She tried to fight him off, but he was too big. The air around him was oppressive with his BO and he'd enjoyed her struggling while he lay on top of her. And his tongue—he forced it into her mouth and when she turned her head, it was in her ear. He was strong enough to hold both of her arms above her head with one of his huge hands, and he used the other to cover her mouth and nose so she couldn't breathe. She struggled desperately but without air she began to black out. When he removed his hand she gasped for breath and he laughed. He did it again and she started losing consciousness faster. She was going to die. When he took his hand away, he spit in her face, he yelled, "Wake up!" and laughed.

Finally, she was too tired to fight and she thought he'd finally take her. But he got angry instead. He swore at her and that's when he reached over and slapped Whoops's face and she screamed. From somewhere deep inside, Danielle found more reserves and almost threw him off. He laughed, again. This was what he wanted. She immediately realized it wasn't sex he craved, what he wanted was violence because seconds after penetration he was done.

He got off her, dressed, and as he left the room, he laughed, "She's all yours, boys," and they closed in on her. They held her down and, one after another, they had her, joking with each other as they did, as if she wasn't there, each of them proving his manliness to the others. She couldn't fight anymore. She couldn't look at their faces and closed her eyes and prayed they'd leave her sister alone. Four, five, six? Maybe more. She was sure some had her twice.

Now she felt dirty, humiliated, violated, and guilty. Guilty of what? She wasn't sure. She wanted to throw up. Waves of anger and hate washed over her like tsunamis. She hated the men who had brought her here, the men who had had her last night, and all the others who lived in the compound. She hated her parents for the disaster that had befallen her — had befallen them all. She hated her old boyfriend for reasons she could not yet conjure. Most of all, she hated herself. The only person she loved was Whoops.

She lifted the covers to look. Her arms and legs were bruised. There was dried blood and semen on her thighs and the mattress. The baby cried without surcease. She was hungry. Danielle didn't know how she'd feed her.

She wondered if she'd get pregnant. At sixteen, she didn't know quite what it took. She knew what they did to her could make her pregnant, but she wasn't sure if it was certain. Then she didn't care if she was. Not yet, anyway. All she cared about right now was Whoops.

There was an argument going on in the other room. The voices were muffled as they came through the wall. She could make out the angry words of a woman saying they couldn't feed them.

How long would they leave her alone in this room without clothes?

The door opened. "She's awake," a woman's voice said as the door slammed shut and she was alone, again.

She could still hear the voices, though they were indistinct and had to compete with Whoops, but one, a woman's voice, was clear. She said, "Tell her to get out here."

The next time she heard the door open a man's unfriendly voice said, "Here. Get up," and she felt something fall on the bed and the door slammed, again.

She lifted her head to see her jeans and shirt. No underpants, no bra, no socks.

She lay her head back down. Whoops kept crying and Danielle pulled her closer. She'd have to get up soon and find something to feed her.

After ten minutes the door opened, again. The woman's voice said, "Get up and get out here before someone comes in here and drags you out." This time the door was slammed so hard the room shook and Whoops got a surprised look on her face and stopped crying for just a moment, then resumed, louder than ever.

"It's okay," Danielle whispered and kissed Whoops's cheek, and she lay there another minute before she reluctantly pushed the covers back and felt the cold air embrace her. She sat on the bed and put on her T-shirt, then stood quickly, hoping no one would open the door while she put her jeans on. She looked around the floor and under the bed for her shoes. They weren't there.

She looked out one of the room's windows. There were trailers all around. She realized there were a lot of people here. There was also at least a half a foot of newly-fallen snow on the ground and more was coming down.

She picked Whoops up, took a deep breath, then went to the door and opened it. It led into a kitchen whose walls were lined with cupboards. The room itself was filled with kitchen chairs, two tables, and one stuffed chair. All the chairs were occupied. There were others standing who huddled near the walls. Everyone looked at her except an old woman in the stuffed chair.

Danielle recognized some of the boxes from her family's van in a corner on the other side of the kitchen. Two girls, about her age, and a middle-aged woman were picking through the clothes. She recognized some as her own.

"Those are my clothes," she said.

"You'll be quiet until yer spoken to," the woman in the stuffed chair said.

"Well, tell those bitches to keep their hands off my stuff."

They ignored her and continued going through the clothes.

"Where's my bra?" Danielle demanded.

No one answered her.

"Where's my bra and underwear?" she asked, again.

"You'll speak when yer spoken to," the old woman warned.

"I *want* my clothes."

"I don't like her attitude," the woman said to no one in particular.

Danielle sensed that statement was ominous, but she persisted: "Where's my family?"

Again, no one answered.

There was a quart-canning jar on one of the counters with white liquid in it. She crossed the kitchen and tasted it. She recognized the taste of reconstituted powdered milk. She poured some into a glass and brought it up to Whoops's lips. The baby drank greedily.

"Do you have the manners to ask?" the woman in the stuffed chair asked.

"She's hungry," was Danielle's response without looking back at the woman.

"I don't like her," the woman said.

"Yeah? Well, I don't like you, either," Danielle said and started going through cupboards. She opened the first. It was full of peanut butter.

"What *are* you doing?" the woman demanded.

"She's hungry," Danielle repeated.

She opened a second and a third and found an open box of Cream of Wheat and poured some into a small cup. There was a sugar bowl on the counter and she poured about a tablespoonful in the cup. She added milk and stirred it with her finger. Then she started going through kitchen draws until she found a spoon.

"Look at her," the woman said indignantly. "She's acting like she owns the place."

Other than the almost inaudible whispers behind her, no one else spoke.

Danielle turned and leaned against the counter and fed Whoops. She glanced back at the corner where the girls and the woman softly argued over the clothes. "Get away from my clothes, you fuckers."

No one said a word and she continued feeding Whoops. But the woman in the stuffed chair got up and came toward her. Danielle was focused on the baby. When the woman reached her, she slapped Danielle in the face harder than Danielle would have thought possible.

"You *will* speak civilly while you're in my house!" the woman yelled.

Danielle was stunned and she forcefully pushed the woman away. "I'll speak any way I want to a bunch of fuckin' rapists and thieves, you dried-up old bitch." She ran back to the bedroom with the cup and Whoops, and slammed the door behind her. She sat on the bed and started to cry. But Whoops ate, so she continued to feed her.

The door opened, again. It was Hank. "Get out here," he growled.

"I'll come out there when I'm damned good and ready."

He crossed the room in two strides and grabbed her with a grip that hurt her arm and dragged her off the bed.

"Let me feed the baby," she screamed.

"Let her feed the baby," the woman's voice called from the other room.

Hank hesitated, then he pushed Danielle, so she fell across the bed spilling half of the cereal, and he left the room.

She put the cup down and rubbed her arm where he'd grabbed her.

"That hurt," she said to Whoops.

"We've got to get out of here," she added, aware none of the words had meaning to her sister, and she resumed feeding her.

When the cup was empty, Danielle checked to make sure the baby didn't need to be changed. Then she took a deep breath and went back into the kitchen. No one met her eye or spoke to her when she reappeared.

"We have rules here," the woman in the stuffed chair said without looking up. "You will speak only when yer spoken to; you will be polite; you will work for what you get; you will not give sass; you will not take anything without permission, including food, whether it's for the baby or yourself, otherwise, we will consider it stealing. If you don't like the rules, there's the door."

"I'll leave, but I want my clothes." Danielle said.

"You'll leave with the baby and what you have on your back. The rest is ours, now."

Danielle would have walked out then and there, but she thought about Whoops. She couldn't take her out into the snow.

Danielle began to cry and her baby sister watched her in amazement.

"Where's my family?" she asked.

No one answered.

"Where are they?"

"Tears aren't going to get you anywhere, young woman," the woman said.

"Where...are...they?" Danielle asked deliberately.

"Last I heard," the woman said, "they were on the road walking south toward warm weather."

Walking, Danielle thought, just like the people they had passed on the road. Walking in the cold, with hundreds of miles to go, no food, and now it was snowing. She knew what happened to them.

She went back to the bedroom and slammed the door behind her. She sat on the edge of the bed. The room was still cold. She looked out the window. The snow was relentless. She pulled back the covers and crawled back under them. She and the baby had to keep warm.

This time they left her alone for quite some time and she drifted back to sleep.

She awoke when she heard the door open. She raised her head quickly and saw a boy, about her own age, standing in the open doorway. When he saw she was aware of him, he stepped in and closed the door behind him.

"Hi," he said.

She didn't say anything.

"My name is Joel."

She lay her head down, again, and pulled the covers up so she didn't have to look at him.

He approached the bed. "Can I sit down?"

When she didn't answer, he sat on the edge of the bed.

"My name's Joel."

"You said that. What do you want?" she asked.

"I just came to say hello."

"Hello. Now, get out."

He didn't move.

"I'm sorry for what's happened to you," he said. "It must be hard to be separated from your family.

"If it wasn't for *your* fuckin' family, or whoever it is out there, I wouldn't be separated from mine."

He was quiet, again, for a minute. "If you just try to get along, everything will be all right."

"If *I* try to get along? I'm not the one who raped someone, I'm not the one who stole stuff, I'm not the one who's keeping someone prisoner. I can get along with anyone who wants to get along with me," she said. "But those guys last night, and that old bag out there, and those girls stealing my clothes…"

"My Grandma's really nice, once you get to know her."

"That old bag's your grandmother?"

"Yeah."

"She's a cunt," Danielle said.

"You shouldn't call her names." Joel said.

Then they were quiet. The only sounds were the muffled sounds coming from the kitchen on the other side of the door.

Finally he asked, "Will you try to be nice to her? I don't want you to have to go away."

"I want to get so far away from here that I'll never remember being here."

Joel paused. "Where would you go?"

"I have family in California."

"California's just thirty miles away," he said.

"Down near L.A.," she said.

"How would you get there?"

"I'll walk."

"It's too cold. You'll die.

"Is that what you bastards did to my mommy and dad and my brother? Make them walk so they'll die?" she screamed.

"I didn't do it…Maybe they got a ride."

"Get real. Have you been out there? Nobody's giving rides. My dad wouldn't even give rides." He wouldn't even take an abandoned baby, she thought to herself, and held her sister closer.

Neither of them spoke for several minutes and she began to wonder if he'd left. She moved the blankets away from her face until she saw him, again. Then she moved them back to cover her face.

"You're pretty," he said.

She didn't like the sound of that. "Go away."

"I'm sorry for what they did to you last night."

"I want my clothes. I want my underwear. I want my shoes. Where's the bra and panties I wore in here?"

"My sister's got your bra. Clothes are in short supply. You're lucky you got anything back."

"You call this lucky?" she asked bitterly.

"No, I guess you wouldn't see it that way. But you are.

"She and the other girls have got most of your underwear, too. They're not supposed to wear them thong things you have. Grandma says they're flossing their crotches when they got 'em on, but she don't know when they got 'em on."

"Were you one of them?" Danielle asked.

"What do you mean?"

She pushed the blankets away from her face, again, and screamed. "What do you think I mean? Were you one of the guys that fucked me last night?"

He looked at the floor and shook his head.

"Why not? Everyone else did."

"Not everyone. Some of us don't think things should be done that way. Uncle Hank tried to make me do it, but I wouldn't come in here."

"He's your uncle?"

"He's kind of a cousin, but I call him uncle.

"How old's your baby?" he asked trying to change the subject.

"Six months. And she's not my baby, she's my sister."

"Oh." Not her daughter. He nodded approvingly.

"For all I know, I might be pregnant," she said and started crying, again. "I can't have a baby. I have a boyfriend back home. I don't know what he'd think if he found out about this."

What would he think? She asked herself. She knew the answer: He said he'd leave her if she got pregnant. Not if *he* made her pregnant; if she got that way at all. So, if it were another man's, even because of rape...

She began drooling as she cried. "I'm not even old enough to have a baby."

"You take good care of her," Joel said softly.

"What?" Danielle asked, choking back tears.

"You take good care of your sister."

"I have to. I'm all she's got, thanks to your family...and she's all I've got."

Joel wanted to say something like, "You have me, too." But he couldn't. He didn't want to hear about a boyfriend, either. He wanted a girlfriend. And Danielle...

The door opened and a thin girl about Danielle's age, with long, straight brown hair stood in the doorway. She stared at Joel for a moment, then left, closing the door behind her.

"Who was that?" Danielle asked.

"Anne."

"She your sister?"

"No, she's new here."

"What do you mean, 'new'?"

"She came in from the road."

"The same way I did, without a choice?"

She knew she was right when he didn't answer.

"What did she come in here for?" Danielle asked.

"I dunno. Maybe she just wants to see who you are."

Whoops began to squirm and Danielle comforted her.

"My grandmother doesn't like her," Joel said.

"Who *does* your grandmother like?"

"Lots of people. You just got to get to know her...and do what she wants you to do."

"I don't want to know her."

"How old are you?" he asked.

"Sixteen."

A long silence followed. Then Joel said, "I'm sixteen, too."

"Why doesn't your grandmother like Anne?"

"She said she's a whiner."

"Is she?"

"Sort of. But I liked her. But Grandma says she's a slacker because she won't work hard. Grandma says that's bad. We can't feed people who won't work hard. And she's slept with almost everyone here hoping we won't throw her out. I don't think it's going to work."

"Why's she let her stay?"

"The guys like her; especially Uncle Hank."

There was another long silence, then the door opened. It was Anne, again. "Can I come in?" she asked.

Neither Danielle nor Joel answered. She stood in the doorway indecisively. Finally, she stepped in and closed the door behind her. She sat on the bed beside Joel. None of them spoke and it was obvious to Danielle that Joel was uncomfortable with her in there.

Soon, the door reopened. It was Hank. "Get out here," he barked at Anne.

"I want her out here, now," Joel's grandmother called from the kitchen.

"She's talking with us," Joel yelled past Hank to his grandmother.

There was a brief silence from the other room, then his grandmother said something none of them in the bedroom caught, except for Hank because he was in the doorway. He glared at the three of them then slammed the door as he left.

"What are you guys talking about?" Anne asked.

Joel didn't say anything. He got up off the bed and left the room. Anne watched him go. Then she turned to Danielle. "My name is Anne."

"I know."

Anne began to rock while she sat on the edge of the bed. "I just got here like a couple of weeks ago." Then she abruptly said, "I don't think Grandma likes you."

"The feeling is mutual," Danielle said.

"We should all be friends. You know, if you just go along with them, they're not so bad. And what else are you going to do, anyway?"

"How'd you get here?" Danielle asked.

"They stopped us on the road," she said.

"Where's your family?"

Anne didn't answer.

"Where are they?"

"I think they got a ride."

"Are you nuts? They're pulling people off the road, stealing everything they've got, then leaving them to die. That's what they did with my family; that's what they did with yours."

Anne looked down at her hands. "You don't know that. Maybe they got a ride."

"You idiot. Have you seen how many people are walking on the roads? No one's picking anyone up. Your family's dead; my family's gotta be dead. And it's all because of those assholes."

"They can be nice, you know."

"Did you get gang raped the first night?"

Anne didn't answer.

"Yeah, don't tell me about them being nice," Danielle said.

"But some of them are."

"Name one."

"Joel."

"You two together?"

"Right now I'm with Hank. But I'm hoping this guy Barry gets me. He seems nice."

"You're with that shithead, Hank?"

"He can be nice."

"The first chance I get, I'm going to kill him."

"You shouldn't talk like that. But Barry's nicer. He's cute. And he's younger, too. He's not old like Hank. Do you know Barry?"

"No. Did *he* screw you, too?"

"He did the first night. But he said he had to, to fit in. He's Abby's grandson, Hank's nephew...and Joel's cousin. But it's different with him and me, now"

"Who's Abby?"

"She's the old lady you got mad out there."

The old lady had a name, now.

"So this guy, Barry, wants you, now after everyone's had you?

"Well...yeah."

"To be his girlfriend?"

"Kind of."

"What do you mean, 'kind of'?"

She didn't answer.

"Does he already have a girlfriend?"

"He's married."

Danielle sat up. "What?"

"It's okay. He said she doesn't really love him."

"So you're going to be his concubine."

"What's that?"

"His fuckin' mistress. His whore, you bimbo.

"This place is a damned zoo," she said to no one in particular.

"There are more men here than there are girls," Anne said.

"So?"

"Well, that's good for us. But we've still got to do stuff or they'll turn us out."

"I'd rather be turned out than live here."

"What about your baby?"

"My sister."

"Oh."

Danielle lay back, again, and hugged Whoops. "She's the only reason I don't run—or kill myself—yet. But, as soon as I can find a way to take care of her, I'm gone. Then I'm going to report these people," she said, and suddenly wished she hadn't. And she wished she hadn't said anything bad about Joel, Hank, or anyone else. Anne had just told her she'd do almost *anything* to stay and that would likely include reporting what she'd just said. "Why'd Joel leave the room?" she asked to change the subject. "It looked like he's mad at you. Is he?"

"Maybe. I think I hurt his feelings."

"How?"

"Because I've been with some of the other guys."

"*Were* you two together?"

"Yeah, the second night, and for a few nights after that. Then I hitched up with Hank…" She trailed off.

"Why'd you drop him?"

"Because he's just a kid. The other guys can keep me here. I don't want to get turned out into the cold."

"I think you should have stayed with him."

"Why? Do you think I made a mistake?"

"I get the feeling he's his grandmother's favorite."

"Oh," Anne said and looked at the floor shaking her head. "Actually, you're right. But I didn't know it, then.

"You gonna try to hook up with him?" she suddenly asked Danielle.

Danielle didn't answer but just gave her a dirty look.

The door opened, again. It was Joel. "You've got to come out here, Anne. Grandma wants you."

She looked at Danielle before she got off the bed. "I'll talk with you, later. We should be friends," she said. "We both need friends."

"Hi, Joel," she said and touched his arm as she passed him.

He pulled away from her touch.

He lingered in the doorway after she left. "Grandma wants you to get up and get busy, too."

Danielle pulled the covers up over her face.

"You've got to," he said. He sounded concerned.

He closed the door and she was alone, again.

She lay there and thought to herself again that she shouldn't have said things about the old lady, Hank, or anyone else to Anne. Instinct told her she couldn't trust her. She didn't know if she could trust anyone. But she had to trust someone for Whoops's sake. She wondered if Joel could save her.

§   §   §

In the kitchen Hank told Anne, "Get out to the barn. You've got work to do."

"It's cold," she said and looked to Joel for support, but he ignored her. She looked around for Barry. He was a large redheaded man with tightly curled hair and a moon face. He looked away from her because his wife, Terry, was sitting next to him. She looked at the faces of others who were there trying to get warm and fed before the day began.

"Get your butt out there, now, girl." Hank ordered.

"What about the new girl? Doesn't she have to work?"

"You never mind 'bout her. Let's go."

But instead of going to the door, Anne walked over to the grandmother who was knitting in the stuffed chair and leaned toward her. She stayed like that for a minute, whispering in her ear, and the woman stopped knitting to listen.

"Okay," the woman said and resumed knitting. "Now, you run along and tend your chores in the barn."

Anne hesitated. She'd hoped the information about Danielle would win her a reprieve from going outside.

"Run along and do your chores," the old woman repeated. "I'm not gonna say it again."

Anne's shoulders sank and she grabbed a coat and went out the kitchen door.

Before Hank could follow her out, the old lady said, "Hank, you wait just a minute."

He hesitated in the doorway and the old lady waited until Anne was out of earshot. Then she said, "Get rid of that new girl."

Joel perked up and had a pained look on his face. He didn't want Danielle to go.

"Aw," Hank said dismissing her with a wave of his hand. "She's okay. I can control her."

"What if the weather warms up?" she asked matter-of-factly. "What if everything goes back to normal and she goes to the authorities? What happens then?"

He didn't reply.

"Besides…" and she mumbled something no one caught.

"What's that?" Hank asked.

"I said, you keep bringing these girls in, but we're not running a whorehouse here."

"We've got to get some women in here," Hank said. "We're two-to-one in guys over girls."

"Yes, we have more guys than gals, but some guys already have a woman…" She glared at Barry who didn't flinch, and his wife, Terry, looked at him and knew the old lady was confirming her suspicions about him and Anne. She got up and left the room.

"I think you'd better go after her," the old lady said to Barry who shrugged and languidly sauntered out of the kitchen to find his wife.

"Get rid of her," she repeated to Hank. "There'll be more comin' down the road that'll be more compliant. But I don't want no more of you guys, who're already hitched, messin' around. Otherwise, it all stops.

"And get rid of that skinny one, too."

"What?" Hank asked.

The old lady waved toward the door Anne had just gone out. "Get rid of her."

"Anne? Why?" Joel asked.

"Because she's a whiner and she's useless and she's gonna wreck a marriage..." She thought about what Anne had just told her about Danielle: that she'd tell the authorities if there were ever authorities again. She knew Anne would go to the authorities, also, if it ever served her purposes. "...and she can't be trusted."

As soon as Hank closed the door behind himself, she turned to Joel and said, "Joel, be a good boy and get that other girl out here, now."

Joel crossed the kitchen to his grandmother, leaned with his hands on the arm of her chair and asked, "Gram, why do they have to go?"

Abby stopped knitting. She loved her grandson. Ironically, he had the same easy-going manner as his grandfather, her late husband, a long-suffering, spineless alcoholic who'd spent his entire marriage committing suicide, one bottle at a time, so he could endure her haranguing ways and abuse. He finally succeeded doing himself in three years before the onset of the ice age. They found him lying in a pool of his own vomit and other bodily excretions right here in the middle of this kitchen floor. But in one of life's incomprehensible jokes, Abby worshipped Joel with as much ardor as she had held contempt for her now dead husband, the man whose character Joel had inherited. Her husband had been a failed project while Joel was a work in progress that she could love. He was at the center of her universe. "Just do as you're told, dear," she said to him, "and we'll talk about it, later."

He let out a deep sigh and went to the bedroom. Just as he reached for the doorknob, the door opened. Danielle stood there with Whoops in her arms.

"Grandma wants you," he said.

Danielle walked back into the kitchen.

The old lady didn't look up from her knitting. "Get out there to the barn and get some chores done," she said. "If you're going to be here, you're going to work for your keep."

"I've got to feed the baby, first."

"Give the baby to Ingrid. She'll take care of it."

"I'll feed her myself."

The woman paused her knitting, but didn't look up. "Then you feed her whatever you find out in the barn."

Danielle sighed. "Who's Ingrid?"

A woman in her twenties rose from a chair and put her arms out to Whoops and Danielle surrendered her reluctantly, but kissed her before she let her go.

"Give her a coat," the old woman said to Joel, "and have her cut kindlin' for my stove. Then have her and the other one do whatever else needs doin'."

Joel got a corduroy coat from one of the hooks near the kitchen door and handed it to Danielle. It was far too big a fit for her, but she put it on. Then she looked down at her bare feet.

"Put on them boots," he said pointing to a well-worn pair sitting against the wall.

She put them on. They were big, too. She knew her feet would be cold in them.

When she and Joel left the kitchen the old woman said, "That little slut is going to have to work before she or her baby get fed."

"How can you tell she's a slut?" Ingrid asked.

"Look at her," the woman said. "Listen to her foul mouth. I can tell.

"I wish the boys would stop bringing these girls in off the road. I know they've got needs. Makes me wonder what shortcomings you girls have that they keep having to bring these tramps in."

She never looked up as she said this. None of the women dared contradict her. And they all hated Danielle and Anne, just as they had the girls before them.

Ingrid held the baby up. "She's cute. And she's so good. She almost never cries. Can we keep her?"

"We're not sullying the bloodline with the blood from some road tramp," the old woman said as she knitted. "You girls should be makin' yer own babies. What's the matter with you?" She stopped knitting and looked around the room. "So don't go getting attached to no strange kids," she warned.

§　§　§

Danielle and Joel went to the barn.

"You're going to have to chop some kindling," he told her.

"How do you do that?"

"It's easy. I'll show you."

He took her to a chopping block and proceeded to show her how to use a small axe to split larger pieces of wood into smaller sticks.

"See, it's easy enough."

But she was distracted when she heard something coming from the loft. It took a minute before it dawned on her Hank was in the loft with Anne. They were talking.

Suddenly, Danielle heard a loud slap.

"Ow!" Anne cried out. "Why'd you do that?"

"'Cause," Hank laughed.

Danielle stared at Joel, but he acted as if he hadn't heard anything. "That's all you gotta do," he said as he handed her the axe and stepped back. "We need a lot of it. Get to it and I'll show you what you have to do, next."

Anne yelled, "Hank, stop! You're hurting me." Then she whimpered.

Suddenly, Anne screamed. "You're breaking my arm."

Danielle cringed. Even Anne didn't deserve this. "Stop him," she said to Joel.

He ignored her.

There was another slap accompanied by another scream from Anne and Danielle closed her eyes. She was afraid she was going to throw up.

"Spread 'em," Hank said.

"Cut the kindling," Joel said.

Danielle opened her eyes. Joel was staring at her. How could he ignore what was going on in the loft, she asked herself.

"You've got to cut the kindling," he said.

So she tried to block out the sounds from the loft and started chipping away at the wood.

But seconds later, Hank came down the ladder from the loft. When he reached the bottom he turned and stared at Danielle. "Ever do a threesome?" he asked her.

She didn't answer.

He laughed.

Anne came down the ladder behind him. The left cheek of her face was red and she rubbed it with her left hand while she flexed the other arm as if it hurt.

"You stack the new load of wood they brought in," Hank said to Anne.

"It's cold," she said.

He kicked her backside harshly. "Get to it," he said.

And she did.

"You, too," he said to Danielle.

"She's supposed to be cuttin' kindlin'," Joel said.

"She'll do as I say," Hank said in a menacing voice.

"You'd better do what he says," Joel said under his breath. Then he sat and watched as the girls stacked the load of firewood along one of the walls. Anne threw pieces up on the stack as it grew and Hank went over and wrenched the wood out of her hands and seethed, "Stack it neatly."

Anne stacked the wood more carefully.

Hank began to do repair work on a skid they used to bring wood in. But he kept watching Danielle who pretended to ignore him.

At first she thought it curious he never said anything to Joel about him not working, but it confirmed what she suspected: Joel was a "favorite."

After a while, Joel got up and started out of the barn.

"Where are you going?" Anne asked.

"It's cold," he said.

"I'm cold, too," she said, but he ignored her and left.

Because the boots were too big and because she had no socks, Danielle's feet got cold, but she didn't complain. But she didn't want to be left in the barn with Hank either. However, she had no choice. So she worked.

They stacked the wood, cut kindling, and cleaned the pigsty. When they were done, Hank came up behind Danielle and grabbed her breasts.

"Keep your filthy hands off of me," she said.

"You got a boyfriend? Did he pop yer cherry, or did I get it, first?"

"If he was here, he'd cut your balls off."

"If he was any kind'a man he'd be here taking care of you," Hank said and laughed.

She wanted to say something in her boyfriend's defense, but what was there to say to this man?

Suddenly, he said, "We're done, for now," and just like that they returned to the house.

§ § §

Both girls were glad to be in from the cold.

Danielle kicked off the boots and felt the mixture of comfort and pain from the suddenly warm floor. It was agonizingly sweet.

She looked around. "Where's Whoops?" She asked in subdued panic.

"What a name for a baby," the old woman said derisively.

"Where...is...Whoops?" Danielle demanded.

No one answered.

"Where is she?" Danielle screamed.

Without looking up, the old lady told Joel, "Go get this tramp's baby."

He left and moments later Ingrid came back into the kitchen. "Look who's here," Ingrid said to the baby.

Danielle walked to meet her and, as she passed her the baby, Ingrid said, "She's such a happy little girl. I already fed her. She eats so well."

Danielle carried the baby to the counter. There was bread on the counter. She tore some off. She opened the cupboard with the peanut butter and took an open one down. She opened a drawer and took out a butter knife. She slathered peanut butter on the bread and started to the bedroom.

"You'll eat with the family," the old woman said.

Danielle slammed the door behind her.

"That gal's gotta go," was all the woman said.

"I thought you didn't want her to eat with us," Joel said.

"I had changed my mind," the woman said, though it wasn't true. "But, if she's too good to eat with us, she's gotta go."

§ § §

Danielle made herself and the baby comfortable. She ate her peanut butter sandwich in the dim light and wished she had brought something to drink with her. But she wasn't going back out there to get anything. She finished the sandwich and lay back on the bed with Whoops and started to cry. She had to think of a way out of there. A way to southern California. A way to be with her family, if they were still alive. Or a way back to Yakima. But the traffic wasn't going in that direction. No one but the Army ever drove north. And the Army didn't pick *anyone* up.

She tried to think of what to do about her predicament. But there were no solutions for her.

After a while, Whoops went to sleep and, laying there in the dark, finally, Danielle went to sleep, too.

§ § §

Somewhat later, she was startled awake. Someone was fondling her.

"Who's that?" she yelled and rolled out on the other side of the bed. She grabbed Whoops.

"It's okay, honey." It was Hank's voice.

"Get out of here!" she yelled.

"Play ball with me and you'll be all right. Otherwise, you and that kid of yours are fucked." His voice wasn't as friendly, now.

She grabbed a blanket and took Whoops into the kitchen and slammed the door on his fading laughter. The kitchen was empty but the weather had cleared and a full moon coming through the windows lit the kitchen. She didn't know how long she'd slept, but it was late. Everyone else had gone to bed. She thought about just leaving, but there was nowhere to go. She wasn't going back in the bedroom while Hank was in there. The only place to sleep in the kitchen was the stuffed chair. She drank some water then sat in the chair and curled herself up. Whoops looked around but let Danielle hold her close and after a while they both went back to sleep.

§ § §

She was wakened in the morning by a sharp slap in her face and the old lady's indignant voice railing, "What are you doing in my chair? No one sits in *my chair* but me."

Danielle quickly got out of the chair clutching her sister. She was too weary to fight. And there was no reason to give an explanation as to why she'd left the bed. No one cared what she said.

The old lady made a production of sweeping imaginary dirt off the chair with her hands while others who had come into the kitchen watched.

Danielle began to make Whoops more Cream of Wheat. This time she made some for herself, too. Then she went back to the bedroom. Hank was gone. She sat on the edge of the bed and fed herself and Whoops.

Looking around, she found a tattered pillow case and tore it to fashion a diaper. After she changed the baby she got under the covers. She wanted to cry but she couldn't cry anymore. She thought to herself she could never cry again. Then it became a promise. She knew she had to get away from these people. She lay on her side and stared at the wall for hours. As the sky got lighter, she fell asleep, again.

Chapter 6
August 27

Peterson lived out his last hours in a coma at the LaCroix compound. But even as he lay dying, with his wife, his brother, and most of his friends at his side, a meeting was held in the living room at the main house of the old ranch.

Louis LaCroix sat at the head of a massive dining table. He looked around the room as if making sure everyone he'd called for the meeting was there. "Who is he?" LaCroix asked softly to open the meeting. His subdued manner and soft voice were not signs of weakness. LaCroix was a large choleric man in his thirties with long black hair, a prematurely graying beard, and large, fleshy ears. He was intelligent and educated. He wore glasses that he kept pushing back on his nose when he was angry and, though he was speaking in a low voice, he was constantly adjusting them, now.

No one answered his question.

"Who's the guy that shot Peterson and killed Anderson, Jamison, and Kyle?" he asked and removed his glasses and placed them on the table.

"His name is Zachary Amaral," a man replied.

"And exactly who is that?" LaCroix's tone was still restrained.

"He lives down outside of Brookings. He married Sandra Gibbons."

LaCroix stared at the speaker. It was Billy Raymond.

"The Gibbonses are gone, aren't they?"

"They cleared out when the going was good," Raymond replied. "Don't know if they ever made it all the way south."

"Wasn't Anderson related to them somehow?"

"Anderson's mom was…"

"It was a yes-or-no question. So, I guess it's yes," LaCroix interrupted. "How do you know it was this guy Amaral?"

"I found the cover from a book with his name on it. It was torn in half and he'd put some M80s on the halves and used cigarettes for fuses."

"M80s? Firecrackers? What the hell were they for?"

There was a long pause. Raymond had to tell how they were outsmarted. "When they went off, he wanted us to think he was still up on the ridge shooting at us. He'd already skied away."

"So, you didn't actually see him to know who he was. You just found a book cover with the name 'Zachary Amaral' on it. We don't even know for sure it was this Amaral character or if it was somebody else who had the book with his name on it. Is that right?"

"That's all we've got to go on," Raymond said.

LaCroix looked around the room without looking at anyone, then let out a long breath.

He looked around once more. This time he looked at all the faces. Very deliberately he said, "I want to know what went wrong. How'd three of our guys get killed and another one's dying?"

"We were chasing him, he got off into the woods, and he had clear shots at us. It was just bad luck," Raymond said.

"No," LaCroix said shaking his head. He picked up his glasses and waved them around. "It wasn't bad luck. Bad luck is drawing to a four-spade flush and catching a heart. This was poor planning. When a dozen guys can't catch one guy…*one guy*…it's because you fucked up."

"He wasn't alone."

LaCroix put his glasses back down and stared at Raymond in anticipation. "No one told me this. There was someone else with him?"

"He had a dog."

There was a long silence. LaCroix suddenly slammed his hand on the table, then lifted his glasses and put them on, again. "A dog…Which one did the dog shoot?" he asked sarcastically. "Peterson? Kyle? Did the damned dog have a sniperscope on his fucking rifle?

"We've been doing this for over two years, with no problems—okay, once we had a problem, but that was two years ago." He was referring to a time when another member of the compound had gotten killed when he and some others tried to ambush a man. "Then, yesterday, you go after one guy…*and his dog*…and you get three of yourselves killed and another guy shot, and it doesn't look good for him. One of the dead, a twelve-year-old boy…" He put his finger to his temple like it was the barrel of a gun, then popped it away like he'd pulled the trigger "…was executed."

"Kyle was fourteen," Raymond said.

"It doesn't matter," LaCroix yelled. "What matters is that you guys fucked up. Why didn't you get him?"

"I wanted to go after him..." Raymond said.

"Why didn't you get him before he got you?" LaCroix asked.

No one answered.

"How'd he get away?"

"I wanted to go after him," Raymond repeated, "but these pussies wouldn't follow with me. Dodd and Scott did, but they kept lagging because they were afraid of the guy."

"We had to get Peterson back," Ted Foy said angrily.

"Lot of good that did," Raymond yelled.

"Why'd he kill Kyle?" LaCroix asked. His voice had dropped off and all the other voices followed suit.

"He shot anybody he could," Raymond said.

"I still don't understand how one man got four of ours and still got away."

A thick silence settled on the room.

"Well, we're gonna have to assume this guy...what do you think his name is?...Amaral?..."

Raymond nodded.

"...we're gonna have to assume he's dangerous. And we can't have someone that dangerous hanging around here. We've got women, kids, and ourselves. We're going to have to get rid of him..." Anger began to show as it welled up in him, again. "...before he kills every one of us.

"I want to know where he lives. I want him done with. I want everyone connected with him done with. And I want to know if he has any connection with old lady Brady and her nephew, Hank. If so, I want them to pay for it, too."

"How are you going to find that out?" Raymond asked.

"How am I gonna find out? Me? I'm not. You are. You're going to ask, that's how you're going to find out. You're going to go there and find out what they know about him."

"What if it's a trap? What if he's with them and..."

"You're going to find that out, too" LaCroix said and took off his glasses, again.

"But..."

"My sister's in the other room crying; she was up all night crying, because you guys got her son killed. You guys know how a mother feels when she sees most of her son's head blown away? Now, you guys go straighten this mess out. And I want that Amaral dead. And if it wasn't him, I want whoever it was dead.

"Is there anything else you got to tell me?"

"We got a bear," Raymond said.

"A bear. That's nice. That's real nice.

"I don't give a shit about bears!" he suddenly exploded. "Get that guy, then tell me you got *him*. That's your job right now. Get this Amaral—or whoever it is that did this. Because whoever he is, he's a menace."

"Should we wear uniforms when we go to the Brady place?" Foy asked, meaning the police uniforms they wore to stop vehicles on the road.

"Do you think the Bradys are going to be fooled by uniforms?" LaCroix asked. "You can go naked, if you want," he said sarcastically. "Just go. But go with a plan. I don't want more of us dead."

Then he sat back and tried to compose himself. "Look," he began, "my guess is this guy's got nothin' to do with the Bradys. I know they've been pains in our asses, but none of those guys on the Brady ranch operate alone. If this guy was one of them, they'd have been out there in numbers. I don't know if this guy's part of a gang or if he's some freak from the backcountry who's down here freelancing. But we can barely deal with the Bradys so we're not going make life harder by tolerating any freelancers."

"That's what we were doing when we saw his tracks," Raymond said. "We were trying to get rid of a freelancer."

"Okay," LaCroix said, "I want you to find that out, too—if he's a freelancer or part of something bigger."

"But, if we kill him first..." Webber began.

"Then kill him after you find out!" LaCroix yelled anticipating Webber's question. He felt as though he was surrounded by idiots.

He took a moment to compose himself, again. "Is there anything else anyone wants to discuss?" he asked.

"Well, one of the things we know about him is that he uses a .30-06 rifle," Raymond said.

LaCroix looked over his glasses. "And you know that because...?"

Raymond reached into his pocket and took out the brass cases he'd found the day before and passed them around the table to LaCroix who examined them.

"These belong to the shooter?" LaCroix asked.

"Yeah," Raymond replied.

LaCroix got up and went to his desk. He opened a drawer and took something out.

When he returned to the table he pushed one of the cases so it slid across the table to Raymond. "That," he said, "is one of the cases you gave me."

He pushed a second piece of brass across the table and said, "And this is from one of the rounds that killed Woody Harris two years ago. Look familiar?"

"They're both .30-06s," Raymond replied.

"Look at the headstamps," LaCroix said.

Raymond examined them and said, "They're the same. What's the L C and 55 mean?"

"Lake City Arsenal, 1955. They're military surplus. The guy you were trying to get yesterday is the same guy who killed Woody. So that seals it: he's been here for at least two years, he's local, he's dangerous, and we've got to get rid of him. You could have gotten him yesterday, but you didn't. This time, you will."

Raymond nodded.

Brian Peterson appeared in the doorway. With just a glance at him, LaCroix knew his brother had died.

"I'm sorry, Brian," LaCroix said.

With that, all heads turned toward the doorway. They understood.

LaCroix turned back to Billy Raymond and addressed him. "First thing I'll do is put together a team, and I want you to lead it out to the Brady place and find out what they know. I don't think they're involved. If they were, this guy wouldn't have been alone. But I want to make sure. Then I want you to go after him.

"But before that happens, there are going to be funerals for the next few days. We're burying Kyle in the morning. I want you guys there. As far as I'm concerned, until Amaral and whoever else involved is dead, I'm holding you guys responsible for my nephew's death. I'm holding you responsible for all four."

As he rose from the table he looked at Peterson and said, "Brian, I'd like to talk with you," and he walked out of the room with Peterson following him. That left about a dozen men in the room who started to argue among themselves, blaming each other for the disaster of the previous day.

Chapter 7
August 27

"Get up," a voice whispered and Danielle woke with a start. She looked out from under the covers and saw Joel standing beside the bed looking at her. He'd closed the door behind him. She sensed he'd been there a while. The room was cold. Whoops was still asleep. She didn't know how long she, herself, had been sleeping.

"What do you want?" she asked.

"You've got to get up. They want you in the kitchen," he said in a low voice.

She pulled the covers to hide most of her head and sighed. She needed more sleep. "Go away."

"You've *got* to come out there," he implored. "They want you."

"It's cold. I was up half the night. Let me sleep."

"My grandmother wants you out there, *now*. I think you're in trouble."

"For what?"

He didn't answer.

"Whatever," she sighed. She knew if the old lady wanted her, it was only for trouble.

"Get out of here so I can get dressed," she said.

He gave her a long, lingering look before he turned and left the room, closing the door behind him. She knew he liked her.

Fuck him, she thought.

She got up slowly. Whoops was now awake and watching her.

"Hey, sleepy eyes, are we awake?"

A fleeting smile crossed her sister's face.

She started to dress but hesitated. She put the shirt on inside out. No sense in stirring up trouble. When she finished dressing, she checked Whoops's diaper. It was soiled. She was changing it when the door opened, again.

It was Hank. "Get out here," he demanded.

"I'm changing the baby."

He hesitated, then slammed the door and left her and her sister alone.

After she changed Whoops, she carried her into the kitchen. There was a crowd. Most were standing. Anne sat in a kitchen chair in the middle of the room, crying.

Hank looked at Danielle and pointed to the only chair that was empty. It was beside Anne. She understood she was supposed to sit there. Given the mood in the room, she complied.

"I don't want no whiner," Abby said. "I want her out." It was clear she was referring to Anne.

Abby stood at the counter between the sink and the stove with her back to the others. She was putting together a stew for later in the day. "There'll be better ones coming down the road."

"What about..." Hank asked.

Abby turned a quarter-turn and Hank nodded toward Danielle.

"That baby yours?" she asked Danielle.

Danielle didn't understand why she was asking the question, but she answered, "Yes."

"How old are you?"

"Sixteen."

"I don't want no road sluts here, either."

"How's Whoops make her a slut?" Joel asked.

"If she wasn't a road slut, she wouldn't have no kid at sixteen,"

"That's not her kid, it's her sister," Joel said.

"Then she's a liar, too, because I just asked her if it was hers and she said it is. I don't truck with liars. And if she wasn't a slut, she'd wouldn't have had no trouble fighting you guys off the other night. I'd have been able to."

"That's because nobody would want to fuck you," Danielle blurted out, and immediately wished she hadn't.

She turned and glared at Danielle and stared at her shirt for a moment. She could read the lettering through the shirt though it was faint and backwards. "Listen to the mouth on that girl," Abby said. Then, to Danielle, she said, "You're not hiding anything with that shirt on inside out.

"Get her out of here. Get 'em both out."

"Why can't you just let her go on the road?" Joel asked.

"Because she knows where we live."

"But you let some others go, and they knew where we live," he countered.

"That was a mistake. It may still be a mistake. But it's a mistake I'm never going to make, again."

Danielle wondered what this line of conversation meant and, when she looked at Anne, who was crying and distraught, it was obvious there was something terribly wrong.

"Grandma..." Joel began.

"Get them out, *now!* Both of 'em!" She commanded and turned her back to them and focused on the stew she was preparing. "I'd give anything for hot running water and a garbage disposal that worked."

"Grandma..." Joel repeated.

"Don't waste no bullet on the baby," Abby said and cut Joel off.

No one said a word for a moment.

"What do you mean by that?" Danielle asked.

Abby didn't answer. She didn't have to. This was her parting "gift" to Danielle for all the insults and rude comments she'd made. Let her think about what it meant when they were on their way out to the field.

"What's she mean?" Danielle asked Joel.

Joel looked away.

"Let's go," Hank said. He motioned with a nod toward the door. "Move it," he demanded.

"Not you," Abby said turning to Hank. "I want Barry to do this."

She glared at Barry. Barry knew his grandmother wanted him to take the girls out to the field because of his liaison with Anne. She'd teach him a lesson, too. This is how he would "undo" cheating on his wife.

She turned to Hank and said, "The CB says there's a pair of cars coming down the road. They's north of Nesika Beach and heading our way. I want you and the boys to put on the uniforms, take the police cars, and go out there and see what they got."

"Aw, let me go out to the road," Barry said.

She turned and faced him. "No, Hank's better out there. You do what I'm telling you to do. Now, get goin'."

Barry pushed himself away from the wall. "Shit," he said under his breath.

"You watch your mouth," Abby warned.

"Come on," Barry said.

The girls didn't get up.

"What do you mean, 'Don't waste a bullet on the baby'?" Danielle asked Abby, who ignored her.

Barry directed the anger he felt toward his grandmother at Danielle and he grabbed her by her hair. She clutched Whoops as he dragged her out of the chair.

"Wait a minute. Answer my question!" she yelled.

Abby still ignored her and, with a kick, Barry directed her toward the door.

"You heard Grandma, she wants you out of here," Barry said forcefully.

But Danielle stopped short of the door. "What do you *mean*?"

Abby continued to prepare the stew at the sink as if the girls had already left. "Betty, get me two more quart-jars of green beans," she said.

Betty got out of her chair and ran to the pantry.

A girl of sixteen named Alice Humphrey confronted Barry. "Can I have the jeans she's wearing?" She pointed to Danielle.

"You're not getting anything of mine," Danielle said firmly.

"Please?" Alice asked Barry.

"We'll see."

"Make her take 'em off so she don't shit in 'em."

"Watch your mouth, young lady," Abby scolded without turning around.

"Sorry," Alice said.

"Why would I shit my pants?" Danielle asked. But Barry pushed her toward the door then grabbed Anne by the shoulder and steered her there, too.

Anne looked at Barry with desperation in her eyes. "Barry, *please?* Don't do this."

"Out!" he yelled at her.

A stocky man named Eddie McFaddin stepped ahead of them and opened the door. Eddie was looking forward to the trip to the field.

"Gram, please don't make them go," Joel pleaded.

"Take him, too," Abby said. "He's gotta see what's gotta be done. He needs to be toughened up."

Barry grabbed Joel and pushed him toward the door ahead of himself.

"Easy on my Sweetie," Abby warned without looking.

Barry eased up.

"It's cold out. I need a coat," Joel said.

Barry grabbed one from the hooks near the door and jammed it into his hands. "Put it on," he said as he pushed his cousin out.

Near the door Hank leaned toward Barry and, in a low voice, said, "You lucky bastard."

Barry nodded. Though he hated having to take the girls out to the field, taking them out there came with benefits.

"Come on," he said to Andrew Ingram who was leaning against the wall. Andrew smiled and followed him out the door.

Close behind was Alice. Now out of the hearing of those in the kitchen she said, "Please, Barry, I want her jeans...and the shirt, I like that, too. I'll make it worth your while."

He was about to say yes when he saw his wife, Terry, had followed them out.

"We'll see," he said and turned away.

Alice turned to see what had caught Barry's attention and saw Terry standing there watching them, and Alice walked back into the house, passing Terry as if nothing had transpired. Terry followed her into the house but stormed off to her room.

Once Barry and the girls were gone, Abby looked absently out the window above the sink and said, "You know, Joel's my Sweetie, but he's gonna have to learn not to be so soft if he's gonna survive in this world. It ain't like it used to be, and he can't be like his grandfather. You gotta be tough or die."

She stopped the preparation and wiped her hands on her apron. She crossed the room to a girl named Clara. Clara was holding her infant daughter, Edna, in her arms.

"Let Granny Great have that little bundle of joy," Abby said and Clara proffered her daughter to the old lady. "Come to Granny Great," she said as she took her. Then she went to her stuffed chair and made herself comfortable with the baby cradled in her arms.

"I don't begrudge those girls anything, but we can't save the world...It breaks my heart to see that baby go...Would have made a nice playmate, wouldn't she," she said raising Edna up in the air. Then she sat her in her lap, again.

"That Danielle girl has quite the mouth on her, doesn't she? And that shirt she was wearing is the disgusting stuff only them sluts wear. She'd have brought us all to grief...that Anne is as useless as a bucket under a bull...and she can't be trusted. She'd sell her own mother out to save her skin."

No one interrupted her soliloquy.

"Now, Colin said he heard on the CB there's more folks coming this way. Hank, I want you and the boys to put on the uniforms and go out and greet them. Don't get in the way of no convoys," though Hank knew better than to do that. "There's some of them comin', too. I hope you know better'n to mess with them. Just the lone cars, or the small convoys."

She stopped playing with the baby and turned to the men.

"What are you doing? Get a move on."

Hank and the others left the kitchen to get the uniforms and guns. After they left, Abby said, "You know, Hank's not a bad man. Sometimes he's a little rough around the edges, but Joel would do a lot better if he was a little bit like him."

They just listened.

"Clara, I want you and Terry to finish the stew."

"Terry's in her room crying. She an' Barry just had a big fight, this morning," Clara said.

"I know. That's why Barry's gotta take the girls out to the field. But she's got to get busy, and she's got to learn to control her man. You go get her, now."

Clara left the kitchen.

"And the rest of you: Clear out! You all got chores if you expect to live here. I'm not feeding you so you can just hang around like barn flies."

§   §   §

In the front yard Danielle stood bewildered in the newly fallen snow and more was coming down. Anne cried hysterically. Danielle was beginning to wonder what it all meant. All she had on her feet were thin shoes. She knew they weren't going to keep their feet warm. Anne was already complaining about snow getting in her shoes.

"This way," Barry said.

Danielle didn't know what "this way" meant. But Andrew and Eddie started walking through the snow. They were glancing at each other and smiling as they proceeded. Barry pushed Danielle in their direction.

"Barry, honey, I'm cold," Anne said.

Barry kicked her. "Get moving."

"But we need better coats."

Barry stepped toward her to kick her, again.

"Okay, okay," she said and turned and began to walk through the snow. She tried to get well ahead of him to keep some distance between them.

Danielle held Whoops close to her to keep her warm. But Whoops began to cry. Danielle knew she was getting cold. They hadn't let her feed her yet and she was hungry.

They crossed what had been good pasture just three years ago. With the new cold weather it didn't support much anymore, and, with last night's snow, there were no signs of life in it at all.

They passed through several stands of trees. Anne cried softly and kept pleading with Barry. "I love you," she said again and again. "I'll do anything for you." She kept complaining that she was cold.

And it *was* cold. Danielle almost couldn't feel her feet, now.

Whoops cried loudly. Nothing Danielle did consoled her.

"Can't you keep that damned kid quiet?" Barry shouted.

"She'll be okay," was all Danielle could think to say. But she couldn't stop her from crying.

They walked quite a ways until they came upon another large field. Barry, Andrew, Eddie, and Joel walked the two girls to the far edge of it.

Danielle figured they were now at least a mile and a half from the house. She saw something sticking out of the snow. It took a moment before she realized it was an arm with most of the flesh gone. There were a few other bones sticking out. She suddenly realized what this was. This was where they took people they brought in from the road when they didn't want them anymore. She began to feel panic welling up inside of her.

She now understood what Abby meant when she said, "Don't waste a bullet on the baby."

They stopped.

"Take your clothes off," Barry commanded. "I don't want ya shittin' in 'em. Those clothes are promised."

The girls didn't move.

Barry stepped forward and punched Anne in the jaw. When she fell in the snow he began to kick her.

"Stop! Stop!" she screamed.

"Get up."

She got dizzily to her feet.

"Now, take your clothes off."

She began to remove her clothes. The jacket, the blouse, the pants. There was no underwear. They'd taken hers, too.

"You, too," he yelled at Danielle, and she began to take her clothes off while she tried to hold Whoops.

Soon, they were both naked except for their shoes.

"What are you going to do with us?" Danielle asked, though everything was now clear to her.

"Pick up the clothes," Barry said to Andrew, and he gathered them up.

"Shoes, too," he said to Anne.

"But my feet, they're already too cold," Anne whined.

He made a fist and started walking toward them. "Shoes too," he commanded.

"Okay, okay," Anne said.

Reluctantly they both took off their shoes and Anne danced from one foot to the other trying to keep them out of the snow.

Barry grabbed the shoes. "You take them," he said as he tossed them to Joel who missed catching them.

Danielle met Joel's eyes and he quickly looked away. He was pale. He looked sick. He knew what was coming.

"Come 'ere," Barry commanded Anne. When she came to him he forced her to her knees. He took his penis out. "Do it."

She stared up at him.

"Do it!" he shouted. "You've always done it good. Now I want you to do it again."

She tentatively took him in her mouth.

"Do it better!" he yelled.

"Yeah, like that.

"You boys should take advantage of this," he said looking at them over his shoulder, then nodding toward Danielle but none of them moved.

"You know, I once read that rich Roman men used to use babies that were still nursing to do this. Maybe that baby would be good for this."

Danielle clutched Whoops closer.

"It's a shame to waste you girls," he chuckled.

Anne pulled her head away.

"Why are you stopping?" he screamed.

"I'm cold. I don't have any clothes on. I'm kneeling in the snow."

"What do you care? You're not going to feel anything in a few minutes, anyway?"

"I can't," she cried.

"Shit," he said and walked around behind her.

"Don't you boys be tellin' my wife 'bout what I was doing with Anne," he said.

He drew a large revolver from under his coat and put it to the back of Anne's head.

"Barry, please don't," was all Anne could say.

The cylinder clicked as it turned when he drew the hammer back. "But you can tell her about this." Anne's face exploded when he pulled the trigger and the snow was speckled with the spray of her blood. She fell forward. Her body twitched and kicked in the snow, but she was dead.

"Look at that!" Barry said. "She's jumpin' like a headless chicken!"

Eddie and Andrew laughed. Joel got paler and started to sway. He was close to passing out.

"I want a piece of the other one," Eddie said and laughed.

"Yeah, I'll have a piece of that," Andrew said.

"After my turn," Barry said.

"You should get some," he said to Joel. "I seen how you look at her. "'less you wanna fuck her dead body, after."

The other boys laughed.

Danielle wanted to run. But there was nowhere to go. She stared in disbelief as Barry, gun in hand, walked toward her. "You do it," he said pointing at his cock.

"Get one of your boys to do it, you fucking faggot."

He slapped her.

She began to cry. Again, she cried like her mother, lowing like a cow. She held Whoops up. "I know what you're going to do. Please, do her first."

"I can't waste no bullets," Barry said soberly. "Get on your knees."

Danielle fell to her knees. "I'll do it. But, please, do her first; I don't want her to suffer. You can't just leave her here to freeze."

"What do you care? In a few minutes, yer gonna be in hell and yer not going to know if she's freezin' or not."

She held Whoops out. "Please."

He wrenched Whoops from her hands and threw her out into the snow.

Whoops screamed. Danielle screamed, jumped to her feet and ran to Whoops and scooped her up in her arms. Whoops was inconsolable.

Barry came up behind her.

"Okay, I'll do it. But I don't want her to suffer. Please, do it." She fell to her knees holding the baby above her head. "I'll suck you, I'll fuck you all. I'll do anything you want. Just don't let her suffer."

"Whatever you want, Honey."

Looking at the boys he said, "Don't tell grandma I wasted no bullet on the baby."

"Well, don't go shootin' Danielle, yet," Eddie said. "I want my turn."

Andrew smiled and he nodded in agreement.

Barry smiled back. He brought the gun up.

Danielle held her sister up in the ultimate sacrifice as they both cried. She clinched her eyes shut and heard the ratcheting of the cylinder as it turned again. There was the shot and she felt a warm spray splatter across her face and body and Whoops abruptly stopped crying.

Now she clutched the baby to her breasts.

Whoops began to cry.

Danielle opened her eyes and began to shake.

Whoops was covered with blood and brains. So was she. She looked up to see Barry still stood in front of her, his body was quivering, a frozen look of bewilderment written on his face, his mouth was moving as if trying to say something. But a large chunk of his head was gone and little spurts of blood squirted out of the chasm where the side of his skull had exploded away. Andrew, Eddie, and Joel were looking around in stunned panic.

Barry crumpled to the snow and lay still.

There was another shot as Eddie's head exploded and he fell.

"Run!" Andrew screamed and dropped the girls's clothes and began to run.

There was another shot and Andrew fell; a bullet in his back.

Joel dropped the shoes and started to yell for his grandmother as he struggled to run through the snow, his feet working like pistons as he tried to escape from the unseen tormentor.

A fourth shot, and he went down. Then, all was silent.

Except for Whoops. She screamed.

Kneeling naked in the snow, Danielle clutched her sister to her body and waited for the final shot.

The snow was cold. It would end, soon.

But nothing happened.

She looked around. A man on skis, dressed in white from head to toe, glided like a phantom across the field. A white dog ran beside him. He stopped when she turned and brought his rifle up. He watched her through his sights for a moment, then lowered his weapon and continued skiing toward her.

He reached them and picked up Barry's revolver. He crouched and rolled his body over and checked his pockets, removing and pocketing what he thought was important, discarding the rest onto the snow. He kept looking across the field from where she and the others had come.

He turned to her. "Are there any others?"

The ski mask, with its gaping hole for a mouth and unblinking slits for eyes, made him appear ghoulish. In his crouch he resembled a wild animal.

He took the boots, jacket, and socks from Barry's body.

He turned back to Danielle and this time shouted his question, "*Are there any others?*"

She shook her head as she clutched her sister.

The dog started licking up Barry's blood and brains. The man stood up and watched for a second, as if not knowing what to do. Then he ignored it. Whoops cried louder.

The man went to Eddie's body. In one pocket, he found another handgun. In another he found some loose ammunition. He put it all in his own pockets. He scanned the tree line in all directions before he took Eddie's boots. Then he stood back, looked at the full body. Eddie was bigger than he, but after some thought he took the shirt and pants.

He looked back at Danielle. "Get dressed," he ordered.

She started putting her clothes on. But she was already shivering violently and had trouble trying to simultaneously hold the baby and get dressed with fingers numbed by the cold.

The man approached her and read her T-shirt:

Fuck Off
or I'll Kill You 'til You're Dead

She turned away.

He reloaded his rifle then continued to the other bodies, taking some things and tossing what he didn't want, into the snow. But he constantly scanned the tree line. He picked up the shoes Danielle and Anne had worn out into the field. He examined them then turned to her. "Did these keep you warm?" he shouted. He sounded angry, but he also sounded scared.

She shook her head again and he threw them away.

He went to Joel's body, removed his boots, and examined them. He threw the first one and it hit her in the hip. When he threw the second one it also hit her, she realized he was throwing them *at* her.

"Those are going to have to do," he said in a voice still laden with fear and anger.

He grabbed Joel's jacket and brought it back to her. "Wrap your baby in this," he instructed.

He held out the socks he'd taken off Joel's body. "Put these on before you put the boots on."

The mask hid his expressions; only his voice and actions betrayed his mood.

He handed her Eddie's jacket after rifling the pockets. "Put this on. It's gonna have to do."

There was a soft gasp from behind them and the man spun around with his rifle to confront the sound.

Andrew was still alive and moaning where he lay in the snow.

"Help me," he begged. "I can't move my arms or nothin'."

The bullet had broken his spine.

The man skied to him and put the muzzle of his rifle to Andrew's head.

Danielle turned away. Despite the fact Andrew had come to take part in her and Whoops's executions, she didn't want to watch when his head was blown off. But after several seconds of silence she turned back. The man still had the rifle about three inches from Andrew's head. But he seemed indecisive. Finally, he lowered it.

"Help me," Andrew repeated.

The man looked back at Danielle and saw she had finished putting her clothes on.

"Let's go," he said.

"What about him?" she asked about Andrew.

He didn't answer; he just skied away.

"Help me," Andrew begged.

Danielle walked to him.

"Help me," he pleaded.

She looked back. The stranger and the dog had already reached the trees.

"I can't move, Danielle."

"I'm sorry," she whispered.

"What about Barry and the others?"

"They're dead."

"You've got to help me, please. Have pity on me."

An odd sympathy welled up in her. But she reminded herself that just moments before Andrew had just stood there and watched Barry shoot Anne in the back of the head. And he'd said nothing when Barry threw Whoops into the snow. And then...he wanted "his turn" with *her* before Barry executed her, too. Now, he was begging her to save him.

She should hate him, but all she felt was pity. "There's nothing I can do," she said.

"Go back to the ranch and get help," he pleaded.

She looked at her sister in her arms. Neither of them would survive if she went back there. "I'm sorry," she repeated and she turned to follow the man in white.

"Danielle, please...help me, Danielle..."

She started toward the tree line.

"...please help me...don't leave me to die...I'm scared..." Andrew called after her as she crossed the field and disappeared into the woods, following the man in the ski mask.

§   §   §

She couldn't keep up. It was difficult to walk through the trees, through the brush, and over fallen logs that were hidden in the snow, while wearing boots that were too big, and all the while having to carry and protect her sister. The boots alternately threatened to fill with snow and to get pulled from her feet.

Meanwhile, the man and the dog maintained a pace that kept them well ahead and often out of sight, and all she had to go on was the trail they left behind. Each time she gave up hope of seeing him again, she'd round a tree and he'd be waiting. But, whenever she got close enough, she was sure he was glaring from behind his mask, and just as she'd reach him he'd abruptly push off on his skis and disappear again.

But one time, he didn't ski off and, when she finally reached him, he stared at her sister. Just as she asked, "Where are we?" he reached to take Whoops from her arms.

"*No!*" she screamed and turned away putting herself between him and the baby.

"Then keep up," he shouted, "or I'm leaving you both here."

She turned back to face him and knew he was angry. She didn't want to think about why he might have "saved" her, but she knew now she and her sister were at his mercy. She asked herself how salvation could so abruptly have morphed into a new nightmare.

He skied away.

She stood helplessly alone and watched him disappear. And once he was out of hearing range she said, "I'm just a piece of pussy for you guys to shoot each other over." "But," she added, "keep your filthy hands off my sister."

She looked around. If she knew where she was, she'd have gone off in another direction. But she was completely lost. And she couldn't go back. There was nothing good in that field and death awaited her if she went back to the compound. For the moment she had no choice but to put herself and Whoops in this assassin's hands and follow him as he led her deeper and deeper into the forest.

Snow kept filling her boots and she stopped again and again to empty them. The socks, now soaking wet, chafed her feet raw.

At one point, she saw him waiting up ahead, but instead of skiing further on, once again he waited. She clutched her sister to herself as she approached him.

He held out another pair of socks. She took them and struggled to get them on while holding Whoops.

He put his arms out to take Whoops.

"*Don't,*" Danielle warned and he lowered his arms.

With the dry socks on, they forged on until...

...they reached a road and he took off his skis.

He waited for her to catch up.

Whoops was crying, now.

He stared at them. "Do something for the baby," he insisted.

"What do you mean?"

"It's crying. Do something!" he ordered.

"She's hungry!" Danielle shouted back at him.

"Feed her."

"Feed her what?" she yelled back.

"What's she eat?"

"Baby food...milk..." Danielle's voice was rising and she held Whoops tighter and backed away. "I don't know. There's nothing out here for her to eat." She ran her free hand through her blonde hair in exasperation. She wanted to start crying. But not in front of this...man.

He abruptly swung his backpack off his shoulders. He took something out and proffered it to her. "This is all I've got."

It was jerky.

She stared at it, looked at Whoops, then looked back at him incredulously.

She thought for several more seconds then, suddenly she reached out and took it from him. She repositioned the baby and started tearing thin strips from the jerky. Whoops screamed in hunger. He saw how awkward it was and again reached to take the baby from her arms.

"No," Danielle yelled and recoiled away from him. She could tell he was angry. The mask was beginning to drive her crazy.

She took the strips and put them in her mouth and, just as she did, he pushed her down into the snow.

But she was on her feet in a flash and she backed away from him. "Why are you being so mean?" she yelled.

"That's for her," he yelled back.

She took the jerky out of her mouth. "She can't eat it like this, you fucking idiot! What do you want me to do, shove it up her ass?"

Defiantly, she put the jerky back in her mouth and chewed it and chewed it and chewed it as she stared at him. When it was pulverized, she brought the baby's mouth to her own and, as if in a kiss, spit the chewed jerky into Whoops's mouth. The baby swallowed it greedily.

She tore off more, chewed it, and repeated the process. This went on for several minutes, on the side of the road, while the snowflakes that danced around them got thicker as if they, too, had come to gather to witness this spectacle along with the man. He watched, first with incredulity, then with fascination, until the jerky was gone.

"That's all I've got," he said. He didn't sound angry, now. "Where do you live?"

She paused a second. "Yakima."

"Yakima, Washington?" he asked.

"Is there another one?"

"What are you doing here?"

"We were trying to make it to southern California."

"Who's we?"

She didn't answer.

She could see his eyes peering out of the eye-slits, his lips moving through the mouth-opening, but the mask still made him appear expressionless. He stared at Whoops again until she got uncomfortable. She began to understand: he wanted the baby.

She backed away from him.

"I've done all I can do for you," he suddenly said. "You're on your own, now."

He turned and nodded down the road. "That's south. Get going. I don't know if anyone will follow us. But sooner or later they're going to discover those guys are missing. You can probably get a ride before they do. The next town south is Brookings. From there it's about five miles to the California border."

"Where are you going?"

The eyes stared out through the slits, but he didn't answer. She knew he wouldn't.

Before she could say anything else, he turned and crossed the road. She was surprised that the dog stayed with her. The man didn't seem concerned.

She watched him put on his skis. Then, just as suddenly as he had appeared that morning, he was gone.

The dog acted as if it didn't know which way to go, but it finally sprinted across the road and followed him.

"Thank you, and good riddance," she said sarcastically to the man who was once again out of earshot.

She wondered why, after he'd saved her, he'd been so mean. Why did he bring her to the road? There was something wrong with him; something hostile about him. She was vaguely afraid to be alone, yet she'd felt more afraid when she was with him. There were reasons to fear all the men out here. Thankfully, he was now gone.

The road had been recently plowed by the Army, but more snow was coming down and the new accumulation was already two or three inches deep. She started walking. Now that she'd eaten, Whoops alternately looked up at her with her happy face and then looked all around at the snow-embraced scenery. She liked what she saw. It was new; it was beautiful.

Danielle knew, unless they got a ride, she was walking to their deaths. She was still cold. She was hungry. They'd given her nothing to eat before taking her out to the field that morning. But why would they? she thought. Food was precious and she wasn't even supposed to be alive now.

Her feet were getting number. She had to walk.

She figured it was about noon when she first heard vehicles. She turned and saw a caravan approaching. She wanted to run, in case they were from the compound. But she had to take her chances. She had to get a ride before nightfall. She raised her hand and waved as the caravan neared and, when she realized they weren't even slowing down, she stepped closer to the shoulder and watched them whiz by.

There must have been thirty cars, vans, and pickup trucks. And just as fast as they'd appeared, they were gone, leaving nothing behind but new tracks in the snow.

A minute later she heard the sound of more vehicles. The second half of the caravan was coming from the north.

Again she jumped and waved and tried to flag them down. Just one car was all she needed to stop. But they roared by just as the others had.

No one was giving rides in the ice age.

She sighed. Then she started walking again…stopping…walking. She wasn't getting far.

Two hours later she heard more vehicles. Again, she turned to face north. And again, she waved desperately as they passed; first the head of the caravan then, a minute later, the tail. And as suddenly as they had appeared, they, too, were gone.

She couldn't help it, she started to cry. Her fate and Whoops's were becoming clear and she was scared. She walked several more hours until she realized the sun was setting. There were no sounds other than branches creaking and snow falling from them into the deserted forest. She knew there'd be no more traffic.

She had to get off the road for the night. She had to find a way…a place…to keep warm. There was no way to light a fire. She didn't even have matches.

When she reached a small bridge, she left the road and went underneath it. She sat down and began to cry. She cried until her whole body was shaking. She couldn't stop. She told Whoops, "I'm sorry." The only other thing she could say was, "I love you. I'll make you as comfortable as I can until the end."

Whoops cried with her: She was hungry again, she was getting colder, and from the odor, Danielle knew she had soiled and wet herself. Danielle had nothing to change her into.

She knew they weren't going to live through the night. They cried for about ten minutes when an animal loomed out of the darkness. She screamed, "*Get away from me!*" and her screaming scared Whoops and she cried even louder.

Behind the animal something else emerged and took on a human shape. "Help me," she pleaded. "Help me. Help us. I'll do anything. Just don't let us die."

He got closer. It was the man on skis. What did he want? He still wore his mask.

"Eat this," he said and he held something out.

She took it with her right hand that was numbed by the cold. But what he handed her was warm. It was meat. It was cooked. She brought it to her mouth and began to eat ravenously and she cried harder.

He held something else in his other hand.

"This is for the baby. I chopped it," he said.

He took a pinch of it and held it to Whoops's mouth.

As a reflex Danielle turned her sister away from him, but he kept his hand out. She stared at it and tentatively turned back and he reached a little further until his offering touched Whoops's lips. Danielle watched as Whoops ate what he fed her.

"It's chopped pretty fine," he said from behind his mask. "She should do okay with it. She won't choke if you feed her just a little at a time," and, when Danielle had eaten the piece of meat he'd given her, he handed her the rest of the chopped meat for the baby. She continued to shake as she cried and fed her sister.

He watched her feed Whoops until that meat was gone.

He offered her a canteen. "It's black coffee. It's cold, but it's okay."

He took out another canteen and poured something from it into the cup that covered it.

"It's water. It's warm. The baby needs it."

He watched Danielle give the water to the baby.

When they finished, he said, "Come on."

She tried to get up but couldn't.

"Give me the baby," he said.

"No!" she screamed. Whoops was the only reason she'd go on living, now. She wasn't letting anyone else help her up.

He stepped back and she started to get up but fell to her knees.

He stepped forward and offered to take her hand, but she said, "I can do this," and she clumsily struggled to her feet.

"Follow me," he said. It wasn't an order and he sounded tired.

She followed him back to the road. He checked once to make sure she was with him, then crossed to the other side. She followed. Whoops kept crying.

They walked through the darkened woods. This time he carried his skis but still stayed ahead. Several times her feet got tangled in snow-covered branches and she fell to her knees, but she'd struggle to her feet and catch up. He kept a fast pace but, unlike the morning, he never got out of her sight. She didn't know how long they walked when she smelled smoke. A little further ahead she could see a small fire flickering and she realized they were in a small clearing.

He motioned for her to sit on a log close to, but upwind from, the fire. He took one of the jackets he'd taken from the bodies and put it over her shoulders as she clutched Whoops to her breasts. Then he fed more wood to the fire. Gradually, it grew.

He had more meat here. He fed some to the dog. He handed her some. Then he sat, peeled off his ski mask, and started to feed himself.

She watched him. She could barely make out his features in the flickering light of the flames. He didn't look anything like she expected. He had a thin gaunt face, though everyone was thin these days. And he had sad eyes, not the angry eyes she had expected. He was younger than she had imagined, though somewhat older than herself. His hair was an off-blonde and his features not unpleasant.

She studied him, but he ignored her.

She wanted to say something.

"Where do you live?" she finally asked.

He stopped eating, looked at her, then went back to eating.

Of course he wouldn't answer. People hid in the ice age.

"You have a nice dog," she said.

He didn't respond.

"I said, you have a nice dog."

"It's not mine."

"Whose is he?"

"I don't know."

"How can you not know?"

"It's just been following me for the last two days."

"Are you going to keep him?"

He shook his head. "Too much upkeep."

"What are you going to do with him?"

"Eventually? I'm going to eat it."

She almost choked on what she was eating and wondered if it was another dog.

"What's this?" she asked.

"Squirrel and porcupine."

For a second, she wanted to retch, but she was hungry, so she kept eating.

She looked around. She was lost, now. What would he do with her, now? What would she be willing to do to keep her sister alive? "What are you going to do with me?" she asked.

"I was hoping you'd get a ride by now."

That wasn't an answer to her question, but she didn't push for an elaboration and neither of them spoke for a while.

Finally he said, "We've got to get some sleep. I want you back on the road in the morning.

"You'll get a ride," he added in a tone that vaguely implied that he felt the reason she hadn't gotten one, yet, was her fault.

He stood up and walked away from the fire.

In the dim light of the fire she could see a burrow in the snow.

He stood over it and pointed to it. "Get in there," he commanded.

There was only one burrow. He wanted her to sleep with him. That wasn't happening.

"I'm staying out here," she said.

In the darkness she couldn't see the incredulity on his face.

He approached her. "Then let me have your baby," he said, "No!"

He seemed to vacillate for a moment. With him this close, she saw a look of disgust on his face.

"You don't deserve that baby," he finally said. "There's some wood there to feed the fire, but you're putting your kid at risk." And with that he went and crawled into the burrow. He took the dog in with him.

"Asshole," she heard him say as he settled into the burrow.

"I'm not the asshole," she said.

It got darker and colder. She sat near the dying fire with Whoops cradled in her arms and rocked her. She wasn't getting in the burrow. She wasn't going to be raped again. She threw more branches on the fire and, though they made the fire brighter, they didn't make her feel much warmer. Within an hour she began to wonder if her feet were getting frostbitten. She started to shiver. She knew Whoops was getting cold.

Whoops began to cry, again. She wanted to cry, herself, but she remembered the promise she'd made to herself. But it was about her sister's survival, now. She wondered if he'd still let her into the burrow. If he wanted sex, what was she going to do? Was she going to give in to save her sister?

She wrestled with her dilemma until she realized she was going to freeze to death. More importantly, Whoops would. She got up and approached the burrow. The way he was breathing, she could tell he was sleeping.

She crouched beside him and whispered, "Hey."

He didn't respond. The dog, on the other hand, lifted his head and watched her.

"Hey," she said louder.

He still didn't answer.

"Hey!" she shouted and was startled when from out of the dark he pushed a small revolver in her face.

When he saw it was her, he lowered the gun. "What do you want?"

"I'm cold."

"I can't do anything about that."

"Can we get in?"

He sighed and sat up. He readjusted the burrow so there was room for her and Whoops. He put them between himself and the dog.

She was sure she knew what he wanted and, if she had to, she'd fuck him. She closed her eyes and wanted to cry. She waited. But he lay down and faced away from her. Soon, she realized he'd gone back to sleep and she lay there shivering, until she got warm. She wondered what she was going to do when he put her back on the road the next day. After a while the clouds cleared and there was a full moon in the sky. The stars looked warm, but the black sky that cradled them was bleak and cold. The forest was noisier than she expected, what with the creaking and crackling of branches and limbs as they now and then shed their snow.

Whoops surrendered to sleep and, at some point, she did, too. And when she dreamt, it was nightmares in which she was lonely, helpless, and scared. In the distance, she saw her mommy, her father, and her brother, Robert, but they were leaving her. Suddenly, she was startled awake. The stranger was now snuggled up to her, facing her, and had a hand cupped over her right breast.

"Stop!" she yelled and jerked upright.

He sat up startled and stared at her in the moonlight. He had the gun in his hand and it was pointed at her face again.

"What's wrong?" he asked.

"Keep your filthy hands off my tits!" she screamed. Whoops began to cry. But she now knew that, even for her sister, she wouldn't *let* a man rape her.

However, all he did was lower the gun and lay down again, facing away as he had earlier. And soon, she could tell from his breathing, he was sleeping, again.

She couldn't believe how readily he went back to sleep. She lay back down, wide awake. She felt Whoops. She was wet but she'd already fallen back to sleep, so Danielle let her be.

She had to get away from this guy. There was something wrong with him. She couldn't figure out how he could have saved her in the morning, yet treat her like this. All he wanted to do was yell at her, push her down in the snow, take Whoops away, and now he was copping a feel. And she knew he was dangerous: She'd already witnessed when he'd killed three men and left another to die. He was one more crazy man, like Hank and Barry. Everything was about violence and sex. But she had to stay with him until she could make her way south. Or until she could get a ride. Or until she could kill him.

Chapter 8
August 27

It was noon before Abby sent a few of the guys out to the field to see what was taking the boys so long. Andrew was still alive when they got there. They brought him home with the bodies of the others.

Had Abby cried, gone on a tirade, or if she'd simply have fainted when she went outside to view the bodies, the others at the compound would have felt better, perhaps even sympathetic to her. Two grandsons and a great nephew were dead. Instead she stood there and viewed them in a stony silence that sent chills through everyone else.

On the other hand, as is often the case, no matter how bad their loved ones treated them in life, many seek — out of guilt, or to find solace, or to obtain the ever-popular "closure" — to canonize the bastards once they're dead. Thus was Barry's wife, Terry Higgins, who upon seeing the body of her philandering husband as he lay on the snow-covered driveway with a quarter of his skull missing and what was left of his brains still leaking out onto the ground, she prostrated herself upon his corpse and cried hysterically belying the fact that he had for years made her miserable and she would have, just that morning, blown his brains out herself if she'd thought she could have gotten away with it.

Andrew would live until just before dawn of the next day. Before he died, he recounted his story, as best he could, of the man on skis and the dog, and how Danielle had left him in the field to die. *That* was when Abby broke out of her silence and went into her tirade. Now there was someone to hate, and that someone was Danielle, Whoops, and the unknown man who had killed her boys. Somehow, Abby Brady was going to get vengeance on the three of them — and anyone else.

That evening, when Hank and the others returned, they were laughing because their foray to the road had been so successful. They'd brought with them two vans loaded with food, clothes, gasoline, weapons, and tools, and six girls, ages eight to sixteen. Behind Abby's back, they referred to the girls as "fresh meat." But their celebration was cut short when Abby confronted them with the news of the massacre in the field.

On her orders, the six new girls, just brought in, were taken out to the barn. Abby didn't want the men to take the chance of walking the girls to the field where the shooter may still be lurking.

Alice, the girl who had coveted Danielle's jeans that morning, stood in the doorway of the barn and watched. She pointed to one of the older girls and said, "Make her take her pants off. I don't want her to shit in them when you do her."

So Hank made the girl take her pants off and he tossed them to Alice with a salacious wink and she smiled at him. The rest of the girls were stripped of their clothes, so they wouldn't get soiled when their bowels let loose. Then each, in turn, as she stood crying, was shot behind the ear with a .22 caliber pistol, the same way farmers often shoot a pig or a cow before butchering it.

Later that night, Abby gave orders that the boys were not to bring anyone back from the road, *ever again*. She further announced that, somehow, Danielle and the stranger, and anyone else associated with them, were going to pay for what they'd done. Though no one understood how this helped, she said shooting the six girls was a start toward retribution.

Chapter 9
August 28

When Danielle woke again it was morning. She sat up in the burrow. The sky was blue and almost cloudless. The man was gone; so was the dog. But much of his stuff was still there. She didn't know what that meant. She lay back down in the burrow. Whoops was still sleeping, but she needed to be changed. She felt between the baby's legs to see how bad it was. She was dry. She was sure Whoops had been wet during the night. She lifted the baby's wrappings. Whoops was wearing a diaper made from a folded-up T-shirt. That meant...

She didn't like that the man had taken Whoops away from her without her knowing it.

She waited in the burrow for what she thought was a long time. Suddenly, there he was, almost as if he'd come from nowhere, with the damned ski mask on. She stifled a scream when he surprised her.

He looked at her oddly.

"You scared me," she whispered.

She saw the skinned carcass of a small animal in his hand and he had the fire going, again.

"We'll eat, then I'll take you out to the road. You'll get a ride, today."

They sat beside the fire and ate in silence. When they finished, he smothered the fire with snow and broke camp.

He put a strip of cloth over her shoulder. It was obvious it had come from the shirt and pants he'd taken off Eddie back in the field.

"These'll have to work as diapers," he said.

He offered to carry Whoops, but Danielle said no. Then they worked their way through the woods and back out to the road. It didn't seem to take as long to get there in the sunlight as it had taken to get into the campsite the night before.

"We're back on Highway 101," he said.

The pristine snow showed that no vehicles had passed during the night.

He stared at Whoops, then at her, then he pointed down the road and said, "That's south. You're on your own.

"Here's some of the porcupine meat. It's cooked. I chopped some for your baby."

She nodded and, just as quickly as before, he disappeared with his dog into the woods.

She was half scared, but also half glad, he'd left. She didn't like him.

She started walking south, again. Sometimes she sat for a while where there was a guard rail, but mostly she walked, her head down watching the ground.

At one point she looked up and there, several hundred yards ahead, a car was parked on the side of the road. She stopped. From where she stood, she could see a passenger-side door was open. So was the trunk. She didn't really want to get any closer, but it lay in her path. There were no tire tracks in the new snow that led up to it. There was no telling how long it had been there.

She was too far away to see any signs of what may have happened to the occupants. They may even still be in the car. She tried to look into the trees ahead, to see if there was anyone lurking there. She raised herself up as high as she could to see if there were any footprints around the car, and there were — or there weren't. From this far away she couldn't be sure.

She looked back and, for a moment, regretted that the stranger wasn't there, but quickly dismissed that thought.

She began to get colder. She could feel the iciness coming up through her feet. She watched her breath condense before her face. She knew she had to keep moving. So she walked again, leaving her own footprints in the virgin snow.

She kept an eye on the car for signs of life and periodically scanned the trees on either side of the road for any movements in the shadows. Whoops began to squirm in her arms and became a distraction.

The closer she got to the car, the more frequently she stopped. She'd hold her breath and listen, but heard nothing. Several times she thought she saw something move in the trees, but decided her eyes playing tricks on her. Driven by the cold, she would walk another twenty or thirty yards, then stop, watch, and listen once more.

Each stop lasted longer. But each time she walked, she got closer. Finally, when she was thirty yards away, she stopped for the last time surveyed her situation and listened. She let out a gasp when she heard something behind her and spun around. It was only snow falling out of the trees she'd passed. Once again, the air was silent.

She whispered to the baby, "Let's go, Whoopsie," and she closed the final thirty yards and was relieved to see the snow around the car was undisturbed. No footprints.

She peered into the trunk. A thin layer of snow coated its contents. But there was nothing there of value: No food, and nothing that would keep her warm.

She rounded the car to the driver's side and peered in through the windows. The cab was empty.

She looked around to assure herself they were alone and never felt so lonely in her life. She could get in the car if she wanted. But for what? She still had the nerrgy to walk and every step forward took her closer to California. She looked down the road at the untouched snow, then resumed walking.

A while later, she heard something coming up behind her. She turned. A caravan. As they got close, she held Whoops up for them to see. She was asking for a ride. If not her, at least for her sister. But like a train, they went by. No eyes behind the windows met hers. There was no pity. As quickly as they had appeared, they were gone leaving nothing but their tread marks on the once clean snow.

A sense of desperation swept over her and she felt rooted to where she stood. It flashed through her mind that her situation was hopeless. But Whoops squirmed again and Danielle looked down at her in her arms, kissed her forehead, and started to walk. Still, in the back of her mind a haunting thought kept recurring: If they didn't get a ride, the very fate she had feared for her sister in the field—freezing to death—was going to happen anyway. She wondered if she'd let Whoops die like that, or bring her death on quickly. It was a decision she didn't want to think about. She tried to think about something else.

Once, she stopped on the road and fed Whoops. Another time, after Whoops had cried for a while, she stopped near a small rivulet that ran beside the highway and changed her. She rinsed the diaper in the water then wrung it out as best she could. The cold water numbed her hands. She slung the wet diaper over her shoulder so it would dry as she walked.

Otherwise, all she did was walk or rest on a guard rail. Sometimes she sang. Sometimes she cried in spite of her promise to herself, but she told herself it was okay to cry if she was alone. But mostly she walked in silence and tried to keep her sister's fate out of her mind..

Hours later, it was getting dark.

And then, there he was, again, with the dog, up ahead on the road. He wasn't wearing his ski mask. He looked angry. She sensed he was mad at her.

When she reached him he said, "Come on."

He skied off onto a trail and she followed him.

She wasn't sure how much longer she could walk.

Soon, they were in a clearing and there it was: another small fire and a camp in the woods.

He pointed for her to sit.

She sat.

He had more meat.

They ate.

He had warm water.

They drank.

"We'll get sleep, then we'll get you a ride in the morning," he said. It was only the second thing he'd said to her since he'd found her again, and this time she got into the new burrow with him, but she realized he still hadn't said anything else. Nor was he going to.

Maybe he expected something from her, this time. But soon, she could hear him breathing slowly and softly. He was asleep. It took her a long time to get there herself, even though she was exhausted. But sleep finally overtook her and she slept through the night. This time he kept his hands to himself

Chapter 10
August 28

The morning of the 28th another meeting was held at the LaCroix ranch; this one on the freshly fallen snow in the circular driveway before the main house. Ten men and two snowmobiles, one with a sled in tow, were assembled. Only five of the men were leaving and they were all well-armed. The sky was a pellucid blue and everyone hoped it was the prelude to another warm spell that would melt some of the snow and bring more traffic down the 101 from up north.

Louis LaCroix had been up most of the night with his bereaved sister and he wasn't in the mood for much talk. He looked about to see who was there, once again counting heads for the mission the men were about to embark on. In his right hand he tossed a shell casing almost rhythmically. It was one left by the shooter two days before. The others knew he carried it now as a reminder of what had to be done.

He continued to toss it while several of the men watched. Without breaking the rhythm, he finally kicked the snowmobile in front of him, to get their attention.

When they were all looking his way he began, "I want to go over the plans once more so there are no doubts. I don't have to tell you: Don't leave here by way of the road. I don't want anyone to go out on 101, today, unless you absolutely have to. We don't need you leaving snow-tracks that this guy—or any cohorts he's got—can follow back. I want us to find him first." He was, of course, referring to the shooter.

"With any luck, the weather will turn warm and melt the snow so we don't leave tracks anywhere.

"Go cross-country," he said. He looked at the disabled red snowmobile that sat just inside the open doors of the barn.

"Be careful," he said. And, trying to break the tension, he added, "They're *not* selling 'em down at Wal-Mart anymore."

A few chuckled politely, but the disabled snowmobile was still a sore subject for him.

He kept tossing the shell casing. It was almost mesmerizing to the others.

He turned to Billy Raymond. With Todd Anderson dead, Raymond was the logical choice to lead the expedition. None of the men liked Raymond but, in this case, that would make for a good leader. And though he was occasionally rash, he'd *lead* the men and he wouldn't send them anywhere he himself wouldn't go. LaCroix also liked the fact that Raymond had pursued the shooter two days before. LaCroix made it clear he would have done the same.

"Billy's in charge," he said. "Anyone got a problem with that, say so now. You can stay here. We got shit that's got to be cleaned out of the pig sty, weather damage repairs that have to be done on the barn, and the solar panels have to be cleaned." The last was a job he had relegated to the women.

No one spoke.

In a voice that was still tired, but suddenly solicitous, he said, "I don't want anyone getting hurt today. I radioed ahead, so the Bradys know you're coming. I didn't tell them why. I don't want to discuss that on the airwaves. But they know we've got a problem.

"But they wouldn't let me talk to Hank or Abby, so there's something brewing over there, too. They're not going to tell me what's up, on the CB, any more than I'm going to tell them. There's all kinds of assholes out there monitoring the channels."

He scanned the men's faces to make sure they were listening.

"When you get there," he continued, "I don't want any of you letting on that we lost four men. They don't need to know our numbers." Three men, he thought before going on; three men and his nephew, and he could add to that the man they lost two years earlier, so there were five. "If it doesn't look good getting into their compound, turn back. Peterson is going to be there to provide cover. Even though they're letting us in, keep in mind they don't like us."

Four of the men nodded. Peterson just stared.

"Remember, I don't want all of you actually going all the way in to the Brady place. Especially you," he said to Brian Peterson, brother of one of the men who'd been killed. "Just you and Fred," he said to Raymond and he nodded to Fred Mayfield. Mayfield was a relative to the Bradys and having blood go along was likely to defuse any hostilities. "I want just the three of you to go on their land, but I don't want Brian to go all the way in."

He turned to Peterson who held a scoped Steyr SSG sniper rifle. Peterson was a taciturn man of average size and average looks. There wasn't much to suggest he was unusual, until you realized he had no close friends — never did, never would — and that what he was best known for, and made him valuable to the compound, was that he was the best shot in the compound; a phenomenal shot. Before the ice age started, he'd been the best in the state, and before that he'd been a premier sniper in the Army and he finished pretty high at the Camp Perry rifle matches in Ohio. There were stories that he took all the toughest sniping assignments when he was deployed to Iraq and Afghanistan. But there were also stories that he sometimes shot civilians just for sport. They'd never been verified, but those who knew him believed they were true.

"I'm not going to tell you how to do your job," LaCroix said, "but remember, your mission is simply to provide cover for Billy and Fred in case they need to haul ass out of there."

Peterson stared at LaCroix without acknowledging what he'd said. He was the one guy who could creep LaCroix out and Louis felt a vague chill as he looked into Peterson't almost empty eyes.

LaCroix then looked at Raymond to make sure everything was understood.

"Got it," Raymond said.

"You guys know what you gotta do and how to do it. Follow Billy. He's a good leader.

"*But no more chances.* Until two days ago, we only had one other incident, and it looks like it's been the same guy each time. That's two strikes. We're not having a third one called on us. I don't want anymore burials. And I want everyone back here from the Brady compound before sunset. We've got more funerals to do."

LaCroix looked at his watch. "Sunset's going to be about eight o'clock, tonight. I want you back long before then."

He suddenly caught and clutched the casing he'd been tossing and asked, "Any questions?"

"What if we see that guy again?" Tom Burke asked.

LaCroix thought about that. "If you can take him alive, fine. I'd like to know who he's with. But no chances. If you have to kill him, kill him; we don't lose any more boys."

He turned to Peterson, again. "Brian, keep the boys safe with your rifle."

Peterson said nothing. The other four nodded.

They started the two snowmobiles and the racket drowned out all other sounds on the compound. LaCroix walked over to Billy Raymond, patted him on the shoulder and nodded, and without another word he turned and walked back into the main house.

Bearing five vengeful men, the snowmobiles started on their journey.

Chapter 11
August 28

The backcountry of Curry County was carpeted with a late August snowfall. Billy Raymond and the four men he led made their way south to the Brady compound, staying east of Highway 101 as they went. Except for some clouds forming to the northwest, the sky was still clear and each man hoped it would warm up enough for the snow to melt. There was going to be enough of it falling in the months to come.

"Eyes open," he had told them before they'd left. The others knew what he meant and they kept a vigil for the shooter who might still be lurking out there.

They reached the barbed wire fencing that marked the edges of the old Brady ranch and parked their snowmobiles at the bottom of a small draw in the shelter of some trees. Jim De Angelis and Tom Burke were assigned to wait with and protect the vehicles while Raymond, Mayfield, and Peterson skied ahead. Fences were irrelevant, now. There were no more range animals to keep in. Goats, pigs, and chickens were all anyone kept anymore, and they kept those penned. So, Raymond cut the fence in the event the snowmobiles had to come in a hurry.

Though now on the Brady property, they still had a few miles to go before they reached the compound.

Raymond and Peterson each had a walkie-talkie and De Angelis had a third one where he waited with the snowmobiles. A fourth, monitoring their shared frequency, was sitting on the desk in Louis LaCroix's office back at the compound.

"Don't use it unless you have to," Raymond reminded De Angelis. "And watch what you say; Louis doesn't like chatter."

De Angelis knew that and resented that Raymond told him the obvious. But he said nothing.

Mayfield tied a white flag to the end of his rifle's barrel and skied at the front of the group, then the three went through the forest along an assortment of old lumber roads and cow trails for their rendezvous with Abby and Hank.

They strung themselves out along the route and were well over half an hour into the ranch when a voice ahead yelled, "Hey!"

Mayfield pulled up short. Raymond, fifty yards behind him, stopped at the same time. He looked back at Peterson who was much further back, but was now fading into the woods with his sniper rifle.

Raymond clicked his walkie-talkie. In a low voice he said, "We've been greeted."

"You all right?" De Angelis asked.

"Yeah, there's someone up ahead."

A staticky voice broke in and said, "How many are there?" It was Louis LaCroix.

"I don't know. I just heard the one voice, haven't seen anyone, yet, but there are probably a few."

"Do you know who it is?" LaCroix asked.

"Haven't seen anyone, yet," Raymond said again.

"Do you want us to come in?" De Angelis asked.

"No, we're good."

"Where's Brian?" LaCroix asked.

"He's back in the trees, but they must have seen him. If they recognized him, they know he's here."

"They know. They're probably listening as we speak. So you boys be careful," LaCroix said and neither he nor De Angelis said anymore. Raymond slipped the walkie-talkie back into his pocket.

On a small hill, some hundred and fifty yards ahead, a man emerged from behind a large oak. He glassed them with a set of binoculars then waved.

Mayfield waved back. "It's Jerry Brady," he called back to Raymond. "One of my cousins," he added.

Relation or not, there was still a lot of distrust in this new world, particularly between the LaCroix and Brady compounds.

"Is anyone with him?" Raymond asked.

"I can't tell."

But Raymond was sure Brady wouldn't have shown himself if he was alone.

Then the cousin yelled something, and Mayfield listened intently. He turned and yelled back to Raymond, "You understand that?"

Raymond shook his head.

"He wants Peterson to get the hell out of the trees with that rifle."

Raymond had to commit to a decision. He was sure the Bradys wouldn't stage an ambush after Louis LaCroix had announced they'd be coming. He looked back along the trail and thought a few seconds. Then he beckoned to the now unseen Peterson.

It was a minute before Peterson came out of the trees. He stood on the trail until Raymond waved him ahead, again. Then the three men skied further on, but they stayed strung out in case it was a trap.

Raymond was relieved when Jerry Brady finally skied down the hill to meet them. Like the others, he was dressed in white and he had a rifle slung over his shoulder. He came up short in front of Mayfield. "What's this about?" he asked.

Mayfield jacked his thumb up over his shoulder indicating he should talk with Raymond.

Raymond got close enough and Brady asked him, "What are you here for?"

"We've got problems."

"Everybody's got problems."

"Yeah, well there's someone out here and we want to know if you know anything about him."

Brady didn't say anything.

"A shooter," Raymond said.

Brady spit in the snow in disgust and Raymond and Mayfield knew he was asking the right questions..

"Have you met up with him?" Raymond asked point blank.

"If it's who I think you're talking about, yeah."

"Have any idea who he is?"

Brady shook his head. "The old lady's wondering if he was someone you guys know, if he'd come off the road, or if there's someone been operating around here we don't know about."

"We think he's old news," Raymond said.

"What do you mean?"

Raymond didn't answer.

Peterson caught up but stood back with his rifle.

"Well, we know who the girl is what's with him," Brady said.

"There's a girl with him?" Raymond asked in surprise.

"Yeah."

"The Gibbons girl?" Raymond asked, remembering what he'd heard Dodd say on the hill two days before about Sandra Gibbons marrying a guy named Amaral. But there hadn't been a girl with him when he killed the three men and LaCroix's nephew, Kyle.

"I don't think her name is Gibbons," Brady replied. "But I never did hear her last name, either. Her first name's Danielle. She used to be here."

"She was here? She's one of your girls?"

"No, no, no. She's from the road." Brady figured folks at the LaCroix compound already knew at least some of what went on at the Brady compound, and about the girls taken off the road. "Do *you* know who she is?" he asked, wondering where Raymond had gotten the name Gibbons.

Raymond shook his head.

"Where'd the name Gibbons come from?" Jerry asked.

It was too long to explain. "It's just a name I heard the other day. But the first name was Sandra."

Brady shook his head. "No, this girl's name is Danielle--'less she was lying to us. She's probably sixteen. But let me tell ya, she's a cunt. Even after everything that happened to her, she stood up to Abby and Hank. That's why we had to get rid of her."

"What do you mean, '...everything that happened to her'?" Raymond asked.

Brady was silent. He didn't want to talk about how she'd been gang raped the first night. Instead, he changed the course of the conversation and asked, "What was your run-in with the guy?"

"He was on our territory. You know we ain't gonna put up with that, even if it's one of you guys. He got some lucky shots in. Got away before we could take him."

"He ambushed you?"

Raymond shook his head while looking ahead. He knew Brady wasn't out here alone. He wanted to see who else was up on the hill. But nobody showed. "No, we were chasing him. *Then* he ambushed us."

Brady looked at Brian Peterson and his sniper rifle. "Where were you?"

Peterson didn't answer.

"Figure it out," Raymond said. "We wouldn't be down here worrying about him if he'd been with us."

Brady didn't press it any further, but he was getting edgy because of Peterson's searing stare.

"The guy got his brother," Raymond said to Brady.

"Dead?"

Raymond nodded.

"Sorry," was all Brady would commit to.

Peterson showed no emotion.

But a casualty, Peterson's brother, had now been introduced into the conversation. Jerry Brady made a mental note of it as Raymond knew he would. Each side was keeping score of how many able-bodied men were at the other's compound.

"Well, he actually ambushed our guys, too," Brady finally said. "Our boys didn't even know he was there. I don't know what he's using, but it looks like you've got some competition," he said sarcastically to Peterson as he looked again at his fancy sniper rifle.

The conversation was going nowhere for Billy Raymond. "Can we go in now?" he asked. "We gotta talk with the old lady and Hank and see what they know and what we can work out...to stop this bastard."

"Got snowmobiles?" Brady asked.

"Not with us," Raymond lied. There was no sense in tempting anyone with something as coveted as a snowmobile that ran.

"Your brother the only one he got?" Brady asked Peterson.

"The bastard took four of us," Raymond blurted out.

"That means he got eight," Brady said.

"He got four of you guys, too?" Raymond asked.

Both men realized they probably shouldn't have admitted to anything. But it was part of a bond that was forming, now. An alliance that would unite two feuding compounds against a common—though unknown—enemy was starting to firm up.

"He got Andrew Ingram, Eddie McFaddin, and two of the old lady's grandsons, Barry Higgins and Joel" Brady said.

"Joel?" Mayfield asked in surprise. He was related to him, Higgins, and McFaddin.

Brady nodded.

"Son of a bitch," Mayfield said.

"We're wasting time. Take us in," Raymond said.

"She's not going to be happy to see anyone," Brady responded.

"We're not here to make her happy. We've got to find out who this guy is, find out who he's working with, and put an end to him and whoever he's operating with. This guy's responsible for the only casualties we've had in three years of doin' this stuff. And that's what we're here for. We want to find out what you guys know and what—maybe together—we can do about it."

Brady thought about it for several seconds.

"Well, she is expecting you. But I don't think she's gonna wanna talk."

He looked back and waved his arm.

Another man came out of the trees and skied down the hill. He stopped when he reached the group. The men from the LaCroix compound recognized him as Steven Ingram, brother of Andrew Ingram who had died in the field.

"We're takin' them in to see Abby," Brady told him.

Ingram seemed uneasy. It didn't take a genius to realize he didn't really want to be there, but he nodded and there was an exchange of pleasantries, condolences, and handshaking and the deal was sealed.

"Sorry about your brother," Raymond said.

"Thanks," Ingram allowed.

"We'll take ya in," Brady said to Raymond, "But I'm warning ya, I don't know if the old lady's gonna want to talk with ya, what with the funerals goin' on."

"Then we'll talk to Hank."

Brady spit on the snow again. Though stupid and dangerous, Hank was a fact of life and a force to be reckoned with at the Brady compound, and he was the person Abby depended on most.

Raymond took out his walkie-talkie, again. "We're going in," he announced.

"I want no more than two of you going in and I want Brian to stay concealed," LaCroix said.

Raymond looked at Peterson and said, "Get into the trees."

"I ain't goin' for that," Brady objected.

"You got all the cards," Raymond said. "If nothing happens, he just sits out here and waits. If you guys decide to fuck with us, we got cover or someone who can get back to the ranch and let 'em know what happened. Peterson's not gonna hurt anyone if we don't get hurt."

Brady shook his head. This was unacceptable.

"Then you tell that dried-up old bag that she can come and talk with us, and you explain why you turned us back."

Peterson had already disappeared into the woods when Raymond started skiing away. Mayfield followed.

"Wait," Brady yelled.

The two men held up.

Brady looked at where Peterson had gone out of sight. He knew he wasn't coming back out of the trees.

"Come on," Brady said. "I'll take ya in."

"You stay here and keep an eye out for Peterson," he said to Ingram.

Ingram's agitation increased. He shook his head. "I ain't staying out here with him. That guy's crazy," he said and started back up the hill.

Brady watched Ingram leave. He looked back at where Peterson had disappeared. But Brady himself wouldn't want to stay out here with Peterson, so he let Ingram go.

"Okay, I'll take you in," he said to Raymond and they started toward the ranch house.

Raymond looked at the sky. More clouds were moving in from the northwest. It could be another storm coming their way. They'd have to get this trip over with, soon. With that thought in mind, he fell in behind Brady.

§ § §

There was a sense of unease when Jerry Brady and Steven Ingram returned with two armed men from the LaCroix compound. Louis LaCroix was fond of saying they both "fished the same stream..." when he referred to robbing the people coming down the 101, "...and there's barely enough there for one compound." But when the LaCroix compound had men out on the road, just because they were further north, they had first pick of what was coming down the pike. There was some resentment over that on the Brady compound just as there was resentment in the communities further south in Brookings, Smith River, and Crescent City toward any town north of them.

Road piracy was largely the way the gangs survived. But they had to be careful how they stopped traffic. One town in California had, in defiance of orders issued by the Army, taken out a bridge to trap travellers going south. The idea was to make them abandon their vehicles. But the Army had orders to keep the road that led to the Hanford Works in Washington State open. No one knew for certain what transpired in the small town of Trinidad, California, just before the Army Corps of Engineers repaired the bridge. The citizens of the town simply disappeared and no one along the route dared duplicate their feat.

But if you stayed out of its way, the military left you alone. The Army didn't care what the LaCroixs did to the Bradys or what the Bradys did to the LaCroixs, nor what they did to those fleeing south on the roads. They left it to them to work those things out themselves. They had to keep key governmental operations going, and there were issues brewing in the most southerly states for which troops were being held in reserve.

Hank was on the porch as Raymond and Mayfield reached the top step. He looked at the two men menacingly as they passed. Both Raymond and Mayfield were wary because they knew of Hank and his reputation. Before the ice age started, Hank sometimes worked on the family cattle ranch and other times he did odd jobs in town. He'd been a hard drinker back in the days when booze was still readily available in the markets and state-run liquor stores, and he frequented the bars in Gold Beach, to the north, and Brookings, to the south, where he long had the reputation as "the man who provoked fights."

Hank was dimly aware that he was stupid, but fully aware that what he lacked in brains he could almost always make up for with brute strength and intimidation. Though arrested many times for DUIs, assault, and disturbing the peace, he'd never been afraid of the police, but he knew others were. Now, with the police uniforms they had stolen from a local police station, he relished the sense of legitimacy and authority he thought the uniform conferred upon him. And with his bearing, when he was out on the road flagging down hapless emigrants, he seemed like a real cop until it was too late and he revealed himself to be a psychopath.

A freshly-constructed casket dominated the living room when they entered.

"That's Barry Higgins," Jerry Brady whispered about the body in the casket. There was a hat on his head to hide the obvious damage. "Andy and Eddie are with their families at other houses on the compound," he added referring to the double-wides that had been moved onto the property to form the compound on what was often referred to as the Brady ranch.

They passed through the room and past the mourners, some of whom looked up to see who they were. They walked down a long hall to the kitchen at the back of the house.

There, a casket rested in front of the stuffed chair where Abby Brady sat slumped and lost in thought. At least fifteen people were in the kitchen, but the room was silent.

"Abby?" Jerry began, "Men from the LaCroix ranch."

The old lady didn't look up.

"Sorry to have to bother you at a time like this," Raymond said.

"Do you realize he's going to have to lay in the cold earth, forever?" she asked bitterly.

Raymond didn't answer. He didn't care.

"Are you listening?" she asked sharply and now sat up in her chair.

"I didn't come here to attend no funeral," he rebutted. "We got enough of those going on at our place."

She looked at him fiercely. "Do you know who did this?"

"That's what I'm here for," he said angrily. "Mr. LaCroix wants to know what you know, and see if you want to work something with us so we can take care of this problem. Am I wastin' my time here?"

She slumped back in her chair.

"I knowed that girl was trouble," she said. "I knowed it the moment I laid eyes on her. She brung nothin' but turmoil, dissension, and sadness here. She had no right to do what she did."

"Is this that Danielle?"

"You don't use that name under my roof," she shouted. "That name will *never* be spoken in this house again."

Raymond nodded to Jerry Brady. He was ready to talk with Hank.

Jerry nodded back and he, Raymond, Mayfield, and Hank turned to leave the kitchen.

"Where are you goin'?" Abby demanded.

The four men stopped.

"You got grievin' to do," Raymond said to her.

"There's always grievin' to do," she countered. "You tell me what you want and why you're down here in the middle of a funeral."

"This isn't the only funeral takin' place," Raymond said walking toward her. He stopped right in front of her. He wasn't afraid of her, but he knew he had to be careful. "We got four of our own down. One's a boy younger than Joel. So don't you go layin' your sorrow on us, we got enough of our own. We come down here to see what we can do about this problem. You? Hank? I don't care who I talk to. This is gotta be nipped in the bud."

"Where are you goin'?" Abby said sharply. This time she was talking to Clara who had gotten out of her seat and hoped to leave the kitchen.

Clara stood indecisively for a moment then sat again.

"You show some respect," Abby warned her.

Several of those who'd been in the kitchen when the men entered now shifted in turn as if making themselves ready for a long quiet vigil.

"Who do I talk to to make some plans?" Raymond asked.

"I want that girl and her baby and whoever it was that helped her to pay for what they done to me."

"There's a baby?"

Abby didn't answer.

"You know, those girls tried to tempt my boys with sex to get them to do things out in that field," she said. She didn't say what field to Raymond.

"There's other girls with them?" Raymond asked. "First there's the guy, then the guy and a girl, then there's a baby, now there's other girls? What are we up against?"

"No, that other one's dead."

One other, he thought. "How'd she die?"

"Never you mind how she died, but she was naked as a jaybird when they found her body out there. That's proof she was trying to tempt them. I always knowed she was a tramp, one of them road sluts that keep showin' up. Those road sluts bring grief with them.

"When are you boys gonna learn that?" she asked looking around the room.

"What are we gonna do, Abby? There's a storm movin' in and we gotta get back. And one of the boys that come with us has his own brother to mourn, but he's here to help settle this shit."

"You watch your tongue in front of my grandson," she snapped.

Raymond rolled his eyes then nodded toward the casket. "Sorry. But we gotta do something. They're still out there. They know where we live, but we don't know where they live, and they're gonna pick us off, one by one, if we don't do something, *now*."

"You work it out with Hank..." she said. "...but you let me know what's goin' on. They're gonna pay for this...everyone's going to pay for what they did to my Sweetie. He never even got to know what life's about. He was so pure. You know, he even cared about that little whore. He even wanted her to stay. And look how she paid him back.

"No more, you hear me?" she yelled looking around the room. "No more tramps, no more sluts from the road," she said.

"Clara, you make me some tea."

Clara leaped from her seat, went to the wood stove, and moved the kettle to a hot spot. She got a cup down from the cupboard and a tea bag from the canister. Abby was the only one allowed to drink tea on the ranch, anymore. Clara wondered what life was going to be like when the tea was gone and Abby had one more thing to bitch about. She hoped someone coming down the road would have some that the boys could take.

"And make certain you let me know what's happenin'," the old woman barked as the men turned again to leave.

Once they were back on the porch, Hank said, "You meet us tomorrow and I'll lead a group of our men and your men and we'll find this bastard."

"You're not leadin' shit," Raymond said. "We'll work with you guys, but Mr. LaCroix isn't gonna have you runnin' our boys."

"Why not?" Hank asked.

"'Cause you're an idiot," Raymond said heatedly.

He was direct with Hank. He had to make it clear, right from the start, Hank wasn't leading anything.

"You know the old beaver pond up near the old lumber camp," Raymond said. It wasn't a question, but he wanted to make sure Hank knew what he was talking about. When Hank nodded, Raymond said, "Mr. LaCroix wants us to meet with some of your boys there tomorrow morning so we can get started on this."

"How many should we bring? We can get a dozen, maybe twenty, guys together..."

"We can't support an operation that big," Raymond said cutting him off. "LaCroix says each compound should send four men. It's probably enough to take care of this guy and it's more than enough to go scouting. If it turns out there's too many of them, we'll know where they are and we can send out a bigger party.

"Bring stuff that'll let you be out for a few days: Guns, food, and extra clothes."

"I'll have to ask Abby," Hank said.

Raymond stomped his foot then started pacing on the porch. When he got back to Hank he got in his face. "She said to work things out with you," he snapped. "If you can't make any decisions, you stay here; send her out to help us."

"We got funerals tomorrow," Hank said.

"We got funerals, too!" Raymond yelled. "And we're gonna have them every day unless we stop the guys doing this."

"There's more than one?" Hank asked in surprise. "Andrew said there'd only been the one."

"You guys already said there's a girl with him!" Raymond shouted, again. "For all I know, he's got a fuckin' army with him. But we're not gonna find out sitting here on our asses at the compounds."

He shook his head. Hank *was* an idiot. "We gotta find out how many more there may be."

"That girl's no problem," Hank said.

"She was in on the shootin' of some of your boys, so she's a problem. Get that straight in your fuckin' head. Why's she with the guy, anyway?"

"Andrew said he seemed to come from nowhere. Maybe he's her boyfriend. She talked about havin' one. Maybe he followed her down the road."

"No, this is a local guy," Raymond said, then paused. "At least we think he is."

"Why would a stranger save her?" Hank asked.

"Save her from what?"

"We took 'em out to the field to shoot 'em." And right after he said it, Hank realized he shouldn't have.

Raymond wasn't going to ask why they were going to shoot her. He'd heard the rumors about what happened on the Brady Ranch. If the snow melted and normalcy came back, everyone on the Brady compound would probably be hung. Of course, given the robberies they had committed on the 101, folks from the LaCroix compound probably wouldn't fare much better. It was ironic, but after you robbed and maybe killed enough, you didn't want the ice age to end. Yet, if you prayed at all, an end to the ice age was what you always asked for first.

Mayfield was looking at the sky. "That storm's getting' closer, Billy. We'd better get a move-on." And it was true, But, mostly, Mayfield wanted to get away from the Brady compound. Relatives or not, he was uncomfortable here.

Jerry Brady and two other men escorted them back out onto the trail leaving Hank behind.

When they reached a point where they were going to split up, Billy Raymond said to Jerry Brady, "I don't want to have to depend on Hank relaying the message. So you tell the old lady we'll meet some of you boys up at the beaver pond at eight o'clock sharp, tomorrow morning..." and he looked at the sky..."unless the weather's really bad. And, if it is, we gotta get out there and find this guy after the storm moves on. Send us something on channel thirteen. We'll monitor it. Just be careful with what you say. No details...

"And see if you can leave Hank here."

"That ain't gonna happen'" Brady said. "She's gonna make sure he comes along. He's the only one she really trusts to carry out her orders.

"You gonna be comin?"

"Yeah. I gotta get away for a few days." He spit in the snow, again. "It's a damned zoo down here," he said shaking his head.

He looked up at the storm moving in and wanted to tell Raymond about them taking the six young girls out to the barn the night before, and shooting them, but he thought better of it. Besides, he shot one of them, himself. He'd liked to have fucked her, first. But you did as you were ordered at the Brady ranch.

Chapter 12
August 29

By morning, a huge storm front was running ashore from San Francisco to Juneau, Alaska.

At the LaCroix compound, Louis LaCroix had contacted Jerry Brady via the CB radio and put off their meeting at the beaver pond. His message was brief, but easy to understand: "Wait 'til after the storm. I'll contact you then." LaCroix's only consolation was that whoever it was they were going to go after was having the same problems with the weather. At least he hoped so.

When Billy Raymond came into the old den in the main house that now served as LaCroix's headquarters, LaCroix was standing at a window watching the falling snow in the newborn dawn.

Raymond stood in the doorway and knocked on the doorjamb to let LaCroix know he was there.

Without turning, LaCroix asked, "Did you hear the radio reports this morning?"

"I don't listen to them anymore," Raymond replied. "I've been busy all morning, anyway."

"This morning," LaCroix said without emotion, "California, Texas, Louisiana, and Florida all announced they've seceded from the Union."

"What?" Raymond's surprise was genuine.

"I think other states—at least the ones that aren't getting buried in snow yet—are going to follow suit," LaCroix added. "Apparently, they don't want to share whatever resources they have with anyone up north."

"Can they do that? Just up and get out?"

"I'm not sure there's enough Federal Government left in Washington, D.C., to stop them from doing *whatever* they want," LaCroix replied.

He glanced back at Raymond. "The governors are telling any military units within their borders to report to state offices and they'll be welcomed."

"Do you think they'll do it?"

"Who knows? It's a dog-eat-dog world out there, now. Some may. But I wouldn't be surprised if some of the Army and Marine commanders stage coups of some kind. And why not? They've got the big guns. I imagine whoever the Marine commander is at Camp Pendleton, down there in southern California, is weighing his options," he chuckled sardonically. "He could crown himself king of Southern California."

"What about the other states?" Raymond asked.

"Most of them here up north don't really exist, anymore. They're just names on the map, now. The Dakotas? The rest of the Midwest? All of the northeast including New England? The Rocky Mountain states? If they're not gone yet, they'll be gone soon. There are still people left in them, but by and large, there are no state governments in them anymore. And if the people still in those states don't get the fuck out, they'll disappear, too."

"I heard the governor of Montana was calling for law and order..."

"Who is he?" LaCroix asked. "He's not someone who was elected. The real governor resigned and went to Arizona after the riots in Helena and Boise. How would you like to have been on the Titanic and, as the bow was going under, have had the captain pass you his hat and say, 'You're in charge, now.'" He laughed again. "Governor of Montana," he said derisively. "He's some wannabe living out a fantasy. He'd better get the fuck out of there before he becomes a Popsicle."

"Are we gonna get frozen out?" Raymond asked pensively.

"Here in Oregon, on the coast? Maybe not."

"Why not?"

"Thank the ocean and the wind."

When Raymond didn't say anything, LaCroix looked back at him. Raymond had a quizzical look on his face.

"Climatologists call that ocean out there a heat sink," LaCroix said. "There's more heat locked up in the water out there than there is in a million atom bombs. That and the prevailing winds that blow over it and come ashore here are the reasons we never used to be too hot in the summer or too cold in the winter. A lot of people used to complain about the summer weather here. They said it was never warm enough because of the ocean. Now that water is all that might save our asses from freezing.

"I read a book in which some geologist said that back in the last ice age, the glaciers didn't pile up here because of that ocean out there. It got colder and things like the redwoods and the sequoias grew further south because the weather better suited them there. But the glaciers never made it all the way to the coast.

"Of course, they may be wrong this time, and we might get pushed right into the Pacific."

Raymond stood respectfully silent and, after a awhile, LaCroix actually had to turn again to make sure he was still there.

"Did you hear," LaCroix asked, as he turned and watched the snow again, "the Mexicans have closed their border? They're not letting Americans come into the country." He chuckled. "Did you ever think you'd live to see that — them sealing it off so *we* can't go down there?"

"I heard De Angelis say something about it," Raymond replied.

"Ironic," LaCroix said. "They've been crossing our border for years, and we never knew what to do about it. Now, they're saying that crossing *their* border is a capital offense. They're shooting people on sight. They're not even letting Mexicans, who came up here illegally, go back to their own country. Now, that's what I call immigration control." He laughed. "They're smarter about it than we were."

"Why'd the states all announce they're pulling out on the same day?" Raymond asked.

To LaCroix, the answer was a no-brainer and he was going to say something insulting to Raymond. But, when he looked back again, he could see Raymond really wanted to know. "You must realize that they didn't decide to secede just this morning. They must have been in touch with each other for quite some time. They just picked this as the time to announce it. I'll lay odds they won't be the only ones. 'The South shall rise again,'" he added with a mock southern accent and chuckled.

"Face it: neither Washington nor the northern states, even Oregon, want the warm states to get out. But the writing's on the wall and, unless they get out, they're going to be drained of their resources until they're as bad off as the Dakotas. Pulling out all at once, they're presenting a united front so if Washington or the rest of the states decide to make threats..."

"What about us? What about Oregon?" Raymond interrupted.

"Nothing, yet. There isn't much of a government left in Salem. The legislature only convened for a week this year. And I don't think the governor's even in the state anymore. According to rumors on the radio, he's somewhere down south."

There was another long silence, and LaCroix changed the subject. "If we can't go after that bastard, today," Raymond knew exactly who LaCroix meant, "at least we can have some proper funerals. Right?"

Raymond didn't have to say anything.

LaCroix continued, "I feel as though this guy's a local; someone we've just overlooked."

"The book cover we found..."

"I keep looking at it," LaCroix said. He picked the two halves of the book cover up off his desk and waved them at Raymond before he dropped them back onto the desk. "It's one more piece to the puzzle of who he might be. I had Goodman get me all the phone books he could find on the compound and I've been looking for the name Amaral so we might be able to narrow our search. I've found three with addresses. They're places to start looking."

There was a staticky voice on the radio.

"What was that?" Raymond asked.

LaCroix listened to the radio intently. "Arizona announced secession about fifteen minutes ago," he said.

The voice suddenly came in clearer. "...unanimous vote of the legislature, joining California, Texas, Louisiana, and Florida in a bid to leave the Union. As of nine o'clock Eastern Time, there still has been no response from Washington. As with the earlier announcements of secession, the governor of Arizona has invited Federal troops within the state..." And the transmission broke up, again.

"Do you really think the military is going to join the states?"

"We'll wait and see. But what other choices do they have? I imagine Washington is all but dead. Not only that, but Florida and California announced they've called their Guard units back in saying they're removing them from Federal control. And they've had the state police in both states close off their borders – their northern borders, of course."

"Like Mexico has," Raymond said.

"Yeah. Everyone's gonna hunker down and take care of their own..." LaCroix said.

"Just like we are," Raymond said.

"Just like us," LaCroix averred. "But I don't think the California border up here is going to be closed. They'll cut it off further south. The I-15 from Vegas was closed a week ago and US 50, between Tahoe and Sacramento, was closed, too. There was a shootout at a place called Pollock Pines, somewhere on the 50, where it leads out to Lake Tahoe. The CHP intercepted a big convoy coming from Nevada. A lot of people are dead. The guys coming in were well-armed and they broke through. I don't know how far they're going to make it. If they penetrate far enough into the state, they'll never find 'em."

"Jesus," Raymond exclaimed.

"My guess is," LaCroix continued, "they're going to close the 101 out there, soon, but probably at the Golden Gate Bridge. They'll close the I-5 at the Vietnam Veterans Memorial Bridge just north of Sacramento. And any other roads coming from the north will be closed. But, wherever possible, bridges will be the key. They'll be the easiest places for the authorities to defend and keep people out. They may even drop some of the bridges."

"Then we're on our own, now." Raymond said.

"We've been on our own for three years. We just never realized or admitted it until now."

"Then there's no law and order either," Raymond said.

LaCroix looked back at him again. "Yeah, there's still law and order. *I'm* the 'law and order' here…well, me and you boys."

Raymond nodded.

There was more staticky talk on the radio.

"What was that?" Raymond asked.

LaCroix shook his head. "I missed it, too.

"I'm going to ask you to do me a favor," LaCroix continued. "I want you to make sure the graves are clear of snow—inside and all around them. I know it's still coming down, but get them as clear as you can. No one's going to want to see caskets lowered into the ground when they're filling up with snow. Make 'em neat and make 'em pretty."

"Sure," Raymond said and turned to leave.

"One other thing."

Raymond hesitated.

"Don't say anything about the states seceding. Let me announce it at the meeting, after the funerals."

Raymond nodded.

But the word was already spreading around the compound. The United States was ceasing to exist.

Louis LaCroix wasn't the only one with a radio.

Chapter 13
August 29

Danielle woke to a cloud-laden sky and snow was beginning to fall. The man was not in the burrow with her.

Neither was Whoops.

She sprung out of the burrow and screamed, "Whoops! Oh, my God, *nooo!* Whoops!"

Just what she'd feared: He'd taken her sister; he'd taken her baby. She fell on her knees in the snow. "I'm going to kill him," she whispered. "I'll kill that motherfucker," and began lowing like a cow, again. She rose to her feet frantically trying to see which ski tracks left their camp. By now, he'd be so far away…but she'd find him…she'd follow him…

"What's wrong?"

She jumped.

On his skis, about fifteen feet from her, was the man in white; the baby cradled in one arm.

"Where did you take Whoops?"

"Who?"

She ran to him and grabbed her sister out of his hands.

"What are you doing with her?" she screamed.

"You needed sleep."

"Fuck you," she yelled then lunged and with her right hand she clawed his face.

He slid back as best he could, but cross-country skis don't like to slide backwards and as she stepped up to him she tripped on his skis and fell into the snow on her sister which both scared her and made her madder.

"Don't take her again, ever," she screamed. "You keep your filthy hands off her. I...will...kill...you...if...you...ever touch her again! *DO YOU HEAR ME?*"

He turned and skied away from her rubbing his face, amazed to see blood.

"She ate," he said without looking at her. "And there's meat on the spit if you're hungry."

She didn't care. She turned and sat down near the fire and hugged Whoops in her arms and cried and shook so violently she was shaking Whoops, who looked at her sister in quiet amazement. "I'm sorry. I'm sorry," she repeated over and over again.

The baby was okay, but she couldn't believe *he just took her.* She hated him, now.

He began to break their camp.

"If you're not going to eat," he said, "I'm packing up the rest of the meat." He spoke in a softer voice, now. The anger he had manifested the day before seemed almost gone. But she didn't care. She rocked Whoops.

When she looked up again, he had finished breaking camp and was standing on the other side of the spit looking at her.

"I'll eat," she whispered. "Just don't you *ever* touch her ever again."

She reached out and took a branch the meat was skewered on. She didn't know how he managed to keep finding animals to kill when she hadn't seen even one.

"What is this I'm about to eat?" she asked indignantly.

He didn't answer.

She looked around for the dog.

"He's running around in the trees," the man said, as if reading her mind.

"Where do you keep finding these things?" she asked.

He didn't answer that, either.

She started to calm down.

She began to eat. It was different. A little greasy, but good. She remembered something she'd once read in a book. It was supposed to be an old French proverb: "The best sauce is a good appetite." She now knew exactly what it meant.

She tore off the tiniest piece and brushed it along Whoops's lips. The baby liked it. She put it in her mouth and the baby swallowed it.

She ate more of it herself before offering another tiny piece to her sister.

This time the baby didn't want it. *So, he had fed her.*

She looked at him. He was sitting on a log staring off into the trees. He was the reason they were still alive.

"I'm sorry," she said softly.

She was sure he'd heard her, but he didn't respond.

She added, "Whoops is all I've got."

"Is that her name?"

She nodded.

He looked at her blankly. "Then count yourself lucky." He looked away.

"What?" she asked.

"I said count yourself lucky you have her."

"What do you mean?"

He didn't answer.

The dog came back out of the trees and approached her. He sat down in front of her and intently watched her eat.

"What's his name?"

Again, he didn't answer.

"*Hello!* What's your dog's name?"

The man looked at her.

"His name?" she asked and pointed to the dog.

"I told you before, it's not mine. I don't know what its name is."

"What do you call him?" she finally asked.

"Stupid."

She shook her head in disgust and went back to eating.

When she looked at the dog again, he was still watching her eat.

She stopped eating.

"Stupid," she said.

She did a double take when his ears went up.

"Stupid," she repeated, and he got off his haunches and started walking toward her.

"That's a horrible name," she whispered to her sister.

The dog stopped just inches from her, sat, and again watched her eat the meat. She tore a piece off and held it out to him.

"Don't feed it," the man said firmly.

She stopped for a second, then gave the meat to the dog anyway.

The man skied over and reached for the meat.

She held it away. "I'm not done eating," she said.

"Give no more to the dog," he commanded.

"Yeah, yeah, yeah," she said and went back to eating.

He skied away.

The dog stayed with her and watched her.

"Come 'ere, Stupid," the man suddenly commanded and the dog reluctantly got up and went to him.

When she finished eating he said, "Let's go."

But she stayed on the log.

"Let's go," he repeated.

"Where are we going today?"

"I'm taking you back to the road. You'll get a ride, today."

She took a deep breath and got up.

§   §   §

He skied ahead as the snowfall picked up. She trudged through the snow behind him.

Soon, the four of them, Danielle, Zach, Whoops, and the dog were on a rise overlooking 101. They stood there a long time while Zach thought.

She didn't say anything, she watched him. It was clear there had been no recent traffic, and there may well not be any more if the snow was too deep, further north.

"How are your feet?" he suddenly asked.

"They're a little numb," she said and, just as soon as she said it, she wished she hadn't told him. "They're fine," she added.

The snowfall was getting heavier and that seemed to concern him.

"Come on," he said, and turned away from the road. He started skiing back into the trees.

It took her several moments to realize they weren't going down to the road.

"Where are you taking us?"

He kept moving and was about to disappear into the trees. If she didn't catch up, he'd be gone. Not knowing what else to do, she followed.

They trekked through the woods most of the day. At their first stop he let Danielle rest and take care of Whoops while he skied off into the trees with the dog.

He left a canteen. The water was warm, so she figured he must have kept it close to his body. She drank some because she was dehydrated, but she saved some and gave it to Whoops. Then she changed her diaper.

Once she finished that, she looked around. They were still alone. She didn't want to see him again. But, if he didn't come back, she wasn't lost. She could follow their tracks back to the road, but where would that lead her?

"Do you want Sissy to sing you a song?" she asked, and when Whoops smiled she sang her a song. Then she did the pattycake song.

Whoops was quiet and smiling and watched her big sister intently. Danielle thought she wouldn't be so happy if she understood their predicament. Her face was pink from the cold, but she liked being carried and liked watching her older sister and hearing her voice. Danielle laid her on her lap and they stared at each other while she sang.

She wondered about her family, if she'd ever see them again. And, if not, how long would it be before Whoops forgot who they were?

Finally she said, "He's a mean man, Whoopsie. He's another nutcase, just like Hank and Barry. He's another fucking asshole. I'm glad Barry's dead. And I promise you, I'll never let this nut hold you again, ever. That's my promise. And the first chance I get I'm going to kill him. Then it'll be just you and me and we can go to southern California."

"Here," he said from behind her and she jumped.

She turned and looked up in surprise. He was holding out some granola bars. Reaching gingerly she took them. After a few seconds of thought she started to break the granola bar up into small pieces into the cup that came with the canteen. Then she poured in some water and placed the cup near the fire.

She wondered how much he'd heard. She hoped not much. Both of their lives depended on being with him for a while.

"I'm sorry. I didn't mean what I said," she finally said.

He didn't say anything.

"I'm sorry," she repeated, in case he'd missed it.

He still didn't respond.

"Okay, I'm not sorry."

He still said nothing.

"Which one do you want?" she asked. "I'm sorry, or I'm *not* sorry?"

"I don't want *anything* from you." He didn't say anything else.

§   §   §

After she fed Whoops, they were on the move, again. This time he made frequent stops so Danielle could rest and take care of the baby's needs. Each time they stopped he made a small fire, melted snow for drinking water, then disappeared into the trees. Almost every time he returned, he had something to eat.

"Where are you taking us?" she finally asked at one stop.

"A place you can rest until the snow stops and there's traffic on the road, again."

So, he was still going to take her back to the road. That was good. But she still didn't like being alone with him. She recalled how Barry was just going to let Whoops die in the snow. Maybe this man would do the same.

"Do you think someone's going to pick me up?" she asked.

"I hope so," he said. Contempt had returned to his voice.

"So, where exactly are you taking us?"

Silence.

He was creeping her out. "*Where are you taking us?*" she screamed.

He stared at her a long time. Finally, he got up. "Let's go," he said and skied away.

Chapter 14
August 29

On the Brady ranch, news of the secessions was greeted with subdued jubilation. The fact that both the Federal and state governments were crumbling was better than a pardon. Not only would past sins not matter, they now had a license to commit whatever mayhem they chose on the 101.

Hank called a meeting in the kitchen of the Brady ranch house to discuss the changes. The room was filled to overflow with the denizens of the compound and he announced the Federal government was no more. To him, that meant the Army didn't exist, either.

Abby sat uncomfortably in her stuffed chair staring at her grandson in the casket before her. His body was pale, almost blue. Though she seemed oblivious to the discussion going on around her, she listened to every word.

"We're on our own, now," Hank said. "We're gonna have to step it up. We gotta get more stuff off the road out there. It's no holds barred anymore. We can do anything we want. We can even take the bridges out so people can't get any further."

Several voices chimed in. It was all good news. It changed the collective mood even though the burials were about to begin.

"No," Abby suddenly said above the din and, when she spoke, the voices died down and all eyes turned to her.

Without looking up she said, "The bridge stays. Folks will just try the inland routes, or they'll come down in bigger convoys than we can handle. We don't have enough people for that. Wait for the stragglers and the small convoys who try to make it. There'll still be plenty of them. They's our bread an' butter. If they thin out, *then* we'll get rid of the bridges.

"Plus," she added ominously, "we don't wanna do nothin' with the bridges 'til we know for sure if the Army's really gone."

The men in the kitchen nodded.

"And no more girls," she said sharply.

Hank looked at Jerry Brady and winked.

Hank was already working out something for that, though Abby didn't know. There was an old shed about a mile and a half from the house where they could take them from now on. They called it "the clubhouse" now.

"But, first things first:" she said, "We're gonna lay our loved ones to rest. They deserve it. Then we're gonna get whoever done this to Joel and the others. Jerry says Louis LaCroix's gonna meet us with a contingent of their guys up at the old beaver pond, when the snow stops. Then we're goin' after 'em."

More heads nodded. A few even clapped. Those who didn't nod acceded by virtue of their silence.

"Now, let's give my Sweetie a proper rest," she said wearily. "I've been up all night. I wanna get this over with.

"You do what yer supposed to do," she ordered Jerry Brady.

And with that Brady stepped forward. In his left hand he held a Bible.

"You do a good reading, now," she warned.

He looked around until the room fell silent.

As Abby had instructed him, he began reading from Ecclesiastes:

> *To every thing there is a season, and a time to every purpose*
> *under the heaven:*
> *a time to be born, and a time to die; a time to plant, and a time to*
> *pluck up that which is planted;*
> *a time to kill, and a time to heal; a time to break down, and a*
> *time to build up;*
> *a time to weep, and a time to laugh; a time to mourn, and a time*
> *to dance;*
> *a time to cast away stones, and a time to gather stones together;*
> *a time to embrace, and a time to refrain from embracing;*
> *a time to get, and a time to lose; a time to keep, and a time to cast*
> *away;*
> *a time to rend, and a time to sew; a time to keep silence, and a*
> *time to speak;*
> *a time to love, and a time to hate; a time of war, and a time of*
> *peace.*
> *What profit hath he that worketh in that wherein he laboreth?*

I have seen the travail, which God hath given to the sons of men
    to be exercised in it.
He hath made every thing beautiful in his time: also he hath set
    the world in their heart, so that no man can find out the
    work that God maketh from the beginning to the end.
I know that there is no good in them, but for a man to rejoice,
    and to do good in his life.
And also that every man should eat and drink, and enjoy the
    good of all his labor, it is the gift of God.
I know that, whatsoever God doeth, it shall be for ever: nothing
    can be put to it, nor any thing taken from it: and God doeth
    it, that men should fear before him.
That which hath been is now; and that which is to be hath
    already been; and God requireth that which is past.

When he finished, Abby said, "Now you find that Twenty-third Psalm and say that, too."

Jerry turned to a marker he'd placed in the Bible.

The Lord is my Shepherd; I shall not want.
He maketh me to lie down in green pastures:
He leadeth me beside the still waters.
He restoreth my soul:
He leadeth me in the paths of righteousness for His name's sake.
Yea, though I walk through the valley of the shadow of death,
I will fear no evil: For thou art with me;
Thy rod and thy staff, they comfort me.
Thou preparest a table before me in the presence of mine enemies;
Thou anointest my head with oil; My cup runneth over.
Surely goodness and mercy shall follow me all the days of my
    life, and I will dwell in the House of the Lord forever.

When he was finished with that, he began reciting the Lord's Prayer.

When Abby joined in, so did others, until the whole room had joined in prayer.

Abby cried throughout.

When they finished, she kissed Joel on the lips. "Granny-great will see you in Paradise, Sweetie."

With that, she stepped back and Jerry closed the casket.

Six men stepped forward and lifted it. They carried it out the door with Jerry leading, Abby in tow, and Hank at her side. The others formed a train behind her. She wailed as she followed it. Like mass hysteria, almost all the women and half the men joined in the wailing.

They trudged through the snow. But when they got to the cemetery, she was startled to see no one had cleared the burial site and the graves were already filling with snow. She started screaming at the men as if they had personally had a hand in the weather.

All the wailing stopped and, as she screamed, men ran and got shovels. They started clearing the snow away.

While she waited, Abby turned and singled Clara from the crowd of mourners. "*You!* You go start me some tea. I'm gonna need something warm when I'm done here."

Clara hesitated. She thought she was supposed to be at the funeral.

"Get movin', girl!" Abby yelled.

With that, Clara returned to the house.

The men holding the casket were unsure of what to do. Its weight was becoming uncomfortable and they started shifting their hands to get better grips.

Meanwhile, the snow removal went on while, all around them, more of it fell, mindless of Abby's wishes.

There were three more funerals after this including Abby's other grandson, Barry, and kin of the deceased were eager to send their own to their final rewards before the accumulating snow made it impossible. But, as per Abby's orders, Joel had to go in the ground first.

Chapter 15
August 29

With a vague uneasiness, Danielle followed the man through the forest. Sometimes, she talked to Whoopsie, other times she sang her songs. But what she was really doing was trying to distract herself from darker thoughts of what might lie ahead. More than once she considered turning around and finding her way back to the road. At times the man was sullen and scary while at other times he was solicitous or he'd become too quiet. But she came to realize that at all times he showed an interest in Whoops and that made her uncomfortable.

Nonetheless, she hugged her sister and trudged on behind him, getting ever further from the road, and taking Whoops deeper into uncertainty and possible danger.

She could barely feel her feet anymore and, as they became number and number, she found herself stumbling as she walked. To keep her balance, she kept her head down, watching where her feet fell every step of the way. She used his ski tracks as her guide. It seemed as if she walked this way for miles until, suddenly, she saw skis and she abruptly stopped. He was standing right in front of her, watching her. She'd almost walked into him.

Behind him was a cabin—an A-frame. About thirty feet from the cabin was a shed. Coming off the side of the cabin, on the same side as the shed, was some framing with nothing attached to it. At the bottom of the framing were logs that seemed to mark the bottom of some kind of structure they and the framing had once supported. On the other side, and apparently running behind the house, was an add-on with a roof canted to shed snow. She turned to look back and saw where their tracks had left the trees and crossed a snow-covered field that lay in front of the cabin.

Without a word, he removed his skis and opened the cabin's door. He stepped aside to let her in, first. She hesitated.

He waited for her to cross the threshold.

A sickness filled the pit of her stomach. She and her sister were at his mercy, now. He could do anything he wanted to them, now. But she walked in.

He looked back at the dog and said, "Stay."

The dog obediently sat in the snow.

To Danielle, the man seemed surprised when the dog obeyed him.

"Take your boots off," he said to her as he crossed the room. They were his only words since leaving the road.

She watched as he unslung his rifle and stood it against the wall. Then he took a handgun from his pocket and laid it on a table near the wall. Finally, he removed his jacket and his boots.

The room was cold. She left her own coat on and settled into a stuffed chair in the middle of the room. She held Whoops in her arms.

Zach kneeled in front of the fireplace insert and opened its door. He made a small mound of tinder inside. Around and on top of the tinder he built a pyramid of kindling. Around that he placed some larger pieces of wood. It would be several minutes before the cabin would begin to get warm.

The ratcheting sound of the revolver's rotating cylinder was unmistakable and, in the same instant, he felt the barrel of the gun pressed against the back of his head.

"Don't move," Danielle said with a trembling voice.

"What are you doing?" he whispered.

She didn't answer.

He didn't move.

She didn't move, either. "You will not touch me," she finally said in a strained voice.

"I won't...I'm gay."

That was a surprise.

"You're not going to hurt Whoops, either."

He shook his head ever so subtly. "I wouldn't...*ever*."

He waited, but she didn't say anything else. But she didn't take the gun away from his head.

Very slowly he turned his head toward her until he was looking into the barrel. The gun was cocked. Her finger rested on the trigger. Whoops was on the stuffed chair in the middle of the room.

He raised his eyes and whispered, "Why don't you put that away before one of us gets killed."

She didn't move.

They stared at each other for several seconds.

Slowly and carefully he reached with his left hand until his left pinky finger touched the barrel and he gently pushed it to his left a few inches while he gradually leaned to his right.

She took another half-step back so his finger wasn't on the barrel anymore, but it was pointed at him, again.

"Uncock the gun," he whispered.

She hesitated. "I don't know what that means," she whispered back.

"Take your finger...*away* from the trigger. It's a hair-trigger."

She didn't move for a second, but gradually she pushed her finger forward and took it out of the trigger guard.

"Thank you," he whispered and let out a deep sigh of relief, but he kept watching her.

He turned his left hand palm up and softly said, "Put it in my hand."

She paused. She didn't want the gun, but she didn't want him to have it, either. She looked into his eyes and he nodded.

She subtly shook her head no.

She'd already crossed her own Rubicon when she put the gun to his head. She had intended to kill him. But she had no plan beyond that. Now, it was kill him or give the gun up and accept the consequences. The consequences could be dire. Whoops began to cry. She stood there longer. The baby's crying became more insistent and intense. They continued to stare at each other, she kept the gun pointed at him. Whoops's cries got louder and started to come in uncontrolled, desperate spasms.

Her resolution began to fade and her sister's bawling became more disconcerting. Whoops needed her. Her hand began to shake. The crying was relentless. Reluctantly and carefully she laid the cocked gun on his palm. Then she watched as he brought his right hand up and, pointing the gun away, he carefully uncocked it.

They stared at each other, again. With the gun now lying in his open right palm, he slowly offered it back to her. "Put this back on the table where you found it," he whispered.

She couldn't believe he was handing it back to her.

"Please," he added.

She took it, turned, and slowly walked to the table where she set it back down. Then she went to Whoops and picked her up.

Once in Danielle's arms, Whoops's crying was reduced to intermittent sobs. Soon, it stopped altogether.

Zach turned his back to her, again, and took a butane lighter from his pocket. His hand was shaking violently. But each fire had to be lit with one flick. As each lighter was emptied, it became a relic. No one was making them anymore. There could be no waste. He'd wait until he stopped shaking.

"Don't ever do that again," he said softly, without looking at her. There was no emotion in his voice.

"Don't ever touch me again," she said softly.

"I haven't, and I won't."

His back was still turned to her.

"Yes you did," she said softly.

"No I *didn't*," he said in a low voice, but with emphasis.

"You're a liar. You felt me up in the burrow out in the woods."

He thought a few seconds and remembered waking up in the burrow to her screams. His hand finally stopped shaking and he lit the fire. With his back still to her he asked, "Is that why you yelled at me then?"

"Of course it was. You woke me up."

"I don't remember doing it."

She didn't know whether to believe him or not.

He hovered over the burgeoning flame and watched it spread from the tinder to kindling. Gradually, the larger pieces began to catch. He closed the insert's door and made sure the vents and the flue were wide open.

"It'll warm up in here pretty quick," he said. He didn't expect a response from her.

She watched him. She didn't think about the gun anymore.

After several minutes she asked, "Who's the woman and the two kids in the picture?" He looked first at her, then to where she was looking. She was staring at a framed photo on the mantel above his head. He stood up, took the picture in his hand, and carried it to a desk in the corner of the room where he put it in the top drawer. Then he went back to his fire.

That's his answer, she figured.

Still not looking at her he said, "When the snow lets up, you're going back to the road."

"Good," she said.

There was another long silence, until he asked, "What was going on back there?"

She didn't know what he talking about, so she didn't respond.

He realized he had to be more specific. "Back there in that field, with those men and the girl?" he added.

"I don't want to talk about it," she replied.

"Okay."

He watched the fire grow.

After another several minutes she asked, "Why'd you let them shoot Anne?"

"Was that the other girl?"

He knew it was when she didn't answer.

"I didn't know they were going to do that to her," he said.

"Why'd you save me?"

"I didn't save you." After a long pause he said, "I saved your baby."

"You'd have let them shoot me if I didn't have Whoops?"

"Yes," he said without looking at her.

"Faggot," she said.

He ignored her.

With the fire now going, he grabbed his sleeping bag and unrolled it on the floor.

Four little holes irregularly strung out in a line the length of the bag, recorded where the bullet had gone through, and there'd be four more on the other side. He started mending them and stuffing back the little bits of down that were leaking out.

For several minutes she watched him close the holes with thick black thread. "How'd you get the holes in that thing?" she finally asked.

He froze for a second, then went back to his task.

He wasn't going to answer her.

She observed how deftly he wielded the needle.

As he finished mending the fourth one, she broke her promise never to cry again.

He glanced at her. She was hugging the baby. She sobbed, but she was trying to keep it quiet.

He turned the bag over.

She was still crying.

"What's wrong?" he asked without looking in her direction.

She didn't answer.

He began mending the holes on the other side.

Finally, between sobs, she said, "I asked him to kill Whoops."

He drove the needle into his finger and it started to bleed, but he still didn't look at her.

She was lowing like a cow, again. "I begged him. I wanted him to…because they were going to leave her in the snow after they shot me and I didn't want her to suffer. I love her, but I held her up…I begged him to shoo…shoo…to shoo…" She was crying uncontrollably, now, and couldn't finish her sentence. "I love her so much. She's all I…" She didn't say anymore.

He finally looked at her. Tears were running down her cheeks in rivulets, her nose was beginning to run, and she was drooling. She clutched the baby to her as if she'd never let her go. The baby was just happy to be held.

He went back to his mending.

Eventually, she stopped.

A few minutes later he was finished with the sleeping bag. When he looked at her again, she was sleeping. It wasn't a restful sleep. Her eyes moved frantically under her eyelids. She was dreaming. Her body twitched even though she was still holding the baby, now sleeping, in her arms.

He was about to roll the bag up. Instead, he took it and draped it over her and the baby.

She woke up abruptly. "Keep your fuckin' hands off of me!" she screamed. Terror was written on her face.

He stopped, then finished laying the bag over them.

"It's okay," he said.

Her shout had woken Whoops who stared up at Zach. For just a second, she smiled.

"I'll take you back to the road tomorrow," he said. Then he crossed the room and put his boots and his jacket back on. He stuffed the Model 60 in his pocket and he went to a closet and grabbed a scoped Winchester Model 70, then went out the door. He didn't look back. He slammed it behind him.

Danielle held Whoops tighter.

"Good," she whispered to the baby. "He's crazy."

Whoops stared at her.

"I hate him," she confided. "I hope he dies out there. I hope every fucking man on this planet dies. They do mean things to girls."

But it was nice having the sleeping bag over her, and the fire was making the room warmer, too. Her feet started to regain their feeling. In place of the numbness, they began to tingle uncomfortably. She held Whoops and tried to put the tingling out of her mind as she closed her eyes, again. Just a little nap, she told herself.

The terrible dreams came back, but she slept through them.

§ § §

The next time she woke, the room was cold. She looked at the fireplace insert. The fire was out. She didn't know how long he'd been gone.

She slid out from under the sleeping bag letting her still-sleeping sister lie on the chair.

She checked the fire though the window on the insert's door. There were still hot embers. She tried to open the door. It wouldn't give at first. Then she saw how the latch worked and, with a little bit of monkeying, she opened it.

There was tinder and kindling on the floor beside the fireplace. She put the tinder in first, then kindling on top of it. Nothing seemed to happen. There were no matches or lighters in sight. She blew on the embers a little and they glowed redder. She blew for almost a minute, but all the tinder did was smolder. She wasn't sure what to do.

Suddenly, the tinder erupted into silent flames that danced off the wood like tiny fairies, and she was relieved. She gently nudged the kindling around with a stick to ensure the flames were in contact with it and it all started to catch. She watched the fire get bigger. After several minutes, she put two larger pieces of wood in and closed the door.

She didn't touch the vents or the flue. She didn't know how they worked. But she squatted in front of the insert and watched. Soon, it was going fine and she put in two larger logs.

She stood up and looked around the room. She walked to the front door and opened it to look out. It was snowing hard and he wasn't in sight. The dog was gone, too. Their tracks had completely disappeared under the weather.

She closed the door and went back to the drawer where he'd placed the photo from the mantel. She took it out. It was a woman and two very young children. The woman was in her twenties. She was pretty. The boy looked a lot like the woman, with the same dark hair.

Danielle looked closer. The little girl was blonde. She had eyes like the man. She wondered what the relationship was since the man was gay. She stared at it for a minute, turning it over in her hands, again and again, to see if there'd be some clue as to who they were. Finally, she put the photo back and looked at the other things in the drawer. There was a large hunting knife. She took it out and examined it. It looked deadly and sharper than hell. She held it in her hand as she continued going through the drawer. There was nothing else there of interest. She closed the drawer, but she took the knife to the chair and stuffed it down between the cushion and the armrest.

Then she went back to the fireplace and saw the fire was sustaining itself. A feeling of accomplishment swept over her. The room was still cold, but it would warm up soon.

There were other things in the room, such as candles that were covered with dust. That meant he hadn't lit them in a while — which made sense since they were a valuable and a difficult-to-procure commodity, now. There were books; so he read. There were tools, ropes, a second woodstove he apparently cooked on, magazines from before the ice age, and doors...

Now, her curiosity overcame her.

One by one she opened the doors. There were two bedrooms. They were cold. It was obvious he lived in this one living room/kitchen area and had sealed the rest of the house off. That made sense, too. One room was easier to heat.

In one of the bedrooms there were boxes of foodstuffs, stacks of clothes, ammo cans, several sets of skis, and some tools. There was also a bathroom, but it looked like the toilet didn't work.

She went back to the chair when she heard Whoops stirring, picked her up, and sat down with her again. That seemed to be enough to make the baby go back to sleep.

Next thing she knew, she began cramping. It had been about a month since she last felt the discomfort of her period. This time she welcomed the pain as it meant she wasn't pregnant. However, she didn't have anything for it. Careful, so as not to wake Whoops, she put her down, again, and went back to the bathroom and looked under the sink. She was relieved to see boxes of tampons; lots of them. That was good because it wasn't likely anyone was making those anymore, either.

She wondered if they belonged to the woman in the photo and if she'd be back. It was clear to her that a woman lived here. Maybe that's where the man went: to get her.

She looked in the medicine chest. There was makeup and there were lotions — not the type a man would use. There was hair spray. She took one of the tampons. Then she took more for the road. She'd need them.

When she returned to the living room Whoops was beginning to fuss. Danielle was sure she was hungry.

She went to the cupboards and found dry milk, cans of flour, peanut butter, and pasta: staple foods that, once they were gone… There were also boxes of cereal, cans of tomato sauce, and a few soups. Maybe the man would let her take some with her when she left.

On the counter near the sink were several one-gallon glass jugs filled with water. She removed the cover from one and smelled the contents to make sure. She put some in a saucepan, which she placed on top of the fireplace insert, covered it, and let it set there to get hot.

Next, she found two large pots in one of the bedrooms. She stared at them for several seconds before she grabbed them. She took them both to the front door and filled them with snow. Before going back into the house, she stared at a little shed not thirty feet away. She went to it and opened the door. One part of it was some kind of workshop with hooks on the rafters. In another part was an outhouse. Since the toilet in the cabin didn't appear to work, she was grateful to know where the outhouse was.

Returning to the house, she put each of the pots atop of the fireplace insert.

Finally, she started dinner for herself and her sister. But this time, Whoops was going to eat something warm. She mixed dry milk and water in a jar and started oatmeal — a lot of oatmeal, she was starving — in a saucepan atop the fireplace insert. When it was ready, they ate. After that, she cleaned the oatmeal pot and the utensils she used, in the snow outside.

Later, when she checked the pots on the insert, she discovered that a lot of snow makes very little water. She found another pot and used it to get more snow that she added to each of the pots on the insert. Feeling a sense of accomplishment, again, she went back and settled into the chair with her sister. She didn't need the sleeping bag over them, now. The room was warm, now.

There was nothing else to do to while away the time, so she talked and sang to Whoops. The baby loved being the center of attention.

Periodically, she fed more wood into the insert and, when she checked the pots, again, all the snow had melted and, though the water wasn't much more than lukewarm, that was enough for her purposes. Placing Whoops on the floor, so she wouldn't fall from the chair, she took the pots out the front door and placed them on the snow.

Now began her task. She washed the diapers she had in one of the pots. Content she had gotten them as clean as she could, she dumped the water from that pot onto the snow and poured the water from the other pot into it. She used that water to rinse the diapers.

She wrung each diaper out. Satisfied with herself, she dumped out the rest of the water and refilled the two pots with snow. She was about to carry them into the house when she screamed. There was the man in white not ten feet away from her watching her. The dog was sitting quietly beside him.

"How long have you been there?" she demanded.

He didn't say anything. He walked by her carrying his rifle and a bag, and he opened the door and stepped inside. But he hesitated and looked at the dog.

"Stay," he said, and the dog sat down.

She followed him in with one pot then returned for the other. She closed the door behind herself and draped the diapers over the backs of the chairs there so they'd dry. The security and peace she had felt when he left earlier now evaporated. Once again, she didn't feel safe. But, mostly, she didn't know if Whoops was safe.

She put the pots on the insert again then, leaving the baby on the floor, she sat in the stuffed chair, again.

In the meantime, he'd taken off his boots and his coat. This time, before he leaned the rifle against the wall, he unloaded it—and he didn't put his handgun on the table. He sat down on the couch but didn't say anything. The way he ignored her, she realized he was preoccupied with other thoughts. When she thought he was finally going to say something to her, she braced herself anticipating the worst.

But he said nothing to her. Instead, he got up and went to the door and opened it.

She could see, just beyond him, the dog was patiently still sitting in the snow. Its tail began to wag when it saw him.

He looked at it several seconds then shook his head. "Come on in," he said with resignation in his voice.

The dog got up and sauntered into the house and the man closed the door. But he watched the dog closely.

It went around the room examining everything with its nose.

It was drawn to the bag the man had carried in and started sniffing it.

"Get away from that," he snapped, and the dog backed away from it.

The man looked as if he were mildly amazed.

But, rather than leaving it there to tempt the dog, he took it to the front door, reached out under the eaves, and hung the bag from a hook there. Then he closed the door again.

She didn't know what was in the bag and didn't ask.

He went back to watching the dog.

"If you see it lift his leg or start to take a crap, yell at him," he said.

She realized he was talking to her.

"Isn't he housebroken?" she asked.

"I don't know."

Next, the dog approached Whoops and the man stiffened.

The dog's head bobbed around as he got closer, as if it were inspecting her not only with his eyes, but with his nose.

Danielle got nervous. "Is he going to be all right with her?" she asked.

"I don't know," Zach said and he started walking toward the dog.

"I'll kill him if he does anything to her," she said.

"We'll eat him if you do," he said simply.

The man said "him," she thought. It was the first time he'd referred to the dog as anything besides "it."

The baby reached out toward the dog, and it backed away. Then it lay down not two feet from her and started licking himself.

"I think it's plain he's been around kids before," she said.

He didn't comment.

"What's his real name?" she asked.

Zach shrugged. "I don't know. I told you it's not mine."

So, we're back to "it," she thought. "Then he's mine," she said and got up to pet him.

"Take it. How are you going to feed it on the road?"

"I don't know. I'll figure it out. And, if I get hungry, I'll eat him," she added, mocking him.

He gave her a disparaging look then walked toward the cupboards and the sink.

"Are you hungry?" he asked.

"We ate," she replied.

He looked at the cleaned pot and dishes on the counter, as if seeing them there for the first time. Then he started fixing a meal for himself.

"You and the baby sleep on the couch," he said. "I'll sleep on the floor."

"You sleep on the couch," she countered. "Whoops and I will sleep in the chair."

"Have it your way," he said.

She'd found an old *National Geographic* to read in the bedroom. She tried not to make it obvious she was watching him eat and, she quite frankly felt he was trying not to let her know that he was watching her out of the corner of his eye.

Whoops fussed from time to time. Otherwise, she was being good, as usual.

But, as the room got darker, it became more difficult for her to read.

When he finally decided to sleep, he brought a blanket to the couch and started to lay down. He removed his handgun from his pocket and suddenly looked at her. She was watching him with the gun.

He hesitated a few seconds. He put the gun under his pillow and rolled over to face away from her.

A while later, she realized he was asleep. It dawned on her she didn't even know his name, nor had he bothered to ask her hers.

But she herself had napped so much during the day, she couldn't sleep now and she sat in the chair holding her sister for hours, torturing herself with thoughts of how she was going to keep the two of them alive on the road. It was conceivable no one would stop to pick her up. And there was also the chance that people from the Brady ranch would find her out there and she was sure they'd blame her for what had happened in the field. She didn't expect to survive a second encounter with them.

Suddenly, the man said something she couldn't understand.

"What?" she asked reflexively.

He kept talking. But it was indistinct and the words were gibberish. He was talking in his sleep.

She listened a few minutes, unable to do more than catch a word here and another there, then he stopped. She could still hear him stirring. But he wasn't getting off the couch. He was thrashing in the dark.

She jumped when he yelled: "*Sandra, no!*"

Whoops stirred.

"*Why?*" he asked in a clear voice. Then his words were reduced once again to gibberish. Occasionally, he moaned.

She quietly got up and in dying light of the fireplace insert she found a candle and lighter. She lit the candle.

He was still talking.

She cautiously approached the couch with the candle in her right hand and Whoops cradled in her left. She leaned over to see his lips moving as he mumbled. Sweat on his face glistened in the candle's light.

He began screaming at this woman, Sandra, his voice alternately fulminating with anger, then sorrow, then fear. She looked at Whoops who watched the man with a look of amazement on her face.

"I hate you. *I hate you!*" he screamed, and Whoops flinched.

She was about to step back when, suddenly, his eyes opened and he lay motionless for half a second. With the speed of a springing snake, he rolled over, cocked the revolver, and pushed it into her face, all in one motion.

She froze. The gun was aimed squarely between her eyes. With her sister in one arm and the candle in the other hand, she was defenseless.

They stared at each other in the glow of the candle for several seconds.

"What do you want?" he whispered.

"You were talking in your sleep," she whispered back.

He pointed the gun away from her and uncocked it. "No, I wasn't."

"Yes, you were…"

"It was just the wind," he said as he stared. But, now, he was looking at Whoops. She felt creepy the way he stared at her sister.

She slowly nodded and said, "Okay," and backed up.

He watched her…he watched Whoops…as she retreated to the chair and fell back into it. She blew out the candle.

The room was quiet, now. The three of them coexisted in the dark. There were no sounds like the man was sleeping, and he wasn't talking. She knew he was lying there awake.

She reached down between the cushion and the arm of the chair and found the handle of the knife still waiting for her like a trusted friend. She'd be glad when she got back to the road.

Chapter 16
August 30

What would have been a late summer rain just three years earlier had come down as snow in the night.

From outside came scraping sounds that woke Danielle. She looked at the couch; the man was gone. She listened intently then rose from the chair, with her still-sleeping sister in her arms, and followed the sounds to the window.

He was up on the roof of the shed next to the cabin, pushing the night's accumulation off. The dog was nowhere to be seen, but his tracks had broken the smooth white carpet of new snow that extended from the window, across the field, and to the edge of the woods.

Whoops woke up in her arms and started to fuss and Danielle changed her diaper, then prepared breakfast for the two of them.

When he came in, the dog wasn't with him. Danielle had Whoops lying in her lap as she fed her. She watched him cross the room, sit on the couch, and stare at the wall. He didn't look at or say a word to her.

She fed her sister, furtively glancing in his direction every now and then, and wondered why he was so quiet.

Abruptly, he said, "It's time to go. You'll get a ride, today."

"Good," she said under her breath. Whoops was done eating, anyway. She put the spoon down and capped the jar.

Suddenly, she felt as though she was going to hyperventilate. She didn't want to ask, she didn't want to beg, she didn't want to hear conditions from him, but her sister's survival was at stake: "I know I'm asking a lot...and I can't carry that much...but can I take..."

"Take whatever you think you can carry for the baby…and yourself," he interrupted, anticipating her question. "There's a canvas sack there. Use it. It has handles."

For some reason he was angry and it made her want to get out of there more than ever.

"Thank you," she said without a trace of sincerity in her voice.

She wasn't sure she should ask the next question, but she had to know: "Who's Sandra?" she asked.

He turned to her and stared a long time. "What do you know about her? Why are you asking?"

"You yelled her name last night…in your sleep…more than once."

"What did I say?"

"Most of it was incomprehensible."

He turned away.

"I was just wondering who she is, that's all.

"What's your name?" she asked.

He didn't answer.

Of course he wouldn't answer. He had just killed three and possibly four men. The reasons why and the circumstances didn't matter. Yeah, he had saved her, but for all she knew, it could all be because he was the craziest man in these hills and crazier than any of the Bradys.

He looked in her direction, again, but he was looking at Whoops. His preoccupation with her sister was another reason to leave.

He got more agitated than ever when she got up, laid Whoops on the floor, and began to pack the bag. He seemed like he wanted to do something but had become aimless. He opened and closed his hands several times and took deep breaths. She began to think he might force her to stay. She tried to remain calm.

She put some of the makeshift diapers, some peanut butter, and a loaf of homemade bread in the sack. She was surprised at how little she was going to be able to carry. They'd have to get a ride the first day or die.

He took something out of his jacket pocket and threw it at her. She picked it up. It was a small plastic bag. Inside were a butane lighter and some heavy twine.

"The string was soaked in paraffin," he said. "It makes a good way to start a fire."

She nodded and put the bag into the sack.

He went to one of the other rooms and returned with a sling. As he came out he slammed the door behind him and shook the A-frame.

"You can carry your baby in this," he said.

She took it, put Whoops in it, and slung her up on her back.

"I'm ready," she said.

His agitation heightened. She just wanted to get out the door.

§   §   §

The dog was outside waiting as they went out and he began hopping around in the new snow cover the moment he saw them. The falling snow was light, but the flakes were big and drifted down like angels in parachutes.

Zach put his skis on and looked at her to see if she was ready. She nodded.

They trekked through the woods. She wondered why he took a new path each time he left or returned.

He skied ahead while she carried Whoops and the dog seemed to find many things to investigate in the forest.

Again, she was surprised when they reached the road. But she was disheartened to see it was covered with a blanket of unblemished snow. There had been no traffic since the day before.

Zach listened, but with the snow muffling all the sounds, you wouldn't have heard a tank until it rolled into sight.

Finally, he skied down onto the road and she followed.

"Okay," he said. "Wait here. You'll get a ride."

"I know," she said as she set the bag down in the snow.

"I want to thank you," she said and she felt unexpectedly scared to be being set on the road this time.

He looked at her, reached in a pocket, took out his ski mask, and put it on.

He turned and skied back across the road.

"Your dog," she yelled.

He stopped. The malamute stood in the road next to Danielle.

"What about your dog?" she asked.

"I told you, it's not mine." With that he disappeared into the woods.

The dog seemed uncertain. He paced back and forth for several seconds until he finally sat on his haunches, next to her, in the snow. He really was hers, now.

She looked up at the clouds and hoped the snow wouldn't get heavier.

"That mean old man is gone, forever," she confided to Whoops. But fear was setting in. No matter how much she disliked him, they'd been safe with him...so far.

The unbroken snow on the road didn't bode well for them, and she knew it. It was deep enough to make walking uncomfortable. So she waited and hoped the traffic would come to her. But when her feet started to get cold, she knew she had to walk. So she did.

The dog prowled around the fringes of the forest as they headed south on the 101. On one of his trips back to her side she asked him, "Have you got a name?"

His ears perked up.

"What do they call you? Spot?...Rover?...Duke?...Doggy?... Stupid?..."

His ears perked up, again.

"Is that *really* it? Stupid?" She laughed. "So Stupid it is. Come on, Stupid." And the three of them headed south on the 101.

Every now and then she stopped to look back. She figured the dog was likely to hear traffic before she did. Sometimes she'd think about the desperate straits she and her sister were cast into. She was free, but she was also lonelier than she'd ever been in her life.

She had to stop frequently to rest. The bag was heavy. Her sister was heavy. She'd look back and all she'd see behind her were their tracks — hers and the dog's — and she'd feel even more depressed. Because Whoops fussed, she eventually took her out of the sling and carried her in her arms. It was less convenient, but they both felt closer this way.

After about an hour, the dog stopped and started barking menacingly. Something lurked in the trees.

She froze. She had no defense against animals or anything else. Panic rose in her throat. She hoped the dog could protect her and her sister.

When he came down out of the trees wearing that damned ski mask, she was relieved and angry with him at the same time. But she wasn't going with him again. He was scaring her again.

"Get lost," she said.

He crossed the road on his skis.

"What do you want? I don't want you here," she said. "Go home."

Without a word, he wrested Whoops from her arms.

"No," she yelled. "Give her back to me."

When she tried to grab Whoops out of his arms, he pushed her down in the snow and started skiing away.

This was something he hadn't done before. She started crying, again. She expected him to fade into the trees, and there was no way she'd catch up with him. Her sister would be gone forever. But he stopped. He was waiting on the other side.

She looked for a rock or something to pick up and throw at him, but everything was covered with snow. She grabbed a jar of peanut butter from the sack and threw it at him. He caught it one-handed. She threw a can of corned beef hash, but he'd dropped the jar and caught that, too.

"Give her back to me," she screamed.

She wasn't going to move, but he had Whoops and he started skiing away, again. She had to follow.

She grabbed the sack, picked up the peanut butter and corned beef hash they'd need on the road, and back through the woods they went.

"Give her back," she kept calling, sometimes screaming.

Several times she fell trying to catch him.

And he'd stop occasionally to see her progress. But he stayed ahead of her.

"Keep up," he commanded once.

"Yeah, if I had a pair of skis like you've got..." She couldn't finish her sentence. She was too frustrated.

He stopped and looked back. "Do you know how to ski?"

"No," she cried.

He shook his head and moved on.

All the way back to the cabin she cried. When they got there, he waited for her by the front door. He pushed the door open, stepped aside, and let her in first. He followed and, before taking off his winter gear he placed Whoops on the chair.

He heard something behind him and turned just in time to see Danielle coming at him with the fireplace poker in both hands. She swung hard and he managed to get his arm up but it glanced off his hand and caught him in the face.

"Don't you ever take my sister from me again!" she screamed. "Do you hear me, you motherfucker?

"Don't you...fuckin' ever...take my sister...away from me again!" she yelled as she swung back and forth with a two-handed grip and, though stunned, he was out of range—until the wall prevented further retreat.

She wound up one more time, as if wielding a baseball bat, then lunged closer and murderously swung again. He ducked under it and it slipped out of her hands and crashed into a glass picture frame on the wall. Glass fell to the floor in a tingling crescendo. But she came at him swinging her fists and kicking with her knees.

He couldn't believe her rage. With his right hand cupped he swung around and caught her on the side of the head and she fell to the floor. She lay on her back stunned for a moment.

He stepped away in horror. Blood was pouring out of the cut she'd opened up with the poker.

She started to move and got up on her knees holding her face in her hands. "You keep your miserable hands off my baby sister, do you understand?" She was crying again, and almost too weak to get up. "Don't...you...ever...touch...her...again."

"Why are you doing this?" he asked.

"*Keep your hands off Whoops!* I don't ever want you to take her away from me again."

"But..."

"*She's all I've got! Keep your hands off of her!*"

"But I'm trying to help you."

"You bastard, you're throwing us out in the snow, that's what you're doing...and don't get me wrong, *we want to go.* I don't want to be in this miserable cabin with you. I hate you. My sister hates you. I should have shot you when I had the chance."

He went to a mirror near the kitchen sink and looked at the gash. He grabbed a towel and used it to stanch the flow. When he looked back at the girl, she was sitting in the chair clutching the baby.

He was confused. "What happened to you back at that farm?" When he looked back at her, he saw she wasn't going to answer. "What'd they do to you?"

"I don't want to talk about those miserable cocksuckers," she said decisively. "And you're just like them."

He turned back to the mirror and shrugged.

"She's your sister?" he suddenly asked.

There was a long pause. "Yeah.

"Does it matter?" she asked when he said nothing.

"Should it?" he asked.

"We've got to get out of this madhouse," she said. She was talking to Whoops, now, but she didn't care if he heard.

He examined his cut in the mirror again as if he was still amazed it was there.

"I want to leave," she said. "But *you're* not taking us back to the road. We're leaving alone. We'll find our own way. I'm never coming back here."

With that he approached her and shouted, "What are you going to do for your sister? You're going to kill her out on that road, you cunt!"

"What?" she screamed. She put the baby down and ran at him.

He grabbed her arms as she tried to claw him.

"Don't you be calling me a cunt, you fucking psycho!"

"What can you do for her?" he yelled.

"What can you do? She needs baby food. She can't be eating all this shit. She needs better food!" she cried. "She needs diapers, decent clothes to keep warm. She's going to die here."

He flinched when she said that.

"And she needs to be away from you! *I* need to be away from you! *Are you listening?*" she screamed.

For a second it seemed as though he wasn't sure what he was going to do. Then he abruptly released her arms and went to the middle of the room. He kicked the throw rug back.

He turned and pointed to the chair where Whoops lay, and commanded, "Sit down!"

She gladly went to the chair, picked Whoops up, and buried her face into her sister as she cried. He bent over and grabbed a large ring up from a recess in the floor. Pulling the ring he opened a trapdoor. Turning his back to the hole, he climbed down a ladder that led to a cellar below. He was down there for just a few seconds before he partially reemerged. He placed two boxes on the floor and, with one good shove, sent them both sliding toward her. He watched her for a few seconds, to make sure she stayed a respectable distance from the trapdoor, then descended again and returned with more.

When he was done, he closed the trapdoor, kicked the rug back into place, and crossed the room to her. He placed the other boxes on the floor next to the chair where she held Whoops and cried. Then he returned to the couch. He kept dabbing at the cut and examining the towel to see if the bleeding had stopped.

For a while she didn't care what was in the boxes. But when she finally looked she saw: Baby food, jars of fruits, vegetables, and boxes of cereal. There was dry milk.

With shaking hands, she took a jar of pureed peaches and opened it. It popped when she broke the seal. She smelled it.

She leaped out of the chair with Whoops in her arms and got a spoon from one of the drawers. She returned to the chair and sat down again and started to feed her sister.

With the first spoonful of peaches, Whoops had a look of amazement on her face. A true ice age baby, she'd never tasted peaches before. She stared wide-eyed at Danielle as she shoveled the peaches into her mouth, and she helped to make room for more by greedily swallowing each spoonful. It was as if she'd been transported to a new planet, and she liked it.

"Why didn't you tell me you had this stuff?" she asked accusingly.

"I forgot…there's more down there. You can take all you can carry."

Back to the road? She glared at him. He dragged her off the road and now he was going to drag her back? He was crazy.

She fed her sister until, suddenly, she stopped and tried some herself, but ate it so fast she started to choke.

She grabbed another jar and opened it. Some for the baby; some for her. Then she stopped. She started to feel guilty. She didn't eat anymore; she just fed Whoops.

He watched them.

"Stop looking at me," she said.

He kept staring until he got up and kicked the rug back again and opened the trapdoor once more. Back down he went down. When he reemerged, he approached her and handed her a fifteen-ounce can of cling peaches.

She stared at it in her hand and started shaking. She started crying again and couldn't stop.

He went to a drawer near the sink and came back with a can opener. Then he went back to the couch.

"When will you let me go back to the road?"

"When the snow stops."

"Thank you."

"Can you promise not to try to kill me between now and then?"

"Can you keep your hands off me and my sister?"

"Yes."

"Thank you, again...and we'll be okay. Next time you take us out to the road, I want you to leave us there. Do you understand? We'll make out."

He didn't reply. He was lost somewhere deep in his own thoughts. "I can't save the world," he suddenly said for what appeared to be no reason at all.

"God, you sound like my father," she said derisively. "He said he couldn't save the world, but now, if he's still alive, he's begging the world to save him."

"It won't."

"I know it won't."

"Where is your family?" he asked.

"I don't know. For all I know, they're dead."

"How did you wind up with those guys in the field? Did they pull you in off the road?"

She didn't answer.

"Are you going to tell me? Did they pull you and your sister off the road?"

"What do you think?"

"What did they do to you at the ranch?"

"What do you think?" she screamed and Whoops flinched.

He didn't respond.

"I have a question for *you*," she said angrily and, putting Whoops down on the chair, she got up.

He jumped up when she got up.

But she went to the drawer, opened it, took out the photo, and brought it to him.

"Why won't you tell me who the woman and the kids that are in the picture are?"

"Put it back," he said bitterly.

"Who's the woman?" she asked, nodding toward the photograph.

Zach ignored her as if her question would go away, but neither she nor her question were going to go away.

"Who's the woman?" she repeated.

"My wife."

"Where is she?"

"She's not here."

"Those your kids?" she demanded.

He nodded.

"Where are they?"

"They're with their mom."

"Where's she?

He didn't answer.

"I thought you said you're gay," she said sarcastically.

"When I said it, you had a gun pointed at my head, remember? I thought it was the appropriate thing to say. Or do you think I'm as stupid as I look?"

"Are you going to go see your kids again?"

"No."

"Don't you miss them? Where are they now?"

He didn't answer.

"Did she leave you?"

"Will you shut the hell up?" he said.

"I'm just asking. For all I know, you murdered them."

She never saw the punch coming. It knocked her out.

Chapter 17
August 30

On the other side of the continent, a man stood at a window. Just four years earlier, such a day in late August would have been called "unseasonably cold." But given the weather of late, it was actually a pretty nice day despite the patches of new snow that lay on the grounds. The sky above was so clear that the sun shown over the landscape sharp enough to hurt his eyes.

"Sir?" a voice deferentially asked. "They're expecting a reply."

The man at the window didn't immediately respond. He knew what the man who had entered his office wanted.

The other man continued, "Hawaii just announced it has seceded. The military needs direction."

An unsettling silence followed. Finally, the man at the window said "I've been kind of expecting this for the last year or so."

The other man waited.

The man at the window continued, "When I was first briefed on the possibilities of a new ice age, by that guy from NOAA...what was his name?" he asked and looked back at the man standing by his desk.

"Benton, Mr. President. Dr. Benton."

The President turned back to look out on the glorious day outside. "When Dr. Benton first told me that we may be entering a new ice age...how did he put it?"

"A glaciation or a glacial age, sir."

"A glaciation," the President said and nodded. "Thank you. Yes, he explained that, technically, we'd been in an ice age all along. It was kind of over my head, at the time. Something about the fact there was still year-round ice in Greenland and Antarctica... I've got that right, haven't I?"

"Yes, Sir."

"It didn't make sense. There's supposed to be ice at the South Pole, or so I thought..." There was a long pause. "...most of us thought.

"When he told me he thought we were entering a new glaciation, my first reaction was, 'What happened to the global warming shit?' But after he gave me the explanation, I asked, 'What happens to the United States if he's right?' I don't want to say I was prescient, but my thoughts were, 'If that's what's happening, this is the end of the world.' Not literally, of course, but it would be the end of the world as we know it. It may even be the end of the United..." He didn't finish.

The other man didn't say anything. He was just awaiting an order from the man who was Commander in Chief.

Another long silence followed until the President said, "Here are my orders: They are to put down insurrection wherever they find it. Any troops joining the seceding states will be considered 'deserters in combat' and will be punished as such. In fact, put it this way: As Commander in Chief, I am ordering that deserters will be shot. And key roads are to remain open. The United States will not tolerate anyone fucking with I-95, I-40, Highway 101 on the West Coast, or any other major arteries. You have a list of them. I want that as an order to the military, and I want it broadcast to the states and the civilian population."

He turned around to face him. "Do you realize that, during World War II, we shot deserters? Not just one or two, but quite a few."

"No, Sir, I didn't."

"We did. I looked it up. There was one, a guy named Slovik. Slovik became a cause célèbre, and there are many who think he was the only one. But, according to Studs Terkel in *The Good War*, we shot quite a few. It's one of those dirty little secrets from American history. And we may have to do it, again. But it won't be a secret. Do you understand the reasons?"

"Yes, Sir."

He turned to face his National Security Advisor, Fred Cotta, and added, "We are a Union, and we will remain that way. That's what I want the Joint Chiefs to know. Tell them to mobilize the troops and keep this fucking country together. If they can't do it, I will replace them with someone who can."

The National Security Advisor nodded, "Yes, Sir." It was the exact message he wanted to deliver to the Joint Chiefs.

"I also want rumors that we may move the capitol further south, denied. We're going to remain here at least another year."

"Yes, Sir. Is that all, Sir?"

"Send Sam in, would you?" the President asked referring to his speechwriter. "He's probably been waiting a while. I want to go over tonight's radio address. I want to deliver it early enough to be picked up on both coasts."

"Yes, Sir," Cotta said, and he left the Oval Office and went to brief the Joint Chiefs on how to handle the secessions that now included nine of the states. In the meantime, Georgia and South Carolina were examining their options to join those seceding. He knew things were going to get a lot worse for everyone before they got better — if they ever got better in the lifetime of anyone now alive.

Chapter 18
August 30

When she came to, she couldn't remember where she was. When she did remember, she didn't know why she was on the couch.

He was sitting on the chair where he held Whoops and was whispering to her. The second he heard Danielle stir, he jumped out of the chair and brought the baby to her. He placed her on Danielle's chest, then retreated back to the chair.

Whoops was glad to see her sister, again.

The side of Danielle's face was sore.

"I'm sorry," she heard him say.

Little by little, she remembered the argument they'd been having. Then, nothing.

"What happened?" she asked. It hurt to talk. Her anger came back to her. "What did you do to me?"

He wouldn't answer.

"Did you rape me or something?" She asked sitting up.

"I didn't touch you," he said. But he wouldn't look at her. "I just put you on the couch."

"What were you doing to my sister?"

"I was just holding her. She was crying."

"You're a shithead: Capital S, capital H."

He could see, despite her combative nature, she was scared. "Shithead's all one word," he said.

"*Oh! Then you know!*" she said sitting up. "You've been called shithead before, so you looked it up. Is that your name?"

"My name's Zach," he said in a soft voice.

"Zach? Did you hear that?" she asked her sister. "His name is Zach. Do you know what Zach means in Greek? *It means shithead!*" she screamed.

"It doesn't mean anything in Greek."

"Oh," she said to Whoops, "did you hear him that time? He's looked it up, to make sure it doesn't mean shithead."

"Why are you doing this?"

"Doing what?"

"Will you stop it?"

"Stop what?" she asked with mock incredulity.

"Stop being an asshole."

"At least an asshole has a function. What's a shithead for?" she asked and clutched the baby to her breasts. Disturbed by Danielle's yelling, Whoops watched her cautiously.

Zach understood that, more than being angry, Danielle was scared. Something had happened to her and soon she'd remember what. He didn't say anything.

She felt her jaw, then she remembered.

"You hit me, didn't you?"

"I said I'm sorry."

"I want to go back to the road, now."

"I'll take you back," he said in a low voice.

She got up from the couch and lay Whoops down on it. She began gathering her belongings quickly and haphazardly. She was so angry she was shaking.

He stood and put on his coat.

"You're staying here," she said when she saw what he was doing. "I can find the 101, myself."

"Put on your coat," he said.

"I don't want you going with me."

"Put on your coat," he repeated.

She continued packing.

She got her sister dressed for the outdoors. Then she started to gather up everything she was going to carry.

"What are you doing?" he asked.

"I'm leaving. What's it look like I'm doing?"

"You're not going to need anything. We're just going out to the field."

She stopped. "What do you mean?"

"I just want to take you to the edge of the field."

She was silent for several seconds. She started to feel panicky and she felt a churning begin in her stomach.

She still didn't move.

"Look, I'm sorry," she whispered and held Whoops tightly.

"For what?" he asked.

"For everything I've done," she said in a low voice. She wanted to be angry, instead she was becoming scared. "For the things I said. I'm sorry. I'm really sorry."

"I'm sorry, too," he said.

"Don't do this to us. Just let us go," she begged.

He stood there for a long moment. Then, as if reading her mind, he asked, "Is this the way your last day at the Brady compound started?"

When she didn't answer he said, "Nothing's going to happen to you or Whoops. I just want to show you something...I *have* to show you something. Then I'll take you back to the road."

"Why are you bringing the gun?" she asked looking at the rifle in his hand.

He looked at it, then back at her. "Have you been watching me?" he asked with a hint of exasperation in his voice. "Do you ever notice what I do?"

He pointed to the door. "I never go through that door without a rifle — and a handgun—even if I'm just going to the outhouse. And if you were going to be here more than another ten minutes, I'd make you do the same."

"I hate guns," she whispered staring at the floor and still clutching her sister to her chest.

"If it weren't for my guns, you and your sister would be dead."

She still didn't move.

"I could leave the guns here, to make you more comfortable, but I won't. Please, come."

"I can't," she whispered.

"Why?"

"I'm going to poop my pants," she said in a high voice.

He took the Model 60 from his pocket and she flinched. He opened the cylinder so she could see it was loaded. He closed the cylinder and tried to hand the gun to her. "Put this in your pocket."

She thought of taking it, but she didn't know what was going on. She looked at the floor again, making herself as small as she could, and shook her head. She couldn't count on her and her sister surviving a trip "out to the field," again.

He reached toward her and stuffed it into one of her pockets himself, but he looked at her accusingly but she didn't know why and, taking her elbow, he steered her to and out the door, leaving the dog behind.

With him still holding her arm, and her clutching her sister, they trudged through the snow until they came to where the field of snow butted up to the edge of the forest. There were three markers sticking out of the snow. Grave markers.

They stood there a long time and she was afraid to ask why he'd brought her there.

Finally, he said, "She couldn't take it. The change in the world, the cold...she kept telling me she couldn't take it. She was always crying. She told me she was always depressed. She said she wanted to die."

He looked at her to see if she was listening, and she was.

He looked at the markers, again. "She didn't like being left alone when I went out to hunt...and scavenge. I kept thinking she'd get used to it...that we could work it out...that I could save her...save us... One day I came home from a hunt..." There was a long pause as if the next words would burn his throat when they came out. "She slit their throats...hung herself in the living room...left a note saying she was sorry, but that she couldn't go on...it was best for her and the kids..."

He started shaking his head and repeated, "She said, it was best for her and the kids." He was getting angry, now, and she thought he was going to cry. "In her note, she asked me not to hate her..."

He didn't go on until he could calm himself down. Then he said, "I can't understand why she had to do it to the kids; why she had to take them away from me. I can't understand why she had to take herself away from me."

"Oh, Christ, I'm sorry," Danielle said.

"You have nothing to be sorry for...but thank you."

"She killed your kids?"

"Yeah."

Danielle started to hug Whoops tighter. She stared at the markers and was afraid she'd start crying. Then she did.

They stood there a long time and some of the words she'd said to him before she went unconscious started coming back to her. And all of his actions, once seemingly random to her, suddenly made sense in her mind. Even the accusing look just before they came outside. It explained his preoccupation with Whoops. It also explained his hostility toward her. The first time he'd ever seen her she was offering her sister up to be shot.

She kept looking from the markers, to her sister, and back at the markers. She couldn't stop the tears running down her face.

"Don't get mad, but do you hate her?"

"Sometimes...usually, I just hate myself."

She looked at him. "Why?"

"Because I didn't see it coming."

"This is why you said you were saving Whoops and not me...because of what happened to your kids."

"I don't know what I meant. I try not to think about it. Except that now and then I think about what I could have...should have...might have...done different. I feel as though, somehow, because I couldn't save them, I must have killed them. I just…I should have listened. I should have realized how depressed and desperate she was. There must have been something I could have done."

After a long moment she asked, "What if you knew what was coming? What if you'd known what she might do? What would you have done?"

He thought about her question. He thought a long time as he stared at the graves. "I don't know. I really don't. Maybe we could have all died together."

"Would you really have let that happen? Would you have just died and let them die?"

"Why are you asking this stuff?"

She thought a second. "That's not an answer to my question."

He thought about it. "No."

"Okay." Then she said, "I think I said, 'For all I know, you murdered them.' Then you hit me, didn't you?" She started crying uncontrollably.

"I'm sorry," he said once more.

"Were you hitting me or her?"

He turned to her defensively. "I *never* hit Sandra. I never even raised my voice to her."

"Then were you hitting yourself?"

He looked at her, again. "I hadn't thought about that one."

"'Cause of what she did…" Danielle said and wiped her eyes off…"that's why you said you saved Whoops and didn't give a shit about me. And is that why you took Whoops from me on the road?"

"I don't know."

"You're not much into self-analysis, are you?"

"No."

"My Mom said men like you are typical guys," she said and laughed through her tears.

He looked at her funny. He was puzzled by her laughter. He said, "I just wanted *you* to understand where I'm coming from. You can pack when we get back to the house. I'll take you to the road."

"Thank you."

But they stood there and didn't talk again while she got her tears under control. Finally, she said, "You hate women…and I hate men. Fine mess we're making of things."

"I don't hate anyone," he said. "I don't even feel anything, anymore."

"Yeah, you do," she said and held Whoops up as empirical evidence of something he cared about.

He shrugged. "Maybe."

"You do," she said and started crying again. "You care about Whoopsie. Thank you."

After another minute, unable to think of the right words she finally gestured toward the graves and asked, "Can I ask...when did...she do it?"

"Last winter. I thought I was over it. I was getting along pretty well...adjusting...until I saw that guy—I don't even know his name—throw Whoops into the snow. When he did that, he was already dead. He just didn't know it. I didn't know why you held her up the way you did...I do, now...but she was safe...he was gonna die before he pulled that trigger ..."

"Thank you," she said again.

"You're welcome."

They stood there staring at the graves longer and she shivered once.

"I'm sorry," she repeated.

"It's okay."

"No, I'm really sorry. I thought you were just a crazy man."

"You thought *I* was crazy? Me?" he asked hiking his thumb at himself.

"Yes. Why? Did you think I was crazy?" she asked.

"I thought you were a lunatic. The way you were coming after me, I had a hard time thinking I was going to let you leave here with Whoops."

"You couldn't tell I was scared?"

"Scared of what? *Me?*"

"Well, look at you. The way you were so quiet...you live alone out here, like a hermit...you kept taking or trying to take my sister away from me...and the way you talked in your sleep..."

"What did I say?"

"You don't want to know, but you were yelling at your wife...and after what those men did to me...and what they were going to do to my sister...and I saw you kill at least three guys...what did you think I was going to think? I thought you were just another dangerous crazy man."

"When you put it that way, I guess I'd have thought I was crazy, too."

"Do you hate me?" she asked.

"No. Why?"

She looked at the grave marker that read Sandra Gibbons Amaral and said, "I just asked."

He went back to staring at the markers.

After another minute she said, "We can stand out here longer than you can. Whoops and I are really becoming pros at being cold."

He shook his head. "You're really combative, aren't you?" he said.

"I'm sorry," she said. "I don't like being this way. I grew up thinking the world was nice. Then the ice age started..."

"I didn't say that as an insult." He looked back at the graves. "If she'd been half as combative as you, we'd still be a family. Whoops is really lucky she's got you."

"Well, she's lucky you came along, too. She'd have died out there on the road...we'd both have died out there if you hadn't taken her from me, wouldn't we have?"

"Probably. I wasn't thinking about it, then. I just did what I did."

"Can I ask you one more question?"

She had his attention."

"If you'd found a live baby in a car on the road, would you take it or leave it to die?"

"I'd take it," he said as if amazed by her question.

"I thought so," she said.

"Why would you ask a question like that?"

"I just wanted to know."

They stood there longer.

"When I said we could stand out here longer than you, I was dropping a hint."

"Oh! I'm sorry. You're cold, aren't you?"

"I'm freezing."

He turned. "Let's go back to the cabin."

On their way he said, "You're not leaving today. I want you to learn how to use that handgun before you leave. You're taking it with you. You'll need it so you can look out for Whoops."

"I told you, I don't like guns."

"I'll show you how to shoot it," he said dismissing her objection. "You're going to be glad you have it."

"Okay," she said, but she wasn't so sure.

They got inside and he casually took off his coat and boots.

"I still have to go to the bathroom," she said.

"Okay."

She left with her sister and went to the outhouse.

When she returned several minutes later he was getting ready to do something in the kitchen.

She approached him but just stood and stared at him.

He stopped what he was doing and asked, "What?"

She suddenly clutched Whoops tighter and said, "I can't believe I'm going to do this, but would you hold her for a second?"

He nodded and she passed him the baby. Without even taking a breath, she took off her own coat and boots as quickly as she could then grabbed her sister back out of his arms. "Okay, that's as long as I can let her out of my reach," she said and smiled. She went back to "her" chair.

He knew that when she let him hold her sister, she was trying to say a lot of things—to both him and herself—and without really understanding why, he felt like a million dollars.

"Do you mind if I ignore you now and do some busy work here?"

"No. Go ahead. I'm curious as to what you do here. Do you mind me watching?"

"Of course not."

He went through one of the doors that led into one of the other rooms. When he came back, he had the large pots she'd used earlier along with a cast iron skillet. He put the skillet atop the stove. Then he stepped outside, and true to form, he took the rifle with him. When he returned, both pots had water in them.

"Where'd you get water?" she asked incredulously. "I had to melt snow."

"I have a well."

"Is this one of the comforts of home you've been hiding from me?"

He smiled and shook his head. "That was something else Sandra didn't have: A sense of humor. Not having one makes a hard life harder." He paused. "I don't know why I'm telling you that."

He took the pots to the stove and placed them on the hot surface. Then he opened the stove door and fed the flames more firewood.

With his back still to her, he said, "Tomorrow morning."

"'Tomorrow morning,' what?" she asked.

"I'll show you how to shoot the gun."

"Okay."

"Then you can leave."

"Okay. It's still in my coat," she added.

"I know. I want you to take it with you whenever you step out that door, even if it's just to go out to the outhouse."

"What do I do with it if I need it?"

"I don't know. I'm sure you'll think of something."

She smiled at his answer, remembering that she'd already cocked it and put it to his head. She continued to watch him.

Then she cleared her throat. "Do you always have to pull that thingy back to shoot it?"

He turned and looked at her for a second trying to imagine what she was referring to. Then he said, "It's called the hammer." He turned back to the stove but spoke louder so she could hear him. "You don't *have* to do that with that kind of gun. You can just pull the trigger. But, if you want, you can pull the hammer back until it stops – they call it 'cocking' it. You do that if you're trying to get an accurate shot. Once the hammer's back, that particular gun's got a hair-trigger. Just a few ounces of pressure from your finger will fire it. Sometimes they call shooting it that way 'single-action mode.' Even though it's a small gun, it's pretty accurate when shot that way."

He kept working.

"It's a little harder to just pull the trigger without cocking it first," he went on with his back to her. "But if you do it that way—just pull the trigger—the hammer will go back and keep going back as long as you keep pulling the trigger back. When you've pulled it back far enough, the hammer is released, it falls, hits the firing pin, and the gun goes off. It's quicker to shoot that way, but not as accurate. They call shooting it that way 'double-action mode.' I'll show you, tomorrow."

"My father had a gun that you always had to pull the hammer back to shoot it."

He nodded without looking back. "That's a single-action revolver. It doesn't have a double-action mode."

He went to the door again. But this time he just leaned out, grabbed the bag he'd hung under the eaves earlier, and brought it back to the stove.

Stupid perked up when he saw the bag. Danielle realized he knew what was in it.

Zach eyed him warily as he walked past him.

"You get none of this until it's cooked," he said to him.

She stayed in her chair with her sister in her arms and watched.

He alternately stood either at the stove or a small counter next to it with his back to her. He emptied part of the bag onto the counter. It was some kind of meat. He started cutting the meat from the largest bones and threw the small pieces into the skillet. Then he took a hammer from the drawer under the counter and began to break up the bones. He put the bones into one of the pots.

The meat smelled good. Too good. She carried Whoops to the stove and stood back but watched it cooking in the skillet.

He glanced back at her. "Try some," he said.

She stepped up, picked up a fork, and reached out to take a piece.

He stayed her hand. "Don't take any pieces except the ones that are well-done."

She hesitated.

"You can take what you want," he explained. "But I don't want you, Whoops, or the dog to have any unless it's well-done. We've got to be careful of trichinosis and toxoplasmosis"

She looked at him askance.

"They're parasites," he said.

She still didn't say anything.

"Trichinosis is caused by the trichina worm; toxoplasmosis is caused by a protozoan."

She still just stared at him and he stared back until she said, "There are no more schools, you know. That's not stuff I ever learned."

"It's not something you'd have learned in school, anyway."

"I'm here to learn it now," she said.

Her attitude surprised him. "Are you sure you won't be bored?" She didn't answer. She waited patiently.

He took a deep breath. "There are something like eight kinds of trichina worms, maybe three of them can cause trichinosis. If you eat meat infected with those, their larvae — their babies — get into your intestines and start multiplying. The newborn larvae can then move through your intestinal walls and get into your bloodstream and lymphatic system. Most people who get infected can fight it off, but the worms can get into your muscles, including your heart and diaphragm — that's the muscle you breath with, and they can also affect your brain. They can cause fever, soreness and pain, swelling..."

"And they can kill you," she said simply.

He paused, nodded slowly, and said, "Yes, it's possible."

"What about the other one?"

"Toxoplasmosis is caused by a protozoan. It's usually not fatal, but it can cause encephalitis, a brain inflammation, and it can also affect various organs like your eyes, liver, and heart. It can even affect unborn babies."

"But it doesn't usually kill you," she concluded.

"No."

"But you still don't want to get it," she said. "You don't want to get *either*," she corrected herself before he could speak.

"Rare meat is not an option anymore," he said. "I either cook it fully or I can it. And, when I'm canning it, the heat from the canning process will kill the parasites and protozoa," he added.

"You're telling me I can't have rare meat? Listen, I haven't even had a *piece* of meat in three years — except what you cooked in the woods," she said.

"Were they okay?"

"Okay?" she asked incredulously. "After three years of peanut butter, rice, lousy bread, rice, peanut butter, some kind of flour mush, some kind of cornmeal mush, rice, peanut butter...and did I mention rice and peanut butter?...I discovered I'm really a carnivore."

And for the first time she saw him smile directly at her. No one other than Whoops had smiled at her in a good while and she still didn't know whether she wanted to be friendly with him or not. But it made her feel good because she knew he'd smiled because of her.

He used the spatula to scoot selected pieces to the side of the skillet where she stood. "Try those. They're done."

She tasted a piece. "Bear meat?" she asked rhetorically.

He nodded

"I think I like it."

"It's not bad," he said. "Take more."

"I'm having trouble chewing. My mouth hurts."

He put the spatula down. "Jesus, I'm sorry," he whispered.

"I'm not trying to make you feel bad," she said offhandedly. "I deserved what you did for what I said to you."

"No," he said turning to her. "No women deserves what I did to you."

"You haven't met Abby Brady, have you?" she laughed.

He looked at her quizzically. "I've heard of her. Is she really that bad?"

"If you have to ask, you haven't heard enough. But maybe you'd actually have to meet her to know what I'm talking about," she said. "In the meantime, keep cooking. Is there a way to cook some so Whoops can have it? She never tasted meat until we met you. And she likes it."

"A carnivore, just like her sister."

He deftly cut a piece that was well-done into very thin slices. He then cut across the slices. He then began to chop what was left.

"I want you to know I'm sorry for what I did to you," he said.

"If you apologize again, I'm going to come after you with the fireplace poker again. Deal?"

He laughed and shook his head. "Deal, I guess. But it'll never happen again, ever."

"Where'd you put the poker?"

He laughed again.

"This is a pretty elaborate rig for canning," she said changing the subject. "My Mom just used a pot with boiling water, and she canned all kinds of things: tomatoes, jam, preserves…"

He interrupted her as he minced the meat. "Tomatoes and fruits can be canned like that. Low-acid things, which includes meats, fish, green beans, asparagus, and a host of other vegetables, stews, and soups, need higher heat. Otherwise, you're risking botulism, and botulism is nasty…I'm not boring you, am I?"

"No. Actually, it's interesting."

"Well, to prevent botulism, you've got to use a pressure canner. The pressure canner lets you get the inside of the canner to a temperature higher than boiling water at regular pressure, and it kills the spores that release a bacteria called *clostridium botulinum*. Those are the bacteria that produce a toxin that can kill you."

"Kill me?"

"Deader than dead, and it doesn't take much."

"Do you drop dead right away?"

"It's a nerve toxin. It takes a while; usually a few days or weeks. But the symptoms usually show up in the first six hours. What happens is it attacks your nerves, your muscles stop working, and eventually you can't breathe. You die of suffocation."

She was quiet while she thought about that.

"What's the food smell like when it's gone bad...when it's got the botulism stuff in it?" she asked.

He turned to her and with emphasis said, "That's the problem with botulism and its toxin: you can't see it, you won't smell it, and it has no taste. But it's one of the most poisonous substances known to man. Just a small taste of contaminated food can kill you."

"Then how do you know if the food's poisoned?"

"You don't. But if you follow the correct procedures for pressure canning, and heat the food to a high enough temperature, and for a long enough time—and to do that you need a pressure canner, not just ordinary boiling water—not only will the bacteria and toxin be destroyed, but the spores that create more bacteria are also zapped so the little bastards can't multiply in the jars."

"What do you do if someone else canned it and you think the food's no good?"

"If you open up a can of stuff, and you're thinking, 'Ah, this stuff may be contaminated,' heat it to one hundred fifty-eight degrees—that's Fahrenheit—for two minutes and you destroy the toxins; heat it to one hundred and seventy-six degrees for ten minutes, and you kill the bacteria, too."

"Isn't two hundred and twelve boiling?" she asked.

He smiled at her. "The schools might be closed, but you know something. If you boil it for a few minutes, you'll kill all the bacteria and it's safe to eat. More importantly, you'll destroy all the toxin, too. *But* it won't kill the spores, which are sort of a hibernating state the bacteria go into when conditions for them become unfavorable. So you can't just boil something, expecting to kill the spores, and call it canned. But the spores alone aren't going to hurt you. It's when they produce the bacteria again, and the bacteria produce the toxin, that you have a problem."

He abruptly turned to her. "Let me qualify that: They won't hurt *you* or *me*. Babies, under a year old, are at risk." He looked at Whoops. "That's why you don't give newborns honey. Honey may harbor some of the botulism spores. You and I can handle them. Little terrorists, a year or more old, can as well. But small babies, like your sister, may not be able to."

She thought about it a second. "Where do the germs come from?"

He stopped and turned to her, again. "You're really interested in this stuff, aren't you?"

"It's interesting," she said.

He turned back to the stove. "They're all around us. But they can't live in oxygen—or an acidic environment like you find in fruit jams and preserves. They're mostly in the soil. But they're not dangerous unless they're in an oxygen and acid-free environment. Then they can start reproducing and creating and concentrating their toxin, again, like in a jar of poorly-canned meat."

She looked at the cutting board he was using. "Are there any here?"

"There may be. But like I say, we usually just coexist with them and they don't bother us."

"How do you know all this?"

"Books. I've got plenty of them. I read them and I remember a lot of what I read. Some of my books are on canning."

"I can tell," she said.

"But," he continued, "when I can tomatoes, I'll just use a hot water bath, like your mother did. The acids in tomatoes and fruits kill them, just like oxygen does, and there's no problem. What you're doing with the hot water bath isn't preventing botulism, the acidity does that for you. What you're doing is killing other bacteria and molds so the food won't spoil."

She laughed. "You're never going to can another tomato for the rest of your life," she said. "There are no tomatoes left to can. They don't grow anymore."

"I grow them," he said.

"You're joking. Nothing grows here anymore," she said.

"Did you notice the frame that's still attached to the side of the house?"

"Yeah."

"It's what's left of my greenhouse. I've got to take the rest of it down because the weight of the snow will ruin it. But I'm going to put a sturdier one up in the spring — if we have another spring, which I think we will. It'll just come later, and we won't have much of one nor much of a summer. So to compensate for the lack of a growing season, I start my tomatoes, and a few other things, here in the house, then I transfer them to the greenhouse and start more plants in the house. Then, if and when the ground warms up enough, I transfer the stuff in the greenhouse to the outside and transfer the new stuff I started in the house out to the greenhouse."

"You're kidding," she said.

He pointed with the knife to the two windows on the far side of the room. "When the greenhouse is, up I leave the two windows open during the day because the greenhouse helps warm the cabin and, at night, the fire from the fireplace or stove warms the greenhouse and keeps the plants from freezing."

She carried her sister to the window and looked at it. She could see where the greenhouse had been attached to the framing.

She looked down at some buckets with plants growing in them then turned to him and asked, "What are these?"

He looked at her funny, as if she should know. "They're tomato plants. They're bare, now, because I've picked them all off."

She read his expression. "I've never seen vegetables growing," she said.

"I forgot," he said.

"That's okay.

"What are these?" she asked observing some smaller plants also in buckets.

"Hot peppers."

She wrinkled her nose and said, "Oh."

"You don't like hot peppers?"

"I don't think so. But I don't know."

"Never had 'em?"

"Nope."

"What's this?" she asked of the next.

"A myrtlewood tree."

"Why are you growing a tree in your house?"

"I want the leaves. Myrtlewood is in the bay laurel family. I use them in cooking."

She looked at the next ones. They were pretty good sized. "More trees you've got started?"

"Marijuana."

"No, please tell me what they are. I'm trying to learn something."

"They're really marijuana."

She looked at him closely to see if she could tell whether he was putting her on or not.

"You're not kidding, are you?"

"No."

"But marijuana's illegal, isn't it?"

"What's legal and what's illegal anymore?" he asked.

She looked back at the plants. "That's true," she said. "What are you growing them for?"

"Historically, weed's been used because it has some medicinal qualities. It's been used for pain relief, insomnia, and things like that. It's also has recreational uses; probably more of that than medical applications. So, lots of people have uses for it, especially now, because of the ice age. It makes a great barter item."

"You're supposed to smoke it, right?" she asked.

"You can smoke it or you can eat it—especially after cooking it into something."

"Do you smoke it or eat it?"

"I never really liked it. I don't particularly like the high from it. I prefer booze. But I've had raging insomnia ever since I was a little kid and about five years ago I discovered it helps me to sleep. Doesn't take much, either, so a little goes a long way.

162 JOHN SILVEIRA

"So, do you smoke it or eat it?" She ran her fingers over the leaves of one of the plants. It was kind of exciting to her to be here with something she knew people used to go to jail for.

"I smoke it."

"What parts do you use?" she asked.

"I smoke or barter with the buds and leaves, I use the stems to make a marijuana wine, I keep some seeds to replant and, because I always get more seeds than I'm ever going to plant, I use the rest of the seeds for bird feed."

"You make wine with them, too?"

"Yeah."

She looked back at him for a moment then she turned back to the plants. She was fascinated.

"It should never have been illegal in the first place," he said.

"Really? Why not?"

"It's my body. I should be able to do what I want with it."

She reflected on that for a moment. "I like the way you think."

He liked the way she thought.

"But I'd grow it now, anyway," he said, "even if I didn't use it, just because other people want it and it's such a great barter item. There are other people here in these hills who use it. But for one reason or another they either can't grow it like I do, they don't have the time to grow it, they can't grow enough of it, or what they grow is of poor quality. A lot of them have used stuff they get from me as barter with the troops to get gas, ammo, or food."

"They trade it with the Army guys?"

"Yeah."

"That's really illegal, isn't it?"

"It's a capital offense, nowadays."

She leaned over to smell the plants.

"Kinda smells like..."

"Skunk?"

"I couldn't think of it for a second, but yeah, skunk."

"What makes yours so good?"

"In the old days," he said, "people used electric lights—they called them grow lights—to grow the best stuff they could. Nowadays, no one around's got enough electricity to power grow lights for very long. Plus, when the lights burn out, you can't replace them anymore. So, compared to the stuff from the old days, what I grow isn't the highest quality, but I've started saving the seeds from my best plants to develop a strain that grows well under these conditions. Folks around here have told me what they've gotten from me is good stuff."

"I'm sorry," she said without turning to him.

"For what?"

"What I said about you…murdering your family?"

"Do me a favor?" he asked.

"What's that?"

"Get me the fireplace poker."

She laughed. "I'll take that as forgiveness. Thank you," she said and, before he could say anything, she asked, "What's this?" She was in front of another group of plants.

"That's sweet basil. The ones next to it are oregano, and the two after those are rosemary. I grow my own herbs, too. I dry them, I cook and can with them, and I use my herbs as barter, too. Life is hard, but people still want food to taste good."

She went back to the biggest pot plant and touched it again. Then she leaned over and smelled it. He could see she was fascinated.

"I like the smell of it," she said.

"Yeah, it's an odd but seductive smell."

She came back to the stove and looked in the direction of the second pot. "You put a bunch of bones in there. Are you canning bones, too?"

"I make my own soup stocks and broths. I extract all the flavor and nutrients I can and put it up in jars. Then I grind the bones up. They make good fertilizer for my plants."

"Where do you put the stuff you can?" she asked looking around.

He looked at the floor.

"Downstairs?"

He nodded. "It's cool down there, but it won't freeze. I keep lots of stuff down there."

"You've got it all figured out, haven't you," she said.

He swept the meat he'd minced onto a saucer and got a small spoon from a drawer and handed the whole package to Danielle. "Here, see how much more she eats."

"Is it okay?" she asked skeptically with one eyebrow raised in a circumflex. "You're beginning to scare me with all this talk about botulism and toxins. It's not going to make her sick, is it?"

"It's cooked completely through. All the bad stuff is dead. The only things in it now that can hurt her are the fats, so she may have a heart attack eighty years from now."

"Should I risk that?" she asked facetiously.

"Gamble. Take a chance."

She took the meat and went back to her chair and fed Whoops.

After a while, and without turning to her, he asked, "Why are you going back to the road?"

It was an unexpected question. "We've got to find our family," she said. "Besides, my Dad said, pretty soon, nothing's going to be able to live up here."

He didn't comment on that and the cabin became quiet except for the hiss of the canner when the water inside began to boil and the baby talk Danielle made to her sister as she fed her.

She was casually aware of him going into the other rooms doing whatever it was he did. She still didn't understand his routines and she wasn't going to be here long enough to learn them. Her prime concern, she reminded herself, was her sister.

But she felt moody. She knew it was going to be tough on Whoops when they went back to the road and she didn't even know if the family she was setting out to find was still alive. The more she thought, the darker and more threatening the world became.

Inexplicably, she started crying, again, and tried to stop, but she couldn't.

He came back into the living room. "What's wrong?"

"Nothing," she said.

"Tell me what's wrong."

"Nothing," she said firmly. "There's nothing wrong. Just leave me alone."

He wanted to tell her, again, that he was sorry for hitting her, but he didn't think that was what was bothering her.

He'd seen this before in his wife. He began to think he'd made a mistake; maybe he should have left her on the road. "I'm sorry I made you come back," he finally said.

"Just shut up," she sobbed.

"I'll take you back to the road, tomorrow."

"I said shut up!"

He went back to the kitchen.

She stared at her sister who stared back as she ate, pausing occasionally to smile.

But Danielle knew why she was crying. For the first time since leaving Yakima, she felt as though she and her sister were safe. And, now, she had to go back to the road. She thought she was starting to go crazy.

Suddenly, he was standing over her. In his hand he had some of the empty wrappers the tampons had come in. "I found these in the old bathroom on the counter. This explains a lot."

For a second she was dumbfounded. Then she said, "Oh," and looked away shaking her head in exaggerated exasperation.

"Remember outside you said I'm a typical guy?" He shook them at her. "Well, *you* are a typical woman, too."

She began to laugh. He shook his head and took the wrappers to the fireplace insert where he threw them in the box where he kept tinder. From there he went back to the stove.

So, he could be funny, she thought. But it was true: Part of what was happening with her was because it was that "time of the month," part was because she was worrying about her family, and another part was knowing she had to go back to the road and risk herself and her sister.

"You know," he began without turning to face her, "I didn't keep track of Sandra's periods. So, sometimes she'd be a real bitch and I didn't know why. And, this was before the ice age. Often, a few days later she'd apologize and tell me she'd bitten my head off because she'd started her period. After that happened a few times, one day she started off on me and I asked her, in the calmest and most considerate manner, if she was upset because she'd started her period, and she really went off and told me not to start writing her moods off because of her periods and to think about what I might have done to upset her.

"Well, a few days later she asked, 'Do you remember how I got so upset the other day because you asked if my bad mood was because of my period...'"

Danielle interrupted, "And she said it was."

He turned his head to look at her. "So you know."

Danielle smiled. "You deserved what you got. You never attribute a woman's mood to her period, even if you *know* that's why she's acting that way—unless you like flirting with death, in which case you should take up juggling with running chainsaws; it's safer."

He turned back to his work smiling and shaking his head.

"Anyway, I'm sorry," he said.

"I'm sure she'd forgive you."

"No, I'm still sorry for what I did to you. I know you don't want to talk about it anymore, but I want you to know it's not something I've ever done before and I promise it'll never happen again. I'm sick about it."

"Apology accepted," she said.

"Thank you."

"You're pretty smart," he said for what appeared to be no reason. "I like that about you."

"I don't know anything," she said. "There are no schools."

"I'm not talking about education; I'm talking about native intelligence. I hope you know the difference."

"I do. Thank you," she said. She liked hearing it.

And suddenly she realized she had to be careful. She didn't want to complicate her life by getting to like him.

Chapter 19
August 31

The following morning was sunny and cloudless and, though it seemed to hold the promise that some of the snow might melt, in reality the lack of cloud cover let the earth's precious heat reradiate back into space and made the day much colder.

Whoops lay on the floor at Danielle's feet, and she and the dog watched each other with genuine curiosity. Danielle liked that he was comfortable with her sister. She sat in her chair and read a book of short stories she'd found.

Zach had been up since before dawn canning more of the bear, but he now sat on the couch. She glanced at him from time to time as he alternately watched Whoops and the dog, then disappeared back into some recess of his own mind, preoccupied with his thoughts. Without saying anything, he suddenly got up and put on his winter gear. She watched as he grabbed his M1 and skis, and went to the door.

The dog met him there and Zach stared at him as if surprised. "You want to go?" he asked.

The dog wagged his tail expectantly.

Zach opened the door and let the dog out first but he paused and said, "I'll be back in a while."

He didn't wait for a response.

She went to the window and watched him put on his skis. With his rifle slung over his shoulder he took off across the field, in the direction of the road, and disappeared into the forest with the dog in pursuit.

Now alone, she walked around the room looking up at the rafters. She realized it was a morbid fascination, but she tried to imagine where Sandra must have been the day he walked through the door and found her hanging. She looked for telltale signs, but if there were any, they weren't obvious. He hadn't said where he'd found his children. She wasn't sure she wanted to know. She shivered. It must be creepy to go on living where all the people you loved had died.

"Maybe he's not so crazy," she confided to Whoops. She was beginning to feel sorry for him and stopped herself.

Whoops began to fuss. She'd woken early and Danielle knew she was tired. She picked her up and walked the floor with her.

After a while, Whoops's head started to bob back and forth until she finally planted it on Danielle's shoulder and she carefully laid her back on the blanket on the floor.

She went to the window again and looked out at the field. She had no idea where he'd gone. She wished she knew when he'd be back.

She didn't like being a snoop. Or maybe she just didn't want to be *caught* being a snoop. But she started inspecting all the candles. She wanted one that had already been lit and found the one she'd used before and got the lighter from the mantel over the fireplace insert. She kicked the rug away and exposed the trapdoor in the floor. She hesitated.

She went back to the window. She checked Whoops, who slept soundly. Taking a deep breath, she opened the trapdoor and stared into the ebony abyss below. She lit the candle and put the lighter in her pocket. Once she was sure the candle was burning okay, she started down the ladder.

As her eyes acclimated themselves to the dim light thrown by the candle, a myriad of pinpoints of light surrounded her. Soon she realized there were hundreds...no, thousands...of jars on shelving that stretched along the walls of the cellar. She got closer to one of the shelves. There were jars labeled "tomatoes" with dates on them. There were too many for her to want to count. She walked slowly along the shelves until she came to jars labeled "squash." There were quite a few of those, too. There were labels that read "venison," "venison stew," "blackberry jam," "carrots," "green beans..." She hadn't seen this much food since before the supermarkets all closed.

She came upon wine bottles and read the labels: "dandelion wine," "tomato wine," "blueberry wine," "blackberry wine," "marijuana wine," — he wasn't kidding — and more.

Beyond that were several dozen jars that read "kochujang sauce." Beneath those words, in parenthesis, were the words "Korean hot sauce."

Further along she saw jars labeled "applesauce." The dates on those were a few years old, and that made sense since the seasons, this far north, were no longer long enough for apples to ripen. He wouldn't be canning applesauce ever again unless he—no, apple trees weren't tomato plants and he wasn't going to figure out how to grow them.

Another group was jars of soup of different kinds, some with old dates while others had dates as recent as the current year. Another bunch was stews and the dates were similar.

All the jars were labeled with their contents and dated.

On the floor there were sacks of rice, sacks of beans, salt, some large cylindrical boxes that read "potassium chloride." This guy could feed himself for years.

There was a table with old bunched-up newspapers. Hundreds of them. She put the candle down and picked one up. There was something round inside. She opened it: a green tomato. She examined a few more—all tomatoes. So, he did grow them. She continued down the line. There were squash—not canned, but *whole* squash. She hadn't seen a fresh tomato or squash in three years. There was a thermometer. She read the temperature: sixty-one degrees.

There was a door on one wall. She hesitated before it. She didn't know if she wanted to know what was on the other side. But unable to contain her curiosity, she opened it. The door was thick and on the other side of it was another room, much smaller and noticeably colder. There were small carrots stacked on one table. Another was piled with potatoes. A third had cabbages. There was a thermometer on the table. She picked it up and held it close to the candle to see what it read: Just over thirty-four degrees. She wondered why he wanted it this cold. There was another instrument she picked up and it read "humidity," whatever that meant. It read "90."

She went back to the other part of the cellar and closed the door behind her.

There were more jars all with dates: "bear meat" ..."wild turkey"..."salmon," there were many of those..."butter/ghee"... Butter? She looked at the jars in disbelief and leaned closer to examine them. She didn't know what the word *ghee* meant, but somehow, he had canned butter. She hadn't had any in three years. Then there was "cheese." She couldn't believe her eyes. But, if nothing else, the stuff in the jars did look like cheese. At the next section of jars she recoiled..."*dog.*" Those had a fairly recent date.

"Shit," she said aloud. "He *is* crazy."

Then there was...she had to lean close to see what they were...cans—store-bought cans—of corn and other vegetables. There were cases filled with boxes of macaroni and cheese. The next thing she discovered was something her father had acquired, just before they left: a reloading bench. This guy made his own ammunition.

She stepped back away from the bench. She didn't know if the candle, this close to the cans of gunpowder, was dangerous.

Stacked against the wall were more boxes. Some were empty, others were not. She opened one of the latter and there were empty jars; the kind he used to can. And there were packages of lids. There were hundreds of those.

Beside them were two large plastic cases. She set the candle down and opened the first one. It was filled with medical supplies: Bandages, tubes of ointments, prescription drugs, and more. She closed it and opened the second one. More medical.

Next to them was another table. She got closer. There were boxes and tubes. She leaned closer to them with the candle to see what they were. Suddenly she shrunk back. She didn't have to be told what she was looking at. The word "Dynamite" was written all over the tubes.

She couldn't go any further. She slowly pulled the candle back and stood there in the flickering light watching the shadows shimmer like ghosts of the bears, deer, birds, and dogs now trapped in the jars.

This guy also had the makings of bombs.

She heard Whoops cry. She'd hoped she'd sleep longer. She got to the ladder and felt scared again. But she paused and went back to look at the dynamite, once more. There was something scary and exciting about it at the same time. This guy was dangerous—she knew that—and...he was cute. No he wasn't, she told herself.

At the foot of the ladder she blew out the candle then climbed back into the light. She closed the trapdoor and readjusted the carpeting just the way it had been. She looked out the window again. There was still no sign of him or the dog. Then she picked Whoops up and sunk back into her chair. She realized her heart was pounding.

"What kind of a man has bombs in his cellar?" she asked herself.

He was nice to her, she reminded herself. And he liked Whoops. But what was he doing with dynamite?

Whoops wouldn't stop crying. So, she walked the floor with her. Then she sat down again and began to rock her while, through her mind thoughts about food, guns, and explosives whirled around in a maelstrom.

The jars labels "dog" really bothered her. Then again, maybe eating dogs wasn't so bad. After all, they were just another kind of meat. She realized it was just that *she* didn't want to eat any of it. And when she thought of dog meat, she pictured the malamute and knew his days were numbered. That wasn't good. She liked Stupid. Maybe she'd take him with her when she left. He deserved a better fate than to wind up canned.

Chapter 20
August 31

Zach reached the 101 and looked down onto the highway from the
trees. The Army had come through during the night. They were the only
ones who cleared the roads. There were new tracks where military and
perhaps some of the emigrant convoys had passed.

He watched the road for several minutes until the dog growled.

"Come on," he whispered and faded back into the trees and the
dog followed.

Moments later he saw a military convoy heading north. There
were trucks and Humvees, with military personnel. One of the Humvees
had an M240B machine gun mounted on it.

He slipped deeper into the trees until he couldn't hear them
anymore.

He had to go back and tell her the road was open and traffic was
passing on it. With the weather turning colder, she might not get another
chance this good to catch a ride.

Then, he reminded himself, he wanted her to learn to shoot the
gun before she left.

He started back to the cabin but, where the trail forked, he
changed his mind and decided to take the long way. The path he followed
paralleled the road before it went through the woods and, at several points
the road and path met again. It was almost too beautiful a day not to be
out. What was his hurry?

Each time the road came into view, he stopped and lingered. Everywhere it was plowed. It was probably open all the way from southern California to Hanford, Washington.

At one point he stopped to inspect the road's condition and the dog's ears perked up. Seconds later there were sounds in the distance. He looked north and, the second he saw it come into sight, he said, "Back!" and he faded back into the trees and the dog, as if on command, followed.

A lone pickup whizzed by. Civilians. There were those who still tried to make it alone or in twos and threes, and many, apparently, made it through.

He looked down at the dog. It was actually *awaiting* his next command.

"Come on," he said and the dog was up and ready to run.

They continued their trip home. But the path he took still wasn't the shortest. It wasn't that he didn't want to see Danielle. Just a day or so before, when she was acting crazy, he wanted her to leave. But after she'd stood there while he canned the night before…company, for the first time in months, was nice. So was having a baby in the house. He'd like her to stay longer. But he couldn't make her stay. That's what he'd done with his wife, and that ended in the worst disaster of his life.

He skied but took his time.

Then, about three miles from the cabin, he pulled up short. About a hundred and fifty yards ahead was a deer. He didn't know where it had come from, and there were damned few left.

The dog saw it and let out a guttural growl.

"Quiet," Zach whispered and, as if it understood, the dog went quiet. But it never took its eyes off the deer and Zach unslung his rifle.

It was difficult to determine if the deer had heard them or seen their movements, but it froze. Then it began a slow but wary saunter across the patch of snow.

Zach had the rifle up. It was a problematic shot from here. His M1 was accurate, at best, to two minutes of angle and from this range, shooting offhand while winded, he'd be lucky if he could shoot a six-inch group. But he had to take the chance. He clicked off the safety and took a small lead, just forward of the deer's shoulder, and as it reached the trees he squeezed the trigger, and the rifle went off like a crack of summer thunder.

At more than two and a half times the speed of sound, the bullet left the muzzle and sped across the snow. Just as the deer reached the trees, it abruptly dropped while all around Zach the crack of the rifle made powdered snow trickle out of the branches and it glistened like stardust in the bright sun. Then all was quiet. But the deer was down.

"Let's go," Zach said and set off on his skis. The dog sped ahead and reached the carcass well before Zach. He was sniffing it when Zach arrived.

With a length of rope he took from his pocket and practiced motions, Zach quickly had the carcass suspended from the branch of a nearby tree and commenced to field dress it.

"No!" he commanded when the dog approached the entrails and the dog shrunk back.

He fished through his pockets until he found a large plastic bag. He put the entrails in the bag. He'd take them back to the cabin and cook them for...what was his name?...Stupid?

He packed the deer's body cavity with snow to cool it quickly. Then he threw the carcass up over his left shoulder and started skiing back on a direct path to the cabin. The whole operation had taken less than ten minutes.

§   §   §

When he came through the door she was in her chair. Somehow it made him feel better that she'd staked out a small piece of territory in his house and was comfortable there. Sandra had never been comfortable in the cabin.

He didn't say anything to her as he passed her but she saw the bag he was carrying and how Stupid was matching his steps and looking up at him in anticipation.

He put the bag up on the counter and turned to the dog and said, "Sit."

Stupid sat.

Danielle watched the scene play out. She was amused that Zach seemed amazed every time the dog listened to him.

She got out of her chair with Whoops in her arms and came to the stove to see what he was doing.

"Why are you cooking all that?" she asked.

"It's for the dog."

"You getting to like him?"

"I want to fatten him up with the scraps I won't use."

Her mood changed instantly. She didn't ask why he wanted to fatten the dog. She thought about the jars downstairs and knew why, and her stomach began to churn. But she couldn't tell him she'd been snooping.

"How's your day?" he asked.

"Whoops has been fussy," she said.

"Is she teething?"

That hadn't occurred to her. "I don't know."

He stopped and looked thoughtfully at Whoops. Then he thoroughly washed his hands and, putting his left hand behind Whoops's head and neck, he used the index finger on his right hand to feel inside her mouth and rub her gums.

"Has she been drooling?" he asked.

"More than usual," Danielle said.

"How old is she?"

"Six months."

"I think I may feel something erupting here...like teeth coming in," he said. "She pooping okay?"

Danielle nodded. "Why?"

"Just want to make sure she's not constipated."

He reflexively leaned forward and kissed the baby on her forehead. "She's probably just teething," he said and turned back to the stove and resumed cooking the entrails.

He didn't see Danielle studying him.

"Can you keep an eye on her while I go out to the outhouse?" she finally asked.

He looked at her kind of surprised. "Of course," he said.

She proffered her sister to him before she realized what she was doing—handing her sister off—and she hesitated like a stutter, as if she couldn't decide if she was really going to do it, then she completed the motion and he took the baby from her arms.

She hurriedly put on her shoes and her coat and went to the door.

"Do you have the gun?" he called after her, and she paused to look at him. She patted the pocket of her coat as if that were answer enough and he went back to cooking the entrails for Stupid with one hand while he cradled Whoops with the other.

She tromped through the snow the thirty or so feet to the shed that housed the outhouse. She opened the door and stepped inside. A pair of eyes were fixed on her. She let out a scream.

She was leaning, with her back against the wall, when Zach burst through the door of the shed with the M1.

The gutted deer was dangling by its neck, its lifeless eyes staring. He thought she was going to cry.

Instead she started to laugh. She turned to him and whispered, "*You are such an asshole!*" But she couldn't stop laughing. "You could have told me about this."

But her smile began to dissolve. "Where's my sister?"

"Oh, my god!" he said and he ran back to the cabin.

Once more alone, she looked at the deer. It was thin, otherwise, it was beautiful. But it was dead. She had to look away and she went through the door and into the outhouse. She pulled down her pants and sat on the hole.

"You are *so* going to pay for scaring me," she said to herself. But she started smiling. She felt foolish for screaming.

When she stepped back into the cabin he seemed contrite.

"I'll teach you to shoot the gun, tomorrow," he said.

She nodded.

He mumbled something else.

"What?" she asked.

"I want to process the deer before we go," he said.

"Okay," she said, even though she realized this meant more time, and took her sister from his arms. "Can I help you do it? I want to see how it's done."

"I'm only doing part of it today. I'll do the rest tomorrow," he said and waited for her reply.

"Okay. But what's this?"

"It's the entrails from when I dressed out the deer. I'm cooking them for the dog."

"Can I help with that?"

"Okay. In a minute."

He put the spatula down and said, "I want you to keep turning this so it doesn't burn."

He'd cut the entrails up into smaller-sized pieces to cook faster and she moved to where he had been standing so she could man the stove.

He went to the center of the room, kicked the rug back, opened the trapdoor, and disappeared below.

When he came back up he had a jar that read "applesauce." He closed the door and kicked the rug back into place.

From a cupboard he retrieved another jar and took a small white pill from it. He popped the lid on the applesauce and spooned some out into a small bowl. Then he took a mortar and pestle from the shelf above his head and crushed the pill.

"This is a vitamin C tablet. I'll dissolve some of it into the applesauce for her. I want you to take the rest."

She watched him stir a little of the white powder into the bowl and the rest into the jar of applesauce.

"This is for Whoops," he said putting the bowl in her left hand, which also held her sister, "and this is for you," he said of the jar as he placed it in her right.

He stuck a spoon into each and took over the cooking.

Once he'd given Stupid some of the cooked entrails, he hung the rest outside the door where they'd remain cold.

Then he began processing the deer. He skinned and quartered it outside, and spent the rest of the day canning meat.

When Whoops stopped fussing, Danielle helped him.

He explained each step to her as he went along and explained *why*. And, from the questions she asked, he knew she was paying attention and catching on.

But, as the cabin got dark, he started acting moody.

All the while, her mood was brightening. She was enjoying herself. She liked learning.

When the last whispers of sunlight were coming through the window, he suddenly said, "The road's open."

"What?" she asked.

"The road; it's open."

"How do you know?"

"I saw it today."

"Oh," she said.

He became more somber. He wasn't sure what all the feelings were that were coursing through him. He wanted to apologize for not telling her about the road earlier. He wanted to apologize, *again*, for hitting her and promise once more that he'd never do it again. But of course he wouldn't do it again; she was leaving.

"What's the dynamite for?" she suddenly asked.

"You've been downstairs."

"Yeah."

"You've been sneaking around," he said petulantly.

She moved closer to him. "Yeah, I've been sneaking around because I want to know what kind of place I have my sister in. But you're not answering my question: What's the dynamite for?"

"I just have it," he said.

"Where'd you get it?"

He looked at her. "You're getting kind of pushy, aren't you?"

She smiled. "I just want to know."

He thought a second. "Back in the day, there was a lot of gold mining in this area. They worked the rivers and the beaches around Gold Beach—that's where the city got its current name, and there was some hard rock mining—you know, the kind where they dig mines into the ground."

"I came across an old mine in the backcountry, and there it was. The stuff is decades old. It's also dangerous to handle because it's so old. I didn't know that when I found it."

"How's it dangerous?"

"Old dynamite can be shock sensitive. Now that I know it, I've got to get it out of here."

"And move it where?"

"I found a place a couple of miles from here. But it will be safer to move when it gets colder. It's less sensitive, then. But it can still go off."

"So you're still going to keep it."

"Sure."

"Why?"

"I don't know. It's just nice to have."

She laughed.

"Okay," he said, "that's the wrong way to say it. I think it might someday be useful. I just haven't thought of all the uses. However, like I say, in the meantime I have to get it out of and away from my house."

"What do you mean when you say it's shock sensitive?"

"Dynamite's usually fairly safe to handle. But old dynamite can become unstable. Dropping it, banging it around, or any kind of shock can make it go kaboom. This stuff is old, and there's enough of it down there to leave nothing but a crater where this house stands."

"This place could get blown to kingdom come?"

"It could. So, let's not play with it while it's down there."

"I certainly won't," she said.

After another minute, she asked, "Why do you have jars that say 'dog' on them?"

He stepped nearer to her and they couldn't get any closer without touching. "Because I can't spell cat," he said.

She looked down at the floor and when she looked up she somehow got even closer, with her face just inches from his, yet they didn't touch. "If we're going to fight," she said calmly, "you can't be saying things that are funny."

He stared at her a long time. "Fair enough," he finally said.

"What's it taste like?" she asked.

"Like cats," he said.

A flicker of a smile crossed her face, but she controlled it.

"You're not fighting fair."

Now *he* smiled. "Okay. I don't really know. It's for 'just in case'."

"What's going to happen to Stupid?"

"No one can support a dog anymore."

"I understand that," she said. "But that's not an answer to my question. Is he going to wind up in jars?"

"Yes."

She stared blankly at the wall. That wasn't the answer she wanted to hear. She couldn't smile, now. He'd already said she could have him, but he'd starve on the road with her. Not only that, a dog made it less likely she'd get a ride and her first priority was the care of Whoops. She went back to her chair, picked up her sister, and held her in the fading light. When Whoops fussed, she fed her more applesauce.

But when she saw him feeding the dog more of the deer's cooked entrails, she couldn't help but see he seemed to enjoy Stupid as much as Stupid enjoyed him. But he was a realist, and she had to be a realist, too, and it made sense that the dog could be viewed as no more than food. But if that's the way things had to be, she wasn't sure she wanted to live in a world like that. She had to get back to the 101 before he did Stupid in.

§   §   §

She didn't remember falling asleep. One minute she started to feel the compulsion to make him like her, even though she wasn't staying, the next she was waking up as Whoops started to fuss. The cabin was dark. She had no idea what time it was and she got off the chair and picked her sister up off the blanket on the floor.

"Shh. Go back to sleep," she whispered holding her sister to her.

But she kept crying.

"Sissy is tired, Whoopsie, please go back to sleep."

She wouldn't.

She checked her diaper. "Shit," she whispered. It was loaded. She didn't want to have to look for a candle in the dark and she didn't want to wake him. She had to figure out how to change her in the dark. A sudden bright light filled the room and made her flinch.

"Where'd you get a flashlight?" she asked.

"I keep it under the couch."

"Where do you get new batteries?"

"They're rechargeable batteries. They're one of the reasons I have the solar panel on the roof."

"Can you pass me a diaper?" she asked.

He came to her. "Will you let me change her?" he asked.

Somehow, it was okay and she gave her up to him.

"Go back to sleep," he said.

"Okay. Just don't put her in any of the jars downstairs," she responded as she lay back.

"I'd have to fatten her up, first."

"That's not funny." she said.

"Yes it is," he said.

And it was. She smiled so he couldn't see her.

A while later she woke up once more to some sounds. It was still dark through the windows, but Zach was sitting on the floor, with his back to her, quietly playing with Whoops in the glow of a candle. Beside them,

Stupid was watching, apparently part of whatever games they were playing.

Had she not been so tired, she'd have joined in. But Whoopsie was safe, so she let herself slide back into the obliterating escape of sleep.

Chapter 21
August 31

Though a large gathering of the men and women, and an assortment of teenagers and children who lived on the compound had assembled in the office of Louis LaCroix, only four of the men, each now dressed in winter camo, were going to meet up with a party from the Brady compound, then head out into the back country of Curry County, Oregon, to find the man who had killed nine of their own.

The others in LaCroix's office were concerned members of the small community and well-wishers who were there to send their men off. There were still others on the compound who had wanted to be at the send-off, but were busy with the funerals or chores. Given the size of the office, LaCroix was glad they hadn't all decided to show up.

He stood in the crowded office and leaned against the front of his desk surveying the assemblage. He was in a better mood than he'd been a few days earlier for the previous meeting.

He turned to confer with Ron Goodman and asked, "Is anyone else coming?"

"Carol Parsons wanted to be here," Goodman said, "but her son got a nail through his foot, so she's treating it. The others are still mourning, doing chores..."

LaCroix waved a hand telling Goodman to stop. His question had already been answered. "You can fill the others in on what happens here, later."

Goodman nodded and, with that, LaCroix turned to the group and announced, "Can I have your attention — now?"

When the voices died down to less than a murmur, LaCroix began, "You all know the situation: Someone out there murdered four of our own—five if you count Woody Harris from two years ago. We've learned he also killed four from the Brady compound. It's created a problem we have to deal with. This may mean our survival. We think we know this guy's name but we don't know where he is. There's also rumors he's got a girl with him…"

Goodman leaned toward LaCroix and whispered something.

LaCroix didn't like needless interruptions and nodded at what Goodman had said to him. "Ron says the girl has a baby with her. But the baby's not a concern for us.

"I've asked around and some of you think you've heard this name before: Zachary Amaral. Of course, we can't be a hundred percent sure he's our guy, but it's all we have to work with. We also don't know if this guy's operating alone or if he's part of a gang. But from what our guys saw, and from what the only survivor of the massacre at the Brady compound saw, we're pretty sure he operates alone." He raised his index finger as a warning. "But we can't be sure."

"One of the Brady guys lived?" a man named Fletcher asked.

"Just until the next morning, then he died. But that's the story he told before he passed."

There was an undercurrent of voices in the room and LaCroix looked at the floor and made it obvious he wouldn't go on until they subsided. He then continued, "We agreed with Abby Brady to send four men from each compound to meet up at the old beaver pond. I chose Billy…" He nodded to Billy Raymond. "…I have a lot of confidence in his leadership abilities…" Raymond nodded grimly and remembered the dressing down he'd gotten in the previous meeting. "…Brian…" He nodded to Brian Peterson who held his Steyr SSG sniper rifle. "…Jim, because he wants to go real bad…good luck…" That got a few laughs, and he nodded to Jim De Angelis who smiled, "…and Fred Mayfield, because he's related to the Bradys, and that may help smooth some of the friction between us and them. You boys know what you have to do, and we want you to all come back safe and sound. Good luck to you all."

He hiked his thumb in Goodman's direction and said to the four, "Ron told me you got all your equipment together and you're ready to go. I also want you to take two of the walkie-talkies…Ron'll give 'em to you."

Raymond nodded.

"But I don't want any unnecessary conversation over them because this guy and any cohorts he has may be monitoring the channels. In fact, assume that every time we talk on these walkie-talkies, they hear what we're saying."

Raymond nodded again and said, "We're all set. Have you found out who the Bradys are sending up?"

"I talked with Jerry Brady. You're going to have to deal with Hank. But Jerry said he's also coming and so are the Ingram brothers: Steven and Vince. Between you, Jerry, and Fred you should be able to keep Hank in line—I hope."

There were scattered snickers around the room.

He continued with a nod to a woman named Karen Peoples and said, "Karen wanted to know why we're not sending you guys out on snowmobiles. I explained they're noisy, I don't want this guy to know you're coming; they're also eating up our fuel and we've got to conserve every drop we can—there are no more gas stations; if it gets too warm in the next few days, and the snow melts, we're going to have trouble getting them back; lastly, this guy targeted one of our snowmobiles already and we can't afford to take any more holes in them. When he hits an engine with the armor-piercing stuff he uses, it's toast." He nodded toward Karen so it was understood that he'd made her concerns known to the group.

"But there's enough snow out there to ski on and you can walk back if it melts, so there shouldn't be any problems.

"You've got enough food for three days. If you don't find him by the beginning of day three, get close enough to use the walkie-talkies and we'll arrange to get more provisions out to you with the snowmobiles or whatever other means available. We've already designated rendezvous points with code names, so we won't have to discuss exact locations over the air."

He looked directly at Raymond. "Now, I was hard on you guys during the last meeting and I still don't know how it all went wrong, but I have confidence in all of you.

"I don't have to tell you that if it turns out this guy's part of a gang *not* to engage them unless you can ambush them and end it quickly. Don't get involved in a prolonged firefight because that's when we're going to take casualties. Come back and we'll go out in force."

There was another murmur through the room.

"Don't you boys go taking any unnecessary chances," Karen said.

LaCroix looked in her direction with a scowl and said, "I can handle this."

Chastised, she looked at the floor.

He continued, "You boys listen to Billy. He knows what he's doing."

Directing his gaze at Peterson he said, "You weren't out there when your brother got killed. If this guy can be taken out with a single shot, I want *you* to do it. It's likely you can end this whole thing with one pull of the trigger and everyone comes home safe."

Peterson nodded and patted his rifle.

"I want all of you back here safe and sound and I want you to keep yourselves and each other safe. This is a team effort and we'll all be praying for you."

A voice in the room asked, "Is it okay if they don't bring Hank Brady back?" and got a lot of laughs.

LaCroix didn't mind that interruption, it loosened the tension, and even he smiled at the question.

"I know how many of you feel about Hank, and I'm not too fond of him either. But after feuding with them the last three years, there's something we can finally work on together. Let's make the most of it.

"Consider this as a 'partnership' thing with the Brady ranch," he said looking at Billy Raymond, "and that you guys have all got to count on each other — and that includes Hank.

"I don't want to hold you guys up any longer. Are there any questions?"

He looked around the room.

"How are they going to find him?" Steve Turner asked. "There's a lot of country out there."

"I've been trying to narrow down the search," LaCroix replied. "Remember when Goodman was knocking on the doors of your trailers asking for old phonebooks, no matter how old? I've been looking through them looking for the name of this character hoping I could narrow our search and give our boys a place to start."

"Not everybody had a listed phone number," Turner said.

"I know," LaCroix said. "I never did. If you looked for LaCroix in the phonebook, I didn't exist. But it's still a place to start, unless someone here can think of something else.

"I've also sent some boys up to the old county offices in Gold Beach to see if they can find the guy's name in the county register or in the deeds. But I don't have much hope for that. But we'll see."

"What about loot?" Goodman asked.

LaCroix turned back to Raymond. "If you catch this guy, and there are goods we can use, take what you can carry. I don't have to tell you to grab the most valuable stuff, first, and you know what that is: ammo, good guns, medical supplies, fuel..." He waved his hands in the air. "You know."

"And there are going to be questions about how to divvy things up with the Bradys," he said to all four men, "but I'm sure Billy can work that out.

"If this guy has a lot of stuff we can use, bring the good stuff, stow the rest, and we can send a party out to get it, later."

"Are the Bradys sending snowmobiles?" a voice asked.

"No," LaCroix replied without trying to figure out who asked the question

"What if we hide the stuff and the Bradys go back for it first?" De Angelis asked.

"If you hide stuff, *we'll* send a party right back out, as soon as you get back here, and we'll get to it first."

He turned to Goodman and loud enough for the others to hear said, "Make provisions for that so we can move fast if we have to."

Goodman nodded.

"Any other questions?"

"What about the chickens? How many are we going to try to carry through the winter?" Trent Powers asked.

Though exasperated, LaCroix smiled and others chuckled with him. "You must be here for comic relief," he said. "Trent, questions about the chickens can wait." He looked around. "Are there any other questions about the expedition?"

Marie De Angelis, Jim's De Angelis's wife, raised her hand and looking over his glasses LaCroix nodded and asked, "What, Marie?"

"The way I heard it, we ambushed *him* and he was just defending himself," she began. "I don't want my husband out there exposing himself if he doesn't have to. Wouldn't it be safer to just leave him alone and he'd leave us alone?"

The reaction was swift. For the first time in the meeting LaCroix raised his voice and, pushing the glasses back on his face he said, "The way he sat up on that hill and picked us off, he was just waiting for us when we were exposed. He shot up our equipment and, don't forget, he shot my fourteen-year-old nephew, Kyle." And putting hand to his temple like it was a gun he said, "He literally executed him."

All eyes were going back and forth from LaCroix to Marie and back again. Other voices chimed in admonishing her for raising the question and Marie now wished she hadn't said anything.

"He was in our territory," LaCroix said angrily, "and now we're going to get him and *his*. I'm sure you won't want your husband out there working while this Amaral guy, or whoever he is, is on the loose. Jim may be next. *We've got to take care of him*."

"Our territory?" Marie started to ask. "But we didn't find him on the compound..."

"That's enough," her husband snapped at her.

Other voices in the room were directed at her and got louder with comments about how they wouldn't feel safe knowing the guy was out there.

Marie could feel the pressure of the group and began nodding her head in acquiescence.

"He's killed our own, now we're going to get him and his," LaCroix now said firmly.

"Okay," Marie whispered while looking at the floor.

"Should we take any prisoners?" Mayfield asked, and the attention was diverted from Marie.

LaCroix rubbed his chin. "Billy and I have discussed that issue and he'll fill you and the other boys in on the details, once you guys are on your way.

"But broadly speaking," he said for the benefit of the others in the room, "bringing someone back here means another mouth to feed. *But,* and this is an important but, if Billy thinks we have to extract information from someone, he's got the green light to bring them in. If he thinks we can ransom someone, *maybe* for that, too. A lot of it's going to be up to Billy and he'll make the call."

"Isn't ransoming someone illegal?" another voice asked. It was Trent Powers.

LaCroix couldn't believe the question. "If someone takes a person from our ranch for ransom, yes, it's illegal. If we take someone, it's not."

That got a lot of laughs, though Powers wasn't exactly sure why, and he wasn't sure if they were laughing at him.

They were.

"Anyone else?" LaCroix asked looking around the room.

No one spoke.

"Then let's get started." But he added, "Trent, why don't you come back in a little while and we'll make a decision on the chickens."

There were a few more chuckles in the room, but Trent nodded, as if struck with his own self-importance.

The last thing LaCroix did, before the meeting was adjourned, was to cross the room to Marie De Angelis and give her a hug. "I know you're trying to help, and you're worried about Jim's safety," he said, and she began to cry in his arms.

Others in the room who had just been castigating her for her errant opinions now clucked in sympathy for her as LaCroix symbolically brought her back into the fold.

"I'm just scared," she said. But she learned never to voice her dissent, again. Though these meetings had a town-meeting feel to them, they were anything but democratic. In the end, only LaCroix's opinion mattered.

"We'll talk about it later," La Croix said. "Now, give Jim a kiss goodbye and wish him luck."

§   §   §

Fifteen minutes later, the four men got a send-off from the crowd of well-wishers, which had grown to more than eighty of the compound's residents, in the circular driveway in front of the main house on the LaCroix compound. With kisses, hand shakes, shouts, and waves, the four moved away from the compound along the old fire road trails, lumber roads, and cow paths that wound through the forest. They were heading for their rendezvous at the beaver pond, though no beavers had been there in years.

None of the other three men in the group mentioned anything to De Angelis about the outburst from his wife. And though there was little talk among them anyway, they didn't speak to him at all. He was good with that. He was still embarrassed by what his wife had done.

They moved along for three miles and reached the beaver pond well before noon and, as expected, they had to wait.

While it's one thing to move through the snow, it's quite another to have to wait in it. Minutes turned into an hour, then two, and the men got cold and were grousing about the wait when Peterson suddenly asked, "What the fuck is this?" His sharp eyes were the first to see someone coming up the trail.

Raymond stood up. "What's up?" he asked.

"Look for yourself," Peterson replied.

Now, all four men were looking down the trail to where some figures had come into view.

Raymond took out his binoculars and glassed the party approaching. There were three men walking, none were wearing skis as the members of the LaCroix party were. The big man was obviously Hank Brady and with his powerful strides he was pulling a toboggan behind him.

"They're dressed like cops," Raymond said. "Who the hell do they think they're fooling?

"Wait a minute…is that the old lady on the toboggan?"

"That's what I was talking about," Peterson said.

"What the hell is she doing here?"

"Well, they did say they were going to send four," Peterson said.

"They're supposed to send us four *men*," Raymond countered and lowered the binoculars in disgust.

"Looks like we're going to have to deal with both Hank *and* the old bag herself," Peterson pointed out.

§   §   §

When they reached the pond, Abby was sitting on the toboggan bundled up against the cold. Hank was wearing his police uniform complete with badge, sidearm, handcuffs, and heavy boots to tread through the snow. Jerry Brady and Steven Ingram were similarly dressed. They contrasted sharply to the winter camo outfits and skis the men from the LaCroix compound wore.

"Good morning, Abby," Raymond said not bothering to try to hide his irritation.

Hank beamed because he could see Raymond was upset. He was still sore from Raymond calling him an idiot when he'd gone to the Brady compound.

"I don't think it's morning anymore," Abby corrected him.

Raymond wasn't concerned with the hour of the day. "What are you doing here?" he demanded.

"We said we'd send four, and there are four of us," she said as if that was all that mattered.

"We need four *men*," Raymond said. "You told Louis that Steven's brother, Vince, was coming."

"You got four of us. Vincent couldn't make it," Abby snapped back, "And my nephew, Hank, is worth two or more of any of you, so there's yer four men."

Raymond got his walkie-talkie out and snapped it on.

"Base," he said into it, "This the field."

"You gotta talk to *daddy*," Hank chided.

Raymond ignored him.

"Base," he repeated, and all that came back was static.

Finally, Goodman's voice came over the walkie-talkie. "What's up?"

"I've gotta talk with Louis," Raymond said.

"What about?"

"Just get 'im!" Raymond shouted.

"I'll see if I can find him. But he's not going to be happy hearing you're calling and breaking radio silence, 'less someone's dead."

"Just get 'im!" Raymond repeated.

Abby said, "Look here, Billy, it was my people and my grandsons what got killed out there. So I'm here to make sure justice is done."

Hank guffawed. He wasn't going to disguise his pleasure at Raymond's annoyance.

It was several minutes before LaCroix's voice finally came on and Raymond walked away from the group.

He explained Abby's presence.

"Abby's there?" LaCroix asked incredulously.

"Yeah. So, what now?" Raymond asked. "We're a man short."

"I'm no happier with this than you are." LaCroix replied. But after a brief pause he said, "You're just going to have to deal with it."

Raymond let out a long sigh. "Okay, I just wanted you to know she's here and give you the heads-up that we're a man short."

"Do your best."

"I will," Raymond replied resignedly.

When he returned to the group he said, "Let's get this dog and pony show moving."

"What d'ya mommy say?" Hank asked.

"Fuck you, asshole," Raymond exploded.

Hank advanced toward him and Raymond was about to get into a fight he was bound to lose when Abby yelled, "Hank, *stop!*

"That's enough," she said when the two men stopped just inches apart with Hank towering over Raymond. "We're not here to fight each other; we're here to get the man who put my Sweetie in the ground. Do you both understand?

"Do you?" she yelled when neither man answered.

Raymond sensed answering her question was allowing her control, so he didn't. "Let's get moving," he said, trying to regain control of the group. "We're going to head east. There aren't that many people living out there, anymore, but we'll look for tracks and, if we meet up with anyone, we'll see who knows what about him."

"I'm not sure that's the best way to go..." Abby started.

"Then you go look for him somewhere else," Raymond snapped. "Let's move. Jim, I want you to take point," he said, meaning Jim De Angelis was to lead. "Brian, you fall back."

De Angelis started to lead at the direction of Billy Raymond with Raymond himself close behind. Then Fred Mayfield and the Bradys fell in. Finally, there was Brian Peterson, bringing up the rear with his sniper rifle.

Raymond tried to keep a pace that would tire Hank, but the big man kept up despite the toboggan he was dragging and Abby endured the rough ride so as to show the men from the LaCroix ranch that Hank was, indeed, worth two or more of any of them.

After an hour, when it became clear he was only wearing out the other men, Raymond slowed the group down; Hank wasn't going to tire. So they settled into a measured and steady pace that took them inland.

Around 6:00 p.m. Raymond told De Angelis to stop. "We'll make camp here," he announced.

The other men from the LaCroix ranch, as well as Jerry Brady and Steven Ingram, were glad to stop.

But Hank directed a barb at Raymond and asked, "What's a matter? Too tired to go on?"

Raymond ignored him, but even Abby was glad to be getting off the toboggan.

They put up tents and Raymond directed the men to build a fire to cook supper and keep warm.

"Keep it small," he warned. "We don't want to be alerting anyone in the area."

But Hank just grinned and built his own fire. He stacked wood until it was a bonfire that probably could have been seen clear to the California border. Raymond was at wit's end with dealing with him. He turned away and hoped tomorrow might bring a new day.

After they ate, De Angelis and Raymond retired to one tent, Peterson and Mayfield to another. Those from the Brady ranch had brought one big tent on the toboggan and they slept in it together.

As they lay in the dark De Angelis apologized for his wife's outburst that morning. It wasn't just an apology to Raymond, it was an apology to the world.

"It's okay," Raymond said. "She's got every right to be scared."

"I'm glad Louis was so good to her. I mean, he handled it well."

"Yeah," Raymond said. "He's a good guy."

"I really like him," De Angelis responded.

From the Brady's tent, they could hear Hank's loud voice. Raymond was sure Hank was loud just to annoy him — and he was right. But he hoped Hank would shut up soon so he could sleep, and he also hoped that there was no one else out there that might hear him and know where they were.

Gradually, the voices in the three tents got quieter as, one by one, they fell asleep.

§   §   §

Meanwhile, back at the LaCroix compound, Louis LaCroix went to the De Angelis trailer. At the beginning of his visit, he spoke angrily as he explained to her how the questions she had asked in the meeting could have upset the morale of the compound. She admitted he was right and began to cry again. With that, he lowered his voice and changed his tone. He explained to her why they had to go after Zachary Amaral and how important she and her husband were to the community. He asked her not to question him ever again and he reached out his arms and she stepped into them and cried. He held her for several minutes.

And while Jim De Angelis was out in the field looking for Zachary Amaral, or whoever it was who had killed the men from the LaCroix and Brady ranches, Louis LaCroix got in Jim De Angelis's bed and spent the night with his wife.

Chapter 22
September 1

In the morning, Zach set up his canning operation again.

Danielle stood by with Whoops in her arms and watched curiously. She wanted to see the steps he went through.

"You do a lot of this canning stuff, don't you," she stated.

"Not really. I don't usually have much to can except after I've harvested my garden. Getting the deer and the bear were purely serendipitous, and you gotta make hay while the sun shines." He paused for a second. "There's an adage that's going to disappear."

"What's the word mean?" she asked.

He thought about what he'd said. "Which one? Serendipitous or adage?"

"The first one; I know what an adage is."

"It means to stumble across something good when you're not really looking for it."

"Like you finding the bear, then the deer?" she asked.

He nodded.

"*Serendipitous*…I like that word," she said, rolling it on her tongue with a smile.

"Serendipitous is the adjective, it describes the event; serendipity is the noun, the event itself."

He could almost feel her filing the word away in her mind. He liked not only that she was smart, but that she was curious and wasn't afraid to ask questions.

"It's been weeks since I last canned," he said returning to their original discussion, "and months since I've canned any meat. So, while I've got it, I've got to take advantage of it."

"Can I help again?" she asked.

"I was hoping you would."

She put her sister on the floor and started doing what he instructed her to do.

He'd brought in a hindquarter from the deer and showed her how to cook the meat, first, then pack the venison into quart jars with some salt, then fill the empty spaces with some of the stock he'd made the day before from the bear's bones. Then he put the jars in the pressure canner.

In a large pot he started making some stew and, again, explained to her what he was doing each step along the way.

Danielle helped herself to little scraps of cooked meat now and then with no complaints from him.

There was a lot of physical contact in the small space in which they worked; his arm against hers, her hip bumping into his. He didn't push for it, but he liked it. He didn't know how aware she might be of it. She seemed oblivious.

All the while, Stupid sat patiently and watched them.

Danielle stopped for a second, then dropped a small piece of cooked venison on the floor in front of the dog. He ate it quickly, then sat poised for more.

"Don't put any more stuff down for him." Zach said.

"Why?"

"Just don't."

"He's hungry."

"I know."

"Then why can't I feed him?"

It was a simple question. She wasn't trying to provoke him. They seemed to be getting along very well, as a team. But he wouldn't answer. She became suspicious.

"Why can't I feed him?" she repeated.

"It'll be wasted," he finally said.

She stared at him but he wouldn't look at her. He just kept cutting the meat. Accidentally, he cut his finger. He rinsed and dried it then put a Band-Aid on it. He'd been pretty deft up to now with his knives, so she thought it was odd that he'd cut himself. He went back to cutting the meat.

"What do you mean, 'it'll be wasted,'" she asked.

He stopped, stared at the wall before him, and said, "It'll make him harder to clean out."

She couldn't believe what she was hearing and she was suddenly angry. "I'm feeding him anyway."

"*Stop!*" he ordered.

"You're not going to kill him!" she yelled.

He stopped cutting. "I'll do anything I want!" he yelled back.

"Why?"

"Because I can't afford to feed him through the winter. Every bite of food I feed that dog is going to be a bite out of my mouth!" he yelled and cut another finger.

"I'll take him with me," she said.

"How are you going to feed him? How are you going to get a ride. He'll starve to death or someone will take him and...and..."

"*Kill him just like you're going to do!*" she screamed.

"What do you care? You're not going to be here."

The commotion started Whoops crying and sent Stupid skulking across the room. He lay down near Danielle's chair and Whoops.

Danielle spun, went back to her chair, picked up her sister, and plunked herself down. She pulled her knees up and stared into space.

Whoops kept crying.

"Shut up!" she screamed. For just a second Whoops stopped and stared wide-eyed at her sister, then she cried even louder.

"Oh, my God, I'm sorry, Whoopsie." She hugged her and started rocking, but the baby wouldn't stop.

"Sissy didn't mean to yell at you," she said softly.

"Come on," Zach said slamming things down on the counter. He headed for the door with dog in tow. In his right hand he had his large, sharp carving knife. He wouldn't look at Danielle as he passed her.

He opened the door and yelled, "Out!" and the dog, not used to Zach yelling at him, cautiously went out ahead of him. Zach followed and slammed the door as hard as he could behind himself.

As soon as he was gone, Danielle started crying and Whoops cried louder, again.

"I can't believe I was getting to trust him," she said to Whoops. "I was even getting to like him. Now I see what kind of jerk he is. I hate him. I hate this whole damned world."

§   §   §

Once outside, Stupid sniffed around in the snow. Zach stood and watched him going from bush to bush looking for new smells.

He lifted a leg and peed.

Good, that would mean his bladder was empty.

Then he defecated. That was even better.

"Come on," Zach said and started walking up to the shed and the dog, as obedient as ever, followed him as he went behind the shed.

Once there Zach stood and watched the dog sniff around in the snow again.

Finally, he said, "Come 'ere boy," and the dog came right to him. It was trusting. It was making this easy.

In one motion Zach reached down, grabbed Stupid by the scruff of the neck and pulled its head back exposing its throat. He would make this quick and painless so the dog wouldn't suffer.

§   §   §

Twenty minutes later he came back in. He slammed the door behind himself and startled Whoops and she began crying once more. He wouldn't look at Danielle as he returned to the stove. He washed his hands and his knife. He was noisy this time as he worked. Twice more he cut himself, swore each time, and had to stop what he was doing so as to clean out the wound and put on a Band-Aid.

"Good," she muttered under her breath each time he cut himself.

But now she had to use the outhouse. She wished she'd gone out, before he'd taken Stupid out.

She held it as long as she could. But, in the end, nature won out and the pressure in her bladder became too much. With a great deal of reluctance, she finally got up, put on her coat, and went to the door with her sister in her arms. As she went outside, she slammed the door behind herself.

"Bitch," Zach mumbled to himself.

"Asshole," she said to herself once the door was closed between them.

She walked up to the shed and the outhouse, but she paused at the door. Her hand reached out, but she couldn't bring herself to touch the knob.

"I could have stopped him," she said to herself.

She reached for the knob, again. But she knew what she was going to see.

She turned, went behind the cabin and, holding Whoops, she struggled to get her pants down. None of this was easy with the baby in her arms, but she managed, squatted, and started to pee. But she couldn't hold the baby, squat, and keep her balance while she was peeing and, when she started to teeter, she did everything she could to protect her sister and..."Ooooh!"...she fell over and sat in her own urine.

"That son-of-a-bitch," she said then got up and tried to clean herself off.

She was cold, she was wet, and she was dirty. But she was done.

When she came back in the cabin, she slammed the door as hard as she could, and threw herself back in her chair.

"I want to leave here in the morning. I don't want to learn to shoot your gun. I don't want your gun."

Without turning around, he said, "It's up to you," and he cut himself, again.

"Shit," he said.

"Good!" she screamed out loud.

In the little time she knew him, Stupid had been such a good dog, she told herself. He'd trusted Zach, trusted her, and liked Whoops. And what had it gotten him? A death sentence. She couldn't imagine how she could have started liking Zach. He was as bad as the Bradys.

There was a sound at the door. She looked at it. She looked at Zach, but he was still busy at the stove.

There went the sound, again.

He turned to her and gave her a petulant look as if she should get off her ass and see what it was.

She carried Whoops to the door and opened it and Stupid came back in and went right to the stove where he maintained his vigil waiting for handouts. Zach fed him a piece of cooked meat.

She went to the stove and stood staring at Zach. He had five Band-Aids on his left hand now.

She continued staring but he wouldn't look at her.

Finally, he put the knife down. *"What?"*

"I thought you were going to kill him."

"I changed my mind."

"Why?"

"I can change my mind, can't I?"

"Are you going to do it tomorrow?" she demanded.

He continued cutting the meat and didn't answer.

"Well, are you?" she asked.

"No," he said softly.

"The day after?"

He didn't like being grilled. "No," he said with a little anger in his voice.

"Next week?"

"No," he shouted.

"Are you ever going to do it?"

"Yes," he said in his normal voice.

"When?"

"On his birthday," he said sharply.

"When's his birthday?" she demanded.

"I don't know, he's a smart dog and he won't tell me."

He cut himself, again.

"Why don't you just cut all your fingers off and can those? It's the only thing you've been able to do right all day," she said.

He tried not to smile. That would be letting her win. Finally, he did. "I thought we were going to fight fair," he said.

She didn't say anything, because she'd smile if she did.

"Why don't you help me?" he asked in a nice voice.

"Okay," she said.

She put Whoops down and washed her hands and Zach took a bunch of cooked scraps and fed them to Stupid.

After she dried her hands, she reached down and petted Stupid on his head, then scratched him behind his ears.

"Oh-oh. Gotta wash, again," she said, and she did.

"I'm glad you're conscientious," he said.

"I've been watching you," she said.

They went back to work and, eventually, because of the small space, there was more contact between them. He didn't want to think about how it was making him feel, but he didn't want it to stop, either. He didn't know if she was aware of it or not.

"Why did you really change your mind about the dog?" she finally asked, but she asked very nicely. It occurred to her that he might just wait until she was gone to do it.

He mumbled something.

"What?" she asked and stepped closer to hear him better, her forearm against his.

"I started to do it, but I realized I like him," he said.

"He likes you, too, in case you hadn't noticed."

Zach stopped cutting and looked at the dog. For the first time, it occurred to him that the dog did indeed like him.

As they finished, he brought in another quarter and they canned that together, working until evening. Altogether, they got thirty quarts of venison and venison stew. Then Zach said they should clean up before the cabin got dark, and they did, neatly and efficiently, as a team.

When they were done, she went back to her chair and read in the gathering gloaming. He then set out some candles for light. She knew this was a luxury, and though it allowed her to continue reading, he seemed to have done it more for himself than for her. He sat on the floor and played with Whoops for hours. Every once in a while, she looked up from her book and watched them. Whoops was bonding with him.

§   §   §

Late in the night she was awakened. The last thing she remembered was cuddling up on the chair in the dark with her sister. Now there was a dim light in the cabin and Whoops wasn't with her.

She looked across the room and Zach had her up on the table and was changing her diaper in candle light.

When he heard her stir, he looked at her.

"She was crying," he said. "She pooped her pants again. I'm changing her."

"Thank you," Danielle said. "Tomorrow morning, teach me to shoot the gun."

"Okay."

A minute later he brought Whoops back to her, blew out the candle, and they both lay in the dark, he on his couch, she in her chair until Whoops started crying again.

"Oh, Whoopsie," she whispered, "I need to sleep."

Seconds later the candle was relit. She hadn't even heard him get up. He came to her.

"I can't sleep," he said. "Let me take her so you can."

"You don't mind?" she asked.

He didn't answer. And she couldn't see his face. All she could see in the dim light were his outstretched arms offering to take her.

She handed her sister to him and said, "Thank you. I'm going to need sleep if I'm going to get on the road."

He didn't say anything. He just took Whoops, sat on the floor with her, and played with her again.

Chapter 23
September 1

The President; his National Security Advisor, Fred Cotta; and his speechwriter, Sam Feinberg were the last to enter the Roosevelt Room directory across the hall from the Oval Office in the White House.

"Ladies and gentlemen, remain in your seats," the President said as several of the men and women began to rise. "We've got a lot to do. Let's dispense with the courtesies and formalities and get down to business."

Although the attendees knew the agenda, he reminded them, "The purpose of this meeting is to map out my *Address to the Nation*, tonight. I'd like this to be quick.

"What's happening with the states?" he asked as he slid into his seat. The question was directed at the Secretary of Homeland Security, Deanna Knox.

"Hawaii just announced secession," she said.

"That makes ten," the President said, though everyone in the room knew the count.

"Intel says that should be the last of them, though we're not absolutely sure which way South Carolina is going to go," she said.

The President looked at her as if encouraging her to continue.

"We're in touch with Governor Brackett and he's assured us South Carolina is with us, but intel says he's fence-sitting," she added.

The President nodded. "Do we know how to get in touch with him?

"No."

"That's not good. If we can find him, I want to talk with him. I don't care what I'm doing. Interrupt me if you have to and let me go tete-a-tete with him. Until we can get some assurances from him, I'm going to assume South Carolina may try to leave, too.

"What about the other governors...the ones in the states claiming to have seceded?"

"They're all incommunicado. But we're still attempting to reach each and every one of them."

"Do we yet know if the secessionists are banding to form a separate country?" he asked, meaning if they were duplicating the actions of the states that had seceded and founded the Confederates States of America during what some called America's first Civil War and others called the War Between the States.

"Not yet," Knox replied. "There was obvious coordination in their announcements, so we assume there's a confederation of sorts, but they haven't announced one yet."

"Is that something we can find out?" he asked Howard Davies, the Director of the CIA.

"We're looking into it, Mr. President," Davies said.

"Let me know what you discover," the President said as he looked down at the sheaf of papers he'd brought with him.

He turned to General Elias French, the Combatant Commander of NORTHCOM. "What's the military assessment, General French?"

The general replied, "We've mobilized troops and we've moved on all ten of the states' capitals—plus Columbia," he added, referring to South Carolina's capital, though South Carolina's status was still not clear. "We've taken several of the governors's mansions and the legislative houses, and we've gone to many personal residences—but we're not sure where they all are and we're stretching ourselves thin as it is. The state legislators we've found say they're not part of the secession, but we're holding them under the *Preventative Detention Act*. But we haven't found any of the *avowed* secessionists, including state governors. We can't even find Governor Brackett," he said referring back to South Carolina's governor. "All of our moves to find and arrest them have been anticipated. They're in hiding. As Secretary Knox pointed out, the secession seems to have been well-coordinated."

"Our political opponents are saying the mass arrests are unconstitutional," the Vice President, Henry Rickers, said.

The President understood Rickers wasn't taking the secessionists's side, he was merely informing him of what they were saying. The President shuffled through the papers before him until he found a page he was looking for and began to read from it, "Article 1, Section 9 of the U.S. *Constitution* states, 'The privilege of the Writ of Habeas Corpus shall not be suspended, unless when in Cases of Rebellion or Invasion, the public Safety may require it.' I want this text to be part of the speech," he said again to Sam, "along with the statement that habeas corpus has been suspended until further notice. Also include that, with amendments to the *Insurrection Act*, passed by the Congress last year, we have the authority to invoke a military presence to stop domestic terrorism and to aid in the event of natural disaster. And right now we have both terrorism and a natural disaster."

In an aside to Feinberg he said, "I would like you to include wording...a summation of both the *Insurrection Act* and the *Preventative Detention Act*."

"Will do, Mr. President," Feinberg said.

"Where are the loyalties of the troops?" the President asked General Winston Turnbull, the Chairman of the Joint Chiefs of Staff.

"Among some units, morale is high. Some, it's not so good. Overall, it's good."

"I'm not asking about morale. Where are their *loyalties*?"

"Frankly, Mr. President, it depends on whether they're being fed. The best-fed units are loyal. Other units would follow anyone who offered them a sandwich."

The comment got the only smile the President would make during the meeting.

"What about the units that are being disbanded?" he asked.

"We've put that on hold," the General responded. "But we don't know how much longer we can maintain them. Too many of the units we've officially discharged have been recruited by the warm states, and some of them have gone over. Others have formed gangs—become road pirates. The ones that have joined the states are bringing their equipment including weapons and ammunition stores with them. If we disband too many units, the states are going to have more armed troops than we will."

He continued, "Though keeping them active is creating a strain on our resources—we haven't the food or medical resources to care for them all—we've determined it is the best action to take in the near-term, unless otherwise directed."

"Have the units that have gone to the states been told they're committing treason...?

"Yes, Sir."

"...and is that your recommendation: To keep the remaining active units active for the time being?" the President asked.

"Yes, Mr. President. Keep *all* the remaining units active until the states are back in the fold. Letting them defect to the secessionist states is unacceptable."

"I agree. But where will the food to feed these units come from? Where do the medical supplies come from?"

"They have to be diverted from the..."

"That was a rhetorical question," the President said. They all knew they were being diverted from the civilian population.

"Yes, Sir."

The President conferred with his National Security Advisor in a low voice for several minutes while the others sat patiently in the room.

"What's the overall food situation," he asked FEMA Administrator Alberto Martinez.

"We can barely provide starvation rations to twenty-five percent of the people in the country and, by the end of the year, that figure will be down to less than twenty percent. To make matters worse, much of the food we try to distribute to the citizens is stolen before it reaches them and it's created a black market of the stolen commodities. But even food on the black market is drying up."

The President didn't say anything, as if expecting him to go on.

"When the ice age began," Martinez said, "the nation had a seventy-two-day food supply. That was seventy-two days with everyone eating pretty much what they wanted. With the current rationing we probably have less than three weeks, and most of that is in the warm states which makes access to it problematic. And, as we all know, we're consuming it faster than we can produce it."

The President paused and made more notes. Then he looked up and asked General Turnbull, "What's happening at the border with Mexico?"

"Americans are trying to enter Mexico," Turnbull said, "but the Mexican government has assembled troops at all the official crossing points and they aren't letting anyone in — even Mexican nationals trying to return home, whether they had come to this country legally or illegally."

The President grimly nodded.

"May I add what I've gotten from National Academy of Sciences, NOAA, and experts with various other groups?" Martinez asked.

"Go on."

"With the abrupt disruption and changes in agriculture occurring all over the world, there isn't a single country with enough food to feed itself. Demographers, the people who study populations..."

"I know what demographers are," the President said sharply.

Martinez nodded without looking at the President. "...and other experts now claim there will have to be a great dying-off before populations can stabilize, and no one knows how long that will take to happen or how much worse the ice age is going to get. But the consensus is that, if this is a full-blown ice age, it's going to last tens of thousands of years."

The President picked up one of his papers and glanced at it. It triggered his next question. "In our last meeting, questions about the roads came up.

What about them? What's happening with the transportation system, General French?"

"Key roads are kept open by the Army. Here on the East Coast, there are points along I-95 where we've had problems with road pirates who have tried to inhibit the flow of traffic. But as the problems arise, we've dealt with them. There are bigger problems along US 101, that runs from Seattle to San Diego. Road pirates there have been intercepting people trying to flee south — robbing them, killing hundreds, perhaps thousands — and they have, on occasion, damaged, destroyed, or blocked roads and bridges to make those fleeing the north easier to rob."

"Where are these people, the ones leaving the north, getting fuel to make the trip south?"

"We can't always be certain. Fuel became something people began to hoard before the gas stations closed, and it has become the most important barter commodity, after food, guns, and ammo. Some, we're sure, has been stolen from military stores."

"Probably much of all those commodities — food, guns, and ammo — come from military supplies," the President said as he made another note.

"How severely do these road pirates disrupt the roads?" he asked.

"Blockades and damage to roads and bridges along US 101 have, in the past, prevented the Army and the Army Corps of Engineers from maintaining the dams on the Columbia River, they've disrupted access to the nuclear facilities at Hanford, Washington, and interfered with the distribution of food and medical supplies. And, now, they could disrupt efforts to stop the secessions."

"Do you think the road pirates are siding with the states?"

"They don't care about the states unless the states come after them, and they don't, anymore. What the road pirates want is to stall traffic so they can prey on the people fleeing south. A year ago we were tasked to come up with a solution. Now, when we discover that a band of road pirates has damaged or blocked roads or bridges, making them impassable, we have elite units," he said with subtle emphasis on the word 'elite,' "from the 3rd Infantry Division, trained to deal with them."

"Let's talk about that," the President said.

General French continued, "Mobile units go in first, deal with those who have created the problem, and they are followed by the Corps which is tasked with the repair of whatever damage has been done..."

"And they have succeeded, so far, in minimizing interference by the road pirates and in restoring the orderly flow of traffic," the President said.

"Yes, sir."

The President nodded and, because California was still the most populous, as well as the largest industrial and agricultural state, and it was a key to maintaining the Union, he asked, "What's happening in California?"

"We still have a presence at most of the military bases including Camp Pendleton, Edwards, China Lake, and other facilities, though troop numbers have necessarily been reduced. The Army now maintains the Golden Gate Bridge, otherwise, the roads and almost all the other bridges are still controlled and maintained by the State."

"Is the Army still at the Golden Gate?" the President asked.

"Yes, but the California Highway Patrol has asked them to leave. They claim the Army is on sovereign Californian soil."

"Have any of the confrontations between the Army and the locals deteriorated...or escalated...into shooting confrontations?" the President asked.

"No. But, as of yesterday, local police forces and the California National Guard are not allowing any movement by the Army, Army supply convoys, or units of the Corps in California, and they're presently stalled and awaiting orders."

There was a silence in the room while the President made more notes.

"Instruct the units at the Golden Gate to stay there," the President said without looking up. "I think it's a strategic point on the 101 and it's symbolic that we keep the bridge."

"I agree," the General said.

As he made more notes the President added, "We are not withdrawing from any of the states. If we can find him, I'll speak with Stottlemyer," he said mentioning the California governor by his last name, "and explain our situation. I'll also explain that we will *not* tolerate interference with Army units in any of the states by *any* state agencies. If I don't get in touch with the governor, we will ask whoever we can reach to convey that message to him and I will also include that message in tonight's address. He won't be able to claim he missed it."

Everyone in the room knew that reaching the Governor was unlikely and it would merely be a perfunctory call, used to buy time while the machinery for getting the Army on the move again was put into gear.

"We need the roads open. We need the transportation links to remain intact to provide food and to stop the insurrection," the President said. "Roads are the glue that's going to hold this country together."

He glanced at Sam Feinberg and, referring to the radio address he was scheduled to deliver that night, he said, "I want it made abundantly clear that the country is still a Union. I also want to emphasize that those advocating or espousing secession are traitors and that those blocking or damaging roads, bridges, rail lines, airports, canals and other waterways, seaports, and anything else of that kind, are committing treason and, under the terms of martial law, will be dealt with swiftly and effectively."

The President continued, "Add...no, *stress*...that the only way we are going to be able to feed people is if we maintain the Union."

Feinberg glanced at the President. He knew there was no way all the people were going to be fed, but he understood the President's motivation for saying this.

"I also want you to include that the secessionists are taking all the food and are hoarding it."

"That could be dangerous," Cotta said. "It's no secret there isn't enough food to feed everybody. We'll have no credibility at all if we claim there is."

"Then make a suggestion."

"Tell them it's the only way to *produce* more food and get on the road to recovery."

The President pondered that. Finally, he said to Fienberg, "Include that. If we can't give them food, let's give them hope," he added.

Or hype, Cotta thought to himself.

Feinberg made notes.

"Let's get back to the problem of the road pirates," the President said to the room. "What about them?"

"They're a problem and we're losing credibility because we're not dealing with them. The states are promising *they* will," Knox said.

"Are they?"

"No. But this is another case where perception is everything. However, intel tells us the states are reluctant to bear down on them because they would like them as allies. Plus, the road pirates are usually not bothering the citizens of the states in which they live, they're preying on the emigrants fleeing from further north. Since the warm states don't want the emigrants and the road pirates have become a deterrent to travel, their activities are tolerated."

"How serious are the road pirates from our point of view?" the President asked.

"May I field that question?" General French asked.

"Go ahead, General."

"Along stretches of the West Coast, from the Golden Gate north to southwestern Oregon, they're very active. Below the Golden Gate there are fewer freelance gangs because south of San Francisco and Sacramento it's law enforcement that's preying on the travelers, and they're doing it with the tacit approval of Sacramento. The legal justification is that if you now have food or fuel, you must have come by them in some illegal manner, so California is using the *RICO Act* to 'arrest' the property — the same thing other states and the federal government have been doing. There's also the perception, from Sacramento's point of view, that the emigrants are not welcome, they're invaders, and the states's actions are tacitly meant to be a deterrent. It's somewhat similar to what happened in southern California during the Great Depression when the locals didn't want emigrants from the Dust Bowl coming into the state and straining the state's resources."

"The difference is that during the Depression law enforcement didn't steal everything you had," the President interjected.

"Times are different, now," the general said and the President acknowledged the statement with a nod.

"Recently," French continued, "we had a problem with a band of road pirates living near Trinidad, California, in Humboldt County, in the northern part of the state. They severely damaged a bridge on Highway 101 and completely stopped the flow of traffic. It was clearly a plan to create a bottleneck where the emigrants were trapped. The trouble was, it also impeded the Army. The Army's 3rd Infantry Division's 1st Brigade moved in with the Corps of Engineers behind them. We don't have the resources to arrest, detain, or imprison large bodies of population. We've already discovered people will break the law simply to get arrested and fed. So we don't do that anymore. We deal with domestic terrorists swiftly and on the spot.

"Frankly, Mr. President, it is widely known that when the 1st Brigade went into the compound, they left no survivors and we haven't had a problem with the roads being damaged or blocked by any of the gangs along the 101, since."

The President didn't comment on the "no survivors" statement except to say, "These are difficult times."

"Further north, along the Pacific Coast," the general continued, "there are still problems with road pirates in Del Norte County, also in northern California, and Curry County, in southwestern Oregon. These counties all lie along 101. These gangs intercept the people fleeing south, rob them, and there have been stories of kidnappings and murders."

"What do you recommend, General?"

"We don't have the resources to deal with it. It should be dealt with as a local police matter, and it isn't. However, as I pointed out, the road pirates now know that if they block or in any way damage the roads, bridges, and key rail lines, the 3rd will deal with them."

"I know this came up in previous meetings. But what I want to know is: Are all of these gangs, these self-styled road pirates, aware of the consequences of blocking or damaging the roads?"

"Yes, Sir, they've all been apprised."

"Otherwise, they're largely left alone?" the President asked.

"Unless they block the roads, yes. Besides, we're afraid if we disrupt the status quo, they will engage our troops in a guerilla war and further dilute our effectiveness in dealing with the states. It's become a temporary live-and-let-live situation."

Finally, the President looked first at General Turnbull then at General French and said, "Gentlemen, your orders right now are to keep posted troops where they are at whatever key roads, bridges, buildings, or other facilities we have deemed important. Inform all resupply convoys they are to carry out their orders and to resupply the units they've been sent to maintain. If they meet resistance, they are to query us, first, and they will be directed as to how they should deal with the problem. Even if I cannot reach Governor Stottlemyer, I expect the Army to keep open the key roads the federal government needs in California, until further notice. Otherwise, deal with the road pirates only when necessary and on a contingency basis, and until we find out whose side they're on. Right Fred?" he asked Cotta.

"Yes, Mr. President."

"With the exception of nonessential units, there will be no more disbanding of the troop units until further notice. They are to be fed, but with ration cuts to all but the most important active units." As an aside to the two Generals he said, "I know what I'm saying is difficult and it is going to stretch your resources until you think they are going to snap, but we're going to have to deal with it for now."

Addressing Secretary Knox he said, "Food stores are to be guarded and maintained. Theft from these stores is to be dealt with severely; it is now, by Executive Order, a capital offense to steal, divert, or interfere with the disposition of the food stores."

He read more from the list for several minutes until he reached a point where he said, "Other than what we've cleared for public consumption, none of what has been discussed here is to go any further than this room, especially with regard to the possible future disbanding of more military units. Anything the public has to know they will hear in my radio address, tonight."

He looked around the table to make sure he was understood.

Turning to Sam Feinberg, then to the others in the room, he said, "I want tonight's address to focus on six points:

"First, I want to begin with efforts being put forth, here in Washington, to cope with the climate change.

"Second, I will reaffirm that all active military units will continue to operate. There will be no future disbanding of military units."

The generals nodded.

"Third, food reserves will be distributed so everyone will get a 'fair share.'

"I want 'fair share' to be in the speech," he said in an aside to Feinberg.

"There *will* be rationing but ample food for all will become available once we're on the road to recovery. Hoarders, whether they obtained their reserves before the ice age began or since then, are required to notify local authorities of their reserves and it will be treasonous to keep reserves concealed from lawful authorities. Any 'surpluses found in private hands will be taken under the terms of the *RICO Act* and the hoarders will be dealt with harshly.'"

"With all due respect..." Martinez said.

The President didn't like being interrupted and glared at him.

Martinez nervously continued, "...are there measures in place to ensure caches of food, medical, fuel, and other supplies will come into the system as they're discovered? What we're finding is that when such supplies are discovered, they disappear before they get into the system."

"We're working on that," the President said.

Returning to his notes the President read, "Fourth...this is the fourth point, isn't it?" He'd lost count because of the interruption.

"It's the fourth," Sam confirmed in a low voice.

"Fourth, secession and insurrection are illegal and will not be tolerated.

"Sam, I want you to include the text from *Article 1, Section 9*, of the *Constitution* concerning the suspension of habeas corpus. It's only about two dozen words...and make mention of both the *Insurrection Act* and *Preventative Detention Act*. I want to stress to the listeners that the country is still under martial law and that state officials—or their agents—participating in secession are outlaws and they are committing treason and will be punished.

"Make it clear what suspension of habeas corpus means and that violators may be subject to court-martial by the various local military tribunals."

Sam made more notes.

The President paused again. "Also, I don't want to use the term 'warm states' in my address."

Sam thought a second and, again in a low voice, he said, "How about 'outlaw states'? Everyone will know what you're talking about."

The President thought a second. "Let me think about that.

"Don't include the message warning Governor Stottlemyer unless we can't reach him by late this afternoon," he said to Feinberg.

"Fifth, any interference with lawful authorities, including military, law enforcement, and contracted agents lawfully acting on the behalf of the United States government, is both terrorism and treason, and will be treated as capital offenses which will be dealt with accordingly, under the terms of the *Insurrection Act*..."

He turned to Sam again. "...put in the word 'swiftly,' too. They'll know what that means. And add that it doesn't matter whether the interference comes from local law enforcement or...find a word for 'private' here so the road pirates will understand I mean them."

Sam wrote furiously but confidently.

The President paused and looked around. "Who came up with this term 'road pirates'?"

"It's just fallen into the parlance," Secretary Knox said.

"I do not want the term 'road pirates' used," the President said. "It's got a romantic connotation and I'd like to avoid it."

"But," he said to Sam, "I still want the wording so it's clear who we mean."

"'Unlawful gangs and terrorists'...we might even add in the phrase 'so-called road pirates,'" Sam said in a low voice.

The President scowled. It still contained the words "road pirates."

"Seditionists, radicals..."

"Come up with something," the President said.

He paused again. He wanted precision in what he said and in a low voice conferred for a moment with his National Security Advisor to ask which point he was on before continuing with, "Sixth, disruption of lines of communication and travel—this includes interfering with the flow of Federal traffic, including military traffic, along roads, bridges, rail lines, and airports, but not limited to those—is a Federal crime and a capital offense and will be dealt with swiftly and without benefit of trial. Furthermore, it will *not* matter whether the perpetrators are road pirates...or whatever substitute for 'road pirates' Sam comes up with...or those following the orders of illegally-acting state government officials, and they will be dealt with accordingly."

"Mr. President, may I make a suggestion?"

It was only because the President valued Fred Cotta's advice that he nodded.

"We can't send an ambiguous message. Everyone knows what the road pirates are. You've got to refer to them directly or you're going to lose some of your audience. Castigate them, demonize them, call them wanton criminals and predators, but you must be clear about whom you are referring."

The President thought about it. "Can you handle that?" he asked Feinberg.

Sam Feinberg nodded without looking up.

The President nodded to Cotta, then asked, "Ladies and gentlemen, are there any questions or other inputs?" he asked.

"I think the message is clear," General Turnbull said.

"It's a very good speech," Secretary Knox said.

There were nods all around.

"It'll be a good speech *after* Shakespeare here gets done with it," the President said, referring to Sam.

"Should you discuss people attempting to cross the border in your speech?" Martinez asked.

"Which border?" the President asked because there were emigrants attempting to enter the United States from Canada.

"The border with Mexico."

He turned to Sam, again. "Make it clear it is illegal and treasonous to attempt to take food out of the country, even if it's for personal use. Otherwise, anyone who wants to leave and go to Mexico or anywhere else is welcome to.

He thought about the second part. *"Don't* put that last sentence in the speech," he said in an aside to Sam.

Feinberg nodded his head in confirmation.

The President continued. "But while we're on the subject of the borders, it's been brought to my attention that we've got to take stronger measures to block the influx of Canadians trying to cross into the country. However, we're not going to address that tonight. It's been pointed out it would be construed as an admission of desperation on our part to deny Canadians entry into the country."

There were nodded assents.

"So, we'll send more troops to likely crossing points, but it will not be publically discussed."

He didn't bother to note that in an earlier meeting they had decided that the military buildup by Mexico, along its almost two-thousand-mile-long border with the United States, that stretched from San Diego, California, and Tijuana, Baja California, in the west to Brownsville, Texas, and Matamoros, Tamaulipas, in the east, could become pretext for future options and actions, since Mexico was now perceived as a candidate for future U.S. expansion if climatic conditions got worse.

The President continued, "I also want a change in vocabulary. We have been using the term 'state of emergency' with little success. We will now invoke the term 'martial law.' 'State of emergency' no longer exists and it will no longer appear in any documents."

"What about the upcoming elections?" Carlos Ruiz, the Attorney General asked.

"It's too soon to talk about that," the President said, though most of those present already knew the decision to cancel them had already been made. Besides, since it was now considered illegal to speak out against the various programs, many of those in the opposition party had already been arrested. It was "necessary."

The President sat back in his seat, a sure sign he was finished with the meeting. "If there are no other questions or inputs," he said, "I'd like to adjourn this meeting. We will meet again tomorrow morning at this same time, after responses to the speech start coming in, and after we receive updates on what's happening with the secessionists."

With that, he rose from his seat. "Thank you for your time," he said, and the others rose with him and the meeting was adjourned.

Two hours later, Sam Feinberg laid the finished speech on the President's desk. It contained the message about secession that was specifically addressed to Stottlemyer, the California governor and made reference to the "outlaw states."

The address was broadcast that evening, and rebroadcast several times over the next several days (and analyzed and reanalyzed by commentators), as millions of Americans listened.

Chapter 24
September 2

Danielle awoke with a start. Her sister wasn't in the chair with her. With panic rising up into her throat she came out of her early-morning grogginess and sat straight in the chair.

She looked around and saw him. He was sitting on the couch watching her. In his lap he held Whoops. He was feeding her. It started coming back to her that she had willingly surrendering her sister to him in the middle of the night.

He was wearing some kind of earphones. "Good morning," he said tentatively. He saw the fear on her face and he took part of the headset away from one of his ears to hear her response.

She leaned back in her chair and, pulled the blanket up over her shoulder and turned away. She sat like that a long time. Whoops seemed comfortable with him and even she was beginning to feel...comfortable. But she was dead tired.

She peered back and he was still listening to whatever was coming through the headphones while he fed Whoops and whispered to her. Whoops seemed rapt as she listened.

"How long can you watch her?" Danielle finally asked.

"I can watch her all morning."

There was a ring of sincerity in his voice.

"Good, 'cause I need sleep before we go," she said as she turned away and pulled the blanket over her face to block the light.

"Go ahead. I'm going to take her out and bait a bear trap with her so we can get more meat."

She was beginning to see he had a sense of humor. "She's tough," she said while smiling, but so Zach couldn't see her. "She'll knock the stuffing out of a bear."

"I know. It was her idea."

Danielle smiled again, but still didn't let him see it, then closed her eyes and in seconds she fell back to sleep.

Chapter 25
September 2

Billy Raymond awoke to the crack of a single gun shot. He scrambled and stumbled from his tent, still half asleep, with his rifle at the ready. De Angelis came out behind him with his own rifle. Mayfield emerged from the tent he shared with Peterson looking confused and scared. Waiting for them, with the rest of the Brady clan, was Hank, his rifle in his hands, and a smirk on his face.

"Time to get up," Hank announced.

"What the fuck are you shooting at?" Raymond demanded.

"You were gonna sleep the day away."

"No shooting," Raymond yelled. "We don't want anyone to hear us."

"There ain't no one around here," Hank said.

"How do you know that?"

"Ain't no one shootin' back, is there?"

Raymond realized Hank was baiting him, but he couldn't help himself and yelled, "What if there's someone close by?"

"Then they knows we're here," Hank said logically knowing it had nothing to do with why Raymond asked the question.

There was nothing Raymond could do. He wanted to punch the bastard, but he couldn't win in a fight with the brute. Nothing short of shooting him would make him back off, and shooting him would leave more than just Hank dead.

"Control him," Raymond yelled at Abby, and immediately wished he hadn't because he was asking her to help lead, a request that was the furthest thing from his mind.

"Okay, everybody," he said, "let's eat and get moving."

"We already et," Abby said.

That meant they'd been up awhile. "Can we do some things together here, so we can run this expedition as a joint venture?" Raymond asked.

"Oh, there you goes usin' them words again," Abby said. "*Expedention, joint adventure...* " She stepped closer to him, as if confiding something: "Let me explain something to ya, Billy, we just gotta find that girl and her boyfriend so's we can kill 'em, then we go home."

"I'm running this show," Raymond said evenly. "It's going to be organized, disciplined, and, when we find them, we've got to find out who they're connected with—if anyone."

"Billy, yer turning this into something difficult," Abby said without raising her voice. "We's just gotta find 'em and get rid of 'em."

"That's not what we agreed to!" Raymond said.

"That's what I agreed to," Abby said.

"It is *not!*" Raymond shouted.

"Keep yer voice down," Hank said smirking again. "Someone's gonna hear ya."

Peterson emerged from his tent. He strolled to Hank and stood in front of him. He didn't raise his voice. "Don't ever wake me up like that again." It wasn't a demand and it certainly wasn't a request.

Hank looked at Peterson and smirked, but said nothing. It wasn't the kind of smirk he wore for Raymond. It was a face-saving smirk, an act of bravado because there was something cold and reptilian about Peterson that put even a brute as big and stupid as Hank off. It was also a certainty that he wouldn't fire his rifle like that during the rest of the trip.

Peterson even put Abby off. Had he been chosen to lead the group, Raymond thought, he'd have been able to control it in a way Raymond himself couldn't; in a way Abby or LaCroix couldn't. But Peterson was neither a leader nor a follower, he was a loner. It was the way he wanted it. It was what made him happy to be a sniper in the Army. And even though Raymond hoped he would back him up in his struggle for leadership with Abby, Peterson manifested no interest in that, either, and that, too, worked against Billy Raymond.

Raymond began to realize that the Bradys were a model of solidarity, even if they were crazy. On the other hand, Mayfield, selected because he was related to the Bradys, not only wouldn't stand up to them, he was avoiding any confrontations; De Angelis was spineless; and Peterson was too preoccupied with whatever beasts ate at him, and that made him a handicap because it was obvious that the most intimidating man from the LaCroix compound, the man Raymond most needed to count on for backup, may as well not have been there, and that made Abby and Hank ever bolder.

It was Raymond—alone—against the Brady clan, and it was clear he was losing. If he couldn't get control, they were potentially all going to be losers. None of this boded well for the expedition. So he tried to reason with Abby. He figured either she wasn't getting it or she just didn't care. But he knew, even more likely, this was how this conniving woman was gaining control of the expedition. She might sound like an idiot, but she wasn't.

Raymond took her aside. "Listen, Abby, this guy we're hunting is dangerous. He's more dangerous than any of us. He's been out here for years, operating right under our noses. He's already taken out nine of us, and we don't even know if he operates alone. There's more people hiding out in these hills. We know that. We just don't know how many or where they are. They may be his friends, and that's not good. When we find him, we've got to find out everything we can. If we find anyone...*anyone else*...we've got to find out whatever we can so's this doesn't ever happen again."

There, he'd said it. Perhaps now she'd understand.

"Billy," she said patting his arm, "yer making more of this than ya gotta. I'll tell you what, you lead us and we'll see what happens. Okay?"

Her response surprised him. Had he gotten to her?

He breathed a sigh of relief and walked to his own men. "Let my boys eat and we'll break camp," he said.

Raymond, Mayfield, De Angelis, and Peterson ate their breakfasts cold so they could set out quicker. They took down their tents, stowed their gear, and were on their way again.

Chapter 26
September 2

The sun slashed like a machete across a landscape and cleaved the world into two jewels; one of razor-white snow, the other of turquoise-blue sky. Its fiery luminescence didn't make the morning any warmer, but it lifted the spirits of the LaCroix/Brady party and made laboring across the countryside more bearable.

The seven men and one woman were strung out over about a hundred yards. Setting the pace was Jim De Angelis. Behind him skied Billy Raymond whose mood, so recently darkened by the presence of Hank and Abby Brady, was brightened by the sun's auspicious promise of the new day and Abby's promise not to interfere with his decisions.

Next in the procession was Fred Mayfield who had removed his skis to trudge alongside his cousin, Jerry Brady.

Before the ice age started, Jerry had been a handyman of sorts. He'd been liked by those who knew him, but nearly invisible, otherwise. When the ice age began, his wife wanted to flee when times turned bad. She took her two children, by a previous marriage, and headed south to San Diego while the getting-out was easy. Jerry stayed because his bonds to his family were stronger than those to his wife. He didn't miss her.

If one had stopped to think about it, Jerry was the kind of man who, in another time and place, could have been a prison guard at Auschwitz. Though initially shocked by how cruelly people so readily treated each other at the beginning of the ice age, he quickly acclimated himself because, like most of us, he could partition his life and his brain into "us" and "them" and turn the people coming down 101 into objects, especially the young girls the Bradys pulled from the road. It was only in his darkest moments, when he thought about what he was doing, that he had reservations or felt guilt. But he always got over those moments and they happened less and less. So, the other night, when he was ordered to shoot the girl in the barn, they first made the girls strip so they wouldn't soil their clothes. Some of the girls from the compound, who had already claimed dibs on what the girls were wearing, stood in the doorway of the barn to make sure the men did it right. Somehow, to Jerry, that all seemed normal, now.

The girl, barely pubescent, was terror stricken, having already watched as her sisters and cousins were executed, and she started to pee down her legs. She desperately cried and looked up at him with fear-filled, pleading eyes, and he used his left hand to gently turn her face away from his, and with his right he brought up a .22 pistol and put a bullet behind her ear and into her brain, snuffing out her existence. When she fell to the floor he felt no remorse and that night he slept like a baby.

Mayfield, although he was related to the Bradys by blood, could not live on their compound. Though the Lacroix compound also preyed on the emigrants fleeing the north, had killed people in some of the firefights that resulted, and had even taken some women, it was easy to rationalize that they were different and only doing what had to be done in a world where you either ate or were eaten. To him, the biggest difference between the Brady and LaCroix compounds, despite the crimes committed by both groups, was that the LaCroixs *weren't* the Bradys.

Prior to the ice age, Fred and his wife had run a small sandwich and coffee shop in Brookings where they made a comfortable living, until his wife had an affair with one of the high school boys they'd hired. The shop fell apart as their marriage unraveled. After the affair died down (because the boy ran off with a girl his own age), his wife left town with a truck driver and Fred stayed on, pumped gas, cooked in some local restaurants, and finally worked as a hand on one of the crabbing boats that plied the waters off the Oregon coast until the ice age ushered in the new era. The crabbing boat was owned by the LaCroix family and, when things got bad, Fred was welcomed onto the LaCroix compound.

Following behind them was Hank Brady. He pulled the sled bearing Aunt Abby with his powerful strides and made fun of the others whenever the pace slackened. But he saved his sharpest barbs for Raymond.

Abby Brady sat on the toboggan Hank pulled as if it were her due. She held herself regally and made eye contact with no one. Though a religious woman, she was now angry with God that He had let a man named Zachary Amaral take Joel "before his time" and, if she could find a way, she was going to take her vengeance on him. In fact, she now saw herself as an agent of the Almighty and imagined herself, as the song said, "His terrible swift sword."

Abby Brady was the one and only person on this planet Hank feared. Abby, on the other hand, feared no one: not Hank, not Billy Raymond, not Louis LaCroix, not the Army, nor the President of the United States, though she was wary of the powers   they might have. And the only person in recent memory who had stood up to her was a girl named Danielle, and Danielle, the shooter, and the baby with the silly name would all be dealt with and pay for taking her Sweetie away from her—as God was her witness.

Behind them was Steven Ingram. Ingram, tall, thin, and nervous, spent most of his life vaguely fearful of every new day. His greatest fear was that people would discover he was a coward. Because of this, he'd always been a hanger-on with bullies thinking that by being their sycophant he would actually be perceived as their sidekick. Ingram admired Hank. Not because he liked him, but because everyone else—everyone but Abby and Peterson—feared him. Ingram lived in dreadful fear of what Hank might, at any moment, do to him. He was often the butt of Hank's cruel jokes, but hoped he disguised his fear when he reacted to them good-naturedly and acted as if they didn't bother him. As much as he admired Hank, he also hated him for the jokes and the way Hank bullied him. Still, he felt a strange attraction to the man, like a moth is attracted to the flame that would kill it. In volunteering for this foray into the woods, to find a "killer" named Zachary Amaral, he hoped to create a reputation for himself in other people's eyes. He hoped he would seem to be more like Hank. He even hoped Hank would develop some respect for him. What he didn't realize was that the only person suffering from all these illusions was himself.

That Abby had a strange affection for him, and often treated him as a surrogate son, made Steven think she saw in him the potential for him to be like Hank. Nothing could have been further from the truth. She loved Steven because he was weak and because of his feckless ways. She loved him the same way she loved her late grandson, Joel, and her dead husband.

But what Ingram liked best about volunteering for this foray into the woods was that he got to wear a police uniform, just like Hank and Jerry did, complete with the Sam Browne belts they'd found, and all the paraphernalia that hangs off a real cop's belt: handcuffs, baton, etc. Furthermore, he believed salvation and redemption lay at the end of this trip, that he could become some kind of hero, and the fact that Hank was saving his jibes for Billy Raymond insinuated this just might happen. Ingram was stupid.

At the very end of the procession was Brian Peterson. He was a quiet, educated man who didn't form bonds easily. He had a coldness about him that put off even Hank and Abby. Though neither manifested fear of him, viscerally both knew Brian was dangerous in a way they were not. The one time on this foray Hank had slung one of his barbs in his direction, Peterson looked at him the way a man looks at a housefly just before he slaps it. Though in what many call a "fair" fight, Hank knew he could kick the shit out of anyone he'd ever met, he avoided a confrontation with Brian the same way a lion would avoid a confrontation with a cobra. You had nothing to fear from Brian as long as you weren't in his way.

In the Army Peterson had been the perfect sniper. Many can shoot well, but few have the patience he had to wait for a target, or the stomach for assassination he possessed. Distant from the others on this trip in both space and temperament, he was content to be at the end of the train. Despite his sociopathic personality, the one person he had loved in his life was his older brother who a man named Zachary Amaral had killed just days before. Somewhere, at the end of this trip into the wilds of Curry County, he would find solace in the deaths of this Amaral, a girl named Danielle, her baby, and anyone in league with them.

§   §   §

Hank was boisterous and talked loudly, though Raymond had ordered them all to be as quiet as possible.

Soon after getting underway, Raymond had appealed to Abby to make Hank be quiet. But he realized, the second that request had come out of his mouth, it had been a mistake. It was an admission he didn't have and wouldn't get control.

As they walked along, Mayfield and his cousin, Jerry Brady, spoke in low tones so the others could not hear them.

"I wish that bastard would shut up," Mayfield said of Hank.

"Everyone wishes he'd shut up," Jerry said softly and both men laughed.

"I think there may be a confrontation between him and Raymond before long," Mayfield added.

"If it's a fight, Billy will lose—and he knows it, so he'd best stay clear," Jerry said.

Mayfield nodded. "I think Billy would turn around and just go home if he didn't feel he owed getting this guy, Amaral, to Louis."

They trudged on further and Mayfield asked, "So what's with this girl Danielle? Why'd she leave your place?"

"She's a bitch; wouldn't show no respect. She fought us every inch of the way. I know you've heard how Hank breaks the new girls in when they come into the compound."

He looked at Mayfield for understanding and Mayfield nodded glumly.

"He claims he calms them down with his dick. But he said she put up the biggest fight of any of 'em. And even after that first night she stood up to him. Worse, the little cunt stood up to Abby. That was a big mistake. Nobody needs a woman like her around."

"So you guys turned her out?"

Jerry didn't say anything.

"Did she run away?" Mayfield asked, and when his cousin didn't answer that question, he asked, "How'd she wind up with the shooter?"

They trudged on in silence and Jerry suddenly asked, "Can you keep this just between you and me?"

"Sure."

"They took her and another girl out to a field. They were supposed to…" He paused. "They were supposed to shoot 'em and leave the baby in the snow. It's always been a plum assignment because the boys like to have fun with them girls before they shoot 'em. But something happened this time. Something went wrong and the boys are all dead. No one knows if the shooter was waiting for 'em or if he just happened along. But we figure he's someone local who's managed to stay out of sight all this time…until now."

"The baby…" Mayfield began and wanted to ask about leaving it in the snow, but he let the sentence remain unfinished.

"Yeah," Jerry said. "That Danielle had a kid with her."

"Do *you* think the girl had a hand in killing the boys?"

"I wasn't there, but it wouldn't surprise me. She's ballsier than you can imagine. She said something about bringing us down. And if you met her, you know if she could find a way, she would."

"What about the other girl?"

"Andrew said they shot her first."

They said nothing to each other for about the next fifty yards.

"How's the old lady been doing, lately…other than Joel getting killed?" Mayfield asked.

"Okay."

"Is she still the bitch she used to be?"

"Worse than ever. There's a lot of grumbling about her at the compound, and she probably knows it. But she also knows no one dares stand up to her as long as Hank's around."

"No one but that…"

"Danielle," Brady said. "Her name is Danielle. Remember it, 'cause she ain't long for this world if Abby has her way — and Abby gets what she wants."

"I couldn't put up with Abby — or Hank," Mayfield said.

"I think there's a feeling that if something were to happen to Abby, the place would fall apart," Brady said. "She doesn't just have Hank to back her up, she has people's fear that if she was gone, the compound can't survive."

"Could it?" Mayfield asked.

"I don't know. They depend on her." What he didn't say was that he did, too, and that without her he was sure the ranch would fall apart and they'd all, including himself, be lost.

But in the light of the new day, what he really wanted to talk to his cousin about was what was happening on the Brady ranch with all the girls. More than Abby or Hank, what held the ranch together was the collective guilt they all shared and Abby used that guilt to her advantage, even though, outwardly, she denied anything was happening.

But how could he explain all this when he himself had become part of the guilt? So the confession burned inside of him like a malignant cancer. Mayfield, on the other hand, had heard the rumors and didn't ask his cousin to confirm or refute them. Thus, as they walked along their conversation turned to old times, dead relatives, and the weather. Safe subjects.

§   §   §

Around noon, Raymond looked ahead to see De Angelis had stopped at the crest of a small hill. He had one arm raised in a signal for the others to stop. He proceeded to lay down in the snow and crawl closer to the crest.

Raymond turned, and he too raised an arm to the others. Each man, as he realized the man ahead had stopped, also stopped and awaited the next command.

Hank yelled, "What's up?"

Raymond made a downward gesture with his right hand, the signal they'd agreed would mean to be quiet, but Hank just laughed his boisterous laugh and Abby sat regally poised on her sled as if ignoring it.

With the entire procession now stalled, Raymond turned his attention back to De Angelis who was peering over the crest. De Angelis finally looked back and alternately beckoned them with his left hand then made downward motions telling them all to be quiet.

There was something up ahead.

Raymond used his arm in the same manner, beckoning the others while at the same time telling them to be quiet, and he went on to meet De Angelis near the crest. He got down low as he reached him and whispered, "What's up?"

"There's a cabin just over the hill," De Angelis replied softly. "Smoke's comin' out the chimney. What d'ya wanna do, now?"

Raymond saw it.

"We'll wait for Peterson before we do anything," Raymond whispered.

From where they lay, they could see a cabin below in a small valley.

"Yup, they're home," Raymond said when he saw the smoke and he looked back to see the others arriving.

Like Raymond and De Angelis, Mayfield and Jerry Brady crawled the final few feet through the snow.

Hank stopped below the crest, Abby stayed on the toboggan, and Ingram stopped with them. Though Ingram was here to see if he could find his backbone, he suddenly lost the courage to find out what was just over the rise.

Peterson, on the other hand, walked past them to join the others at the top. He knew what he was here for and hoped to end it all with one or two carefully placed shots. He felt a certain amount of exhilaration rising up in him that he hadn't felt in years. He embraced his rifle like he'd just recognized an old friend he'd thought he'd never see again. When he got close enough to the ridge, he too got down and crawled the rest of the way to their position.

Raymond was surveying the area below with his binoculars and Peterson took his own out from inside his jacket and glassed the cabin and its environs.

The cabin was set against the trees. There were solar panels on the roof. Not only was there smoke from the chimney, there were tracks, some leading to a shed about thirty feet from the cabin.

"How do you take them?" Raymond asked Peterson.

"Wait. No sense in risking any of our own. There may be others there or even people out in the trees. We don't even know if we've been seen."

"Pussy," Hank said and, when the others turned to him, he was now standing right behind them in full view of the cabin and he was grinning.

"Get down and be quiet," Raymond growled in a whisper.

Hank smiled.

De Angelis said, "There's a dog down there, too. He's behind the cabin, now. The wind's right, so it won't smell us and it won't hear us if we're quiet."

"We ain't gonna wait all day," Hank said in his loud voice.

Turning again, Raymond whispered, "Hank, get down and keep it down."

Hank grinned again and snorted. He stepped to the top of the ridge knowing this would piss off Raymond.

"Get down," Raymond ordered in a loud whisper.

Instead, Hank turned and walked about twenty feet from the group.

Raymond shook his head, but he was glad Hank had gotten out of sight of the cabin below. He turned back to observe what was going on down the hill. "A couple of us should circle around to surround the place," he said softly.

"You make the assignments," Peterson whispered.

Lying in the snow, Raymond took stock of his men. He had only seven to work with since Abby had come along. But he was sure the seven of them would be enough.

He said, "Fred, I want you and Jerry to cut around through the woods and cut off any escape." Putting the cousins together made sense to him. They were more apt to cooperate with each other. "And be quiet about it."

"Brian," he said to Peterson, "Give Fred your walkie-talkie."

Peterson took it from inside his jacket and handed it to Mayfield.

Looking back at Mayfield, Raymond said, "Don't use it unless you absolutely have to; only if you see trouble or if they're trying to escape out a back door."

He looked around back to see what Hank was doing. In full view of the others, he'd dropped his pants and was defecating in the snow.

"Jesus," Raymond whispered and shook his head. The others glanced back and grimaced in disgust.

Abby had joined them and tried to stay low without lying in the snow. Behind her was Ingram, still hanging back and afraid to see what was on the other side of the ridge.

Abby quickly got uncomfortable trying to crouch on her old legs. She'd obviously decided not to lie down like the others. She suddenly stood up in full view of the cabin, turned, and went back to her sled.

Raymond shook his head again. But he was sure they still hadn't been seen.

"There's the dog," Peterson whispered.

Raymond looked back and there was the dog. It was white. It had come out from behind the cabin, stopped, and stared into the trees where they hid.

"Don't move, and be quiet," Peterson whispered.

"That fuckin' dog don't know we're up here," Hank suddenly said.

With that the dog started barking.

The door to the cabin opened and a woman briefly appeared. Then she disappeared, closing the door behind her.

"Shut the fuck up," Raymond said in a threatening voice.

Hank just smirked and in the same voice he'd been using said, "Well, looks like they know we're here, now."

"Fred, Jerry," Raymond said, "get going and work your way around..."

But, before the men could move, the first bullet from the cabin came up through the trees and all the men hunkered down beneath the branches, including Hank.

The dog started across the field in their direction until a voice from the cabin called it back.

The dog stopped, then started racing back to the cabin.

"Take the dog!" Raymond commanded.

Peterson's rifle came up quickly, he gauged the dog's direction and speed. Even for a superb marksman, a running shot is difficult. But Peterson pulled the trigger, and the dog was about thirty feet from the door when it fell. He worked the bolt to chamber another round as a matter of habit.

"Good shot," Raymond said.

It lay still for a moment, then its front legs started moving as if it was trying to swim through the snow. Raymond looked at the dog through his binoculars.

"You broke its back."

Peterson looked down through his scope, again, but Raymond immediately said, "*No!* Don't waste good ammo."

Peterson took his eye away from the scope.

The others fired at the cabin. Peterson lay there watching the window near the door through the crosshairs of his scope. Just one motion through the window and he would send a minion of death into the cabin.

Sporadic shooting went on for nearly sixty seconds until Peterson suddenly yelled, "Wait!"

The front door of the cabin opened a crack and a white flag dangled out the door.

"Hold your fire!" Raymond yelled.

A few more shots rang out.

"Hold your fucking fire," he yelled, again.

An abrupt silence fell over the forest. Then Hank laughed.

Raymond turned to Abby and said, "You tell that son of a bitch to hold his fire or I'll put a bullet in him."

"Those people have to pay for what they did to my Sweety," Abby said.

"We have to find out who those people are connected with before we do anything to them," Raymond snarled. "So *you* control him, or *I* will."

"Hold your fire," Abby said to Hank.

Hank smirked, again. "Sure." And he brought his rifle down.

"What now?" Peterson asked.

Raymond considered his options.

"I'm going in," he finally said. "Watch the windows and the door," he said to Peterson. "Any movement and send a bullet in."

With that, he was on his skis and going down the hill

§   §   §

Raymond stopped about fifty yards from the cabin. "Come on out," he yelled.

The door opened slowly and the man stepped out with the white flag in his hand.

He stood on the top step.

"What do you want?" he asked.

Raymond approached him.

The others were now coming down the hill, three on skis, two walking, and Hank was running down doing a remarkably good job of staying ahead of Abby and the sled.

The man seemed relieved when he saw Hank, Jerry, and Ingram in police uniforms.

"Who else is in there?" Raymond asked.

It's just my girlfriend and our daughter," the man said.

Raymond said, "Tell everyone to come out or we'll riddle the place with bullets until it's quiet inside."

"You can come out, honey. It's just the police."

A woman holding the baby came out.

"That ain't the bitch," Abby said of the woman in the doorway when she arrived.

"What do you want?" the man asked.

"We're looking for Zachary Amaral," Raymond said.

"Who?"

"Do you know Zachary Amaral?"

The man looked surprised.

"Yeah, but you're not going to find him here."

"Where is he?"

"Last I knew, he was living up river. He has a cabin a few miles up. What did he do?"

"Never you mind."

"What do they want?" the woman asked.

"It's okay, honey," he said. "I've got it under control."

"Are you looking to arrest him?" the man asked, his hands coming down.

"Keep your arms up," Raymond warned, and the man's arms went back up. "Tell me where his cabin is."

"It's hard to explain how to get there," the man said. But he explained as best he could with Raymond making mental notes of every detail.

When he finished, Raymond asked, "You guys friends?"

The man was guarded. "Not really. We did some trading with him a year or so ago. But we ain't seen nothing of him since his family died."

"What do you want to do?" Peterson asked.'

"Look around, but we're done here," Raymond said.

From nowhere a shot rang out and the man crumpled onto the snow.

The woman shrieked and ran out to her boyfriend.

Hank laughed, the barrel of his rifle pointing at the body now in the snow.

"What did you do that for? You fucking idiot!" Raymond yelled.

"They gotta pay," Abby suddenly said. "He admitted he knows the guy who shot my Sweetie. Every one of these people gotta pay for my Joel, my Sweetie, for what they done to him."

The woman was on her knees beside her boyfriend, hysterically screaming. She put the baby on his stomach and cradled his head. The man looked confused. He was gasping, trying to talk to his woman, but no words came out. He was dying.

Hank suddenly grabbed her by her hair and jerked her to her feet and the man's head fell to the ground. He looked at his girlfriend, tried to speak, and died.

"My baby! My baby! Let me have my baby!" the woman screamed.

Abby solved the problem when she pointed a small handgun at the baby and announced, "They're all sinners."

"*No!*" Raymond yelled, but it was too late. Abby stopped the baby's cries when she sent a bullet through its head.

"What did you do that for?" Raymond yelled at Abby.

"They's livin' in sin," Abby said. "What does it matter to you, anyway?"

Then, yelling at everybody, Raymond asked, "What are we doing?"

The woman was frantic, now. But she couldn't match Hank's strength and he ran her back into the cabin while holding a fistful of her hair and he slammed the door behind them.

From inside they heard the woman scream and beg.

"Stop him!" Raymond demanded of Abby.

But she walked away saying, "They're sinners. They're all sinners."

And it became clear to Raymond and everyone else that the real leader of the group was Abby Brady.

From inside they could hear the woman call her boyfriend's name; she called the baby's name. She begged Hank for mercy. It went on for a minute.

As if bound with invisible shackles, Raymond was riveted to the spot where he stood.

Then it was quiet.

A minute later, the door opened and Hank stood on the top step, his police uniform covered with blood. He hitched up his pants, buttoned them, buckled his belt, and zipped up his fly. He stepped back into the cabin and, when he reappeared, his right hand was behind him. He was smirking, again.

He sauntered down the steps, hesitated, then in one motion, he brought his arm from behind himself and threw the woman's head, eyes wide open, mouth agape, into the snow where they all stood.

"You fucking asshole!" Raymond screamed. "What are you doing this for?"

"They gotta pay!" Abby screamed. "Everyone's gotta pay."

"But they didn't do nothing."

Abby stepped up to him. "Someone's gotta pay. They gotta pay. Everyone out here's gotta pay for what they done to my Sweetie."

"These people didn't do it!" Raymond yelled.

"They's friends of his. You heard 'im: They made trades with him. They's his friends, so they gotta pay."

"We've just gotta stop this *one* guy who's killing us and keep him from killing any more of us," Raymond yelled at her.

She fearlessly got right up in Raymond's face. "That's exactly what we're doin', Billy," and Raymond stepped back.

"If you ain't got the stomach for what we have to do, *go home.*" she said.

The baby was dead; the woman was dead; the man was dead. Things were completely out of Raymond's control.

"Take the bodies out back," he finally said. "We'll stay here tonight; we'll move on in the morning."

He turned to Hank. "You too, fuckhead. Get the body out of the cabin and put it out back."

But Hank just laughed at him. "Do it yourself," he said and walked away.

Raymond didn't know what to do.

In the end, he had Jerry Brady and Mayfield take the woman's decapitated body from the cabin.

Mayfield puked as he helped carry her out. Jerry wanted to puke, but he couldn't. He was already used to this kind of thing.

Raymond walked to the dog that now lay in the snow. Occasionally it paddled with its front legs and whined. Mostly it just lay there confused by its predicament and watched the others.

"Sorry about this, fella," Raymond said, and he kneeled beside the dog and with a .22 he took from his pocket he dispatched the dog and ended its terror and misery.

He stood up and announced, "Let's look in the cabin. We'll reprovision with what they've got here."

Abby said nothing. Hank was already back inside the cabin going through stuff.

"What are we doing?" Raymond asked Peterson. "There was no reason to kill those people."

"You read stuff about things like this," Peterson said.

"What do you mean?"

"Massacres, looting, pillaging, putting people in ovens…It's in the Bible, it's part of history. The Europeans have done it in all their intramural wars, African ethnic cleansing, we did it to the Indians, the Nazis to the Jews, French revolutionaries to each other, leftists to rightists and rightists to leftists, the religious, the nonreligious, we all do it. We've done it since before history was written. But you can't comprehend it when you just read about it. And you don't believe it when you're in the middle of it; worse, you become inured to it when you're a part of it, especially when there's too much of it." He looked at Jerry Brady when he said that. "You know what Stalin said? 'A single death is a tragedy; a million deaths is a statistic.'"

"What about you?" Raymond asked. "How do you feel about this shit?"

"The important question is: How do you feel about it? How do you feel about being part of it?"

Raymond was horrified. "I'm not doing this stuff," he said.

"But you're standing by and watching it happen…and so am I."

"So, what do we do?"

"You can only stop what *you're* doing," Peterson offered. "But that's not going to stop *them*…" he said referring to the Bradys. "And you won't stop me. There's a man out here, maybe more than one, who killed my brother." And he let it hang.

"We're all going to go to hell over this," Raymond said.

"We're already there, Billy. We've been there since the day we were born," Peterson said and walked away from him.

§   §   §

They stayed the night in the cabin. Abby got the big bed, Hank took a smaller bed, everyone else slept on the floor. Raymond, Jerry, and Mayfield slept the sleep of the damned. The others slept as though they were without souls.

At twilight Raymond woke to the sound of Abby giving orders. He rolled over and saw Hank, Ingram, Jerry, and even Mayfield bringing furniture and boxes out onto the snow.

"What are you doing?" Raymond yelled at Abby.

She didn't answer him.

He went to the door and looked out. She had the men putting things in the snow away from the cabin. There was a treadle sewing machine, rifles, shotguns, boxes, chairs, and a desk. Mayfield was passing by him with jewelry in his hands.

"Put that shit down," Raymond ordered.

Mayfield hesitated, then he placed the jewelry on the kitchen table.

"You take that stuff outside," Abby calmly said to Ingram and he gladly rushed in to follow her orders and scooped up the jewelry.

Peterson watched Raymond and when Raymond's eyes met his, neither man spoke until Peterson said, "I'm going to get something to eat," and he turned back to the stove on which he'd been heating some canned beans.

"Okay, everybody eat," Raymond said to no one in particular. "Then let's get the hell out of here."

After breakfast, they assembled outside. LaCroix's orders were to split whatever loot they got. But, as if the loot was cursed now, Raymond didn't want any part of it. Besides, he had a more important task at hand: he still had to find Zachary Amaral and the girl...what was her name he asked himself?...oh, yeah, Danielle.

So he started ordering the men to "suit up" for the trip up river. He gave instructions saying, "Leave this shit here," as he waved a hand at the booty in the snow. "We'll come for it later."

The men hesitated.

"Abby said we're taking it, now" Mayfield said.

"The fuck we are. Get moving," Raymond shouted.

"We're burning it down," Abby announced.

"The cabin? No, we're not," Raymond countered and got in her face. "We're going to take what food we can carry so we don't have to go back to the ranches yet. And we're going to stow the rest so we can come back for it on our way back."

"We're burning it. I don't want no one living here, again," she said.

"I'm running this expedition," Raymond yelled.

"Oh, listen," Abby said with a contrasting calmness, "he uses a big word like 'expedition,' again, and thinks it makes him look smart."

He lowered his voice. "Look here, Abby, I'm leading this hunt. If you don't like my orders, go. Go home. Me, Brian, Jim, and Fred will continue on looking for this guy. We don't need you; we don't want you. Get out."

"You're not the boss of me," Abby said. "We're as much a part of this as you are. *You* go home if you want. We know where they live, now, and I'm here to make sure..." and her voice suddenly started getting louder, "...the people who laid my Sweetie in the cold ground, before his time, *pay*. They gotta pay. Everyone out here's gotta pay!"

"If you're staying with us," Raymond said deliberately, "you will obey my orders."

She said nothing.

"Shit," Peterson gasped.

Raymond turned. Hank had used kerosene he'd found inside and he'd torched the cabin.

"Well, it looks like it's settled," Abby said.

"There's food in there. We could'a used the solar panels!" Raymond yelled.

"Too late now," Hank said with his smirk.

Raymond stood once more riveted to his spot and watched the flames engulf the cabin.

§   §   §

Thirty minutes later they started off across the field. Abby sat at the front of the sled because the back end of it was stacked with the sewing machine, the weapons, some other furniture, and boxes. When there was no more room to put anything on the sled, she made Ingram and Jerry Brady carry stuff. Jerry looked ridiculous carrying an antique chair in each arm and his rifle slung over his shoulder. Ingram was carrying a small oaken escritoire. Because he was a relative, she'd tried to bully Mayfield into carrying a small box with some fine china in it, but he knew he'd never be allowed back at the LaCroix ranch if he did, so he refused and Ingram had to carry that, too.

The loot now slowed the party, except for Hank who heckled the others whenever he had to stop and wait for them. Despite Abby and all the goodies she'd piled on the sled, he didn't slow down even a step with his powerful strides.

Behind them the cabin still burned sending a plume of smoke off into the grey morning air. Yesterday's sun had promised a new and better day but had failed to deliver. The grey clouds now coming from the west forebode of darker things to come.

Chapter 27
September 2

The second time Danielle woke that morning it was to the sounds of the canner hissing and Zach speaking in a low voice. She knew it had to be around noon.

She turned to look, and Zach was now at the counter with his back to her. He was putting more meat into jars. Whoops was propped up with blankets and pillows and he was explaining to her in a whisper how he was canning the meat and why he was doing what he did. Even if Whoops couldn't understand a word of what he was saying, she enjoyed watching and listening to him.

Danielle got off the chair and stretched. She still felt groggy.

He glanced back and said, "Good morning," for the second time that day. He didn't say it in the sarcastic tone of voice her father used when she slept late. He said it sincerely.

"Mornin'," she offered through a yawn as she approached the stove.

She looked up at strips of meat on a rack a few inches above the woodstove. Each strip was set about half-an-inch from its neighbor on the rack. If he was trying to cook it, it was too far from the heat.

"What are you doing with that?"

He looked to where she was looking, at the meat. "I'm dehydrating some of the meat to make jerky."

"What's that all over it?"

"Pepper, garlic powder, a little crushed rosemary..."

"Ooo! I haven't had jerky since before...well, you know when."

"I know."

"I didn't know you could make it. I thought it all came from stores. Can I try some?"

"There's some finished in the jars on the shelf," he said.

She took one of the jars down, opened it, and took some out.

"Why's it in jars?"

"To make sure it stays dry...put the cover back on. Jerking meat preserves it because it reduces the amount of water in it, and bacteria and molds won't form if the amount of water has been sufficiently reduced."

There he was, she thought, lecturing again. But she liked it. She liked learning.

"But," he continued, "the jerky starts to absorb water from the air as soon you're done dehydrating it. If it absorbs enough, the bacteria and molds start to thrive, and the meat goes bad. The stuff drying up there on the rack will go into the jars as soon as it's dry enough."

"When it's jerked?" she asked.

He smiled. "Yeah, I guess you could call meat that's been dried 'jerked'."

"Is that a word?" she asked.

"If it wasn't before, it *is* now."

Although she hadn't asked, he added, "I'm getting the jars warm so that they'll have as little moisture in them as possible when I put the jerky in them, and when I put the lids on, as they cool they'll form a partial vacuum."

"You read that in a book?"

"Heating the jars? No, that's one I figured out. I don't know how effective it is, but I haven't had any spoilage since I started doing this, five or six years ago."

She began to eat a piece. "This is good stuff, you know?"

"No, I didn't," he said dryly.

She laughed. "Be nice to me and I'll let you have some."

"Really? Then I guess I'll have to be nice to you."

"Is Whoops helping?"

The baby glanced at her when she heard her name.

"Oh, yeah. She's making sure I don't do anything wrong."

Danielle looked at the operation. "Why don't you get everything closer to the stove so it'll dry faster?"

"You don't want it too close. The idea is to dry it out without cooking it."

"You figured that out, too?"

"No, I read that in a book."

She smiled. "I've got a lot to learn."

He sighed, without realizing he had, because she wasn't going to learn it from him; she was leaving. But he said, "Yes, you have."

She thought about what she was eating. "What kind of meat is it? Did you and Whoopsie catch the bear?"

He smiled again. "It's venison."

"That's what's hanging out in the shed, right?"

"That's what *was* hanging in the shed," he corrected her. "You've already helped me can most of it. The last batch is in the canner. I'm using the rest to make jerky."

She looked at the pressure canner still hissing away.

"Why do you do both?"

"By canning it I can use it in meals; jerking it I can carry it when I go out, without weighing myself down unnecessarily. Also, I'm simmering the bones and anything else I won't eat or tan and making stock that I can use later in soups and stews."

She hefted a piece of the jerky. "Yeah, it's pretty lightweight. Can I take some with me?"

He mumbled an answer.

She stepped closer, her right forearm against his left, and asked, "What did you say?"

In a voice louder than necessary he said, "When you leave, you can take anything and everything you can carry." His enthusiasm had abated.

She ignored his mood change and asked, "May I help?"

He stopped, looked at her, then at what he was doing.

"Wash your hands, then start cutting strips."

"That's all I get to do, cut it into strips?"

"Oh, no. You said you want to learn. You're going to do it all. And it's easy.

"See how thin these are?" He was pointing to what he'd already cut. "Cut them that thin—that's so they'll dry out faster—then I'll show you how to put a mixture of seasonings on it. After that, we'll put them on another rack and start them dehydrating, too."

"I'm glad you didn't 'do' Stupid."

She let her right arm brush against his left and he cut his finger.

"*Damn!*" he said, He washed the wound, squeezed out some of the blood, and reached for another Band-Aid.

She smiled to herself and began to cut the meat into strips.

After she'd cut enough of it, he showed her how to sprinkle the seasoning mixture over it. Without prompting he also explained how, someday, he'd be making his own garlic powder from what he grew and that he already grew his own rosemary and some other herbs which he dehydrated.

"I'm going to have to produce my own herbs and spices or eat everything bland, from here on out," he said.

She liked his confidence.

"You've got quite an operation going here."

"It pays off. It feeds me and, by staying busy, I don't go crazy."

He stopped and turned to face her. "Keep in mind, there's not much else to do. There's no TV anymore, not that I watched it before, but there's no Internet anymore, no shopping malls, and no nights on the town. I've got just so many books to read — though I often find new ones when I go out scavenging — and there's no one to talk with. All that's left is to can, hunt, scavenge..." He brought his hands palms up to emphasize that that said it all. "Otherwise you stare at the walls and go crazy."

"I can see," she said in a tone that implied he already was crazy, and he eyed her critically.

"Now," he said, "put what you've cut and seasoned on another rack and place it above the stove so they'll dehydrate."

She did. But when she finished she turned without a word and walked back to the middle of the living room.

He didn't know what she was doing and after a few minutes he turned around. She was getting her stuff ready to go.

"I'm going to make room for some jars of jerky," she said.

He mumbled something she couldn't quite hear.

"What?" she asked.

"You won't need jars," he repeated. "I'll put it in some plastic bags. They're lighter and you can just toss the empty bags when you're done with them."

She returned to his side and, somehow, her right arm was against his left, again.

"How long's this going to take?" she asked as she surveyed the project. He didn't answer.

"I want to learn to shoot my gun, now" she said, changing the subject.

He was quiet for a second. He took a deep breath. "Okay," he said. "Let me finish this."

"So, how long's it going to take?"

He paused. "There's a lot to do."

"Go ahead. Finish what you're doing. It's just that I'm never going to get out of here at this rate."

He didn't say anything. He just kept working.

She stood and watched until she said, "Instead of me just killing time, show me more," she said.

He was glad she wanted to learn more. He was glad she wanted to stand beside him.

He talked about other things he was doing, too. He explained how he was growing a few hot peppers and he digressed to explain how he saved seeds for everything he grew and why so-called heirloom vegetables were better for him to grow than the hybrids most people had grown before the ice age.

Chapter 28
September 2

In Washington, D.C., a sergeant in Air Force Intelligence read an alert on his computer that the most recent satellite observations showed a patch of infrared where an infrared signal shouldn't be. Something was burning in the forest near the Oregon coast. It wasn't a particularly significant piece of data. It was just one incident among many.

But he added it to his incident report and, four hours later, sent the intel to a superior. From there the report began its arduous rise through the bureaucratic chain of command until a captain brought it into the office of a Colonel Atkinson who leafed through all the incident reports, too tired and bored to read any of them.

"What have we got today?" the colonel asked.

"Movements, manhunts, fires, snow..."

"Manhunts?"

Atkinson didn't know what to make of it. By itself, the information meant nothing. And it was just one of a pile of memos.

The captain was in charge of Intelligence in the two northern California counties, Humboldt and Del Norte, and the southernmost of Oregon's coastal counties, Curry and Coos. Highway 101 ran through all four. Of the first memo he said, "We've intercepted messages between some groups of road pirates in the area. They're looking for somebody named Zachary Amaral and a girl named Danielle—no last name with Danielle. It isn't clear why they're wanted."

"Do you know if they had anything to do with this..." the colonel paused, "...fire? That's all it is, isn't it? A building or something burning down?"

"We can't tell, Sir. There *is* a cabin at the location. That's probably what's burning."

"Well," Atkinson said dismissively, "as long as they leave the roads alone, we don't care what they do to each other."

The military had neither the resources nor the incentive to mediate local feuds. The memo would go no further unless there was something definitive that required intervention. Then it would be passed onto the Army's Third Infantry Battalion.

Chapter 29
September 2

When they had the last of the venison either on racks or in jars she suddenly asked, "Are you done here?"

He didn't reply.

"Show me how to shoot my gun," she demanded.

"Tomorrow," he whispered.

"No! Now!"

He paused. Then he said, "Okay."

"Good. But this is going to take a minute," she said and grabbed her sister and started wrapping her in some blankets. "I want Whoops to be warm."

"Wait, I've got stuff," he said and went to one of the closed-off bedrooms shutting the door behind himself to keep the heat in the main room.

When he was gone too long, she started wondering what the "stuff" was and she went to the door and opened it.

He had his back to her and he was going through boxes.

"I'll be right out. Close the door so we can keep the heat in there," he said, and she closed the door and returned to Whoops.

When he came back he had his hands behind him and he approached her in her chair. But his eyes were on Whoops and, as he leaned toward her, he asked, "You know what I've got?"

Whoops watched him with her happy face.

He brought his hands out to reveal a little pink snowsuit.

"*Ta-da!* See if this fits her," he said to Danielle.

She took it and tried it on her sister. "Look, Whoopsie, a new snowsnoot.

"It fits perfectly," she said to Zach. "It's even a little big. She's got wiggle-room, so she can grow into it."

"She can have it," Zach said.

She thought a second and knew who must have worn it before. She stood and gave him a hug and said, "Thank you."

Her hug lasted longer than it had to and he hugged her back. Her body felt good against him. And when they stopped hugging, they were both awkward.

But she regained her composure and stepped back and looked at the floor. She was almost hating to have to say what she was about to say: "Show me what you've got to show me, so I can go to the road."

All she got back from him was, "Okay," as he nodded exaggeratedly, but his heart was not in what he said.

"Oh! Wait!" He went back into the other room and returned with some women's boots.

"These will probably fit you. They may be a little big and if they are, you can wear heavy socks with them."

"Thank you," she said as she took them.

"They were...um..."

"Sandra's," she said completing his sentence.

"Yes."

Then he fished around with his arms in the air as if searching for words and finally said, "Let me show you how to shoot a few guns. I want to do that before you go."

"A few? Why?" she asked.

"Well..." He was at a loss for words.

"Sounds like this could take all day," she said.

He didn't reply.

"Okay," she said. "I'd actually like to see more than one gun."

"Good," he said, and he went to the closet and pulled out several long guns.

She shook her head and smiled as she watched him.

"What kind are those?" she asked.

He started to fumble for words, again.

She liked him when he was confident, but she found him charming when he fumbled for words.

"It's okay, just bring 'em," she said.

"I just...I think you should learn to shoot a few guns," though he couldn't think of a reason why.

"You said that," she said.

"I know," he said because there was nothing else to say. "But we can't do too much shooting because every round we shoot is a round I can't replace—except for reloading. And even then I have just so many bullets, shot, primers, and powder."

"Okay."

He opened the door and stepped aside to let her go out first. Stupid was waiting for them.

"Wait," he said and he ran back into the cabin and disappeared in one of the bedrooms.

When he returned he had a cardboard box and a blanket in one hand and two sets of ear protectors, the ones shooters often call 'Mickey Mouse ears,' along with a set of binoculars, in his other.

"What's the box for?" she asked.

"Whoops; I don't want her too close to the shooting. It's bad for her ears. We'll put her in the box on a blanket. With that and the snowsuit..." he paused.

"...she'll be warm," Danielle said finishing his sentence.

"Yeah."

"Okay," she said.

The man who had shot four people in the field was falling apart over her and her sister, right before her eyes. She was fascinated.

Zach put the box in the snow in a sunny spot away from the cabin. "She'll get some sun here, but not in her eyes," he said. "Vitamin D...sunlight," he added pointing to the sky.

He seemed so awkward that Danielle wanted to laugh, but she didn't. "That sounds good," she said.

After they made Whoops comfortable he trod through the snow and hung a target on a stump about twenty feet distant and three more targets, one above another, on an old dead tree about twenty-five yards away. When he returned he took one set of "ears" and started to put them on her.

She stood still and let him.

"Adjust them so they're comfortable on you," he said.

She adjusted her hair around them and watched him in anticipation as he put the other set on himself.

"Do you have the Model 60?" he asked.

There was some hesitation until she reached into her pocket and took the handgun out and pointed it at him.

With his left hand he pushed the gun away from himself.

"The first thing you've got to learn is not to point the gun at anyone, unless you intend to shoot them."

"Sorry," she said.

His awkwardness had suddenly disappeared. In her eyes it was almost like a personality change taking place within him. He was back on his turf, now. He was sure of himself with the guns, just as he had been with his canning and jerking of the meat. She liked that about him.

"Don't let it happen again," he said.

"I won't," she said and she smiled.

He didn't.

"Let me have it," he said.

She did.

He opened the cylinder, unloaded it, and reloaded it with some rounds from his pocket.

"These are lighter loads I've loaded myself. They're thirty-eights."

"Doesn't mean a thing to me," she said.

"Doesn't have to, right now. But it will, someday."

"Ya think, huh?"

He ignored that and held the gun out for her to examine and he asked, "Do you see how there's a groove in the top of the frame of this gun?"

"Yes."

"It's what they call a fixed sight." He handed it back to her and said, "Hold the gun up so you're looking down the groove to the end of the barrel where the front sight is."

She did.

"Are you looking at the front sight through the groove?"

"Yes."

"Get the top of the front sight level with the two sides of the groove."

"Okay," she said.

"If you look beyond the front sight, that's about where the bullet's going to go if you fire the gun now, as long as you keep the back sight — which is that groove, the front sight, and the target lined up."

"That's all there is to it?"

"Yes. At least at the range we'll be shooting. But I want you to hold it with two hands so you're comfortable. With a two-handed grip you can aim and control it better."

"So, once the back sight and front sight are lined up, even if I move the gun, wherever it's aimed, that's where the bullet is going?"

"That's right."

He turned her toward the target and stood behind her.

"See the target that's closest? Aim for that."

She brought the revolver up.

"*Wait!*" he said. "Cock it."

She looked back at him and he knew she didn't know the meaning of the term 'cock.'

"Pull the hammer back."

She smiled.

"You did this the first night at the cabin," he said reminding her of when she had threatened to shoot him. He reached around her with both hands, cradled her hands with his left and, with his right thumb he pulled the hammer all the way back. Her hands were soft and warm.

He took his hands away.

"Now that it's cocked, it will take very little for the gun to go off. When you have the target in your sights, pull the trigger very gently and..."

The gun went off. He could see a hole in the eight-ring.

"Cock it once more and shoot again."

She pulled the hammer back and seconds later he could see a hole in the nine-ring.

"That's actually pretty good," he said.

"When you cock it and shoot it, it's called single-action mode. This time I want you to try aiming and shooting it in what's called double-action mode. Instead of cocking it, just pull the trigger. It's going to be harder and not as accurate."

"Then why do it?"

"When shooting in self-defense, you don't always have the luxury of the time to cock it, first. Sometimes, you have to get the shots off as quickly as you can while still trying to be accurate. But shooting in double-action mode will not be as accurate.

"There are three shots left in this gun. Aim — *quickly* — and just pull the trigger — three times — while trying to shoot as accurately as you can."

She began to pull the trigger and stopped, but let the trigger go back to its original position and said, "The gun moved a little bit when I started pulling the trigger."

"That's why it's not as accurate to shoot this way. Let me tell you a story. I don't put much stock in cowboy stories, but did you ever hear of a guy named Wyatt Earp?"

"I think I saw a movie about him and his brothers."

Zach nodded. "Well, there's a story about him. It may be apocryphal, but someone is supposed to have once asked him how you were supposed to act in a gunfight and he replied, 'Take your time...in a hurry.'"

She laughed. "That's funny, but it sounds true at the same time. You'd be scared in a situation like that, wouldn't you?"

"Scared and, if you're not careful, reckless," he said.

"Scared and shitless," she corrected him. "So, you want me to take my time in a hurry," she added.

"Another thing he is reputed to have said is, 'Speed is good, but accuracy is final.'"

"Sort of the same thing in different words," she said and smiled at him. Then she turned and started to bring the revolver up but hesitated again and looked back at him. "What's 'apocryphal' mean?"

He liked her sense of curiosity. First it was about what he was canning; now it was about the words. "Fictitious; something that may not be true."

She aimed and fired three fairly quick shots. The first hit the five-ring and the other two missed the target completely and dug up some snow near the stump.

"That's okay."

"It was lousy," she countered.

"It was good for the first time. You just need practice."

"Will you let me try it in the future?" she asked.

"Yes," he said with conviction. But what could she possibly mean by "the future" when she was leaving today, or at the latest, by tomorrow? It seemed like it was the right time to ask her to stay, but how could he when the last one, his wife, killed herself when he tried to make her stay? The words wouldn't come out.

He asked her for the gun and he thought their fingers seemed to linger on each other's longer than necessary, as if they were trying to intertwine with each other. He asked himself, how that could happen without her being aware of it? How could it be so provocative to him, yet, from what he could tell, it meant nothing to her? How could she be so oblivious? Did she realize how she was making him feel?

He reloaded the gun with the .357 rounds and pocketed the .38 brass. Then he picked up a big rifle, ejected the en bloc clip, and said, "This is an old M1 Garand. It's the rifle used by this country in World War Two, Korea, and even in the early days of Vietnam."

As he went to put another clip in, she pointed to the one he'd removed and asked, "How come those bullets have black tips, but the ones you're putting in don't?"

Holding the black-tipped cartridges up he said, "These are M-2 armor-piercing rounds. They have a carbide insert that'll go through a lot of barriers, including a measured amount of steel, and still do destruction. The regular ammunition…" He held up the other clip. "… is called M-2 Ball, and it's pretty powerful and it'll probably do enough damage to a vehicle's engine to stop it. But the armor-piercing makes it more certain."

"That's why you got it? To stop cars and trucks?"

"That's part of the reason. I once read that during World War Two the American troops in Europe complained that their ammo was useless against German personnel carriers. The personnel carriers had armor plating. Not much, but enough to stop the M-1 ball."

"M-2 ball," she corrected him.

"Yeah, that's what I meant...The military started equipping soldiers at the front with this stuff and it did seem to even up the score a little."

"You've got stories about everything, haven't you?"

He nodded.

"So, it's more apt to shoot *through* something?" she asked.

He nodded, again.

"How do you know all this stuff?" she asked.

"I read a lot and I remember a lot of what I read."

"Yeah, you said that."

"I remember saying it, too."

She laughed, again.

"Let me see 'em?" she said pointing to the armor piercing ammunition.

He handed her the clip and their fingers were briefly all over each other and he started to crave more of that skin-on-skin contact with her.

He took the clip back and pocketed it. "This isn't all that easy to shoot. First, it's heavy. Second, you have to put the clip in like this..." And he began to push it in. "...and force it down with your thumb, and get your thumb out of the way before it gets mashed..." And he let the bolt slam forward driving a round into the breech. "Third, it's going to kick quite a bit until you get used to it."

He clicked on the safety and handed her the rifle.

She took it and gave him a deadpan look. "It's heavy."

"That's what I said."

"*But it's heavy.*"

He smiled.

He turned her around.

"Bring it up," he said, "aim, and try shooting at the topmost target."

She started to raise the rifle. "It's heavy."

"Use your trigger finger to push the safety forward."

She tried to push it forward. "It's hurting my finger."

"Yeah."

She lowered the rifle. "It's heavy, it's going to try to eat my thumb when I load it, it's going to break my finger when I try to push the safety off, and it's going to beat me up when I try to shoot it. I want to try shooting something that's nice to me. Why'd you get it, anyway?"

"Did you say all that without taking a breath?"

"Yes. So, why'd you get it?"

"I got three of them. They're old, but they're very durable, reliable, accurate, fire a good round—and, 'back in the day,' I could get surplus ammo for it that was cheap, spare parts that were plentiful, and they're almost as good as a lot of rifles that would have cost me three and four times as much. So, I got three of these instead of one of those."

"It's heavy," was her reply, but she smiled and asked, "Can I try another one?"

"Sure. But this one kicks, too."

He handed her the Remington 870 and their fingers met, again. They both acted as if nothing had happened.

"This is lighter," she said with a big smile.

"That's going to make it harder to shoot; the lighter the firearm, the more you feel the recoil."

"I wanna shoot it."

"Okay."

"It looks mean," she said.

"It is."

"Have you ever shot anyone with it?" she asked.

He thought she was almost turned on by the thought of it. This, from the girl who had just recently said she hated guns.

"No," he replied. "But, if I had my druthers, and barring someone wearing body armor, at close range I'd rather have this in my hands than anything else."

"What kind of gun is it?"

"It's a 12-gauge shotgun."

"Isn't this the kind of gun that you shoot from one side of the street and wipe out everyone on the other side?"

"Only in the movies. I've got various loads for birds and small game, but there isn't much use for them, now. I've also got some that have slugs; good for big game..."

"Not much of that either..." she said, but looked at the dog, "...except for you, Stupid."

The dog's ears went up at the sound of his name.

Zach smiled. She wasn't going to let go of his past intention to off the dog and can him.

He continued, "Like I said, they're good for big game, if you can get close enough for an accurate shot. For self-defense, if you hit a guy in the torso with one of these it's pretty much *sayonara*.

"But the round I like best for it is the double-ought buck. One shot at close range sends nine balls, each the diameter of a .33 caliber bullet, at about thirteen hundred twenty-five feet a second, and they hit all at once. It's like shooting someone nine times, all at once, with a .32 caliber pistol."

"How much do they scatter?" she asked.

"With the double-ought, the spread is about one inch for every yard. So, at six feet it's like a two-inch circle. At fifteen feet they make about a five inch circle. At the range we're shooting, twenty-five yards, figure it'll be about two-feet wide."

"That rocks. I wanna shoot it," she said giddily.

"It kicks."

"I don't care."

It entered his mind, again, that she *was* getting aroused. But, just as quickly as the thought entered his mind, he dismissed it. She was leaving.

He stepped up behind her and helped guide the butt of the weapon to her shoulder and his left wrist accidentally met with her left breast. He took it away, but she hadn't flinched and she didn't say anything.

"Hold it tight against your shoulder. It's going to come back hard and, if the butt isn't snug against your shoulder it's going to hurt like hell.

"It's going to hurt anyway," he added, "but shooting it right lessens the pain."

"Does it hurt you?"

He thought a second. "Not any more. You shoot it a few times...actually, a few days...and your brain learns to ride with it and it doesn't hurt anymore. It's the learning curve that's hard, especially on someone as small as you."

"Okay. Outta the way; Danielle's got a shotgun," she said.

He stepped back and she brought it up.

"Wait," he commanded, and she paused.

"Kind of lean into it a little bit because it's going to try to push you backward. It's going to hurt..." His voice trailed off.

She leaned too far forward and he said, "Not *too* much." Then he added, "You'll understand how much you have to lean into it after the first shot."

She repositioned herself. "Can I shoot now?"

He stepped forward and said, "This is the safety. Push it so it'll fire."

He stepped back. "Anytime. Take the top target."

There was a short pause, then the shotgun went off. "Shit!" she screamed when its recoil pounded her shoulder. "That hurts!"

He thought she was going to cry, so he started to reach for it saying, "Let's try a different one."

She pulled it to her breasts. "No, I want to shoot it again."

"Why?"

"You said it's powerful. If it's that good, I want to know how to shoot it."

He thought about it. The logical thing was to point out she wouldn't be there to shoot it again—ever. But he didn't.

"But first," she insisted, "show me what kind of bullets it shoots." She was rubbing her shoulder and he knew she was going to have a bruise.

"Call them rounds—or, in the case of shotguns, shot shells—not bullets," he said.

"Aye, aye, sir."

He hesitated and wanted to say something to her. Something about staying longer. But the words he was trying to find were like mosquitoes in the dark that are hauntingly close but always out of reach. He started thinking he couldn't let her and Whoops go back to the road. But he reflexively looked up at the graves. When he tried to make Sandra stay, she found a way out and took everything that mattered to him with her.

"Well?" she asked and he snapped his attention back to her.

"It shoots lots of different loads," he said and took a round containing double-ought buck from his pocket. "But most of them look sort of like this."

"God. They're big."

"Lotta lead inside, lotta powder, lotta power," he said. "It's what you're shooting now."

"And we all know size matters," she said.

He wasn't sure if she realized how loaded that comment was.

"Can I see the target before I shoot again?" she asked.

"Yeah."

They walked up to the target.

"One shot made *all* those holes?"

"Yeah."

"Now I *really* want to shoot it again."

"It's your shoulder."

"I'm a big girl."

They walked back and she assumed the stance, again.

"How many times can I shoot it?"

He took a deep breath. "Every round you shoot is gone forever. But there are four more rounds in the tube."

"Can I shoot them?"

"Yes," he replied. "But you have to work the slide between shots. Jack one into the chamber."

She looked at him quizzically.

"Bring it up to your shoulder. Your left hand is on the pump. Pull it back toward you to eject the spent shell, then push it forward to load a fresh round into the breech. Do it quick. Shoot it, pump it, shoot it, pump it, and keep doing it until it's empty. Be a man about it."

She smiled, brought the gun up, and worked the pump to load another round in the breech. "Like this?" she asked. She was learning fast.

"That's right," he said.

She acquired the target, pulled the trigger once…jacked the slide…twice…jacked the slide…three times…jacked the slide…fired the final shot, jacked the slide again and stopped.

She turned to him. "Was I man enough?"

It was his turn to smile. "Did it hurt you?"

"I wanna cry, but I'm a man, now, so I can't," she said and rubbed her shoulder. "It hurts, but I like it—the gun, that is, not…" and she rubbed her shoulder some more, "…what it does to me." She handed him the shotgun.

He nodded. He admired her spunk.

"Maybe…" She paused. "…later I can try the M1?"

"Sure."

She looked at the targets. "Let's look at them again," she said, and he put it down with the other guns and they walked back through the snow to the target.

"Did I hit it every time I shot it?"

"Looks that way. You're a natural."

"Yeah, I'm amazing," she said with a smile on her face.

They walked back to the guns and when he started to hand her the AR-15, she said, "That one's ugly." She examined it closely while he held it. "But it's a beautiful kind of ugly.

"Kinda like you," she casually threw in and he didn't know how to take that.

"Does it kick, bad?"

"Almost not at all."

She looked at him skeptically. "You're not lying, are you?"

He stared back at her without saying anything.

And, as if that were answer enough, she said, "I trust you. Let me shoot it."

Elation! She trusted him!

"This is a Colt AR-15 H-Bar," he said before placing it in her hands. "All the H-Bar means is that it has a heavy barrel. I'm not sure what's gained and what's lost with it, but it was the only one I could find and afford before the weather changed. So, when I found it…"

She nodded. He didn't have to finish the sentence.

"The barrel makes the rifle heavier than it has to be, but I was told the larger barrel also dissipates the heat better, which presumably makes it a little more accurate, and it makes the gun a little steadier when you're trying to place shots precisely."

"Whatever that means. I wanna shoot it," she said impatiently taking it from him, and he laughed.

He showed her how to work the bolt, then he showed her the safety and made her alternately turn it from fire to safe, back to fire and then safe, again. Then he said, "Pull the trigger."

She looked at him quizzically and said, "It's not loaded, yet."

"Pull the trigger."

"Okay,"

She tried to pull the trigger. It didn't *pull*.

"It won't fire with the safety on," he said. "Now, flip that thing to the 'fire' position."

She did.

"Now, pull the trigger."

It clicked.

"That's how the safety works," he said.

He took a loaded magazine from his pocket and showed her how to put it in. Then he had her work the bolt, again.

"Now that the magazine's in and, you worked the bolt, there's a round in the breech," he said. "It'll fire, now. Put the safety on."

She did.

"Can I ask a question without upsetting you?" she asked in a serious tone.

"Go ahead."

"Did *she* like guns?"

He shook his head no, and with that she brought the rifle up to her shoulder.

"You've got to flip the safety off before you shoot," he instructed, and she flipped it off with her thumb. Then she took it down from her shoulder.

"It won't hurt?"

"I promise," he said.

She smiled and brought it up, again. "I trust you."

He got that heady feeling, again.

She brought it down, again. "The sights are different."

"Oh, put the safety on," he said and abruptly stepped forward until he was behind her and adjusted the rifle back up to her shoulder, "It's a peep-sight. You get the top of the front sight in the middle of the ring…" and, without intending it, his wrist was on her breast, again. This time he left it there. He thought, she must know it's there, but she didn't act as if she'd noticed anything. But now a flood of unexpected emotions he'd been holding back coursed through him.

"And whatever's in a line with it, is where the bullet is going," she said finishing his sentence.

"How far's it shoot?" she asked.

"I read that the bullet will go a couple of miles, but the reputed effective range is just a few hundred yards, depending on the rifle, the round, and the shooter. I guess there are guys who can make it effective to six or eight hundred yards. I can't. What I've done is I've sighted it so it's zeroed at fifty yards and, because the bullet travels through the air in a shallow parabolic arc, the bullet stays within point of aim from just beyond the barrel to about two hundred and forty yards. After that it drops seriously, It'll only be about seven inches low at three hundred yards. But if someone's three hundred yards away, I'm going to be running; it's not likely I'm sticking around and risking my life."

She laughed. "But three hundred yards is pretty far."

"Sometimes. If they're shooting back, it's like they're next door. Now, line up the sights," he said and stepped away.

"I can shoot?" she asked without looking back at him.

"Go ahead."

"It's...not too...heavy," she said spacing her words as she sighted in on the target. Then she was quiet until she pulled the trigger and the gun barked.

She looked back at him, but Zach was watching the target through the binoculars.

"That's pretty good," he said. "Shoot again."

"I don't have to work the bolt again?"

"No. Each time you fire it, now, it'll jack another round in until the magazine's empty."

She looked back through the sights. Three seconds later she fired again then lowered the rifle.

He shook his head when he saw the new hole right next to the first.

"Three more," he said.

She nodded and brought the rifle up again and took her time acquiring the target... "Whoops," she said and flicked the safety off. She looked through the sights again, then fired the rifle once...twice...three more times, in the space of about five seconds.

When she finished, she hugged the gun to herself. "This is *mine*," she said. "I love this gun."

"Put the safety on," he commanded, and she realized she'd made a mistake. She liked that he was on her about it.

It was his turn to sound skeptical. "You say you haven't shot before?"

"No," she said giddily. "Am I doing all right?"

He shook his head in disbelief. "You're doing very well. Some people are just naturals."

"Did you do this well when you first shot?"

"No. I had to work at it."

"Are you good now?"

"Yes."

First, he picked up the brass from the snow and pocketed it. Then he started to walk toward the target. It had been clear through the binoculars that three of the five rounds were within the confines of the 10-ring and the other two had hit just below, in the 9-ring, but he had to see it first hand.

He'd only gone a few steps when he felt a sudden sickening thud to the back of his head.

He spun around in anger.

Danielle was bending over making another snowball as fast as she could. The rifle was leaning with the other guns against the stump beside her.

It took him a second to realize what she'd done. When he started running at her she dropped the uncompleted snowball and, yelling, *"Ohhh!"* she ran as fast as she could to her sister and had her out of the box and up in her arms just as he reached her. She held Whoops up as a shield and he stopped.

"You'll hurt Whoops!" she yelled. She was laughing.

He glared at her. "You can't hold her forever," he said.

"Yes I can. I love my sister. I can hold her for a million years."

He took a step closer but instead of stepping back she scrunched her upper body in the almost impossible task of hiding behind the baby as she laughed.

He got closer, almost face to face with her and grabbed her shoulders. She was about to say something else when, suddenly and impulsively, he kissed her on the lips.

He held the kiss until her shoulders slumped. Her grip on her sister slackened and she started shaking her head. She twisted her shoulders to get out of his grip and, when he released her, she took a step back.

With her eyes cast to the snow and her head still shaking "no," in a flat voice she said, "Don't you ever do that again...*ever*. I want to go back to the road, *right now*."

He wanted to say, "I'm sorry." He wanted to say it was a horrible mistake. He wanted to say something to make up for his impetuous act, but there were no words in the universe he could find. Whatever it was that he thought was developing between them, it wasn't there. He brought his hands up, and still, no words came out. "Sorry," was all he could muster and he slowly turned and, now defeated, he started back to the cabin.

He'd gone four steps when he felt another thud to the back of his head.

When he turned, Whoops was back in the box and Danielle was trying to make another snowball, but there was no time. He was coming after her.

She threw the snow down, grabbed her sister in her arms, and started running, yelling *"Ohhhh! ...Whoopsie, run for your life!"* She was laughing. Stupid was barking and leaping in the snow.

Zach caught her as she turned and tried to push him away. She was falling backwards with him, Whoops between them, Stupid barking, trying to include himself. He had her pinned in the snow and she laughed as she tried to keep the snow out of her face.

"You're treacherous!" he yelled.

"It's payback!" she screamed. "You deserve *every* mean thing I do to you, 'cause *you're* mean. You could have told me about that damned deer.

But *nooo*," she said, no longer laughing but wide-eyed and staring up at him from the snow. "You had to make it a complete surprise and scare the pants off of me. Do you realize that every time I've gone out to the outhouse I was afraid I'd run into a bear or a mountain lion or the boogieman? Then I opened that door and a *dead* deer was hanging there...and *you didn't tell me!*" she screamed.

"Then the way you were always taking my sister away from me..." she yelled. "Wait," she said in an ordinary voice, "we can't count that 'cause you were being nice." Then she yelled, again, "But I didn't know you were being nice, so that counts against you, too."

"What?" he asked incredulously.

She started laughing, again. "Yes, that counts against you, *too*.

"And then you didn't tell me you'd changed your mind about Stupid. *Nooo*, I had to find that one out for myself, too. You're an asshole. I was out here peeing in the snow behind the cabin, so I wouldn't have to see him hanging dead in the shed, and I slipped and wound up sitting with my bare butt in *my own yellow snow*."

He started laughing.

"It's not funny," she insisted, though she herself couldn't stop laughing. "You're an idiot. *You're* the one who should be named Stupid."

Then, she raised her head out of the snow, her face just an inch from his own and in a mean voice she said, "But you're not even good enough to be called Stupid. From now on, I'm going to call you Shit Head, capital 'S' capital 'H.'" She dropped her head back and kept laughing.

"We're back to that? You're going to call *me* Shit Head?"

She stopped laughing, smiled sweetly and said, "If you're nice to me, I'll call you *Mister* Shit Head." Then she laughed, again.

He didn't move off of her.

They stopped talking.

They stopped laughing.

They watched each other's eyes.

His head got closer.

Whoops started crying.

He let his lips touch her lips ever so lightly it was almost as if it wasn't happening. But she lifted her head a little and, with her free hand on the back of his head, she pulled him down until there was full contact. They stayed like that until Whoops's cries turned into a howl. Their lips parted.

"There's something else," she said.

"What?"

"Neither one of us is perfect...well, actually, you're not..."

And he smiled.

"...but stop treating me as if I'm Sandra."

She was serious, now. "When we first met, I knew you didn't like me, and later on I came to realize it was because of Sandra. And now, I know you like me, but you're being overly nice to me, and it's still because of Sandra. Don't get mad at me for this, but I'm *not* Sandra. Start treating me like I'm Danielle."

"How old did you say you are?"

"Seventy-two."

He smiled. "Deal."

He got off her, and he helped her to her feet.

Whoops was wailing, now, and Danielle hugged her, then she held her in one arm and brushed the snow off her with her other hand.

"Oh, no, she's cold," she laughed. "She's got snow in her new tiny little snowsnoot. Let's take her inside and get her warm."

Zach didn't say anything but he took her elbow and guided her to the long guns. He gathered the three of them in one arm. A sense of relief swept through both of them as they walked back to the cabin—the four of them—and with each step her right arm bumped his left.

"We're even, now," she said with finality. "You can't do anything mean to me or you start a whole new round. And if you think I was bad this time...'treacherous,' you said?...." She let it hang there.

"I'll do anything I want," he countered.

"Not if you know what's good for you," she warned.

"Have you *always* been a bitch?"

She thought a second. "Yeah. That's why those men were going to shoot me in the field."

"Really?" he asked.

"Yes," was her one-word reply, and he knew she was telling the truth.

He put his left hand on the small of her back and kept it there until they reached the cabin door. He opened it and let her in first. They spent the rest of the afternoon cleaning up and moving jars and jerky to the cellar. He talked to her about the guns and told her about the air rifle he had in the closet that allowed him to keep his shooting-eye on the cheap. "Rounds of ammo for my rifles were up to over a buck apiece when the ice age started, but I could get a thousand pellets for the air rifle for less than fifteen dollars and keep in practice."

"And I'll bet you've got more than a thousand pellets—a *lot* more."

He smiled that she would know.

Early in the evening they sat on the couch together and talked.

When it got dark, he opened the couch into a bed and they slept on it together.

Chapter 30
September 3

"Why are you being so quiet?" he asked.

They'd awakened early and he'd taken Whoops into the bed between them.

She threw an arm over him. "I'm just thinking," she said.

"About what?"

There was a long pause.

"Why I'm doing what I'm doing."

"What are you doing?" He knew what she meant: sleeping with him. But he wanted her to talk about it.

"I haven't told you what they did to me at that..." The only word she could find was "...place."

"You don't have to."

"I want to, but not now. It still hurts," and she started to cry.

When he reached to touch her face she said, "*No!* I'm okay. Just let me get over it."

"When you're ready," he said.

"Okay." She knew he wanted to know, but she was glad he wasn't overtly inquisitive because she wasn't ready to confront her feelings. "But first I want to tell you, the other girl who was out in the field, her name was Anne, and she was hoping that by sleeping with every guy there, she'd be safe. She was trading sex for security. Now, I'm wondering if that's what I'm doing to save me and Whoops."

"Did you offer them sex?"

She looked at him accusingly. "No," she said curtly. "They just took it...except in the field. That's when I told them I'd do anything if they wouldn't let Whoopsie suffer," and he knew she'd hit a sore spot when she started to cry, again.

He reached to hug her and she said, "Don't do that right now. Just give me a few seconds." And he took his arm away.

"First," she said, "I want you to know, that what they did to me has changed me; it's left a scar on my soul. Does saying it that way sound right?"

He thought she sounded like a poet, "I understand what you're saying," he said.

"They've made me realize what people can be like; that they can be animals who will do anything they can get away with, if they're given half a chance. They've made me hate people. And they've made me feel dirty about myself. It's not something I would have believed could happen to me. I feel as though I won't be clean until I can go back and kill every one of those bastards."

"Be careful," he said.

"Careful of what?"

"You don't want to become like them."

"What do you mean?"

"You don't want to become the kind of person you hate."

"If it meant I'd be able to kill them all, I wouldn't care."

A long silence ensued. She knew what she said affected him.

Finally, he asked, "Did you feel dirty last night?"

She wanted to be careful with her answer. "A little bit, at first, but you were so gentle and caring..."

She let him kiss her.

"Can I tell you something else?" she asked.

He nodded.

"I told you that you scared me when I first met you. Even though you saved us, Mostly, I was scared of you because of what they did to me, what they were going to do to Whoops, and what they did do to Anne. I didn't know what you were going to do to me or Whoops. But I didn't have any choice; I had to go with you. I couldn't admit it to myself, then."

"I'm sorry I scared you," he said.

"You scared the shit out of me," she laughed. "I told you before, you were so quiet. And it seemed like you were always watching me and I didn't know why. It was creepy. But now I think I know why you were that way."

He was confused. "Why?"

"I think you wanted to see if I was going to be like your wife. You don't want to go through that again. You're not mad at me for saying that, are you?"

He thought that was insightful. "I was watching you. I didn't think about why. But maybe that was why I did...how old did you say you are?"

"Never mind," she said. "I tried to hate you because you scared me because you wouldn't talk to me and you kept taking Whoops away from me."

"Sorry."

"Don't say that. Now I know why you were doing it...now that I know what happened to your kids. But if you'd had said something...about why you were taking Whoopsie away from me..." She thought a second. "I probably wouldn't have believed you. Not at first, anyway."

He laughed.

"Don't laugh at me," she said, and he just laughed harder.

She hugged him.

"Can I ask you a question?" he asked.

"Sure."

"Do you like me now?"

"A little bit," she said holding her hand up with her thumb and index finger about a quarter inch apart.

"That's better than nothing," he said.

She laughed. "It's a start."

They lay there and stared into each other's eyes.

"Zach," she finally said, "I want to go back to the road. I want to go down south and find my Mommy and my Dad and my brother, Robert. I have to."

She could see the effect saying that had on him and she continued, "But, then again, now I want to stay here with you. We're safe here...me and Whoops...and I'm starting to like you...Okay, not just starting. I think I liked you right from the start, when you saved us in the field. But like I said, I was scared of you, too, and I didn't trust you. The way men are treating women now, in the ice age, I think you had to prove yourself to me just as much as I had to prove myself to you. And, even though you *did*, you proved yourself again and again and again, I was so scared, I couldn't see it."

She hugged him again while trying not to squish her sister. But Whoops seemed to like where she was.

"I guess you're right," he said. "But I think I was making you prove yourself to me, too. And I'll tell you, you also did it—proved yourself—again and again and again. But I was skeptical. Even though I loved Sandra...and I still do...I don't want to go through what I went through with her, ever again."

"And?" she asked. "Where's that leave me, now?"

"You're different. *But*...until yesterday, I thought you didn't like me...or couldn't like me. I actually started to think you were just plain loony."

She laughed. But he could feel her tears running off her face and onto his cheeks.

"Hey, it's your turn not to laugh," he said. "I entertained the notion that you were either a psychopath or a homicidal maniac."

She laughed again.

"I told you not to laugh."

"I'm not. I'm smiling out loud."

"I want you to know," he said, "Whoops and I talked about you and we decided you can go back to the road *anytime* you want. But she said she's going to miss you if you do."

"Oh," she said and laughed again. "*She talked to you about this?*"

"Yes. It was a very nice conversation."

"What else did she say?"

"She said Stupid would miss you."

"And what else?"

"She said I'd miss you, too."

She gave him a kiss. "Would you? How much?"

He held his hand up with his thumb and index finger about a quarter of an inch apart.

She laughed and kissed him once more.

"Why would you miss me?"

"Because you're the best piece of ass within thirty miles."

She punched him. "Tell me why? Really. I have to hear it."

"You already know why," he whispered.

"Would you make me stay if I wanted to leave?" she asked, and as soon as she said it, she realized it might be the wrong question. "Sorry. I shouldn't have said it that way."

"It's okay. I didn't *make* Sandra stay. She tried to stay with all her might. She just wasn't cut out for it. And because I didn't know what to do about it, I was less than helpful to her. I think that made it worse for her."

"Do you feel guilty about that?"

"Of course I do."

"What would you have done...if you'd known what she was going to do?"

"Don't think I haven't wrestled with that question. But I just don't know...really, I don't."

"That's okay," she said.

"Can I ask you something else?"

"I think you're going to, anyway."

"When you called me the C-word…" She hesitated. "Were you really calling Sandra that?"

"You're not going to let me forget saying that, are you."

"I'm not holding it against you. It's just that, after hearing you talk in your sleep…"

"What did I say?"

"I don't think you really want to know."

He thought a second. "Was I saying things about Sandra?"

She nodded. "You were yelling at her."

He realized she was right, he didn't want to know. But he said, "I've been taking a lot out on you because of her, haven't I?"

"It's okay," she laughed. "I can take it. Last several days, I've discovered I can take a *lot* of shit and still bounce back."

That was another difference between her and his wife, he thought. He hugged her harder. He thought he should feel guilty, but he didn't.

"Can I ask you about your kids?" she said.

"Go 'head."

"What were their names?"

"Sarah and Matthew."

Now that they had names, she started to cry. "Tell me what they were like."

He thought a few seconds. "Matt was quiet, always watching, introspective, and very sensitive. I didn't think he was built for the ice age."

Probably like his mom, she thought.

"Sarah, on the other hand, was insane; she bounced off the walls, she was funny and daring. She was a real daddy's girl. Even at five, she insisted on helping me with everything. She was trying to grow up as fast as she could. If she'd had her way, she'd have run the house, done all the chores, and eaten all the applesauce downstairs."

She laughed again. "They're beautiful in the pictures I've found."

"And now they're dead," he said.

She put her hand on his chest so she could feel his heart. "They're always going to be alive in here," she said.

He hugged her for a long time and when he let her go they lay there without talking for a while. Whoops seemed to be interested in the world around her and they watched her look at the ceiling, the blankets, and at them.

Finally, Danielle said, "I know what we did last night…several times, in fact…but I still don't want you to see me with nothing on."

"Is that why you have the covers pulled way up over you?"

"Yes, and I'm not getting out of bed."

"It's okay," he said.

"I know I'll get used to you seeing me, but, right now, I'm still kind of embarrassed."

"That's okay, too."

"But I'm not sorry about last night," she averred.

"Can't say I am, either."

"But I am sorry about one thing."

He looked at her inquisitively.

"My period. I'm glad we put the towels down, but I think I still made a mess of the bed."

"We did."

"How do you know?"

"I looked."

"You looked? You saw me naked?"

"Yes."

"While I was *sleeping*."

"Yes."

"Now, I *am* embarrassed."

He kissed her. "It's not as bad as you think."

"You don't have a lifetime supply of tampons here, do you?"

"No."

"What happens after they're gone?"

"You make that stuff, just like they did in the old days."

"How?"

"There are a few ways. One way they used to do it was to use cotton materials and stitch a pad that was a dozen or so layers thick, then maybe four inches wide and a foot long. It'd have a couple of 'tails,' one at each end that would tie around a belt that fit around the waist. After each use it was rinsed out well, washed, and dried for future use."

"Kind of the way we're making diapers for Whoopsie?" she asked.

"Yeah. And another way was to make a cloth pouch that could be filled with dried grass or leaves and worn the same way. After it was used, you threw away the contents, washed the pouch, and reused it."

"Figures you'd know stuff like this. Let me guess, though: You read it."

"Yeah."

"Like I say: It figures."

They lay there another few minutes and watched Whoops.

Finally, she said, "I'm going to have to take a shower or something."

"On any given morning, there's only enough water for one shower. Then we'll have to wait a few hours."

"Then we'll have to take one together."

"But I'm not supposed to look," he said.

"Shut up."

§   §   §

They got up, showered together, and dressed. She watched as he made breakfast and she was starting to learn where he kept the food. Afterward, he put on the set of earphones he'd had on the day before.

"What are you listening to?" she asked.

"News and weather."

"What is that contraption?" she was examining the piece of wood on the table with the wires and clips hanging off of it.

When he told her it was a crystal radio, she asked, "Are you telling me that's actually a radio?"

He put the earphones on her head.

"I hear something," she said. "Voices." She looked around. "But what's it plug into? Where's the electricity come from?"

He took the earphones off her and thought a second. "I'm going to give a brief explanation of how this thing works and I'm probably going to lose you. But here goes because these are things you should now know:

"Light waves and electricity are displays...manifestations, if you don't mind me using a big word...of the same force. It's called the electromagnetic force. And radio waves are a form of light waves, but they're invisible. What a radio station does is use electricity to turn sound into electrical impulses, and it uses the electrical impulses to produce radio waves and sends them out in all directions through the air.

"Now, what a radio does is reverse the entire process. It absorbs the radio waves through its antenna and turns them back into electricity. Then the electricity is turned back into the original sound. The problem is that radio waves don't produce that much electricity, so you don't get much sound. That's why we need the earphones. But modern radios contain things called amplifiers that amplify the electricity so they can make a louder sound and you don't need earphones."

"Okay."

She followed him! He liked that.

"But why don't you just use a real radio?" she asked.

"I'm telling you, this *is* a real radio. It's the way the first radios were built. It's simpler, more primitive than modern radios. I have modern radios here that I can plug in if I want, and I have a few solar panels on my roof to produce electricity so I can run 'em. But I discovered that modern radios create electrical waves that can be detected. Decades ago, back in World War Two, American soldiers in Europe weren't allowed to have personal radios, when they were too close to the front, because the Germans could detect them and could figure out where they were. So, the G.I.s resorted to making radios like these, that can't be detected. Instead of referring to them as crystal radios, they started calling them foxhole radios. But it's the same thing."

"And," she concluded, "when they used those, the Germans couldn't detect them and find out where they were."

"That's right."

"And you don't want anyone to detect you, either."

"No. One of the rumors is that the Army is using detection equipment to know where people are. Whether it's true or not, I'd just as soon keep as low a profile as possible. I don't bother the Army, and I don't want them to bother me."

Danielle said, "My Dad used to say, 'Just because you're paranoid doesn't mean they're not out to get you.'"

He smiled. "It's true."

"Where did you get the plans for the radio?"

"Off the Internet, when there still was one."

"I should have known."

"Listen to the news and the weather," he said and she let him put the earphones back on her. "We're picking up a radio station out of Crescent City, just over the border in California. But don't believe everything they say. They'll be taken off the air if they don't spout the approved line.

"I also listen to some of the 'Jesus' stations because they often have news that isn't filtered by the government. Though their views and analyses are often skewed toward religion and salvation, I can often get a sense of what's really happening locally from what they have to say."

"Is this the Crescent City station?" she asked.

He nodded. "They're replaying the President's Weekly Address in about five minutes, if you want to hear what he has to say."

She listened to the end of the news broadcast. The weather followed. After that the station segued into the replay of the President's address. It ran about ten minutes and, when it was over, she removed the headset and asked, "Does the government really have food to be distributed?"

He shook his head. "Not enough to save very many people. Food is so scarce, most Americans are going to die if they're not dead already."

"The government would take everything you've got if they found out where you are, wouldn't they."

"In a heartbeat," he replied.

"Is there really a revolution going on in the country now?" she asked. "Is that why he's talking about the outlaw states?"

"It's really a war of secession." He explained what secession meant. "What we now call the warm states can barely feed themselves and they don't want to share what they have with anyone else. It's a matter of survival. So they've seceded and they're either setting up a separate country or they're forming a bunch of independent countries. I don't think we can be sure, yet. But, in the meantime, they've formed an alliance."

"The President says there'll be penalties, without trial, for anyone damaging roads maintained by the Army. He's really talking about the road pirates, isn't he?"

"Yup. They've already warned people about the roads and bridges and they're making examples of anyone who goes against the warnings. It's pretty well known that about eight months ago they killed hundreds in a compound near Trinidad, California, because they destroyed a bridge on the 101 so they could stop traffic and rob the caravans. But the story goes that, because the Army uses that bridge, too, they went in and killed every man, woman, and child living there. No one's done any damage to the 101 since."

"That's why the Bradys don't do it?"

"And that's why the LaCroix's won't do it either," he said.

"That means the 101 will remain open."

When he didn't respond to that, she knew he wanted her to stay.

"I can't imagine why anyone would become a road pirate. Can you?" she asked trying to change the subject. But she became uncomfortable when he didn't answer right away.

Finally, he said, "I can understand why people do it."

She pulled back to look at him to see if he was serious. He wasn't smiling.

"I didn't expect that answer from you. I expected a big 'No.'"

"It's not something I'd want to do," he said. "But I'm not going to starve to death for some ideal. And, now that you and Whoops are here — and I hope you stay — what do you think I'd do if it came down to a choice between becoming a road pirate and watching you two starve to death?"

She still wasn't happy with his answer, not after what road pirates had done to her and her family.

He could see it in her eyes. "I understand why the road pirates operate as they do," he quickly said. "Everyone in the world has gone into survival mode; those who don't are almost certain to die. I just found a better way to stay alive than they did. But I also started preparing before the ice age. I didn't know what I was preparing for back then: epidemics, an asteroid hitting, the ice age...whatever. Even just losing my job. I was just getting ready for *any kind* of catastrophe and the ice age came along."

"But you're saying you'd become a road pirate," she said flatly.

"Only if I had to...really had to."

She had to think about that.

"What would you have done if you'd become a road pirate and had you found me and Whoops on the road?

"I *did* find you," he reminded her. "And I'd have treated both of you exactly as I'm treating you now."

She was quiet, again.

"It's a new world out there, isn't it," she eventually said. "A whole new set of rules and realities."

"Yes," he said.

"I don't like it," she said.

"After what you've been through, you shouldn't."

They were both quiet for a while. Gradually, without realizing it, she moved closer to him. Eventually, she was hugging him again.

"What are we going to do today?" she finally asked.

"We're going to check the tomatoes downstairs and start making and canning relish using some of the green ones. We're also going to check and see if the seeds I have near the window have dried sufficiently to save for next spring. And if you're going to stay with me, you're going to get one or two more shooting lessons. But we can't have too many…"

"…because every shot is a round that's gone forever," she said finishing his sentence.

He smiled. "You're catching on. So I'm going to show you how to shoot my air rifles. But I can already see you're a natural, so it won't take long for you to learn to shoot well.

"And you're going to have to learn to ski, can, hunt…And you're going to start reading some of the books I have here."

"Am I going to have to do all this today?" she laughed.

"You've got fifteen minutes. Then there's a pass/fail quiz at noon."

"What if I fail?"

"Whoopsie said she'll miss you."

§   §   §

In the evening, he grabbed a rifle and went out the door. She figured, since it was almost dark, he was just going out to the outhouse.

She looked up at the bare mantel for a moment. She got up and carried Whoops to the desk. From the drawer she took the photograph of his wife and two children and returned it to its place on the mantel. She stared at it, and the woman and the kids stared back at her with their pre-ice age smiles. She tried to imagine what they were like before the world went to hell and before Sandra had murdered their children and killed herself. She looked at the children. They were beautiful. She looked at Sandra and wanted to hate her, but she couldn't. But she couldn't understand her either.

She went back to her chair.

He came back in and passed the mantel several times without seeing it.

One time, he started to pass it, but suddenly stopped. He took a step back, and stared at the photograph for a long time. He was surprised she had put it back up. She was telling him something. It was something important: She could live here with him *and* their ghosts, and she could be comfortable. He knew Sandra could never have done that.

He approached her in her chair, hesitated, leaned over and kissed her. It wasn't a long kiss, but she knew what it was for.

Chapter 31
September 4

Since leaving the burning cabin behind, the LaCroix/Brady expedition had found nothing. They followed the verbal directions they'd received from the man Hank had killed, but came up empty. Arguments broke out between Abby and Raymond as to which of them had heard the directions correctly, but Raymond and several of the others were beginning to think the man had either intentionally or inadvertently given them erroneous directions to the Amaral cabin.

In the meantime, for the last two nights, they had, at Raymond's insistence, pitched camp near one of the feeder creeks that fed the larger creeks that ultimately fed the Pistol River. Raymond hoped the sounds of the flowing water in the creeks would drown out the noises Hank made.

So, this morning, the Fourth of September, they awoke to the new day and another leaden sky of unbroken clouds that threatened to storm. But, with eight mouths eating, their provisions were disappearing fast and Hank insisted on, and received, the rations for three men. When Raymond pointed out that burning the cabin had destroyed food stores that would have made it possible for the party to have stayed out longer, without having to backtrack to a reprovisioning point, Abby chastised him for making a big deal over things that couldn't be changed.

"Spilt milk, spilt milk," she said to Raymond and walked away shaking her head.

Hank's logic was, "Just eat what we got, *then* worry, Billy." He laughed as he said it because he knew it annoyed Raymond.

Raymond asked, "If you were bringing the toboggan, why didn't you load it up with more food?"

"Why didn't you tell us to?" Abby asked from afar.

I didn't know you were bringing the toboggan."

"Why didn't you ask?"

"Why would I have asked that?"

"See?" she said and walked further away.

They were cunning, not geniuses, he told himself.

"The next food stores we find will *not* be destroyed," he told them both, but when they didn't acknowledge him, he didn't push the point because he couldn't afford to lose another argument. His leadership was already tenuous.

The day wore on uneventfully except for Hank's relentless baiting of Raymond and, as there was nothing to report, they maintained radio silence. No one in the party talked about the slaughter of the young couple and their child at the cabin, but it weighed on several of them. Today, however, Raymond was so tired he found he could push that atrocity to the back of his mind.

Near noon he finally suggested they call in and turn back to get reprovisioned at one of the preselected rendezvous points, and while several of the members of the party were willing, Abby said there would be no turning back, not until they found the people who had murdered her Sweetie. Hank backed her up. Reprovisioning would split the party up, and Raymond wasn't willing to do that.

§ § §

The day's dreariness deepened as the expedition journeyed further east into the backcountry. Jim De Angelis was forty yards ahead of the party while the other seven, including Brian Peterson, had now bunched up as they came through the trees and brush. Jerry Brady and Steven Ingram still struggled with the looted furniture they carried, while Hank towed the sled that carried Abby and the rest of the loot from the cabin they'd burned. However, with the load, the weather, and the bad nights of sleep, even Hank was beginning to tire. Those from the LaCroix compound, carrying lesser loads, were less tired, but still exhausted.

Hank's barbs at Raymond and the others ceased because even Abby was getting tired of hearing them and she finally told him so. Besides, Hank had served her purposes and Raymond had to know, by now, he was no more than the titular head of the expedition and that, though he would never admit it, any order he gave only stood if she approved it. In effect, she was now in charge.

They marched on, each man and Abby lost in their own thoughts and Raymond was trying to decide how soon they should make camp and how to explain he was calling in for a reprovisioning rendezvous, regardless of Abby's wishes, when, from ahead, Jim De Angelis came hurrying back through the trees.

"A cabin, a cabin, there's a cabin up ahead," he said in a low voice. It changed everything.

Hank perked up. "Cabin!" he exclaimed in a loud voice. This would be another opportunity to annoy Raymond and he opened his mouth to proclaim the sighting of yet another cabin but a voice beside him said simply: "Don't do it."

Hank hadn't realized Brian Peterson was standing right beside him, Though he towered over the sniper, the reptilian look in Peterson's eyes was unmistakable and the words Hank was about to proclaim died on his lips. Hank, never afraid of another man in his life, found Peterson eerily disconcerting.

Raymond witnessed this and again wished there was some way to enlist Peterson's support so that his grip on the leadership would be secure. He'd have to wait and see. He turned his attention back to De Angelis and, as Jim reached the group, Billy asked him, "What did you see?"

"A cabin up ahead. It's occupied. Smoke's coming out of the chimney and there's tracks all around the place.

Raymond turned to Abby, "Let's keep it quiet," meaning, let's keep Hank quiet and he immediately wished he hadn't said it. Reflexively, he was seeking her support—her permission—and he was acknowledging that he couldn't lead the expedition without it.

Without waiting for her reply he said, "Brian, let's go up front and see what it is."

He, Peterson, and De Angelis made their way through about twenty yards of trees which abruptly terminated at the edge of a snow-covered field.

There it was: a cabin. Several yards away from it was a shed that likely housed an outhouse. Between the cabin and the shed was a well-worn path in the snow. Smoke languidly drifted out of the cabin's chimney.

"What do we do?" De Angelis whispered.

Before Raymond could answer, the door to the shed opened.

§   §   §

Zach walked out of the shed. Stupid awaited him.

Zach was close to euphoria. He was happier than he'd been in over a year. There was a sudden sense of family and a purpose to his life. Danielle and Whoops were not replacements for his wife and children, but somehow they managed to banish the ghosts that had been living in the cabin. His home was no longer haunted. The memories of his family could stay, but the grief that had accompanied them was now easing itself out the door. He could move beyond their deaths and make a new life for himself.

Had he not been so euphoric he'd have been paying attention to Stupid who was staring across the field into the trees.

The dog let out a guttural growl.

Zach ignored it.

When Zack was just ten yards away from the door of the cabin, Stupid barked once and started off across the field. Zach froze.

"*Stop!*" he yelled at the dog, and he did.

Then Zach thought of how odd it was the dog had barked and he reached toward his pocket where he had the Model 60 as he scanned the tree-line at the edge of the field. There was something wrong with the way it looked; something unfamiliar in one spot where the trees and the field met.

He broke for the house.

§   §   §

"Take him!" Raymond said sharply to Peterson who had already unslung his rifle and was watching Zach through the scope and, though it was a difficult shot, he deftly pulled the trigger and Zach went down.

The dog started running toward Zach.

Working the bolt smoothly he took a second shot and the dog spilled over into the snow.

This was why Peterson was here.

He was beginning to top off the magazine when he realized Zach was up and lunging toward the front door of the cabin.

By the time he got his third shot off the door had slammed and the bullet splintered part of the wood.

Without thinking, Raymond shouted, "Let's go!" and he started skiing across the field.

Behind him, De Angelis and Peterson followed.

Having come up behind them, Ingram and Jerry Brady started down though the field, too. They were still carrying the furniture, Fred Mayfield ahead of them trying to catch up to Raymond, and Hank was running as he pulled Abby on a wild ride across the snow. With his giant strides, Hank overtook Mayfield.

It was sheer inspiration that prompted Raymond's charge and he was suddenly overcome with exhilaration and felt exonerated, he felt he'd reclaimed his position as the leader of the expedition as they charged toward the cabin.

§   §   §

Inside, Zach lay on the floor bleeding. Danielle rose from her chair with her sister in her arms. She was confused and horrified.

Zach tried to get to his feet but couldn't, something inside was broken; his pelvis? his hip? his femur? He wasn't sure. Getting to his feet was all but impossible, but he tried.

Bullets started coming through the walls and he fell again and screamed at Danielle to get on the floor.

She did.

They lay there, about ten feet apart while large caliber rounds splinted the wood in the walls around them.

It suddenly stopped.

"Come out here or we'll torch the place," a voice from outside yelled.

Zach stared across the floor at Danielle who looked terrified.

"Come out on the count of three or we'll fill the place with bullets and burn it down," the voice outside commanded.

"One..." the voice began.

"...two..."

§   §   §

The door opened and Zach, hanging onto the jamb, emerged limping from the cabin, his right pant leg was matted with blood. He used all his effort to stand.

"*It's him! It's him!*" Ingram cried. Making a positive ID made his day. "He's the guy I hunted with. *He's Zachary Amaral.*"

That was exactly what Abby wanted to hear and she smiled a sinister smile as she got off the toboggan and approached him.

Zach hopped down the stairs onto the snow and Mayfield and his cousin, Jerry, each grabbed one of his arms and he groaned in pain as Mayfield frisked him and found the Model 60 in his pocket.

"This is a beauty," Mayfield said looking at the little .357 revolver and he pocketed it.

"Do you have that bitch Danielle here?" Abby demanded.

"Please leave us alone," Zach begged.

"*Is the bitch here?*" Abby screamed.

Danielle appeared in the doorway with Whoops in her arms and wearing a dress that once belonged to Zach's wife.

Abby smiled again. "You're *both* going to pay for what you did to my Sweetie," she said. "*All three of you are going to pay!*" she screamed.

"Leave Danielle and her sister alone," Zach pleaded. "I'm the one you want."

Abby just couldn't get rid of her smile.

"What are we going to do with them?" Jerry asked.

Abby suddenly yelled, "*Hank! No!*"

He had his rifle leveled point-blank at Zach, but he hesitated at Abby's command.

"Not yet. I want him to see what happens to his girlfriend for what they did to my Sweetie. They gotta pay," she said. "They gotta know," she added, her voice rising. "*They gotta suffer for what they done!*"

Hank snorted a laugh at Abby. He looked at Zach, leaned his rifle against the side of the cabin, then with a flourish he undid his Sam Browne belt from around his waist and let it drop to the ground as if he were dropping his trousers. Zach knew what the gesture meant.

Raymond had nothing to say. He knew what was coming. He hoped the girl's and the baby's deaths would be swift. He tried to detach himself from the scene.

As Hank's approached, Danielle retreated inside with Whoops tight in her arms.

"Get out!" she screamed.

But Hank ascended the stairs in a single bound, stepped inside, and slammed the door behind him. The door and walls couldn't contain the muffled voice of Danielle alternately swearing and screaming. "Leave my sister...No!...stop...leave my sister..." Hank's lusty laughs and insults were mixed with Danielle's defiance and Whoops's desperate cries. There was a sickening thud.

Zach struggled and got a rifle butt in his face, from Jerry, for his efforts. He wasn't sure if his jaw was now broken or not. But his strength was gone. He couldn't help Danielle anymore.

She was screaming again.

"She'll learn," Abby said to Zach, then she spit in his face. "Eye for an eye, tooth for a tooth. It's the last thing she's gonna to learn. Then you'll learn it. You'll learn what it's like to have something taken away from you...*just before you die.*"

There was another sickening scream from within the cabin and Abby smiled.

Then it was silent. The snowflakes came down like fairies floating around them, unconcerned with the human drama unfolding in their midst.

Neither Raymond nor Peterson could look at the cabin. Still holding onto one of Zach's arms, Fred Mayfield just stared at the snow at his feet.

"Wait'll you see the surprise Hank has for you," Abby hissed at Zach. "You'll regret what you did to Joel, what you did to my Sweetie. It's the last regret you're ever gonna have...*you goddamned son-of-a-bitch!*" she screamed.

As those words came out of her mouth, the cabin door was flung open.

Danielle stood in the doorway bathed in blood from her hair down to the hem of her dress. She held something in her hands.

§　§　§

Inside the cabin, Hank had dragged Danielle around the room by her hair while she screamed and swore. She held onto Whoops with every ounce of her strength. But she didn't have a quarter of Hank's strength and he threw her to the floor as he laughed.

"Whore," he called her.

She desperately rose to her feet like a boxer trying to last out the final round of a title bout and Hank threw a punch she tried to shield the baby from, but part of it caught her and part caught Whoops whose desperate screaming and panic filled the room. He threw another punch and knocked Danielle off her feet again. Miraculously she got up, once more, still clutching her sister. She desperately fought her way to "her" chair and fell into it.

Hank's pants dropped down around his feet and he stepped out of them. He had an erection. This was the moment he'd come in here for. He was on Danielle like a lion on a lamb and in a flash tore open the top of her dress exposing her breasts.

"You may as well enjoy this, whore, because..." He hesitated, "First we gotta get rid of this little piece of shit," he said.

As he grabbed Whoops and tried to wrench her from Danielle's grasp, she desperately held on to her sister with her left arm while her right hand fished down between the cushion and the arm of the chair. Hank began to choke her with his other hand. Her hand searched. She was beginning to pass out. She hoped Zach hadn't already found...and suddenly her hand wrapped around its handle. In one motion, she pulled the hunting knife out from under the cushion and whipped the razor-sharp blade across the left side of his neck, neatly severing the carotid artery, and just as quickly brought it back and slashed the other side. Their eyes locked as he grimaced, her own eyes looking deep into his with homicidal hatred as she showed him the blood-soaked blade.

"You fucking asshole," she said.

"You fuckin' cunt," were the last words ever to form on his lips. He stood up trying to hold his life fluid inside his body with both hands, but geysers of blood, pumped by his giant heart, sprayed from between his fingers hosing both Danielle and Whoops. The look on his face was profound surprise. He was dead before his stinking corpse hit the floor.

In a flash she put her screaming sister on the seat cushion and she was out of the chair and across the room to the closet.

§   §   §

When she threw the cabin's front door open, all eyes turned. And there she was, her dress torn open to her waist, her body and clothes drenched with Hank's blood, the Remington 870 coming up murderously in her small hands.

Mayfield, holding Zach by his left arm, suddenly realized the shotgun was pointed at him. The first time she pulled the trigger she sent nine balls of double-ought buck into his face and neck. Four of them penetrated his brain, two reaching all the way to his medulla oblongata, one of them causing hemorrhaging in the lateral medulla. All involuntary muscle control in Mayfield's body ceased and he had a total loss of coordination as he slumped against Zach. He wasn't dead, yet.

In a panic Jerry Brady released Zach's right arm and Zach, keeping his balance on one leg, caught Mayfield's falling body and pulled his Model 60 from Mayfield's pocket. With a calmness that surprised even him, he put the gun against Jerry's head and blew his brains out. Jerry crumpled like a paper bag full of fresh shit. Zach let the paralyzed Mayfield slip to the ground.

Respiration was now impossible for Mayfield. As he lay in the snow fully conscious of the maelstrom of screaming and shooting that raged around him, he became witness to his own death by suffocation—and there was nothing he or anyone else could do about it.

Danielle immediately jacked in another round into the chamber and she brought the shotgun to bear on De Angelis. With a squeeze of the trigger, nine red dots appeared on his chest and she ensured he would never learn that Louis LaCroix had fucked his wife.

Now, for the first time in his life, Brian Peterson, the hunter, was the hunted. The man who had calmly drawn a bead on his victims more than forty times for the Army and a dozen times for Louis LaCroix was, suddenly, the prey instead of the predator as Danielle brought the shotgun to bear on him as she worked the slide on the shotgun. Never having been the prey before, panic had a profound effect on Peterson and he fumbled as he unslung his prized rifle from his shoulder and, though he got his shot off first, the experienced sniper was too hurried, too panicked, and his bullet merely splintered the door jamb three inches from Danielle's head.

Danielle was too focused to flinch.

Peterson, his training finally kicking in, expertly worked the bolt of his rifle to get a second shot. He wouldn't miss again.

However, with an almost Zen-like calmness, Danielle, now a half-second ahead of the master marksman, took just enough time to be precise and, as he slammed the bolt home on his sniper rifle, she sent nine balls of death screaming down the barrel of the 870.

What a difference that half-second made. In what some might call poetic justice, Peterson now knew what many of those others, who had had the misfortune to have appeared in his crosshairs, had learned before: With nine balls striking his neck and chest, and both carotid arteries spewing blood, he had only seconds of consciousness left before he was dead.

As he dropped his rifle and slumped to the ground, Danielle jacked a fourth round into the chamber.

Abby, Raymond, and Ingram had been too surprised by the sudden commotion to react and, before Danielle could snuff out their existences, they threw their arms up in surrender. Her finger, already putting pressure on the trigger, she paused.

The air was abruptly and eerily still except for Whoops's painful screams in the cabin and Stupid's desperate whines on the snow.

The only surprise to both Zach and Danielle was…

…neither of them shot anyone else.

The snowflakes still swirled around them like the chorus in a Greek tragedy — witnesses but uninvolved.

No one spoke. Danielle looked down the barrel moving the sight at the end of the tube from one to another of them because she *needed* a reason to pull the trigger again. But none of them moved. None of them gave her an excuse. She didn't know it, yet, but this would create a new problem for her.

"How's Whoops?" Zach asked breaking the silence.

"She's okay," Danielle replied in a monotone that told Zach that, somehow, Hank Brady was no longer a problem; he was dead. But he couldn't imagine how Danielle could have survived the onslaught of the brute.

"Are you okay?" Danielle asked.

"I'm not sure," he said.

Danielle watched the three as she stepped down the stairs to reach him. Abby began to lower her arms and Danielle brought the 870 back up. "Keep your hands up."

Abby's arms went up again.

"What happened in there?" Zach asked. "I didn't hear a shot."

"I didn't need a gun for that piece of shit," she said.

Abby and Raymond glanced at each other.

"Is any of that blood on you yours?" he asked.

"It's all Hank's."

Even Zach couldn't believe her words. Still trying to stand on one leg, he was losing blood and in imminent danger of falling.

Abby's arms started coming down again.

"Put them *up!*" Danielle yelled.

"My arms are getting tired," she complained.

"Put them *on top* of your head," Zach ordered. "All of you."

They did.

Danielle nodded. She liked that. She studied the situation.

"Can you get yourself into the house?" she asked Zach without taking her eyes off the three of them.

"We've got to do something with them, first," he replied.

"That's not an answer to my question," she said and, enunciating each word deliberately, she again asked, "Can you get yourself into the house?"

"Yes, but…"

"Can you get Stupid into the house?"

Stupid was up on three legs. The femur on his left rear was shattered beyond repair and the leg was dangling by shreds of muscle and skin. He gingerly licked his wound.

"I think so. But we still have to…"

"I can deal with them," she said. She was getting testy.

"But we've got to do something, *now,*" he said emphatically.

"Get Stupid into the cabin," she said without taking her eyes off them.

Zach teetered on his good leg. He was beginning to feel woozy. He sensed his and Whoops's fates were now in Danielle's hands. Whoops was screaming. He didn't know if he was losing his mind along with his blood, but he was going to trust her, now.

"Get Stupid in the cabin," she repeated.

"Come 'ere, boy," he said and turned to go up the steps with Stupid in front of him

"Wait!" she yelled.

Chapter 32
September 4

No one knew why Danielle shouted, "Wait," but they all froze their eyes on her.

The moment Abby, Raymond, and Ingram surrendered, it became clear neither she nor Zach could bring themselves to simply execute them, though it was clear that, had the tables been turned, those in the Brady-LaCroix party would have no trouble murdering Zach, Danielle, and even Whoops.

It was also readily apparent to Abby and Raymond that Zach and Danielle's reluctance to shoot them could work to their advantage. With Zach's wound he would not be on his feet much longer and, once he was down, they would have only the young girl to deal with. They just had to bide their time until she made a mistake with a lapse in judgment or attention. It was inevitable.

Danielle was aware Zach was succumbing to his wound. Whatever had to be done, she would soon be doing alone. With a glance at him and Stupid, she wasn't sure if either of them were going to live. There was no 911 to call, no doctors, no hospital to take him to. If he died, she and Whoops were alone in the world, again.

With everyone now staring at her, she looked around. There was Ingram in his police uniform and still wearing his Sam Browne belt. With an eye on the three of them she went to the body of Jerry Brady. He too had worn a belt with the same police paraphernalia Ingram wore. She thought a few moments, then quickly stooped, took the handcuffs from the belt, then stood, again.

"What are you doing?" Zach asked.

She didn't answer. She kept as much of her attention focused on the other three as she could.

She went to the Sam Browne belt Hank had dropped in the snow. As she stooped to retrieve the handcuffs, she stopped and quickly brought the shotgun up. "Put your hands back up on top of your head," she yelled sharply at Raymond. Raymond's hands had been gradually coming down. She was scared and anything any of the three survivors did made her nervous. He put them back up. With an eye on him, Danielle retrieved the cuffs from Hank's belt.

"How do these work?" she called back to Zach.

"They go on real easy. To get 'em off, usually one key fits all."

"Where's the key?"

"I can see a key ring on the belt on the ground."

She glanced down at Hank's belt and quickly stooped to retrieve it, still keeping a wary eye on what Abby, Raymond, and Ingram were doing.

"Which key?"

"The little key with the circle at one end," Zach replied,

"Where's the Model 60?" she asked.

"Why?"

"I may need it," she said.

He hopped up behind her and slid the revolver into a pocket of the dress. "There are only four rounds left in it," he whispered.

"That's okay. Get in the cabin, throw my coat and the boots out," she said and, with the muzzle of the shotgun leading her, she approached within ten feet of the trio.

"Take your coat off, Abby." she ordered.

"It's cold," Abby said.

"If you don't take your coat off, in two seconds, you won't feel a fucking thing."

"Listen to her mouth," Abby said and Danielle brought the shotgun up and rested the sights on her.

"Okay," Abby said and quickly let her coat drop to the snow.

"Hands back up on your head."

Abby's hands went back up on her head.

"Your turn," she said to Ingram.

Ingram was too gutless to protest and he let his coat drop into the snow then he put his hands right back up on his head.

She nodded to Raymond and, seeing as the shotgun was now aimed at him, he followed suit. Why not, he thought? He had only to wait until this young, dumb bitch made the mistake that would get her killed.

His coat dropped, but he stood and stared at her defiantly.

"*Get your hands back up on your head!*" she said.

He was testing her and he could see he was making her nervous. That was good. His hands went back up, but slowly. It was just a matter of time.

"What are you going to do with us?" he asked.

Danielle didn't answer him. There was something going on in her head, he thought.

She nodded toward Ingram and said, "The handcuffs you've got on your belt; take them, and handcuff Abby's left hand to that guy's right hand."

Sensing Raymond was a bigger threat than the others, she brought the shotgun up to bear on him as a warning against resisting, and Ingram did as he was told.

"Tighten them," she said.

"Careful!" Abby yelled as he did, but it was too late and Raymond and Abby were now bound to each other.

She threw the other two sets into the snow at Ingram's feet.

"Take those and put a set on each of your wrists.

"*Do it!*" She yelled when he hesitated, and he did.

"Now, handcuff your right wrist to that other guy's left hand."

Ingram hesitated when Raymond glared at him.

"Do it," Danielle ordered again.

Ingram put it on him.

"Make sure it's tight."

He did.

"Now, handcuff your left hand to Abby's right hand.

"Not that way," she shouted. "I want you to go around the other way."

"But we'll all be back-to-back," Ingram said.

"That's right. Now, *do it.*"

Raymond suddenly realized the girl was smarter than he'd thought.

Ingram did as he was told and, this time, he made them tight without having to be asked.

Danielle got closer and checked them.

She looked back at the steps. Zach had thrown the coat and boots out. She backed up, sat on the steps and, while watching them, she quickly changed into the boots and donned the coat. Then she was back on her feet.

"Now, let's go back to the road," she said, and the three started trudging through the snow to the edge of the field with Danielle behind them. Through the trees, the snowflakes, and the cold afternoon air they went. Raymond now realized the pistol hidden in his pocket was inaccessible. But, if she was going to shoot them, she'd have done it long ago. He could wait for an opportunity.

It wasn't easy for the three to walk through the woods handcuffed as they were. Either someone was walking backwards or all three of them had to step sideways through the snow. They fell frequently, particularly when going through thick bushes or stepping over deadfalls, and, whenever Raymond fell, they all fell and had trouble getting back to their feet. Abby and Raymond constantly bickered with each other. Abby beseeched Danielle to take the handcuffs off her but all Danielle would say was, "Keep walking."

Raymond and Abby complied because each was anticipating the moment when they could reach the handguns they had concealed. But, because of the way they were bound together, reaching them was all but impossible, and Raymond realized an accurate shot would be impossible with each of his hands handcuffed to someone else, even if he had the gun in his hands right now. So, he and Abby bided their time, expecting a better opportunity.

Abby fell again and they stopped. She lay in the snow and asked, "Can you please free me, dear? I'm not the danger these two are to you."

"Can you guys drag her if I shoot her? Or should I shoot you all before we reach the road?"

"I'll drag the dried-up old bag if I have to," Raymond said.

Ingram bemoaned his fate, but Abby struggled to her feet.

§   §   §

They reached the edge of the road.

"Stop!" Danielle commanded.

She placed the key on a stump.

She spoke to Ingram. "Work your way over here and get the key."

They all had to move together so Ingram could reach it.

"I want you to unlock the cuffs," she said, but she explained how she wanted it done and, soon, they were freed of each other but each of them was standing with a set of cuffs on one wrist.

"What now?" Raymond asked. His opportunity was almost here, but she still had the shotgun pointed in his direction.

"Take your clothes off."

Raymond looked at Abby. He looked at Ingram. Neither had moved and he knew, with his clothes off, the gun would be out of reach.

"I'm not taking my fucking clothes off."

"You're not?"

"No."

"I'm not getting naked in front of these men," Abby said. "It would be a sin."

"You're not taking yours off, either," Raymond said to Ingram. "I'll beat the shit out of you if you do."

Ingram said nothing, but he was more afraid of Raymond than he was of Danielle even though she had the shotgun.

Danielle stared at them wordlessly.

"What now?" Raymond asked her. He pretty much had her where he wanted her. All he needed, now, was a momentary lapse in her judgment and he had her.

"I don't know who you are," she said to him, "but you *really* don't know how pissed off I am and you should be listening to me."

He still didn't move and the other two weren't moving if he didn't.

"Take 'em off," she repeated.

He shook his head "No."

She didn't know what to do and took a deep breath. She had to make a decision and, not sure of what to do next, she let her gaze drop to the snow. It was the lapse Raymond had been waiting for and what happened next was a blur. His hand went into his pocket and he brought up a Kahr .40 caliber handgun.

Danielle saw the motion in her peripheral vision and, though he managed the first shot, it's not that easy to shoot a handgun accurately. His shot went wide but with a two-handed grip he was zeroing in on her. But Danielle was already in motion and with a gentle squeeze of the trigger she sent a load of double aught buck into his chest. Raymond fell to his knees as Danielle jacked the last shell into the chamber and swung the shotgun smoothly to Abby. Abby now had a small pistol in her hand. Realizing she was about to die, she quickly threw it onto the snow and put her hands back up.

Raymond was gasping. He had a look of amazement on his face as a torrent of blood poured from his mouth. He quickly went into shock from the loss of blood, fell facedown, and proceeded to die.

Once again there was silence until Danielle said, "Remove his clothes."

With the shotgun pointed at them, Abby and Ingram hurriedly removed the clothes from Raymond's body.

"I want you to pick up that gun up by its barrel and toss it in this direction," she said to Steven.

He complied and threw the Kahr and it softly landed in the snow at her feet.

"I want you to do the same with the other one."

He threw Abby's gun toward her.

"I'm going to say it one more time and, if you don't do as I say, I'll kill you both right here. I want you to keep your hands in sight and take your own clothes off—both of you."

They began to undress until they were down to their underwear.

"Everything."

Abby hesitated and Danielle looked down the barrel at her and was about to pull the trigger.

"Okay!" Abby yelled.

"Steven, I don't want you looking at me!" Abby screamed.

Abby and Ingram quickly took off their underwear.

"What are you doing?" Abby demanded.

"Shoes too."

"But the snow is cold."

"If you don't take them off, you won't have to worry about how cold it is," and she brought the shotgun up once more.

They took off their shoes.

"Steven, handcuff yourself to Abby."

"What are you doing," Abby asked.

"Do it, Steven."

He did.

"Down to the road...*now!*" she yelled and, when they hesitated, she had the scatter gun up once more.

"My feet are freezing," Abby complained as she and Ingram negotiated their way down the bank to the 101. "Don't look at me!" Abby yelled at Ingram again.

"Please, let me at least have my shoes," Abby cried.

"Start walking," Danielle said.

"We can't walk like this," Abby complained.

Danielle picked up their clothes and shoes.

"Throw me my shoes," Abby demanded.

But Danielle had already started back into the trees. But she stopped when she heard something. She came back out of the trees, again and looked north.

It came into view over a rise: A car—then another, and another. It was a caravan.

Abby and Ingram first looked north then at Danielle. Then they looked north again.

The vehicles came closer, one after another like pearls on a string.

Glancing back and forth from the cars to Danielle and back again to the cars they were unsure of what Danielle might do if they tried to wave them down. So, at first, they tentatively waved their arms. But their gestures became frantic when the cars were upon them.

"Help me!" Abby yelled.

"Stop! Stop!" Steven shouted.

"Please!" Abby implored as the cars zoomed by. "We'll pay you," she screamed.

The convoy didn't even slow.

When it had passed, they looked back at Danielle.

"This is how you've left people," Danielle said then started crying. "You made my Mommy and my Dad and my brother, Robert, freeze to death on the road and this is how I had to stand in the field waiting to die with my sister." She couldn't stop crying now.

"Anne, I'm sorry, I'll make it up to you," Abby beseeched her.

"Anne is dead. My name is *Danielle!* she screamed. "Remember my name, and take it to hell with you. My name is *Danielle! Danielle!*"

"I'm sorry, 'Danielle' is what I meant to say."

Danielle didn't answer.

"I'm sorry," Abby said. "It's not what I wanted. I didn't know what they were going to do to you. *Please*, let us at least have our clothes. I promise, you can come back with us. We'll take care of you. You and your daughter."

"*My sister!*" Danielle screamed.

"Your sister," Abby corrected herself. "We'll take care of you both."

They started walking toward her and Danielle calmly brought the shotgun up and they stopped. Ingram knew she'd kill them as quickly as she'd killed Raymond moments before.

"Start walking," Danielle said.

"At least let us have our shoes," Abby implored.

Danielle said nothing.

"Do the Christian thing?" Abby screamed.

"The Christian thing would be to shoot you, so you don't suffer. But I'm not that gracious. You're going to hell, and someday I'll join you there for what I'm doing to you. But it's worth it."

With that she turned and walked about thirty yards into the forest. She couldn't hear or see them anymore. She sat on a stump and began to cry. Vengeance didn't feel as good as she had hoped it would. She began to puke. Zach's words came back to her: "Careful you don't become what you hate."

"I'm becoming just like them," she cried. "I'm becoming Abby Brady." She puked again.

She wasn't sure how long she sat there. Five? Ten? Twenty minutes? She had to return to the cabin, but she'd give them their clothes and they could figure out what to do from there. But, when she reached the road, they were gone. She looked north and south. They were nowhere in sight. She dropped their belongings—their shoes and clothes, less the two handguns—on the side of the road in case they returned.

Strangely, she started to hope they were all right and she turned and started making her way back to the cabin, back to Whoops, back to Zach, and back to Stupid, trudging through the snow but looking back frequently and hoping she wasn't followed.

Chapter 33
September 4

She returned to the cabin as the snowfall was picking up. She was cold and tired. But she couldn't stop to rest; there were still things to do. Four of the bodies lay in front of the cabin and were slowly disappearing under a blanket of white. They couldn't stay there.

She stepped into the darkened cabin and flinched because Hank's body was closer to the door. She pointed the shotgun at it and approached it cautiously. From beneath half-mast eyelids, his eyes stared, vacant and unblinking. He was dead.

Despite his wound, Zach must have tried to drag him out, but was too weak or too much in pain to get him any further. The couch was pulled out into a bed and he was on it. She stepped closer; Whoops was asleep beside him. On the floor next to them, Stupid lay motionless. She leaned over Zach and was relieved to hear him breathing. She put her hand on him. He was cold. She got more blankets and piled them on him and her sister.

Without knowing exactly what she should do, she knew Stupid's leg was shattered beyond repair. She sensed there was only one way to possibly save him. Her hands shook and she cried her eyes out as she took one of Zach's boning knives and knelt beside him. Stupid lifted his head and watched. He either couldn't feel his leg or he knew what she about to do and did nothing to stop her. When she had cut the splintered part of his leg away, he put his head back down and lay motionless. She didn't expect him to live, but he was still breathing.

She went to Zach and felt his face again. It was sweaty even though he was cold.

Whoops was awake now and watched her. When Whoops smiled, Danielle started to cry again. Her little sister didn't know how bad things were, but her world was all right when Sissy was there.

The next thing she did was to get the tattered, blood-spattered dress off and change into jeans and a sweater, and she put the coat back on. She went to Hank's body and emptied his pockets. Then she tried to move him closer to the door. He was huge. She pulled but found she couldn't move him all at once. So she dragged one arm, then the other, then a leg, then the other leg, then the torso, just to move him a few inches. Then she started the whole procedure over again, with the arms, the legs, and the torso. Inch by inch and foot by foot she got his body closer to the door.

It took ten minutes, but she finally got it to the threshold and she rolled it down the steps.

She hoped it would be easier to drag his corpse through the snow, but it wasn't. It just seemed to want to sink in.

She looked at the toboggan still covered with the plunder from the cabin down river. She got an idea and unloaded it.

Dragging it to the edge of the forest, she brought back branches and brush and formed a thick bed on the snow about forty yards from the cabin.

Then she dragged the toboggan to the woodpile behind the cabin and loaded it up with firewood. She dragged it back to the bed of branches and created a layer of the split wood on top of the branches. Atop that she laid more dry branches and kindling. Over that she piled more firewood. She knew what she wanted: an inferno. Once she was satisfied with what she had done, she dragged the toboggan to Hank's body and tried to move his corpse onto it, but the toboggan kept sliding. Finally, she found the solution and rolled him onto it. It wasn't easy but she managed.

She pulled the toboggan to the pile of wood and started to move his body up onto the impromptu platform. First, one arm, then the other, then his upper body. She tried to heave the rest of him up onto it, and began swearing when she couldn't. After ten minutes, she was sweating profusely, but she finally had his whole torso and arms onto it, got his legs up, and rolled him to the middle.

The sun was almost below the tops of the trees.

She returned to the others and, one after another, searched their bodies. She found more weapons concealed under their clothes and placed those, and whatever else she thought useful, aside. Then she loaded Fred Mayfield's body onto the toboggan and took it to the pyre and got him up on top of it. Next, she rolled the body of the cuckolded Jim De Angelis onto the toboggan and brought him to the pyre. Then Brian Peterson. And finally Jerry Brady. The whole operation took over three hours to complete because she had to stop frequently to rest. But once she was done she covered them all with more branches and firewood.

The last of the day's light was fading in the western sky. She stood and examined her accomplishment.

She was too tired to think about what she was about to do now and too numb to cry.

Her hands were rubbed raw, her arms and legs were aching, her feet were cold and numb. She did not realize she was beginning to manifest symptoms of exhaustion. She could hear her sister crying inside the cabin. She was barely able to strike a match to light a piece of tinder. It caught. But she had another ready, just in case. She watched the flame. She knew each match lit was another match gone forever in a world where she may never be able to get another one.

The fire spread slowly. She helped it by moving some of the burning kindling to other parts of the pile. The nascent flames ate their way through more and more of the tinder and branches, picking up speed as they raced through the seasoned wood. They were like hungry insects settling in to feast on a piece of carrion. More and more they grew into the conflagration she had hoped for. They greedily engulfed the bodies one after another. The only sounds were the growing whisper of the flames and crackling of the branches. The snowflakes fell silently all around her and the rest of southwestern Oregon. It would all be over, soon.

She watched with tired eyes until a horrific scream filled the night. A man rose up out of the pyre. She had no way to know his name but Jim De Angelis, his arms flailing, his clothes awash in smoke and flames, rose to his feet. Her screams joined his. What had she done? She backed toward the cabin in terror, her hands to her face, and watched through her fingers as he howled and tried to brush the flames away from his face. Large pieces of skin came off with every swipe. He kept screaming. He turned and saw her and tried to walk toward her but the logs were unsteady and he fell to his hands and knees. Smoke poured off of his body. "*Oh, God!*" he shrieked. "*Oh, God!*" He tried to rise again, but he fell into a position like a man in prayer and moaned. She began to cry uncontrollably. She watched as the flames swaddled him and he stopped moving. The fire was making him its own.

For his sake—for her sake, she hoped he was now dead.

Whoops became more desperate and demanding inside the cabin.

Sparks rose heavenward to mingle with the snowflakes that were falling…into Hell, she told herself.

She backed toward the cabin and sat on the front steps, her face buried in her hands. She prayed they were all dead, now. She hadn't intended any of them to suffer. But, she asked herself, what if she had realized he was still alive? What would she have done with him? She didn't have an answer.

Finally able to move again, she went back to the pyre and threw more wood atop the blaze to keep it going. But the flames were getting too hot and she had to back away once more.

Finally, she turned, and went back into the cabin to check on Zach and her sister.

She leaned over him. He was barely breathing, but he periodically moaned. She touched him. He was still cold.

She picked up Whoops to console her and realized she herself was still crying. She embraced Whoops until they both stopped. Regaining her composure, she realized her sister needed a diaper change. She needed to be fed. Mundane tasks still had to be performed in the midst of death and horror.

The image of the tortured man kept flashing through her brain, so she jumped when a voice came out of the darkness: "I want you to leave."

It was Zach.

With Whoops in her arms, she went to him.

"I want you to leave," he repeated.

"How are you feeling?" she asked.

He brushed her question aside. "You've *got* to leave," he hissed. "Will you?"

When she didn't answer, he suddenly reached out and grabbed her arm with his strong hand and pulled her down so she had to sit on the bed. "Promise me you're going to leave," he insisted.

"You're hurting me," she cried, but he wouldn't let go.

"Promise me you'll take Whoops and get out of here," he demanded.

"Why?"

"More of them are going to come."

She didn't know what to say.

"*Promise me!*" he yelled

He wasn't going to let go until she answered his question. "I promise," she said.

"I'm sorry," he whispered and his grip slackened. "I don't want to hurt you."

He looked away and stared off into space.

"Who was screaming out there?" he finally asked.

"No one."

"Was there someone out there with you?"

"No," she said. She couldn't talk about the man. In her mind he would forever be screaming and writhing in the flames. She looked at the door and half expected him to come through it smoke and flames pouring off of him.

She put Whoops back on the bed and stood.

"Where are you going?" he whispered.

"What's in your medical kit downstairs?"

He looked at her funny.

"What do you have for infections?" she asked.

"Antibiotics aren't going to help me," he said.

"That's not an answer to my question. What do you have for infections?"

He had to think. "There's ceftriaxone...and cephradine..."

She'd never heard of them. "Are they good for infections?"

"Yes...Are you and Whoops okay? Are you hurt?"

"We're okay," she said. "I'll be right back."

She took the flashlight from where he kept it under the couch and turned it on. Going to the middle of the room, she kicked the rug back, opened the trapdoor, and went down the ladder to the cellar. She went right to the kit. After rummaging through it she found plastic pouches that said ceftriaxone sodium on them. There were directions on the packages: She had to mix the powder inside one of them with water, put the mixture in a syringe—she found several of those in the kit—and inject it deep into muscle tissue. She took a deep breath; she could do that.

She searched deeper. There were several plastic bottles that read cephradine. That was the other drug he'd mentioned. She wasn't sure which would do what. But the instructions on one of the bottles of cephradine read: "Take one (1) every twelve hours until gone."

There was another bottle. This said "morphine." She knew what that was for.

She took several pouches, a bottle each of cephradine and morphine, and a syringe and went back upstairs.

She hydrated the ceftriaxone sodium at the sink and filled the syringe.

She went to him.

"What are you doing?" he asked.

"Lie still," she said.

She'd cleaned the boning knife and began to cut away his pants. When she brushed her hair back, she got blood on her face. She didn't care.

She tried to be careful but he groaned in pain as she peeled the fabric away, but he didn't resist.

With his leg exposed, she used one smooth motion to inject the needle into his thigh and slowly pushed the plunger and watched as the solution in the barrel disappeared into his leg.

When she looked at his eyes again, he was watching her.

"I'm going to get you some water and I have some pills I want you to take," she said.

"I want you to leave," he said.

She went and got a cup of water and returned and had him take a pill from each of the bottles. He groaned again as he made the effort to raise his head, but he took them.

"You've got to leave," he said with his head back on the pillow.

She ignored him. She made sure Whoops was comfortable beside him and went to the door. Reluctantly, she made herself look out the door at the inferno. The man's body had fallen over as if into a fetal position. Thankfully he was as dead as dead can be. The flames were consuming him along with the others. The snowfall was getting heavier.

She descended the steps and got another load of wood on the toboggan and brought it back to feed the flames, but every time the burning logs shifted she flinched afraid it was another body getting up.

When she returned to the cabin, she sat on the bed again. His first words were, "You've got to leave. More are going to come to find the ones we killed."

"I can't," she said.

He grabbed her wrist again. "You *have* to," he said with his voice getting louder and Whoops started crying. "Neither you nor your sister are safe here, now."

She shook her head. "The weather's moving in. We'll never survive on the road," she said.

"Get me a pencil and paper. There are other people hiding in these hills. They're my friends. I'll draw you a map. You can go to them."

She shook her head again and started crying. "I don't want to go. I want to stay here."

He tightened his grip on her arm until it hurt her. "Leave!" he shouted.

"I'll stop them!" she screamed back and Whoops cried harder.

"How?" he asked in an angry voice. "You're just a girl."

She didn't answer. She wouldn't look at him.

Now he begged. "Please leave before they come. *Please.*"

She shook her head.

"Why not?" He was angry again.

"I told you, I'll stop them," she whispered and wiping her eyes and her nose with her other hand she got more of his blood on her face.

"You and whose army?" he mocked her.

She hung her head and he thought she was going to cry. But she didn't.

"What else can go wrong?" she whispered.

"Nothing, if you'll leave."

She looked at him quizzically, then said, "I don't mean for us; I mean for *them*. What else can go wrong for them? What can *I* make go wrong for them?"

"What are you talking about?"

She didn't answer. She leaned over and kissed him and his grip on her arm slackened, but he didn't let go. She hugged him, but when he groaned she realized she was hurting him, so she stopped.

"What are you talking about?" he repeated in a whisper.

She couldn't answer. He'd think she was crazy. Even she was starting to think she might be crazy. But she had a plan.

Chapter 34
September 4 - 5

"There's nothing you can do," he whispered. "Take your sister, get as far away from here as you can."

Suddenly, she pulled away from him and stood up.

"Where are you going?"

Without answering, she left Whoops beside him, took the flashlight, went to the middle of the room, and descended back into the cellar. She could hear Whoops still fussing up above. She let the beam of light lead her through the darkness until it shone on the boxes of dynamite. She stepped closer and looked at them pensively for several seconds. This was her Rubicon. She had to make a decision.

Finally, she lifted one of the boxes and, clutching it carefully, climbed back up the ladder. She put it in the middle of the floor and went back down for another. Box after box, she brought them up afraid that if she dropped any of it...

She couldn't believe how much he had down there but, once she had it all upstairs, she took it outside, one box at a time, and loaded them each onto the toboggan.

When that was finished, she returned to the cabin. Zach's eyes were closed and he was breathing deeply.

She picked Whoops up and checked her diaper. She was still dry. She grabbed extra diapers and some food for both of them and stuffed it all into her pockets. She put the baby sling on her back, got her sister in it, and adjusted it. She took the AR-15 from the closet and stuffed some loaded magazines into other pockets. Last, she took one magazine, put it in the rifle, jacked a round into the breech, put the safety on, and slung the gun over her shoulder.

"I want you to leave," he whispered.

She ignored him. She was afraid if she went back to him he wouldn't let her go.

Outside, she got into the toboggan's harness and leaned into it. At first the sled wouldn't budge, but she used all of her might and the snow suddenly released its grip and the toboggan began to slide across the field. When she reached the trees, the last thing she did was look back. The pyre burned brightly; the cabin looked serene in its glow. She hoped Zach would be okay, and off into the woods she went with nothing but the flashlight to show her the way. Because of the weight of the baby, the rifle, and the toboggan, she had to stop frequently to rest. She was cold and tired but tried not to think about either. However, it had now been twenty hours since she'd slept and she felt it.

Here and there she snagged her ankles on a buried branch and fell to her knees. But each time she rose to her feet, leaned into the harness, and moved on only to get the toboggan caught on brush, branches, or rocks, patiently free it, and go on, only to fall or get stuck, again.

She came to a hill and thought at least here it would be easy to go down. It eluded her what was going to happen until the toboggan sped up and suddenly was hitting her from behind. She got out of its way as it slid past, only to fall again and this time it dragged her through the snow to the bottom where it stopped only after it crashed into a tree. She lay there grateful it hadn't exploded. Now she worried about how much "shock" it was going to take to set it off.

Whoops was screaming. Halfway back up the hill the flashlight glowed in the snow where she'd dropped it. She got up, removed the harness, and climbed back to get the light. All the while poor Whoopsie howled.

She took her sister off her back and sat in the snow to inspect her.

"Oh, you got snow in your tiny little snowsnoot again."

Whoops was inconsolable.

Danielle cleaned the snowsuit out as she laughed, then she held her sister to her until she stopped crying. Finally, she returned to the toboggan and stared at it. Boxes that were already open had spilled their contents onto the snow and she had to pick them up. "You bastards had better blow up when I need you to," she said to the dynamite.

She shined the flashlight all around and discovered she was in a gully.

"Shit," she whispered.

She tried to pull the toboggan up the other side, but it was too heavy; she was too small. She tried to think her way through her new problem.

Finally, leaning the rifle against the tree, she carried the dynamite, one box at a time, up the hill. She kept her sister on her back.

When the toboggan was manageable, she grabbed the rifle and pulled the toboggan up the hill where she reloaded it and continued on.

§   §   §

She was more cautious, now. She didn't want to chance another crash. But the price for caution was time. So, with snow still falling, it wasn't until the first grey light of dawn that she reached the field that lies just east of the 101 where it crosses a bridge over the Pistol River. She stopped to rest and stared at the bridge. She was tired to the point of exhaustion. She leaned back into the harness and dragged the toboggan until she was beneath the south end of the bridge.

From up close and below, the bridge looked invulnerable. The concrete girders were massive. Just moments ago the dynamite on the toboggan looked like a lot; now, she wondered if there was enough. Maybe her plan wasn't going to work.

She looked back out to the field. If the explosion took place there, it would have less effect, she reasoned. Far enough away and it wouldn't affect it at all. So closer is better. It should sit as close to the bridge as possible. There was a small space where the bridge and the embankment met. That's where the dynamite would have to go.

She leaned the rifle against one of the pilings, took Whoops off her back, and set her down near the toboggan. She then took the first box, carried it up the embankment, and put it in place.

Box after box, she carried them up and packed them in the space.

"This had better work," she said to herself again and again. But each time she stopped and looked at the bridge, she was racked with terrible doubts.

With half the boxes of dynamite in position, she started a trip back down and, in horror, saw Whoops holding a stick of the stuff and waving it. She couldn't even imagine how she'd gotten it.

"*Whoopsie!*" she screamed.

Now the baby was banging it on the ground.

Danielle tumbled down the embankment in her hurry to get to her. She was covered with dirt when she reached her sister and grabbed the stick as Whoops was about to bang it on the ground again.

She smiled when she saw Danielle.

Danielle took a deep breath and smiled back. "You're going to kill Sissy and Whoopsie," she said.

Whoops now had a full-on happy face.

"You're a terrorist," Danielle told her.

That made Whoops smile even more.

She grabbed her sister and squeezed her.

Now she stared at the stick in her hand. What *was* it going to take to detonate one? She put it into one of the boxes and moved Whoops away from the toboggan. She then resumed bringing the rest of the dynamite up and placing it under the bridge. The process was tedious and tiring.

Once she was finished, she retrieved her sister and picked up the rifle.

Towing the toboggan behind her, she walked back into the field. She looked back and decided to go further. She also had to get closer to the river to get an angle from which to see the boxes. Finally, she stopped and looked back again. This seemed like a safe distance. She would do it from here.

She was shivering, now, and sleepy. She had more doubts than ever.

She laid the rifle down and, remembering what Zach had done, she took Whoops yet another fifty feet away and lay her on the toboggan so the report from the rifle wouldn't damage her ears. She returned to the rifle, picked it up, and tried to steady herself as she looked through the sights.

She hesitated and listened intently when she heard something. *Vehicles!* She quickly prostrated herself in the snow and saw the first vehicles of a caravan approach the bridge from the north. She kept herself low and watched it pass. She could hear Whoops begin to cry. She didn't move. She waited a few minutes until she heard the second half of the caravan and watched as it, too, crossed the river.

By now, Whoops was howling. But Danielle knew there was no way they'd hear her in their closed vehicles as they passed by.

Once the caravan was out of sight she lay still another few minutes until she was sure no one else was coming.

By now, she was shivering violently. She stood, looked back at her sister, then turned back to the bridge and brought the rifle up. She looked down through the peep sight once more, through the swirling snowflakes, and tried to place the front sight on the dynamite. She was shivering too much. But she pulled the trigger. The round hit concrete. She looked down through the sights, again, and after several seconds she pulled the trigger again. The bullet struck closer, but she realized she was shaking too much to shoot accurately and, under the circumstances, that wasn't going to change this morning.

She recalled Zach's words: "Every round fired is a round gone forever."

She lay back down on the snow and rested the rifle on its protruding magazine. It was steadier, now. She stared down the sights once more and watched the front sight trace a very small circle that kept passing rhythmically over the target. She tried to time the movements of the sight and, just as it was passing over her target, she gently squeezed the trigger.

The sudden overpressure and displacement of air that accompanied the explosion was nothing she expected.

"*Mommy!*" she screamed and closed her eyes as the expanding cloud of smoke and debris engulfed her. When she opened her eyes again, the air was filled with flying pieces of the bridge. In the periphery of her vision she realized huge chunks of it were still climbing into the sky. They looked beautiful. But there was something wrong. Mouth agape she realized they had to come down and the biggest chunk had reached its apogee and…it was coming down, down, down, with increasing velocity. From deep within her throat she once more yelled, "*Mommy!*" Leaping to her feet, she ran to her sister, and threw herself on her hands and knees to shield her. Eyes closed, the debris rained down on her. Pieces struck her. Some hurt. But the biggest piece was still up there.

A dull thud shook the earth. She didn't dare open her eyes. From the sound, she could tell less and less was returning to earth. Finally, it was quiet again. She lifted her head and opened her eyes. There it was: A piece as big as a small car less than three feet from her and Whoops. She looked back down. Whoops was smiling at her with her happy face, glad to see her sister, again.

"Are you happy to see Sissy?" Danielle whispered and Whoops flailed her arms and smiled some more.

She kissed her then slowly got to her feet with her sister in her arms. Most of the debris had disappeared into the snow. Only chunks too big to have completely buried themselves offered any evidence of what she'd done.

She looked back at the bridge. It was hard to tell what had happened to it from where she stood. She was afraid it was still intact.

If this wasn't enough…

The snow was falling harder.

She carried her sister to the 101 and climbed over the guardrail. It was there she saw the gaping hole in the bridge's roadbed, big enough to stop traffic. When she reached it she could see the rushing waters of the Pistol River below. She let out a sigh. Nothing wider than a bicycle was going to get over it, now.

She kissed her sister again. "You're stinky," she said.

She pulled a diaper from one of her pockets and, spreading her coat so she could lay her down on the bridge, she changed her. Whoops ignored the cold and seemed more fascinated by the snowflakes coming at her and, with her arms waving, seemed to be trying to catch them. Relieved, Danielle could now laugh at her as she changed her.

She looked around. Even at the end of the world, she wanted to dispose of the dirty diaper properly. She laughed at herself. Still, she couldn't bring herself to throw it in the river, so she just left it on the bridge.

Shivering and sleepy, she started trudging back through the field. She headed up the Pistol River, back toward the cabin, with her sister on her back, the rifle slung over her shoulder, and dragging the empty toboggan behind her.

The snowfall got heavier. Each flake that fell in one of her tracks filled it minutely. With the billions that were falling that day, her tracks completely disappeared in two hours.

§   §   §

When she reached the cabin, she was in agony with chilblains from the cold running through her feet and legs and almost crazy with fatigue and hypothermia. The funeral pyre still smoldered, but the powdery snow all around it was already a foot deeper. There were still some partial skeletal remains. The fire needed to be fed again. But Whoops was wailing, hungry, and soiled again and they entered the cabin.

She knelt before the fireplace insert. There were embers. She placed a layer of tinder and wood on the glowing coals. As soon as the flames started, she changed and fed Whoops then took her to the bed and placed her between herself and Zach. She was freezing. Zach was burning up with fever. Somehow, they'd help each other.

But if the the Bradys and LaCroixs came back now, there was nothing she could do to stop them. She was, after all, just a girl.

Chapter 35
September 5

In an office at the Pentagon, an Air Force captain stood before the desk of his superior. "Reports from one of the convoys, Sir," he said to the colonel seated behind the desk. "Someone's blown up a bridge on the Pistol River. Nothing's going to move, either north or south, until it's repaired."

There was a long pause. "Where the hell is the Pistol River?" the colonel finally asked.

"Southwestern Oregon."

"On the 101?"

"Yes."

"What's it called again?"

"Pistol River. It's the name of both the river and an unincorporated area. I don't know if it's a town or what."

The colonel squinted at the captain. He stood and looked at a large wall map behind his desk. It showed all the points of interest on both coasts. "Pistol River?"

"It's on the southwest coast of the state, Sir."

The colonel had to get close to the map to find the dot associated with the name Pistol River.

"Who the fuck ever heard of the place?"

The captain didn't answer.

"Had you *ever* heard of Pistol River?"

"No, Sir."

"Was it rebels?" the colonel asked.

"We don't think so, Sir."

"Who's there?"

The captain looked at the paper. "There are two compounds, two of the biggest on the West Coast, located in that area…"

"Road pirates?"

"That's what we think. One of the groups is…" The captain looked at some papers in his hand. "…the Brady compound; the others are the La Crocks. Each one has maybe two hundred residents. And, like I say, they're two of the biggest gangs on the 101 corridor."

The colonel turned to the captain and held out his hand for the paper.

The captain passed it to him. The colonel looked at it and handed it back. "The name is French. It's pronounced 'la-croy'" he said.

"Sorry, Sir."

"Is it a big bridge?"

"No, Sir. But the water in the river is running high and the officer in charge of the convoy said nothing's getting across it until the Corps repairs it."

Looking back at the report the colonel asked, "Were these assholes told what would happen if they fucked with our roads and bridges?"

"Yes, Sir; months ago.

"There's a detachment in Crescent City…" the captain said.

"Huh?"

"It's the last city in northern California before you cross into Oregon…they can move in just a few hours and deal with them."

The colonel sighed. "I'll take it upstairs. It's their decision. But I think we both know what's going to happen." With the wave of his hand he dismissed the captain.

"What if they didn't blow up the bridge?" the Captain asked.

"It won't matter. Examples have to be set. Besides, if they're ballsy enough to blow up a bridge, they're probably siding with the rebels, anyways."

As the captain turned to leave, the colonel said, "I like that, though."

The captain paused and asked, "What's that, Sir?"

"What you called them, 'La Crocks.' These road pirates are crocks of shit."

The captain smiled a perfunctory smile and left.

Chapter 36
September 5

Danielle woke to the sound of shuffling and groaning and sat up with a start. She saw Whoops was lying on the floor dressed in her pink snowsuit again. The sounds that had awoken her were Zach as he tried to make his way around the cabin using a broomstick as a crutch while dragging his bad leg, and groaning with every move he made.

"What are you doing?" she shouted.

"Trying to get you out of here."

"I'm not going anywhere," she retorted.

He stopped and looked at her. "The hell you aren't."

"I'm not going anywhere." She leaped from the bed and tried to lead him back to it.

He pulled his arm away and she caught him as he almost fell.

"You're leaving," he insisted.

"*No!*"

"You're leaving," he said louder.

"Why?" she shrieked and started Whoops crying again.

With sheer agony he pulled her to the window and pointed up the slight hill to the grave markers which just barely stuck out of the new snow. "That's why."

It struck her, this was about her and Whoops—and it was about his family. He was trying to exorcise the beast that had been feeding on his soul since they had died—deaths he blamed on himself. And his redemption was to save her, but most of all, he had to save Whoops. Right from that moment in the field when he shot Barry and the others, it had been *all* about Whoops.

And, Danielle realized, this was all that had kept her alive, too, ever since she'd been separated from the rest of her family: Whoops. If she stayed and the Bradys and LaCroixs came♥ back, everything she and Zach had done could all be for naught.

"If I could, I'd leave with you," he said softly. "But you'd never make it with me."

She didn't move.

"You realize I don't want you to go, don't you?"

She said nothing.

"You realize it, don't you?" he asked gently.

She nodded.

"But you have to, for your sister."

"I know," she said.

"Will you?"

"Yes."

"Do you promise?"

She nodded again.

"I'll help you get ready," he said.

"I can do it myself."

"No." He got up again. He was unsteady on his feet.

"Would you sit down," she asked, "and let me do this? I know how I want to do it."

She quickly handed him some paper and a pencil. "Draw me the map to your friends's place."

He nodded and began to draw the map, quickly and skillfully.

"They're last name is Short," he said as he drew. "His name is Peter; hers is Margaret. They've got a baby boy. They're good people. They helped me when Sandra and the kids died. They'll take care of you, too.

"You can come back when this is over," he added.

But she knew he was just saying that to make sure she left. After the Bradys and the LaCroixs arrived, there would be nothing to come back to.

"Do you have the Model 60?" he asked.

She patted her pocket.

"Take the Colt."

She slung the AR-15 over her shoulder.

"Get the flashlight," he said.

"I have it," she replied and bit her lip. She was starting to have doubts about leaving. She was losing it.

"Get some of the extra batteries I charged."

She nodded and did as she was told.

"Take some food," he said and tears started running down her cheeks

"Take enough for at least a day—in case you get lost," though he was sure she wouldn't.

"Are you ready?" he asked.

She nodded.

"I want you to leave, now. I want you to find the Shorts before it gets dark. I've written a note on the back of the map that will explain who you are."

"They can come back and help you," she said.

"*No!* Don't let Peter come back here."

"Why?"

"There's nothing he can do alone."

She realized Zach wasn't going to let his friend come into a situation that could cost him his life. She, herself, wouldn't do that to a friend, either.

"Okay," she said.

She came and sat on the edge of the couch. Their eyes locked.

"Go, before they get here" he said.

She didn't move.

"Go," he repeated.

Instead, she got up and went to the sink.

"What are you doing?" he asked.

She hydrated another pouch of ceftriaxone sodium. She brought the loaded syringe, along with the bottles of cephradine and morphine and a glass of water, back to the bed.

"You've got to leave," he said.

"Lay back," she ordered.

He complied and she injected him with the syringe. Together, they watched the syringe empty into his thigh.

"I want you to take these," she said, and gave him a pill from each bottle.

He took them.

"Leave," he whispered.

She hesitated.

"Leave," he whispered, again.

"I   will."

"Leave," he said when she didn't move.

She rose from the bed without looking at him and picked up her sister.

She slowly opened the front door. When she closed it behind her, she sat down and the girl who blew up the bridge at Pistol River started crying, again.

But he was right. If she stayed, Whoops was at risk. Who knew how long it would be until the Army arrived? Or if they'd even deal with compounds this time. Staying here was fraught with danger and uncertainty. If anything had ever made sense in her life, it was to take her sister and run now. "You're the most important thing in my life," she whispered to Whoops, then hugged her and cried like there was no tomorrow — because she didn't want tomorrow.

Whoops watched her with concern. She didn't like it when Sissy cried.

Danielle rose to her feet. She had to leave before she made a mistake and changed her mind.

Across the field she went and, when she reached the trees, she looked at her map. She was sure it was drawn well enough to find the Shorts. A few hours, at most, and she and Whoops would be safe. But darkness was going to be upon her if she didn't make haste.

She stepped off into the trees but hesitated to look back. If the Bradys and LaCroixs returned, he'd be alone, but she and Whoopsie would be safe. That's what he wanted. That's what she wanted.

"I wish I hadn't fallen in love with you," she said to the cabin.

Chapter 37
September 5

A second joint-party departed from the Brady and LaCroix compounds. This one was in search of the seven men and Abby Brady, who had left, days before, but who had not made radio contact in two days.

This time Louis LaCroix himself joined the searchers. They travelled on snowmobiles over the new snowfall, going south on US 101 until they saw a distant figure staggering northward. They pulled up and LaCroix glassed the figure with his binoculars for several seconds until he exclaimed, "It's Abby."

When they reached her they found a frostbitten and incoherent Abby Brady dragging the frozen body of Steven Ingram to whom she was still handcuffed. She was delirious and oblivious to the facts she was both naked and dragging Ingram behind her.

Without a key for the handcuffs one of LaCroix's men, Goodman, had to use a Bowie knife to cut Ingram's hand off, so as to free Abby. After they bundled her in some jackets, one snowmobile took her and Ingram's body back to the Brady compound, while the other two, one carrying Louis LaCroix, went further south until they came to the bridge at the Pistol River.

It was then that the enormity of what they witnessed fell instantly on LaCroix.

The bridge was impassible.

"This is not good," he said as he surveyed the damage.

"They'll fix it," Goodman said, referring to the Army.

"I don't care if they fix it or not. They're going to blame us."

"But we didn't do it."

"It won't matter!" LaCroix shouted. "They're going to blame us — and the Bradys..." He didn't have to finish that sentence. Goodman and the others knew what it meant.

"So, what are we going to do?" Goodman asked.

LaCroix looked at something on the roadway. "What's that?" he asked.

"What's what?" Goodman asked.

"The thing on the piece of rubble, dammit," he said pointing.

Goodman picked it up.

"It's a used diaper," he said.

"A diaper?"

"Yeah. Full of shit," he said as he handed it to LaCroix

LaCroix didn't know what to make of it and threw it into the rushing water below.

There was nothing left to do at the bridge. "We've gotta go back," LaCroix said.

They sped north to the Brady compound. When they arrived, it was clear Abby was dying. In her final hour, as she slipped in and out of unconsciousness, she recounted to LaCroix what had transpired on the expedition and the confrontation with Zach and Danielle: Hank was dead, Jerry was dead, and Steven was dead, as were all four of the men from the LaCroix compound. But she kept coming back to one name: Danielle. Danielle, she said, had killed everyone. Danielle killed Hank without a gun. She shot it out with Brian Peterson, and *she* won. "Danielle is Satan incarnate," she said. "She killed the others and now she's killed me."

"You'll be okay." LaCroix said.

"No, I won't" she said.

She pointed a finger at those in the room and warned, "She said she's gonna bring us down. She didn't say how, but the devil's in her. She's gonna do something to bring us all down unless you stop her. It's up to you, or yer all dead. My time's over."

She seemed to stare off beyond them and said, "Hi, Sweetie. It's granny-great...come to be with you." Those were her last words. She slipped back into unconsciousness and, minutes later, she stopped breathing.

§   §   §

"So, who blew up the bridge?" Goodman asked. "That guy...what's his name?"

"No," LaCroix said. "Abby said he'd been shot. It couldn't have been him. From what Abby said, he's gotta be dead by now."

"Then who?"

He thought about the diaper left on the bridge. Was it a calling card? If the bridge was impassable, the Army was going to come after someone, and that someone would be the people at the LaCroix and Brady compounds. "It's the girl. It had to be …what's her name?" he asked.

"Danielle," Goodman replied.

"She got a last name?" LaCroix shouted.

Nobody knew.

"It had to be that fucking…Danielle," LaCroix said.

"But they say she's just sixteen."

"You should'a seen what she was like," one of the Brady men said. "She wouldn't back down from Abby or Hank. Even after the guys raped her, she kept comin' at 'em. She said she was gonna get us. That's why we had to get rid of her."

LaCroix considered other alternatives and other possibilities. Who else could have done it? he wondered.

"She done what she said she's gonna do," the man said. "She killed the people we sent out there. Abby said so. She even killed Hank. Nobody could kill Hank. She killed your guy, Peterson. Nobody coulda killed him. Now she's blowed up the bridge."

What kind of sixteen-year-old girl could possibly have killed Billy Raymond. What kind of girl could have killed Brian Peterson? Peterson was the most dangerous man LaCroix had ever met; even more dangerous than Hank. And what kind of girl could have killed Hank without a gun? His head was swimming in the possibilities, but he kept on coming back to Danielle. Could this girl he'd never seen, the one they were calling Danielle, have done it all? If not, then who?

"We've gotta kill her," LaCroix finally said. "But first we've gotta deal with the Army."

"But the Army don't make deals," Goodman said.

"They've gotta. We've got nowhere else to go. "We've gotta make them see what really happened. Maybe *they'll* kill her."

§   §   §

He returned to his own compound and held an emergency meeting. First, he told the families of Bill Raymond, Fred Mayfield, Brian Peterson, and Jim De Angelis that they were gone, killed by someone named Danielle. They would try to recover the bodies, but first the Army would be coming because of the bridge. They had to deal with the Army before they could do anything else.

However, within an hour there were those who were slipping out of the LaCroix compound. Further south, at least a dozen people stole out of the Brady compound. Some were heading north to Gold Beach where they hoped they'd be welcomed by the few who still inhabited the small town. Others went south toward the larger town of Brookings. They left because, like everyone else, they'd heard what the Army did when it arrived.

But LaCroix was determined to reason with them. He'd be on their side. He'd explain to them what happened and help them find that bitch, Danielle, the girl who had killed so many of them, and then blew up the bridge.

But when the Humvees and armored personnel carriers appeared at the compounds, men garbed in head-to-toe camouflage, armed with M16A4 rifles, and wearing body armor poured out of the vehicles, as low-flying helicopters swooped in over the trees. And though there were those who thought they could reason with them, including Louis LaCroix who greeted them with a white flag, there was not one among the officers or enlisted men who had orders to reason with *anyone*.

Not a man, woman, or child was left alive at either compound.

Epilogue
April

It had been a hard winter and the spring that followed came even later than the spring of the year before. But the springs were going to come later and later, from here on out.

Zach worked beside his cabin in the April sun carefully putting the fiberglass panels back on the soon-to-be-resurrected greenhouse. This year it was going to stronger so he could leave it up year-round. He'd already started his tomatoes, potatoes, beans, squash, and several different fast-growing greens inside the cabin some eight weeks before. Now, with the weather changing, it was time to finish putting the paneling up and move the plants out. There was still snow in the forest and in the field and, as he limped about, he had to be careful of his footing. He was never going to walk normally again.

Yet, he considered himself lucky. According to UN estimates he'd heard on the radio, almost a billion more people had died in the last six months. The world's population had been reduced to less than two billion and no one was sure when it would bottom out. Yet, he not only survived, he had actually put on five pounds over the winter.

Stupid suddenly growled and started across the snow in the three-legged gait he'd perfected.

Zach looked and there were three skiers far off in the upper field. The lead skier was waving.

"Sit," Zach ordered, and Stupid sank to his haunches but he was tense, alert, and awaiting the command that would send him through the snow.

Zach grabbed his M1 Garand in his left hand and his binoculars in his right.

But even without his binoculars, he could tell one of skiers was a woman carrying a child. There was also a dog with the group.

He brought his binoculars to his eyes and glassed them. It was the Shorts.

He set the rifle down, raised his left arm, and waved them in.

Stupid had seen the dog and got off his haunches, "Sit," Zach repeated, and the dog did, but he whined. He hadn't seen one of his own kind in over seven months.

"Quiet," Zach commanded.

But for the first time in memory, you'd have thought Stupid was being tortured and he let out intermittent and impatient squeals.

Zach began to walk across the melting snow to meet the visitors.

When they reached him, he shook hands with Peter Short who asked, "How you doin', Zach?"

"Fine," he replied. "And you?"

"Great," the man said.

"And how are you doing, Margaret?" Zach asked the woman holding the child.

"I'm wonderful," she replied and she unconsciously hiked the little boy higher in her arms as if showing Zach one of the reasons life was so good.

Margaret was a "serious" woman and she and her husband, Peter, had been married almost six years.

"Is little Peter doing okay?" Zach asked as he reached and patted the boy on his cheek. But the child shyly turned away into his mother's arms and buried his face into her neck. It had been so long since he'd seen him that he didn't remember Zach.

"Getting' ready to get your garden in again?" Peter asked.

"Oh, yeah. If we have another good year, I'll have enough tomatoes and squash..."

"What happened?" Peter asked nodding to Zach's legs. The limp couldn't be hidden.

"Nothing serious," Zach said.

"I can look at it," Margaret said.

"It's okay," Zach responded.

"We'd also like you to meet Helen Russo," Margaret said.

Helen was a beautiful woman in her mid-twenties with straight black hair cut off at her shoulders. She had a smile that could have melted the snow and even in her winter clothes it was obvious she was athletic and trim. She removed her sunglasses and her eyes were as deep and as green as emeralds.

"It's nice to meet you," Zach said and reached to shake her hand.

She removed her glove and placed her hand in his. It was warm and soft. She confidently made eye contact and smiled a smile that could make flowers bloom.

"It's nice to meet you, too, Zachary. All Peter and Margaret do is talk about you."

Zach couldn't help but smile himself.

Margaret kept glancing up at the edge of the field where the graves of Zach's wife and children were. Peter and Margaret were the first people Zach had come to see when he'd come home and found his children dead, his wife hanging in the living room...and the note. The snow had been cleared away from the wooden headstones and there were wreaths on the markers that made them look fresh and well-kept. Margaret wasn't sure if this was a good sign or bad.

Standing there, Zach and Peter talked about the snow, the weather, the state of the country, the secession, jumping from one subject to another in a desultory fashion that made Margaret realize they were avoiding talk about what really mattered: the reason they had brought Helen.

"Zach," she interrupted, "We came out because we thought you and Helen should meet. We've talked about you so much that she said it would be nice to pay you a visit, so..."

She stopped in mid-sentence and she, Peter, and Helen looked beyond Zach to the cabin.

Zach turned to see where their gazes had gone.

"Who's the woman?" Margaret asked in a low voice.

"That's my wife," he replied.

Looking tired and frail, Danielle stood in the doorway with the shotgun. Clutching onto the skirt of her dress, Whoops stood beside her and stared at the strangers.

"Go over and say hello." Zach said to Margaret and Helen.

The two women glanced at each other, then skied to the cabin and, when she reached the front door, Margaret said, "I'm Margaret Short."

Danielle recognized the last name. It was the one Zach had put on the map he'd drawn so many months ago.

"This is Helen Russo," Margaret continued. "My husband and I are friends of Zach and...we were friends of Sandra's, too."

Still holding the shotgun in her right hand, Danielle stared at the women and unconsciously let her left hand fall and hold her stomach.

"How far along are you?" Margaret asked.

Danielle looked down at her stomach. "Six months, we think," she said in a tired voice.

"The little girl yours, too?"

"Yeah...she's my sister."

Little Peter hugged his mother, but he watched Whoops with curiosity.

"Did he get you from the road?" Margaret asked.

Danielle didn't like the way she asked if he'd gotten her "from the road" and asked, "What do you mean by that?"

Margaret didn't reply. But she looked toward the graves again and said, "He keeps the graves up well."

"I keep the graves up."

Margaret looked back at her curiously. "Did you know them?"

"I know them, now," Danielle replied.

"How old are you?" Margaret asked nosily.

"Why are you asking?" Danielle asked with an edge creeping into her voice. She kept glancing at Helen. She'd overheard part of the conversation when they'd arrived and it was easy for her to guess why they brought this woman.

Coming up from behind, her husband said, "Because she's a busybody. Hi, I'm Peter Short and if you promise not to make any jokes about my name, neither will I."

It took Danielle a second to get the joke and suddenly she smiled and covered her mouth in embarrassment.

Margaret, however, didn't like her husband cutting her off and it showed on her.

Helen, on the other hand, was looking Danielle over. She'd come here to meet a man and suddenly discovered there was competition from…a girl "from the road." In the dog-eat-dog world of the new ice age, another woman's man was fair game if he was any good.

But Peter was just the opposite of his wife; he was a friendly guy used to defusing the confrontations she created. "How do you like living out here in the woods?" he asked.

"I love it," Danielle replied.

"Who's the monster?" he asked looking at Whoops.

Danielle smiled at him for that. "She's my sister."

"What's her name?" Peter asked.

"Whoops."

"Whoops?" He laughed. "Aw, come on, no one's really named Whoops. What's her real name?"

Danielle smiled at the way he asked the question. "Audrey. But she doesn't know it."

Peter thought a second. "I like Whoops better."

"So do we," Danielle said.

He looked from Whoops, to Danielle, back to Whoops, and finally back to Danielle. "Yeah, I can see the resemblance, now…except Whoops is pretty."

Danielle was startled for a second, then she began to laugh.

Margaret looked at Peter. "That's a perfectly horrible thing to say, Peter. Danielle's beautiful..." And as soon as the words were out of her mouth, she wished she hadn't said them. After all, they'd brought Helen here to meet Zach. "But not as pretty as Helen," she added awkwardly.

"Whoops..." Peter said thinking about the name.

"What did you say your name is?"

"I didn't."

"What is it?"

"Danielle."

Peter's humor suddenly abandoned him. He looked at Margaret, then at Zach, then back at Danielle.

"Did you come from the Brady compound?" he asked.

Danielle didn't answer. Inside she began to panic. She looked at Zach and the sudden silence became awkward.

"They say only one girl ever got away," Peter continued. "They'd raped her then tried to kill her, but she got away and, when they came after her, she killed a bunch of them. Then she came back at 'em and brought them down, along with the LaCroixs. Her name was Danielle. That's what they say, anyway, and she had a little sister with a funny name, but no one can remember what it is. And you..."

"It's just a coincidence," Zach interrupted almost too quickly.

Danielle forced a smile at Peter who scrutinized her closely. But Margaret and Helen looked at each other as if trying to decide what to do next.

Finally, Margaret said, "Hi, Audrey."

Whoops ignored her.

"You should call her by her real name so she knows who she is," Margaret said accusingly.

"'Whoops is just fine," Zach said.

Margaret leaned toward Whoops with her son in her arms, to introduce him, and said, "This is Peter, Junior," but her son recoiled back in his mother's arms though he kept staring at Whoops intensely.

"Where's your family?" Margaret asked.

"This is my family," Danielle replied.

Zach could see Margaret had Danielle on a short fuse and he suddenly asked, "Would you folks like some coffee?"

"You have coffee?" Peter asked incredulously.

Margaret didn't like that the conversation was again diverted from her questions.

"I keep some stashed," Zach said, "and, every once in a while, you find some in the abandoned cars on the road."

"They say the military left a truck that broke down; had a lot of coffee, cans of beans, sugar, 5.56 ammo, and who knows what else. It was supposed to be going up to Hanford. They left it on the side of the road a few months back, while they went to get a repair crew, and when they returned the next day, most of the stuff that was on the truck…"

"Don't know anything about that," Zach said cutting him off, again. "But I have a few bags stashed."

"How much?"

Zach smiled and said, "Actually, quite a bit."

Peter laughed and shook his head. "Maybe we can work a trade," he said.

"What have you got?" Zach asked.

But before he could answer Zach's question, Peter looked out in the field and said, "Well, look at that."

They all turned in the direction Peter was looking and Stupid and the Short's dog were unabashedly answering nature's most basic call near the woodpile.

"That's the first dog—and certainly the first female dog—he's seen since we got him," Zach said.

"They aren't losing any time," Peter laughed. "It's amazing what they know how to do without being shown. You get the dog from the road?"

"Nope," Zach said in all seriousness, "He got me from the road."

The answer didn't mean anything to Peter. "Not many people would keep a three-legged dog," he said.

"He's only got three legs?" Danielle asked incredulously. "I'd wondered why he walks funny, but Zach wouldn't tell me."

Neither Margaret nor Helen thought that was humorous, but Peter and Zach laughed.

"Girl's got a sense of humor," Peter said. He was getting to like her. "But it's too late to stop them now. Is he a good dog?"

"He's the smartest dog I've ever known in my life," Zach said seriously. "He was a real survivor when he had four on the floor, and losing one hasn't slowed him down one bit.

"Once I could get back on skis," he added, as he patted his bad hip, "he went out with me whenever I hunted or scavenged. He's got an almost preternatural sense for finding game. And he doesn't spook it. I couldn't have fed him if he wasn't as good as he is. We even expanded the pantry over the winter because of him. He's carried his weight."

"Well, I know you," Peter laughed, "and if you're willing to take a three-legged dog with you into the ice age, he's gotta be good stock." He laughed again. "You can have the pick of the litter if she takes."

"They're tough to feed," Zach warned.

Of course Peter already knew that, but he said, "So I've heard. But they're worth their weight in gold, when they're good. And he must be good."

It was clear to Margaret the men were going to talk about nothing that mattered to her. Finally, she said to Danielle, "I can help you."

She nodded toward Danielle's stomach in a perfunctory manner when Danielle looked at her.

"We don't need any help," Danielle replied. She already didn't like either of the women.

But Margaret went on. "I'm a nurse-practitioner," she said. "I've delivered babies. I've dealt with prenatal and postnatal problems. I can help you with your pregnancy, if anything comes up."

Danielle reiterated, "We don't need..."

"*Danielle*," Zach said sharply. He looked up at the graves then looked back at her. "We'll take *all* the help we can get."

Danielle looked at the graves, then at Zach, then Margaret. "I'd appreciate your help," she said.

"Maybe this is how you guys can get some coffee," he said to the Shorts.

"I can come by every few weeks," Margaret said to Zach.

"Are you spotting at all?" she asked Danielle.

"I did a few weeks ago, but Zach made me rest. I'm okay, now."

"Do you know what gauge that is?" she asked nodding toward the shotgun that was still in Danielle's hands.

"It's a 12-gauge," Zach said.

Margaret hadn't wanted the answer from Zach. "Do you know how to use it?" she asked Danielle.

Danielle again looked at Zach, then back to Margaret. She'd already killed four people with it. But all she said was, "I'm learning."

Margaret didn't hide the skepticism in her voice as she said, "Good. You know, they can be dangerous around children."

Danielle realized Margaret was treating her as if she were a little girl and the thought crossed her mind that she'd like to shove the muzzle of the shotgun up the woman's butt and pull the trigger. But she didn't say anything. And neither did anyone else for several seconds.

"So, how come we never met you?" Margaret asked.

"You were supposed to meet her last fall," Zach said. "But she wouldn't go away like I told her to."

Margaret looked quizzically at Peter. But Peter was laughing and he asked Zach, "What does that mean?"

"It means he was trying to get rid of me, but I wouldn't go," Danielle said with a slight smile.

"Some women are just like that," Zach said knowing, had she not turned back, he'd have died.

Peter knew something had intentionally been left unsaid. He wanted to know what it was.

"Come on in," Danielle finally said and stepped aside. "I'm making pancakes if you're hungry."

"Pancakes? I'm starving," Peter said. But, as he started up the steps, he paused to observe small holes in the door, punched through the wood. They looked like bullet holes.

And when they entered the cabin, Zach suddenly realized that somehow, sometime during the winter, the cabin had become Danielle's territory, and even if no one else had realized it, not a one in the four of them had even asked to go inside while she blocked the doorway. It was an animal thing, a territorial thing, that everyone had subconsciously respected until she invited them in. She not only ruled his heart, she ruled his hearth.

Once inside, Peter looked at the other side of the door and realized the wood had been splintered, then repaired, incontrovertible evidence, in his mind, that the cabin had been under siege. "What happened to the door?" he asked Zach.

"It's always been that way," Zach replied.

Peter knew it hadn't. But something else caught his eye. "Holy cow!" he exclaimed and walked to a table near one of the windows where Zach and Danielle had started some marijuana plants. "Get a load of these, Margaret...Helen. These are going to be good."

"They look better then the ones you had last year," he said to Zach.

Margaret examined them. "Look at these," she said to Helen. "Aren't they beautiful? Zach has a way with growing things, and he uses a lot of it for barter. We're going to have to trade for some of this when it comes in. I've got patients who need it."

"Where'd you get the maple syrup?" Peter asked when he spotted it on the table.

Zach shrugged.

"They say there was maple syrup on that Army truck, too. Do you know how rare maple syrup is nowadays?"

"The Army should be more careful with their trucks," was all Zach would allow.

Peter laughed and said, "They say a couple of officers got busted for losing the stuff and the guys who were supposed to stay with the truck got discharged. That was a tough break for them because the Army's where it's at, if they'll take you at all, 'cause you know you'll still get three squares a day; more than the rest of us can count on.

"So how much of this stuff have you got?"

"Quite a bit," Zach replied.

"Well, you can eat just so many pancakes," Peter said holding the bottle up and letting the light filter through its amber contents.

"I can use it to make maple mead and maple wine," Zach said.

"You can?"

"I've already got some started. But I've still got enough syrup to use for bartering. Got a lot of flour, too, and it won't keep as well as the whole wheat kernels I've got stored, so we can work some deals there, too."

"Did you hear that?" Peter asked Margaret without looking at her.

"I heard it," she replied.

As he looked around the cabin, Peter realized there were other holes in the walls and even some of the fixtures. A real firefight had happened here, and Zach and Danielle weren't saying anything. But Danielle looked too small to be..."But, you know," he said, and looked at Danielle as he changed the subject, again, "that girl that brought the Bradys and LaCroixs down, *her* name was Danielle and she had a little sister..."

"Just a coincidence," Zach repeated.

"She's too young," Margaret said.

"Too young for what?" Danielle asked. She knew she was being put down by Margaret, but she didn't know what to do about it.

Margaret didn't answer. But by eliciting this reaction from Danielle, she'd made her point.

"She's all that kept me alive in the months after..." Zach began, then paused, "...my accident. If she hadn't been here, I'd be a goner by now. In fact, Stupid wouldn't be alive, either."

"Who's Stupid?" Margaret asked.

"The dog."

"But," Margaret protested, "you said he was a good dog."

"Margaret," Peter said, "it's a name...like *Whoops*. If Zach kept him through the winter, he's gotta be good."

Once again, Margaret didn't like Peter stepping on what she had to say. She set little Peter down on the floor and, though he was a year older and much bigger than she, Whoops circled him like a shark and he held onto his mother's leg like a drowning man clutching flotsam watching Whoops with undisguised alarm in his eyes.

Peter looked at Danielle again, then he looked Zach dead in the eye and asked, "Got any idea who blew up the bridge that crosses the Pistol River?"

When neither Zach nor Danielle responded, another long, awkward silence ensued. Danielle held her breath as she watched Zach. Peter was watching it all.

"Danielle..." Zach finally said, and she thought she was going to freak out. "...and I heard about it, too, on the radio. And I say good riddance to both the Bradys and the LaCroixs."

"I'll second that," Peter said.

Danielle suddenly stepped closer to Zach and whispered into his ear.

"The lady of the house has just informed me that I'm not being a good host. Would either of you like a glass of wine while we talk?"

Helen nodded and Peter clapped his hands, "Oh, one of Zachary Amaral's famous homemade wines," he said.

"You're not having any wine," Margaret said to Danielle.

Danielle looked to Zach for support, but he seemed oblivious. He was more intent of basking in the attention from his guests, especially Helen's. But she was reaching the end of her rope with Margaret. However, all she said was, "Why don't all of you sit down at the table and relax," and she went to the stove.

As they sat, Peter said, "Your wine reminds me of something I want to tell you about: Me and Dennis Brown were out scavenging a few weeks ago. Do you remember there was a hermit living way up river, on the south bank of the Rogue—Jerrys Flat Road?"

Zach turned his palms up and said, "I don't know who you're talking about. I didn't really live here until after the ice age started."

Peter continued, "Well, the old codger's disappeared and we were scavenging through his house and we found eight cases of gin in a root cellar; like the guy was stockpiling it."

Zach nodded. "Sorry *you* got to it first."

Peter laughed. "I mention it because we gotta work a trade."

"I've got uses for gin," Zach said. "We'll work something out."

"So, how'd you hurt your leg?" Margaret asked Zach.

"Like I said, it was an accident."

"You really should have someone who *knows* what they're doing look at it."

With her back to the room, Danielle cringed and dropped her spatula. Picking it up, she cleaned it off. She couldn't help feel that all Margaret's comments, especially that one, were meant to batter her.

And they were.

"It's okay, now," he said.

He could have said again, "Danielle takes care of it," Danielle thought, but he didn't. She was going to kill him.

"Did you hear about Ted Hathaway, his girlfriend, Carla, and their daughter?"

The Hathaway homestead was about four miles from where Zach and Danielle lived. "Apparently the LaCroixs and Bradys killed them and burned their place down while they were out looking for the Danielle woman."

"I went by their place a few months ago," was all Zach would allow. "I saw what was left. I didn't realize that that's what happened to them."

"So do you think the glaciers are going to come down to us?" Helen suddenly asked Zach. Danielle looked over her shoulder and saw this woman smiling at Zach with those beautiful green eyes…and her hand had reached out and tapped Zach's, and he wasn't pulling it away.

He smiled back and said, "I don't know. We'll just have to watch them."

"What do we do if they do?" Peter asked.

"We'll all go south; shoot our way into Mexico."

The four laughed while Danielle brooded at the stove.

"Southern California, south of Bakersfield is in a civil war," Peter said.

"I've been following it on the radio," Zach said.

"Everything north of the Bay Area and all of Oregon south of Eugene is now…"

"Jefferson," Zach said, as he opened the wine and named the new country that had been formed by secession. "Heard about that, too."

Peter paused. "Then you *must* have heard the stories they're telling about Danielle." He wasn't giving up. "They're on the radio and all over the CBs. They're talking about her from Seattle to San Diego and all the way back East. She's become an inspiration to those trying to stand up to the road pirates and she's even become an icon to those in the secession movements. As corny as it sounds, they're calling her a symbol of someone who'll stand against injustice and stand up for freedom and, lately, there's plenty of the former and almost none of the latter. She's become a 'Joan of Arc' for Americans." He kept watching Danielle for a reaction. He noted her motions at the stove were slowing, as if she was listening nervously. He just wanted a clear sign that would confirm or refute his growing suspicions.

But neither she nor Zach said anything as she returned to the table and put a large plate of pancakes on it.

Peter wasn't sure what to make of their silence. "So, what *do* you think about the Danielle stories?" he asked.

"Peter, will you lay off?" Margaret asked sharply.

"No, it's okay," Zach said as he poured four glasses of wine. "Here's what I think," he said and raised his glass in a toast and said, "Here's to the state of Jefferson…Cheers."

"Can I join in?" Danielle asked with a glass of water in her hand.

"What do you have in that glass?" Margaret asked.

"She knows enough not to drink; not while she's pregnant," Zach said.

"It's good you've got her trained," Margaret said and Danielle wanted to throw the water at her.

And Helen, in the meantime, sat there looking beautiful.

After the toasting, the four began to eat while Danielle went back to the stove.

Turning in her chair, Margaret said, "You know, dear, you have to use a little more heat, these pancakes are heavy."

Danielle was stunned and she approached the table to take her plate. "I'm sorry," she said in a hurt voice.

"No, no," Margaret said coldly, "I'll eat them. Waste not; want not."

Danielle realized Margaret had nailed her again.

Looking around the room, Margaret saw all the photos of Sandra and the children. "It's nice to see you're adjusting," she said to Zach then pointed to the photos.

When Zach realized what she was referring to, he said, "Danielle put them up. I didn't."

Margaret made no comment about that.

But more and more, the conversation excluded Danielle.

And when Peter described "the real Danielle," he talked about the shirt she wore that read something like: "Fuck off or I'll kill you 'til you're dead," and Danielle froze.

Peter was watching her intently, now.

Danielle put the spatula down and crossed the room. He watched her stop at a laundry basket. She picked up a folded black T-shirt. It was the only thing she removed from the basket. She took it into another room. When she returned, she was empty-handed.

He stared at the door of the room she had gone into. He wanted to see that shirt.

Back at the stove, Danielle began banging things around and suddenly realized she was playing into Margaret's hands. Both women were reducing her to the level of "kitchen help." But she couldn't help it. With Zach paying so much attention to Helen, she never felt so alone in her life.

At that moment, Whoops grabbed little Peter's arm and he cried. Margaret reached out and grabbed Whoops's shirt and dragged her to her.

That was it. Danielle grabbed a knife. She wasn't putting up with this woman's shit anymore.

But before she reached the table, Zach reached out and grabbed Margaret's wrist. "Let go of my baby," he said. His tone of voice had completely changed, it wasn't one of friendliness.

Margaret released Whoops who was looking at the two adults confused.

"Let them fight their own battles," Zach said.

"I don't like the way she's grabbing my son," Margaret retorted angrily.

"If he can't fight his own battles with a girl half his size, put a dress on him," Zach said sharply.

They all suddenly looked at Danielle. She was standing at the table with the large knife in her hand. She was suddenly awkward and indecisive and she realized even this, too, played into Margaret's game.

She took another step, but toward Zach. "This is the knife you've been looking for," she said softly.

He hadn't been looking for a knife. He knew exactly where each and every one of them was. But he suddenly realized why she had it in her hand. He smiled, shook his head at her, and she thought he was going to laugh.

Instead, he said, "I'm glad you found it. I thought it was lost forever. Thank you."

She handed it to him and forced herself to smile.

"I love you," he said unexpectedly.

"I love you, too," she replied. And now her smile was genuine.

She went back to the stove.

Zach didn't flirt with Helen again.

Helen no longer flirted with Zach.

Margaret began to fidget.

Peter tried to keep the conversation going, but Zach kept breaking out in inappropriate laughter.

"What's so funny?" Peter asked.

"It's nothing," Zach said, but he couldn't look at Danielle. It was completely clear to him, now, why she was reacting as she was. If anything, it made him love her more than ever.

Peter sighed. "It's late, we should be going," he finally said. He sensed the visit was over.

"Before you go, let me load you up," Zach said and, with that, he kicked the rug back and went down to the cellar. When he returned, he had several boxes so that, when they left, Peter, Margaret, and Helen had plenty to carry besides Peter Junior: Coffee, flour, maple syrup, and some 5.56 ammo.

"Come back with a sled in a few weeks, and we can complete the deal," Zach said.

Peter agreed. He also got Zach to promise he'd make more crystal radios because he had "customers" for them. He promised they'd return for more "stuff" and bring some of the trade items he'd promised Zach and Danielle, and Margaret would come so she could check on Danielle's pregnancy. No mention was made of Helen returning. In a few months, there might even be a puppy he said.

And they left.

§   §   §

Peter led the way through the field and, when they entered the forest, he stopped to let his wife and Helen catch up.

"They were acting so funny every time I mentioned 'Danielle,'" he said. "Do you think she could be the Danielle everybody's talking about?"

"Of course not," Margaret replied disdainfully.

"Why not?"

"I knew right away she's not."

"How?"

"First of all, she's not that smart. And when I saw her standing in the doorway with the shotgun, *I* wasn't impressed. She didn't even know she was holding a 12-gauge. Zach had to tell me. And did you look at how big she is? They say the *real* Danielle killed Hank Brady with her bare hands. That's the clincher. You met Hank. He was a monster. There's nothing to that little bitch. I could snap her like a twig. And that woman, Abby Brady, she said the *real* Danielle used a 12-gauge. What's she weigh? A hundred-ten pounds knocked up? A 12-gauge shotgun would knock that little tramp on her skinny ass. Furthermore, the Army experts said when the *real* Danielle blew up the bridge at Pistol River, she had to have used at least five hundred pounds of explosives. The *real* Danielle could have done it. The *real* Danielle's an Amazon. But that little shit couldn't have gotten that much stuff out there. She's nothing but a spoiled city girl. She can't cook, she can't carry on an intelligent conversation, she can't even take care of Zach. She's a…she's a…" She almost couldn't say it. Then she did. "*She's a cunt.* There, I've said it. Okay? Are you happy? If it wasn't for her pretty face, Zach wouldn't have a thing to do with her. And she's not even that pretty."

"But her name. And she's got the baby sister with the *funny* name. There's something about her…personally, I think she's a tough little girl. And when I talked about the shirt Danielle was supposed to have worn, she went right to the laundry basket, took a shirt out of it, and put it in the other room. Did you see her do that?"

"No. You're imagining things."

He wasn't dissuaded. "Then, the way they got quiet every time I asked about her past and how she and Zach had met…and did you look around their house? It was the scene of a firefight, Margaret."

With her voice rising in anger, Margaret said, "Danielle's probably not even her real name. All Zach did was go out to the 101 and find himself a young piece of useless pussy like a lot of guys are doing nowadays, like the Bradys did, and even the LaCroixs sometimes did. Don't you even dare insult the *real* Danielle and compare this girl to her. Helen's more like the real Danielle," she shouted. "This one's going to wind up hanging herself from the rafters, just like Sandra did. Do you know how many imposters are saying they're the *real* Danielle? There are hundreds claiming they're her. This one's just another wannabe."

"But she wasn't posing," Peter said. "And neither she nor Zach ever said she was the real Danielle. In fact, *everyone* wants to talk about the legend of Danielle, but they're the first people I've met who don't. Every time I brought her up, *they* changed the subject, not me. They're hiding something."

Clutching her son, Margaret ignored her husband's protests and, in a voice now frosted with disdain, she got closer to him and said, "I'm disappointed with Zach. Sandra must be spinning in her grave. Someday, he's going to realize he's made a big mistake. He'll rue the day he missed out on, Helen. The *real* Danielle is a legend, Peter. People are naming their daughters after her. If we have a daughter, I'm naming her Danielle. She's changed things here on the coast. If this one were the real Danielle, I'd be on my knees before her. We'd all be on our knees. Zach would be on his knees. This little...little..." she groped for the word, "...*whore*...is nothing but a road slut, and Zach's choosing her over Helen. I'm sorry we brought Helen out to meet him."

"But there's something about her," he insisted. He was beginning to get angry.

Enunciating each word so there'd be no mistaking what she meant she said, "It's exactly what Zach said *twice*: Did you hear him? He said *her* name, the weird name she calls that little rat she's got: *It's just a coincidence*. And now she's got Zach calling it his; that's an insult to his own children."

"Come on," she said self-righteously to Helen. The conversation was over for her and the two women shoved off on their poles. "Did you see the way she keeps house?" she asked Helen as they skied away.

Peter looked back from the edge of the forest at the cabin and thought about Margaret's words. She was right, the real Danielle had done things no man he knew could do. He couldn't imagine how the girl in Zach's cabin could have killed Hank Brady without a gun or how she could have blown up the bridge, and no one could have won a shooting duel with Brian Peterson. The real Danielle really was the stuff of legend. And this young girl was small and *seemed* to be so vulnerable. He saw the way Margaret browbeat her and pushed her around. But there was still something about her...

He thought about the way she looked when he first saw her standing there in the doorway with the shotgun, defiant and protective. There was nothing small about her then.

He stared at the cabin and shook his head. "There's something going on here," he said to himself. "There's something going on."

But he wasn't going to solve it today and, with that, he skied off to catch up with the women.

§ § §

With the cabin quiet again, Zach watched Danielle go to "her" chair. She reached down between the cushion and the arm of the chair and took out the hunting knife. Without realizing he was watching, she returned it to the drawer in the desk. He knew she must have put it there before she'd gone to the door. But he didn't say anything. And he knew she'd leave it there, under the cushion, forever, were it not for Whoops scampering around.

"I don't like her. I don't like either one of those women," she said.

"I don't know Helen," he said. "We'll probably never see her again. But you'll get used to Margaret."

"I don't like her. She doesn't like me. And she's nosy."

"I know, she's officious, obtrusive, impertinent, and meddlesome. But you'll get to like her once you get to know her. You just have to know and accept her limitations."

"With every question she asks, she's really asking something else, and she acts like people don't know what she's doing. And she's going to do more of it when she comes to check on my baby. Why didn't you say something when she was prying?" Her voice was rising.

"What was there to say?"

"And did you see how they talked? They were excluding me...and they knew just how to do it. And they were treating me like a servant in my own house. She was trying to make me look like an idiot, and...Zach...she succeeded."

He thought she was going to cry.

"I didn't know there was anything wrong with my pancakes..." she said.

He cut her off. "*No*, listen. Basically she's a good person. But she's got some faults—*major* faults. Not everybody's going to measure up to what you want. We all have faults..."

"Speak for yourself," she said angrily as she slammed things while she cleaned the kitchen.

"...and you're going to have to learn to accept them," he continued. "Nosiness is one of her faults. And you're going to find out she's very judgmental, too. But she's still a good person—and we need the Shorts. However, in spite of her faults, you dealt with her very well."

She continued cleaning up the plates and putting things away, banging cupboard doors and slamming down pots and pans as she went.

"I heard them talking when they arrived," she said and spun around to face him. "They came here because they wanted *that* Helen to meet you, didn't they?"

"They're just trying to help. They didn't know about you until they got here."

"And you liked her."

He fished for words. "She was nice…"

"Well, once they saw me, those two shouldn't have been making it obvious what they were here for and making me feel small in my own house. That hurt me, Zach. That just hurt." She slammed the skillet down and turned to him. She was trying not to cry but tears started running down her cheeks. "And you saw what Helen looks like, she's beautiful and you were flirting with her, and I'm all fat and ugly…"

So, that was what she was afraid of: losing him.

"You're not fat, you're pregnant."

"…and you just sat there…Why are you smiling at me? *Stop smiling!* I hate you smiling when I'm mad."

He wanted to say that the people in whose minds she had become a legend would be surprised to find out, not only did she not want that reputation, but that she was still soft and vulnerable and too young and innocent to understand the wiles of two older, more experienced, and manipulative women. But he didn't. Instead he spoke his second thought: "It's nice to see you're jealous — that I mean so much to you. And you're right, I liked the attention she was paying to me." He was hoping he wasn't hanging himself with that admission. "But it was wrong of me. I wasn't thinking about how it would make you feel. I think you're just unsure of exactly how much I love you."

She didn't deny it. She wiped away her tears, but they were followed by more. "Shit Head," she called him. "And *he's* nosy, too," she added. "But, at least with him, you know exactly what he wants to know when he asks you something. And you know how to answer him. But even he wouldn't give up. He kept asking about…you know…who I am. He *knows*, Zach. Or at least he suspects. And that scares me. I don't want anyone to know who I am…I don't want the Army looking for me and Whoopsie…or you…"

"It's okay. I understand," Zach said cutting her off, again. "But now you've met them, and there are others hiding in these hills you have to meet. Some of them you're going to like, some of them you won't.

"But I want you to keep reading the books." He was changing the subject, again. "We've got boxes full of them. Keep reading and we'll talk tonight. In the meantime, I've got to get the greenhouse up before it gets dark."

"I'm too tired to read."

"Then lie down for a while."

"No. The house needs cleaning."

"You're nesting. Will you lie down…"

"*No!*" she shouted defiantly and stopped in the middle of wiping off the table to glare at him. "I'm taking care of my family. Can't you understand that?"

"Let me finish," he said calmly. "Will you lie down when you finish this?"

"Yes. But you go out and finish assembling the damned greenhouse. There's going to be another mouth to feed before you know it."

"I love you, you know."

"I know you do, and I love you," she said angrily.

He approached her to kiss her.

"Not now," she said. "I'm not in the mood."

But he grabbed her wrists and pulled her toward himself and when she tried to pull away, he was too strong and he pulled her closer.

"*Don't!*" she yelled.

But he wouldn't stop. When he tried to kiss her, she turned her head. So he kissed her on her cheek. "You're beautiful," he whispered.

"*Stop!*" she insisted.

He kissed her temple. "I love you."

"*Don't!* I told you I'm *not* in the mood..." she screamed.

But she couldn't get away from him and she was weakening as he entangled her heart with his warm words and strong arms and his kisses, just as he had done all winter, and she finally let herself fall into his arms. She let him kiss her lips.

"You just won't give up, will you?" she whispered.

"I'll *never* give up on you," he said.

"I love you...*Mister* Shit Head," she whispered.

He could feel the tension pour out of her as he held her, like air whooshing out of a balloon, and he held her in his arms for about a minute.

He whispered, "I live with a legend, you know? I live with the Danielle everyone's talking about, from Seattle to San Diego and all the way back to Washington, D.C."

"I don't want to be a legend. I just want to be happy," she whispered back.

"Let me make you happy," he said.

He could feel her arms begin to tighten around him.

Suddenly she yelled, "*Whoopsie! Stop!*"

When Zach looked over his shoulder, Whoops was trying to drag the dog by his tail. She stopped and looked at Danielle for just a moment. Then she went back to pulling its tail. Stupid ignored her.

Danielle still held onto Zach. When her anger was completely drained out of her she whispered, "Do you like my pancakes?"

"I love them."

"Are they heavy?"

"I'd tell you if they were."

"You're a liar."

"I know, but they're not heavy."

"What do officious, obtrusive…and those other words you used mean?" she whispered.

"Nosy."

"You could just have said that," she said, but she kept her head against his chest so he couldn't see her begin to smile. Then, after another few seconds, she whispered, "You said we all have faults…What are mine?"

"Oh, Danielle, don't ask me that, *now*. It's too late in the day. Ask me in the morning when I have all day to tell you."

"What?" She pushed him away. "Get out of here and get some work done," she yelled. She was trying not to smile again, but he knew she wasn't angry anymore.

He put on his jacket and turning to Stupid he said, "Come on, big guy," and, when the dog got up, he pulled Whoops, who still had a grip on his tail, so that she tumbled to the floor.

Man and dog went out the door, one with his permanent limp, the other with his dumb-ass, three-legged gait.

Danielle finally smiled at their backs as they left.

§   §   §

When she finished cleaning, she picked Whoops up and went to the window and watched Zach as he reinstalled more of the fiberglass paneling for the greenhouse.

They had tomatoes, squash, and potatoes to bring out there when he finished. Beans, too; he said they'd have to plant legumes to put nitrogen back into the soil. He explained the milpa gardening used by the Indians of Mesoamerica where many vegetables were planted together because they complemented each other the way plants in a natural ecosystem do. Planting beans with the corn would allow the beans to climb the corn stalks into the sunshine while, at the same time, the beans were fixing nitrogen into the soil the corn to grow. He told her to read the books and she'd understand. There was so much for her to learn. And there were more plants they had started in pots some two weeks before that would have to stay in the cabin longer, and still more they'd started from seeds just yesterday. Zach told her he liked to stagger his plantings.

She reflexively put her hand on her stomach when the baby kicked and she thought about her "other" family. In her imagination Mommy, Dad, and Robert were down in southern California, warm and enjoying life. She knew there were impossible odds against them having made it there, but this was the way she wanted to remember them. But she wasn't going down there.

Watching Zach work on the greenhouse she realized this was her life, now. This was her family and this was what she wanted. She flinched and gasped when she saw a two-by-four he had just leaned against the framework suddenly fall and hit him on the head. But, when he merely pushed it back to where it had been standing, and went on with his job, she relaxed, again.

She left the window, took the 12-gauge, and put it back up over the front door. That was where she wanted it. The AR-15 was in the closet. Her sister was in her arms, her baby was in her tummy, her husband was rebuilding the greenhouse, the Model 60 was in her pocket. This was how she lived and no man or woman, no road pirate, not the Army, nor the ice age were going to take it away from her...ever.

Afterword

Danielle Kidnapped is the first novel in a trilogy that is set in the next glacial epoch of the ice age we currently live in. The next two titles will be *Danielle Discovered*, to be published in 2013, and *Danielle Betrayed*, which will be published in 2014.

When asked why a sixteen-year-old girl is the central character, my stock answer is that if I'd focused on a twenty-eight-year-old ex-Navy SEAL, you'd expect him to survive. So I chose someone you wouldn't think could make it: A female with one foot still in her childhood and the other in womanhood. Then I imbued her with intelligence, determination, and a will to stay alive against all odds to see where those attributes might take her.

About the Author

John Silveira lives in a haunted house on the southwestern coast of Oregon with a houseplant named Spaz. Besides writing, he whiles away his days photographing the local wildlife, playing poker and chess, and drawing women. You can view his photography at:

http://www.backwoodshome.com/blogs/WhereWeLive/

Made in the USA
Charleston, SC
02 January 2013